MINA FORD
studied languages and spent a year living in France, before
working for a French media company in London. After
several years of tube rage, she decided to escape to the
relative peace and quiet of Bath, where she wrote her
first novel, *My Fake Wedding.*

mY fake WeDDing

Mina ForD

RED
DRESS
I N K
™

First North American edition April 2004

MY FAKE WEDDING

A Red Dress Ink novel

ISBN 0-373-25054-1

Visit Red Dress Ink at www.reddressink.com

Printed in U.S.A.

For my parents

I would like to thank, in no particular order, my friends and family for their faith in me during the writing of this book: Mum, Dad, Ginny, Reuben, Faith, Rob, Nick, Pat, Basha. Also my editor, Marion Donaldson, at Headline. And last, but by no means least, my brilliant agent and very good friend, Judith Murray, without whom this book would certainly not have seen the light of day.

PROLOGUE

'**I**'m getting married.'

'What?'

Chins bounce off the parquet as my best friends digest my latest announcement. To be perfectly honest, I'm even a bit gobsmacked myself.

Six months ago, I vowed I'd eat my own hair and choke on a fur ball before I sold out. I'd chew toenail clippings before I bought the big marshmallow frock, squodged my great pork chop feet into a pair of foolish kitten heels and let some pig dog man in a ridiculous brocade jerkin drag me, kicking and screaming, to the altar. Now look at me. Katie Simpson, self-confessed singleton, about to renounce my precious independence and become Mrs...

Buggeration.

Mrs what, exactly?

As it strikes me that, in all the dizzy excitement of the past couple of days, it's never even occurred to me to ask what the buggery bollocks his surname is, I tell myself it really doesn't matter in the slightest. It could be Pratt or Shufflebottom for all I care. It could be Clutterbuck or Blenkinsop and I really wouldn't give a flying fuck through a rolling doughnut.

It's not as though I intend actually *using* it, for Christ's sake.

At least, not for very long anyway.

But I'm getting ahead of myself...

Chapter 1

New Year's Day. Four months, three weeks and two days after I walked into Jake Carpenter's bathroom to find Fishpants Fraser, the Balham Bike, strapped spread-eagled to the heated towel rail, cheap cerise g-string hooked over one foot and Jake's moony white bum hammering away like a roadbreaker between her duotanned thighs, I flump onto my squashy caramel suede sofa. Peeling a crust of chipped lime green glitter polish off my big toenail, I glance through the personal ad I scribbled on the back of a fag packet last night, while heavily under the influence of a bag of custard doughnuts and a bottle of cheap vodka.

'Gawky ginger spinster, with lard addiction and weird gay man obsession seeks non-ginger, sport-hating, gay-looking straight male for meaningful relationship. Manic channel flickers, compulsive PlayStation addicts, mother fetishists and those with big boffin hair need not apply.'

I take a giant slurp of banana milkshake, hoick up my sloppy tartan jimjams to hack at an ingrowing hair on my shin and scan my ad one more time. Then I scrumple it up into a ball, cheerfully chuck it straight at the waste bin.

And firmly resolve to stay single.

It's one-night stands all the way from now on.

That bit about me being a Ginge isn't totally accurate. I've recently gone Nectarine. That's what it said on the packet, anyway, although having seen the results, I think Neon Satsuma might be more appropriate.

The part about me looking for a man isn't strictly true either. I might be single, but I'm not one of those mimsy whingers you see forever cluttering up the bars in Dean Street, flicking their hair about and blubbing into their Chardonnay because they've got fat bums and no bloke.

Not me.

I'm not saying I'm perfect. Sometimes, I can be a right cow. I've been known to do wees on people's toothbrushes when they annoy me. I'm morbidly fascinated by news of terrible tragedies in the papers. Quite often, I don't wash up for a week. Oh, I have my faults all right.

And crap taste in men is fairly high up on the list.

I am one tragic cow when it comes to choosing a partner. For a start, I was born with a wonky Gaydar. I'm a serial fancier of gay men. Show me a rampant homosexual male and I'll try and get off with him. My judgement is famously bad. According to my personal Love File, I've met 'Mr Right' no less than three times. Oh, the first one reeled me in gently all right. Paid for everything, cooked me sumptous three-course dinners, bought me trinkets when I was depressed and was completely unselfish in bed.

Or so I thought.

It was when I opened my twenty-fourth birthday present that I discovered what he was really after. Tearing off the glittery pink paper in excitement, I was utterly gobsmacked to find myself gawping at a studded dog collar with matching lead. And then he hit me with it. Told me he'd always found sex with me a bit tame. Apparently, I could do so much more for his libido if I could only see my way clear to going down on all fours and barking like a dog once in a while.

It was all I could do to manage a feeble 'Woof' before bursting into tears, grabbing my coat and getting the hell out of there.

I fell in love with Mr Right The Second for a very simple reason. He ate fast. Which made me look positively dainty in restaurants. Unfortunately, it wasn't long before all the chomping and slurping got to me and I started to hanker after a rather more sophisticated line in dinner party conversation.

Then along came Jake. And I only went and fell for him. Hook, line and crotchless knickers.

I've reeled, dazed with shock, from every relationship I've had the misfortune to totter into. Since I hit puberty, the needle of my Bullshit Barometer has wavered permanently on 'Dangerously High'. I've taken so much crap I'm a prime candidate for Toxic Shock.

After the Fishpants fiasco, I was a walking bloody sewage farm.

I reckon it's high time I settled for life in the single groove. OK, so it's not particularly groovy right now, but things change, don't they? At least I'm big enough to admit that in the race for romance, I'm a non-runner. On my personal Valentine menu, Bloke is Off.

I've done relationships and I prefer cake. Look at all the misery Jake caused me. And he wasn't even on a par with Happy Shopper Arctic Roll. Oh no. My mind's made up. Absolutely the only men I'm having any truck with in future are Ronald McDonald, Mr Kipling and Nick O'Teen.

You know where you are with them.

And, while we're on that subject, just so you know where I stand food-wise, I'll tell you that I don't do dieting. I do pork pie sandwiches and black pudding fried in lard instead. I'll jam down anything, apart from Liquorice Allsorts and the horrid jellery bits you get in fried eggs that look like snot. I gave up calorie counting two years ago, when I was breaking up with Tom. Tom was a poet who worked in Baby Gap to make women think he was sensitive. It was only when I'd finally decided that even if he wasn't Mr Right, he was Mr Very Bloody Nearly, that I found out he was in possession of one GBH conviction and one (very current) wife.

Which made him Mr Not On Your Fucking Life.

I felt such a tit. I was mainlining strawberry Pop-Tarts and tins of Devon Custard quicker than I could flip the switch on the toaster, and realised I had quite enough on my plate without fretting over whether I'd soon be tucking my stomach into my knicker elastic. I'd have plenty of time to whinge about my weight when I looked as though I had a packet of crumpets tacked to my thighs and my minky had vanished under Michelin Man rolls of lard.

Then I met Jake.

And suddenly, the world became a happier, shinier place.

Jake, Uberbloke, graphic designer and driver of gleaming red Surrogate Penis, smarmed his way into my life just over a year ago at a hair gel launch in Kensington. Obviously, I usually wouldn't have been seen dead at such arse-kissing events, but this one had been organised by my oldest friend Sam. Sam was blessed at birth with a smile like a synchronised swimmer's and had a natty, built-in bumlick function that ensured he was well on his way to becoming Top Banana at a PR consultancy in Noho (that's the top end of Tottenham Court Road to me and you). The launch marked a pivotal point in his career and he begged me to go along to make up the numbers. And despite the fact that I'd rather have knocked back a litre of Toilet Duck in one sitting, I dutifully bigged up my hair, dusted myself in sparkles and poured myself into a spangly acid-green frock, all so I could stand, pigeon-toed with anxiety and feeling as out of place as a foreskin at Hanukkah, while Sam whizzed around proffering trays of angels on horseback to whinnies of marketing girls in Bacofoil dresses. As I expected, it was the very worst sort of party: the champagne and air-kissing kind, where everybody hates everybody else and pretends that they don't, and people are so obsessed with their image that no one actually gets to have any fun.

Especially not me.

I was abandoned in my usual party spot, in pole position for the buffet and shovelling in salmon and cream cheese pinwheels with one hand, while desperately trying to balance a glass of fizz and a Marly light in the other. As usual, I cursed myself for being a jelly-spined wimp who could never refuse an invitation. It was always the way with me. When put on the spot, I fished around for a suitable excuse before giving in, gushing that I'd absolutely lurve to come to Jemima's Virgin Vie party or Nux Vomica's Mexican-themed evening, or whatever hellish event I was being invited to. Then, when it got nearer the time, I found myself praying for a contagious dose of ebola and wondering if it even might be worth enduring the humiliation of ringing the hostess and bandying the diarrhoea word about.

The night I met Jake, I was as sickeningly healthy as ever. I was freezing my tits off in my minuscule frock and spangling hopefully at no one in particular, when there was a tap on my shoulder and I wheeled round to find myself nose to double chin with a seven-bellied monster with big microphone hair. This prime specimen wasted no time in engaging my left breast in lengthy conversation on his favourite subject. Himself. He was a trader, he told me, puffing himself up so he looked bigger than ever. In the City. What he traded, precisely, I didn't have a bloody clue, but as long as it wasn't bodily fluids with me I wasn't complaining.

In any case, I hoped my boob was listening in case there were questions later, 'cos I sure as hell wasn't. I was working out how long it would take me to get to the exit. Should I just make a break for it, or should I take off my shoes first in case I fell arse over tit on my way out? When Microphone Hair finally stopped to draw breath, remembering his manners for long enough to inquire of my nipple what it did for a living, I was so shell-shocked that I grabbed the underwire of my Wonderbra, waggled it up and down and shouted, 'Come on then. Answer the man.'

It was loud enough for a gaggle of designer girlies next to me to hear. Sucking their heads out of their arses with a collective Phwopp, they stopped bitching for long enough to turn and bog at the fishwife who'd actually had the audacity to pitch up in head-to-toe Topshop. I turned tomato. Fervently, I prayed for the floor to turn into a wobbling mass of pink blancmange so I could gracefully sink through it.

Miraculously, salvation appeared in the form of a twinkly-eyed, curly-haired pixie who flashed me a conspiratorial smile before grabbing my arm and saying, 'There you are, darling. I've been looking for you everywhere.' Then, flashing me a smirk of pure mischief, he stage-whispered, 'He takes photos of other people's dangly bits for a living. You don't want to get yourself mixed up with him. Name's Jake by the way. How do you do?'

It was fate. Jake had rescued me from the pages of *Readers' Wives* and I was smitten. He whisked me off to Soho for greasy Chinese, then came back to mine for 'coffee'. From there, I went on to disprove the SOFA (Sex On First Acquaintance) curse, which states quite clearly that if you are one of those trollopy strumpets who shags on a first date, you are unlikely ever to see the other person involved again.

But Jake was too good to be true. And the sex was bloody marvellous.

At first.

We made the Kamasutra look like Topsy & Tim. We bonked everywhere. Under piles of coats at parties, giggling like teenagers. In a plane toilet on the way to Amsterdam. No stone was left unturned in our search for New Places To Shag.

And Jake taught me a lot. I never realised a Toblerone had so many uses.

Unfortunately, the excitement wore off pretty quickly. Six months in, I found myself secretly making shadow pictures of butterflies and bunny rabbits on the wall above the silhouette of his humping buttocks, just to pass the time. But I decided to give him and his sloppy technique the benefit of the doubt. After all, it was only natural for things to get samey after a bit, wasn't it?

Hell, what did I know? Still, one thing's for sure. If I'd found out earlier that he was wearing a Jake-flavoured groove in Fishpants Fraser, Gateway To The South herself, I'd have done more than practise a spot of discreet shadow graffiti. I'd have sodding well asked him to pass me an ashtray to prop on his bum.

Well, I won't be putting myself through all that bollocks again. Being single, I tell myself firmly, is going to be just great. Think of the advantages! I'll be able to wear my ripped Levi's— the ones Jake hated, with the arse hanging out—on a daily basis if I feel like it.

I'll be able to grow my pubes down to my knees.

Watch crap TV without having to pretend I'm being ironic.

Walk round the flat covered in moustache bleach.

And leave leg stubble in the bath any time I damn well please.

Oh, and while I'm at it, I won't give myself hives every time the phone goes and it turns out to be just one of my friends. Janice, maybe, with news of a lorry driver she's picked up over the all-day breakfast at South Mimms Services. Or George, calling to report a nasty bout of carpal tunnel syndrome. So all in all, life should be a lot easier.

My first day of Official Singledom coincides with the first Fag Hags and Slagbags lunch of the year. I'm meeting my three closest friends so we can trough pizza together. And if I don't hurry up and get ready, I'm going to be late.

Buggering ballbags.

I shuffle into the hall, knocking over my milkshake glass and sending a gloopy yellow river oozing across the floorboards.

Dashing upstairs, I shake a couple of breakfast Doritos out of my orange corkscrew curls before jumping into the shower and scrubbing myself down with tangy grapefuit shower gel to blitz away the last of my vodka hangover. I wait a couple of minutes for my deep cleansing seaweed mask to take effect, then it's out again, skidding across the swamp I've made of the bathroom floor to wrap myself up in a fluffy white bath sheet and hot-foot it to the bedroom, almost tripping over Graham and Shish Kebab, who are curled on the landing like fat ginger croissants.

There's no time to blow dry, which means I'm going to end up with a halo of frizz round my head like an alien from the Planet Pube. I scrub in a mountain of Frizz-Ease to remedy the situation as best I can, and find a lemon-yellow scrunchie to scoop the whole lot up into a jaunty ponytail with. It does make me look a bit 'Estate' but there's no time to worry about that now. I slap on powder to sort out my skin, which currently resembles the contents of a tin of SPAM, then cake on spidery mascara and a slick of lip gloss where necessary. A rummage through my knicker drawer heralds nothing but period pants, but that doesn't matter today, seeing as pulling opportunities will be limited. I add faded Levi's, a chunky black jumper, one pink sock and one nasty peach one, then pull on a pair of stinky-cheese trainers and head for the stairs, locating keys, fags, purse and mobile phone on my way out.

The freezing air hits me straight in the chest. Christ. The streets of Balham are deserted. Everyone else is sensibly tucked up inside; hutched up cosily in front of the telly with their left-over boxes of Black Magic or squabbling over Trivial Pursuit. Shivering, I slip my hands into the pockets of my tatty leather coat and trot onwards past the Dog Shop, thanking my lucky stars that I've thought ahead for once, and have a full pack of cigs on me so I won't have to brave the retch-inducing stench of damp Alsatian today. I trot past the house with the vomit orange paintwork and the swirly green fireplace tiles on the outside windowsills. Along by the deserted school playground and under Pigeonshit Bridge by the tube station. Past various kebab shops and dodgy burger joints until, after a couple of minutes, the neon pink sign of our favourite pizzeria comes into view and, already drooling on the garlicky scent which wafts into the damp, exhaust-filled air of the Balham High Road, I push open the door and glance around for my three best friends in the world.

Chapter 2

I'm last to arrive as usual. There they are, already comfortably installed at our favourite corner table. Janice, picking at the olives and filling the ashtray with tab ends coated in her trademark Harlot Scarlet lippy. Janice is absolutely my best girlfriend, because she's VGV, which in Katie-speak stands for Very Good Value. Almost eight inches shorter than me, she has boobs like beach balls, more curves than spaghetti junction and a mass of bubble curls the colour of lemon drops, which she wears as big as humanly possible in an effort to make her look taller. Janice is brilliant fun, expects little entertainment in return and, despite the fact that she'd probably describe herself, somewhat annoyingly, as having 'bags of personality' and can be bloody bossy and a bit muff before mate-ish sometimes, I love her to bits because she'll do absolutely anything for a laugh.

George, one deliciously pert buttock raised slightly from the Formica chair as he rummages in his bum cheek pocket for Sobranie fags, is perched opposite her. Clad in a skin-tight, ice-cream pink T-shirt, a pair of silver hipsters and a clonky pair of biker boots, he looks ashen. His eyes have sunk almost entirely into his head and he's obviously knackered. Which is hardly surprising. It's the first of January after all, and George is a gay man. He'll have spent last night tripping his tits off on disco biscuits and dancing to Dana International.

'Been up all night, have we?' I tease him gently.

'Does Judith Chalmers have a passport?' he grumbles, proffering an unusually pasty cheek.

I grin at him and look across the table at Sam. He is, I have to admit, looking very slightly uncomfortable. But it doesn't take a genius to work out that this is because Janice has practically superglued herself to his side. Poor Sam. Janice has fancied him ever since I introduced them during college days. Any mention of his name in her presence has been accompanied without fail by much phwoar-ing and raising of her clenched fist in a suggestive manner. Sam is terrified of her. I don't dare tell Janice this, but he's been known to suggest he'd rather sleep with his grandmother. He says it's because she looks too much like a drum majorette for his taste, though George reckons it's more to do with the fact that Sam is a closet queen. But then George always says that about straight men. Especially when he wants to sleep with them.

George, I'm very much afraid, is a tart with a capital T.

I've known Sam a lot longer than the other two. Janice and George are friends from college, whereas Sam and I lived next door to one another as kids. We spent our formative years puncturing each other's Space Hoppers and generally causing as much damage to the other's few belongings as possible. I broke his swing ball; he hacked off Football Sindy's legs with a Swiss Army knife. He stamped on my Buckaroo; I threw all the bits of Operation down the toilet. We were expelled from playgroup together for swinging on the chains in the boys' toilets (at my instigation) until they broke under the strain. Sometimes, we had great fun.

And sometimes we didn't.

When we were four I cracked his head open with a sandpit spade because my mum let him sit on her lap. Which, I thought, was absolutely fair enough. His noggin bled so much his angelic blond hair turned strawberry pink. Shocked, I forbade him to tell a soul. And like the loyal bud he's always been, he suffered in silence. I wasn't found out until we sat down to watch *Playschool* and my mum noticed the raspberry blobs rapidly appearing across the back of her wicker swing chair. Oh, I was all for sharing, as long as it wasn't my sodding stuff that got shared. I was an only child, for Christ's sake. I was sensitive.

Somehow, Sam and I have managed to stay friends. I suppose it helps that my mum and his dad still live in the same street, nipping in and out of each other's houses for sherry and swapping vegetable marrows and runner bean crops as and when the fancy takes them.

Sam's changed a bit since we were kids. Now, six feet three and with a shock of sand-blond hair which refuses to behave, no matter what expensive goop he slathers all over it, Sam throws himself with gusto into everything he does. He takes huge bites out of life as though it were a great big toffee apple. Women adore him. He says 'Jump', they ask 'And would you like me to wear knickers?' He only has to snap his fingers and they come running, frothing at the gusset. I think it must be his enthusiasm. It's not as though he's particularly good-looking.

OK, so there was a time when I sort of fancied him. I let him finger the strap of my trainer bra outside the cinema when we were fourteen. But that was only because he bought me a family size bag of Revels and let me eat all the Malteser ones.

Oh, and we snogged each other once at our end of A-level party. But I put that down to too much Thunderbird.

Then Janice spots me, jumping up from her chair and enveloping me in a huge, Giorgio-scented bear hug.

'Someone smells nice.' I squeeze her back. 'Classy bitch.'

'And you look brilliant,' she tells me, even though I know I look like a big ginger pineapple.

'Do I?'

'Course you do. God, you're such a lucky bitch, Katie, not having any tits.'

'Er...thanks.'

'S'true.' She looks miserably down at her own chest, sticking her jaw out like us women always do when we check out our cleavages. 'Everything I wear hangs straight from my nips and makes me look preggers.'

'You look great,' I tell her.

And she does. Her clingy black long-sleeved T-shirt emphasises her glorious sweater-girl curves and her pancake-flat stomach. But I can tell she doesn't really believe me.

We both blame her insecurity on the workplace. She's got a very good job in advertising. Unfortunately, it means that she's forced to sit next to tossers who come out with ridiculous stock phrases, like 'Hold on, Roger, let's get our ducks in a row on this one', and 'We're not sure how this one's going to pan out, Frank, so we'll just have to suck it and see'. All the women who work there wear a lot of black and are so thin they haven't got bums. Soon, they're probably going to have to cushion the loo seats to avoid facing legal action relating to injury in the workplace. Poor old Janice works in a bum-free environment. Her surroundings are arse-lite. And the pressure to look emaciated is enormous. She's tried every diet fad going. The Hay. Weight Watchers. The Elton John. The diet which let her eat anything she wanted, as long as she only ate one of it. Aerobics. Swimming. Trampolining. She even tried to get me to join Bums and Tums with her. Which, of course, was totally impossible. My idea of exercise is bending down to put a couple of pains au chocolat in the oven to warm through. And I'm allergic to those cheesewire leotards that slice you right up your bum.

At the moment, she's following the advice of some diet guru or other who's advised her against keeping any food in the house. But it's not working too well. By bedtime, her tummy's rumbling so much she's frenziedly scoffing whole jars of vitamin tablets and tubes of Setlers Tums, just to keep the hunger pangs at bay.

The poor love. It's not as though she has an eating disorder. She just wishes that she did. She spends a lot of time being pissed off that she doesn't have the willpower to be anorexic. For her, anorexia is an impossible goal. A bit like seeing a pair of Dolce & Gabbana shoes she knows she'll never be able to buy, even if she saves up for a decade.

'I'm starving.' George pulls a candy-pink fag out of the pack and examines it carefully.

'Don't worry,' I assure him. 'It doesn't clash with your T-shirt. What about you, Sam?' I ask as he gives me a big New Year smacker on the cheek. 'Are you hungry? What are you having to eat, you fat bastard?'

'At least I can put on weight if I want,' he teases me. 'Which means I don't have to go around looking like a lanky ginger hockey stick.'

'Ha ha. Come on, let's order. I could eat a scabby donkey.'

'I'm going to have whatever I like as well.' Janice looks at the menu resignedly, struggling with her desire to look like a Belsen victim versus her craving for cheesy garlic doughballs, spaghetti carbonara and double chocolate ice cream.

'Might as well,' I encourage her.

'Sod it,' she agrees. 'I can always yack it up later if I feel like it.' *She wishes.*

We order mozzarella-stuffed mushrooms, well-dressed salads and enormous pizzas all round and demand a new bottle of white wine. George orders two pizzas. He feels so terrible he thinks he's having meningitis, so he reasons he might as well. But that's nothing new. For a start, he goes out clubbing so much he's always completely hanging. And he's a classic hypochondriac. He's got a big *Book of Symptoms* at home, which he flicks through at random, convincing himself he's got raging symptoms of each and every disease in it. AIDS figures weekly. As does emphysema. Last week he was absolutely positive he had deep vein thrombosis. The week before it was CJD. And he's had rickets and shin splints God knows how many times.

I love these lunches. Love the fact that my three best friends all get on so well. And, while we wait for the food to arrive, we chatter like sparrows, each telling the others what we've been up to over Christmas. Sam, lopsided baseball cap on head, tells us how much his niece loved her Wendy house. And then, bright-eyed with excitement, he rolls up the sleeves of his baggy sweatshirt and yatters about his new house. He finally moved in a week before Christmas and he can't wait to get going on the decorating.

'Wait till you see it, Ginge.' He winks at me. 'It's fantastic. Loads of light. And when I've decked it all out, I'm going to use one of the upstairs bedrooms as an office.'

'What for?' George's big brown eyes glint mischievously. 'I'd have thought you'd be needing the extra bed. Then you can get the next old slap in before the last one's vacated. You won't even have to wait for the sheets to cool. Just roll her into the damp patch and move on.'

'Like you're so chaste.' Janice waves her cigarette around so that a big carrot of ash drops into my wine. 'You've had more men than my ruddy mother. And that's saying something.'

I feel sorry for Janice's mum. Just because she refuses to tell Janice who her father is, we all assume she doesn't know. Which is, more than likely, complete bollocks. And if you actually sat Janice down and asked her, she'd probably admit that she's never seen her mum with a man. But we all prefer the slagbag story. It's much more fun.

'Can we get back to me?' Sam is laughing.

'Me now. Me now,' I tease him.

'Don't you want to know why I need an office?'

'Not really,' I joke, lighting myself one of Janice's fags and jabbing him in the ribs.

'I'm going to set up my own business,' he announces proudly.

'What as?' George asks. 'A male escort?'

''Cept no one would have to pay him,' I say. 'Would they, Sam?'

'Depends who's offering. Obviously I might do discounts for very good friends. But you three buggers'd have to pay full whack of course, the amount of piss-taking you do. Anyway, a couple of the clients at my place have been a bit disgruntled recently and I'm sure I could persuade them to come with me. I sometimes think they'd prefer the more personal touch.'

'Not too personal, I hope?' Janice laughs.

Sam rolls his eyes to heaven.

'That's cool,' I tell him. 'Even if it's a bit scarily grown-up. C'mon, you two. A toast. To Sam's new business.'

Janice and I clink glasses enthusiastically and then George, anxious to gossip, lights yet another fag and tells us how his job on a TV culinary dating show is going. The week before Christmas a gay couple won a holiday to Martinique on the strength of their steak and kidney pie. Understandably, they were jubilant. And, at the celebration party afterwards, George managed to separate them.

'I had one in the stationery cupboard over the staplers and took the other into the Ladies.' He giggles naughtily. 'Though, looking back, I think giving out my mobile number afterwards was a bit of an error.'

'To which one?' Janice asks.

'Both.' George laughs. 'They wrote it down on separate pink Post-its. Barry found my number in Steve's pocket and clicked. They rang me from the airport. I ruined the holiday, apparently. I mean God only knows what it had to do with me. I got all the bloody blame, obviously. I certainly don't remember promising to be faithful to either one of them. They should have been mad at each other.'

'Have you heard from them since?' Sam asks.

'No.' George tosses his head back and exhales smoke through his nostrils like a dragon. 'I went home for Christmas. Drank port and lemon and played Scrabble with Mum. Chucked my mobile in her fish pond.'

'And did you tell her?' I ask, suddenly serious. George, though aged nearly thirty and camper than *Carry On Camping*, still flatly refuses to tell his mother he's gay. It's something to do with her being elderly and he being her only child. Stupid, I call it.

'No.'

Sam pours more wine and we all agree George is lucky not to have been sacked. Janice says she wishes she *could* get the sack, because she hates everyone at work so much, and I say I probably *will* get the sack if I don't make a start on the article I have to finish by tomorrow morning. Then we all clink glasses again, amidst a chorus of Happy New Years. Which sets Janice off again.

'Resolutions. Who's got resolutions? And I don't mean stupid, shallow ones, like more Croissants for Breakfast.' She takes one last drag of her fag and stubs it out in the butter dish.

Croissants for Breakfast is Janice and Katie shorthand for cunnilingus, the inference being that cunnilingus doesn't happen very often, and is therefore a lot like having croissants for breakfast instead of toast.

'Or getting rid of your duty friends,' she says. 'I don't mean that.'

'What's a duty friend?' asks Sam.

'They're the ones who always call you,' I tell him. 'You never call them because you don't give a toss if you never see them again.'

'Exactly,' Janice agrees. 'But they're always so bloody thick-skinned.'

'They steadfastly refuse to fuck off,' I explain. 'The only way to really get rid of them is to have them killed.'

'I mean,' Janice lights another cigarette and gulps more wine, 'we should all think of something really life-changing we'd like to do this year.'

'Like what?' I ask. It's OK for her. She has a proper career. So does Sam. The PR company he works for is probably one of the top three in the country. Even George has a better job than me. And he doesn't need one. He has a trust fund that'll

keep him in DKNY knickers for the rest of his life. But his work
as a researcher on the TV show—*Ready Steady Shag, Can Shag,
Will Shag*, something like that—means he gets to meet lots of
people to have sex with. Which he likes. Hence the Steve and
Barry story. He picks off the cream of the gay contestants, ruts
them senseless over the urinals then drops them like a hot shit
sandwich. He doesn't even seem to actually do any real work,
judging by the number of emails he sends me on a daily basis.

Mind you, neither do I.

I have a crap job. I just drift through life expecting that one
day I'll find out what I want to do for a living.

It hasn't happened yet.

'Do you want to hear what mine is then?' Janice asks. 'Or not.'

'Not,' George says.

'Yes we do,' I say. 'Don't we? Sam?'

'Yes.'

Janice takes a deep breath, puts both hands palms down on
the table and looks at us intently.

'This year,' she breathes, 'I'm marrying a rich man.'

'How do you know?' George asks.

'Because I'm going to have a bloody good try,' she says.
'That's how I know. I've had enough of pissing about with men
my own age.'

'You mean the kind who boast about how many pints they
can neck in a session and spend their spare time fantasising about
shagging Lara Croft and lighting their farts?' I say.

'Exactly.'

'That counts you out then, Sam.' I giggle.

Am I imagining it, or is that a flicker of relief I see pass across
his face?

'Don't worry.' Janice slaps him playfully on the knee. 'I'm
going older this time. 'S the only way. I'm going for gold.'

'Old gold,' I say thoughtfully.

'I don't even care about looks,' Janice drivels on. 'Although
I don't want a fat one. Or a ginger.'

'Thanks.'

'Sorry, Katie. No offence.'

'None taken.'

'I'm interested in finance, not romance,' she carries on. 'It's hello hard cash, goodbye hard cock from now on in. You can't have it all. These days, you have to look at a relationship as an alternative PEP. Or a TESSA.' She giggles. 'Transferring Expenditure to Someone else's Savings Account.'

Sam looks shocked. As well he might. Janice is just like him and George. Known for working her way through men like a fly through shit. She needs regular and varied sex like I need fags, chocolate and beauty products in nice packaging. Her last three boyfriends have dumped her because they've caught her boffing someone else. How on earth is she going to stay faithful to one man? Particularly one who's old enough to be her father.

'You're not going to go really old?' George looks worried. 'Not, like, incontinence and dribbling?'

'I might.'

'Jesus.' He rolls his eyes. 'That is sooooo Jerry Springer.'

'Sod off.' Janice nudges Sam. 'What about you, Sammo? Any resolutions? Apart from becoming your own boss?'

'I don't know.' Sam looks embarrassed. 'I'm thirty this year. Perhaps it's time to settle down with that special person.'

'Yeah, right,' I snort. 'Likely! If we saved the condom from everyone you've humped and dumped, we'd have enough rubber to bungee jump from the top of Canary Wharf. Don't pretend you want to change now. You couldn't if you tried.'

'What happened to Pilaff?' asks George.

'Pia,' Sam corrects him.

'Poor Paella,' I say. 'He dumped her.'

'She dumped me, actually,' he says.

'Only because you made it quite clear the contents of her knickers no longer interested you,' I say.

Pia was just one more in a long, very thin line of Sam's silly bits of fluff. She lasted three months, and I hated her with a passion. Partly because she was gamine and chic and really suited short hair, whereas I am none of the above, but also because she would keep on insisting she came from Tenerife. Which, as I've tried to tell Sam, time and time again, is nigh on bloody impossible. You don't come from Tenerife, for fuck's sake. It's a holiday destination.

Still, I can't help feeling a bit sorry for the poor cow. Anyone could see Sam didn't really love her. He took me out for dinner on her birthday because I'd just been dumped. She must have been a bit doolally in the first place to have been so totally sucked in by him.

'She sensed he was cooling off so she asked him to go for a walk on Wandsworth Common,' I tell the others. 'Wanted a chat.'

'Actually—'

'Shut up, Sam. I'll tell it. I know it better than you.'

'That's because you make half of it up.'

'Shh. Anyway, they drank a bottle of wine in the pub first. Then, when they sat down to talk, he fell asleep. The silly bitch waited an hour and a half for him to wake up. And when he did, guess what?'

'He gave her the old "it's not you, it's me" bullshit and left?' Janice hazards a guess.

'Spot on. What a waste of a Saturday afternoon. She could've gone shopping instead.'

'You bastard, Sam,' Janice says. But she bats her eyelashes at him as she says it. His eyes widen in terror and he shifts away from her slightly.

'You are a bastard, Sam,' I tell him. 'You're a Quick Erection, Instant Rejection merchant just like the rest of them.'

'I'm not.'

'You are. You wouldn't have got away with that with me, you wanker,' I tell him, in no uncertain terms. 'I'd have got your knob out and left you there with it lolling out of your flies. Not that anyone would have noticed, what with you having a dick like a bit of Heinz spaghetti.'

'And how would you know?' Sam grins.

He has a point. I might have known him all my life but Sam could have a willy like a lump of baloney sausage for all I know. I change the subject. 'What about you, George? What's your New Year's resolution?'

For a second, George looks uncharacteristically wistful.

'A baby,' he says firmly. 'I'd like to get a baby. My maternal instincts are kicking in. I could hardly dance in the club last night because my biological clock was drowning out the beat of the music.'

Oh good giddy God.

'And I saw a lovely one the other day in Harvey Nicks.'

'Clock?'

'Baby,' he says despairingly. 'Great cheekbones for one so young. And it was wearing this gorgeous little Gucci cashmere thing with poppers. Don't suppose you'd care to oblige, would you, Katie? Provide the oven if I supply the bun, sort of thing?'

'Fuck off,' I tell him. 'I wouldn't bonk you if you were the last man on earth.'

Actually that's not true. George isn't the sort of man you'd kick out of bed for farting. If he were straight, he'd be quite a catch. I, for one, would shag him like a shot. It's my personal tragedy that he is, as my mother puts it, 'riding the other bus'. If he offered me the chance of a quick bunk up I'd leap at it like a Jack-in-the-box. But it's not very likely, I'm afraid. George has always preferred to go in the back door. Gusset-wise, he's as safe as industrial-strength Durex.

'Don't be ridiculous,' he scoffs. 'You haven't got a penis. Why would I want to shag you?'

'What then?'

'I thought we could baste one,' he says. 'Like Max and Jacqui did in *Brookside*. You've always said you don't want your own kids.'

'Too bloody right,' I mutter. 'Giving birth gives you Stilton cheese veins in your legs and bunches of grapes dangling out of your bum.'

'We're eating,' says Sam, rubbing a hand through his shock of hair and making it stick up even more.

'What's your point?' George asks innocently.

'My point,' I tell him sternly, 'is that I'm blithered if I'm widdling the equivalent of the Empire State Building through a drinking straw just so you can satisfy your ego by carting it around like a Prada handbag. The answer's no, George. N bloody O.'

'You wouldn't be able to cope with the birth,' Janice points out.

'Neither would Katie.' Sam shovels in doughballs.

'The blood and the stitches would make you barf,' I remind George.

'Probably wouldn't need stitches, the men you've had,' Janice jokes. 'Be like waving a finger of fudge round the Lincoln Tunnel.'

'Speak for yourself,' I say. 'I'm not the one who stakes out haulage companies in search of nice bits of rough. What if you didn't like the look of it?' I get back to George's and my imaginary basted baby. 'You wouldn't be able to send it back. You can't just order a baby as if it's a pizza and then return it if you don't like it. What if it comes out dog ugly?'

'It won't,' he says confidently. 'Luckily for me I've got an exemplary gene pool, sweetie. No one eats cheap beefburgers and oven chips in my family.'

I look longingly at his snake hips, six-pack abs, chocolate-brown eyes and jet-black hair, cropped close to his scalp to show off an immaculately chiselled jawline.

'I'm sure you have,' I tell him. 'But I'm a bit of a ginge, in case you hadn't noticed. And you wouldn't want one of those soiling your precious gene pool, would you?'

'You can't tell for sure what it'll look like until it comes out. It's a bit like a genetic tombola in that respect,' Janice tells him. George looks blank. He clearly hasn't got a clue what a tombola is.

'Not true actually.' Sam waves his fork around and tucks into more pizza. He's chosen the one with the egg on top, I notice. Typical bloke thing to do. 'We'll soon be able to choose exactly how our children look.'

'How fabulous.' George puffs himself up. 'They'll all come properly accessorised. The world will be full of beautiful people. Just like me.'

'It sounds awful,' I say. 'We'll be overrun with Mail Order Infants. Embryos To Go. Delivery will take on a whole new meaning.'

'You'll even be able to order a whole stock of spare parts for the baby in case something goes wrong with it,' Sam says knowledgeably.

'Shut up, smart arse,' I tell him.

'Yuck.' Janice drinks more wine and drunkenly lights the wrong end of her cigarette. 'Like a Foetal Exchange Mart.'

'I'm not having your baby, George, designer or otherwise,' I say. 'In nine months' time the novelty will have worn off and I'll be stuck with it. You can't take babies to nightclubs, you know. Even if you do dress the poor little buggers in leather and sequins.'

'What about you, Katie?' Sam, shovelling in garlic doughballs, wants to know. 'What's your resolution?'

Everyone turns to stare at me.

'Yes,' Janice says 'What is yours?'

For a second, I'm stumped. Then I remember my Vow of Singledom.

'To have a nice time,' I announce.

'What?'

'Yep. On my own. I'm giving up on relationships altogether,'

I inform them coolly. 'Can't be buggered any more, if you must know.'

'You're what?' Janice looks astonished.

'Oh God,' moans George. 'You've come over all lesbian, haven't you? You're a ruddy great carpet muncher and you're too afraid to tell us.'

'I said I was giving up on relationships,' I tell him. 'Not men.'

'What about sex?' Janice looks horrified.

'Janice, you're the last person to try to tell me you have to be in a relationship to have sex with someone,' I say.

'True,' she admits.

'The men I meet are about as useful as chocolate tampons,' I say. 'So I'm going to follow the BLAB principle. Behave Like A Bloke.'

'What?'

'Fuck 'em and chuck 'em. Hump 'em and dump 'em. Blow them off then blow them out. I'm going for a one-night stand record.'

'But you'll be crap at that,' Janice says. 'You'll end up doling out charity fucks like there's no tomorrow. Shagging people you feel sorry for. Look at that computer spod you bonked at college. What was his name? Bruce?'

'Bryan,' I mutter through gritted teeth. 'His name was Bryan.'

Wine comes out of Janice's nostrils. Even Sam's trying not to piss himself laughing.

'Bryan,' Janice snorts. 'He wore mustard Y-fronts and—'

'Yes, yes,' I assure them. 'It was all absolutely hilarious.'

I spent a week in the bath, scrubbing myself down with shame, after Bryangate, and I still haven't been allowed to forget it. Oh, he seemed handsome enough when I snogged him over the pool table in the Union bar. But by the time we got back to his black ash bedroom, the effects of the seven pints of Snakebite and black I'd consumed had worn off enough for me to notice that his hair was lank and greasy and he was speckled

with whiteheads. But, being the non-confrontational type, I fig-
ured it was probably less hassle just to brace myself and let him
get on with it.

God, perhaps they're right. I'm completely shit at shagging
around.

But then I won't know unless I try, will I?

Chapter 3

Did I say how much I hate my job? I write for a glossy lifestyle magazine, which isn't as glamorous as it sounds. Office life isn't really my thing, for a start. Oh, it's OK for nicking stamps, making long personal calls, slagging off the outfits in *Hello!* and comparing sandwich fillings, but apart from that, I don't see any advantages from where I'm standing.

My one saving grace is that I'm allowed to work from home sometimes. Which isn't actually all it's cracked up to be either. It's not all lounging around on designer sheets with a state-of-the-art laptop, dressed in wisps of powder-blue and drinking out of big cups to make your hands look dainty, like they make it look on American TV shows. I have motivation issues. I hate having to chain myself to my geriatric Mac with nothing but a box of fondant fancies and a walnut whip or two for company, forcing myself to write something intelligent and witty, when I'd far rather be slumped in front of the telly in my friendly old PJs, posting in Pepperamis and watching Judy 'WishIwasthinagain' discuss teenage bulimia.

Until now.

Recently, I've found myself actually enjoying going into work on the odd occasion. Just before Christmas, the *Suki* magazine office acquired its very own Mr Diet Coke Break. Fresh from the land of kangaroos, koalas and Kylie, David—or The David, as he's been nicknamed, due to his striking resemblance to Michelangelo's equally luscious masterpiece—is over on a sabbatical from Sydney, and he's had everyone's La Perla in a veritable twist since he wandered through the door of the features office. He sits opposite me, which gives me lots of opportunity for bashful flirting, and I have to say the view has improved considerably since all I had to stare at was Fat Claire's Cute Cats calendar on the slightly grubby stretch of wall between my desk and the coffee machine.

Because of this, I make more of an effort with my appearance than usual, pulling on clean, black bootleg trousers and a pale pink V-neck, which reeks only slightly of fags from its last outing. I even do make-up, disguising the luncheon meat effect of last night's bottle of red wine on my cheeks with a layer of tinted moisturiser I've had knocking around the bathroom for yonks, and sweeping shell-pink blusher over the place where my cheekbones were last spotted, circa 1992. Then it's off to the tube, where I spend an unhappy forty minutes jostling along on the Misery Line with my nose jammed into someone's beef stew armpit. Personally, I think travel on the London Underground should be gratis. There's nothing enjoyable about it, after all. And there's nothing worse than shelling out the best part of a hundred quid a month for the pleasure of getting to work, when I'd far rather be cocooned under the duvet with a bag of Jelly Babies and a good book. Especially at this time of year.

I emerge at Sloane Square and walk the long way to the IBS Magazine building so I can have a calming fag before I go in. The familiar tsunami of lethargy washes over me the second I drag my heels up the steps and I illegally grind out my fag on the wall by the front door. There's something acutely depressing about the smell of our building, new carpet mixed with stale coffee grouts, that makes me want to spin on my clumpy boot heel and run for the hills.

Or the shops at least.

Marsha, the toxic receptionist, glances up from painting her talons purple as I slope in, wincing at the cheerful vase of fat crimson poppies and hot pink peonies on the reception desk.

'Good Christmas?' I ask, more out of politeness than anything else. Actually, I couldn't care less what sort of sodding Christmas she's had. She's so up herself I doubt she even noticed anyone else was *having* Christmas. She probably thinks the whole damn festive season was laid on just for her.

'The best,' she purrs. 'Did I tell you we were going to the Maldives?'

'About a thousand times.'

'My Bradley proposed on the beach. Sooo romantic.'

She waves her hands around a lot as she speaks, so that I can't fail to spot a rock the size of Gibraltar winking away in the shaft of sunlight that comes from the window. Still, if she actually thinks I'm jealous she's even thicker than I thought. I'd drink sick before I'd touch Her Bradley with a ten-foot pole. Marsha's Bradley is about as attractive as school mince. He wears too much aftershave and he looks twelve. In fact, the only reason Marsha herself is interested in him is that he's seriously loaded. He works on the LIFFE floor in the City, which suits him down to the ground. Marsha's Bradley is a LIFFE. A Loud Ignorant Fucker From Essex. A Bish Bash Bolly Boy. A Lobbo Yobbo.

'Late again,' Marsha singsongs as I shuffle miserably towards the lift. 'And you had a lot of time off before Christmas as well. Missed all your deadlines. Imogen was reely furious.'

That's a very bad habit of Marsha's, mistaking me for someone who gives a toss.

'I had gastroenteritis,' I lie.

'Ooh, lucky you,' she breathes. 'I bet you lost loads of weight. Just in time for the party season too.'

'Er, right.'

The office is already humming with activity. There's Melanie the Mouth. Spreads office gossip like cheap margarine and is about as harmless as a redback. Delilah, who has neck cords from too much dieting and always looks as though she's knocked back a petrol and floor polish cocktail. Audrey, who's just popped out a pair of twins and has breasts like nuclear warheads. Men swarm round her like flies round a fresh cowpat and she says it has done wonders for her sex life. Hilary, who never speaks but spits in her boyfriend's sarnies every time they have a row. Fat Claire, her flabby chip shop arms on display as usual. She's into all that holistic claptrap. Aromatherapy. Reiki. All manner of herbal hocus-pocery. I don't know why she bothers. It's obvious it doesn't work. Otherwise she'd have managed to feng shui her cellulite or something by now and her double-decker arse would be a thing of the past. There's Serena Bumlick, the office brown nose. Her tongue is permanently wedged so far up the editor's bottom, I'm surprised she ever manages to get any work done.

Jabba the Slut, all fifteen stone of her, wedging in an iced bun.

And so on.

'Hi, Katie,' calls Audrey, dabbing at a milk spot on her silk blouse.

'Hi,' I say. 'Did the twins enjoy their first Christmas?'

'Oh, they did.' She immediately starts talking in a stupid goo-goo voice. 'Ickle wickle Theo and Toby had a wonderful time. Loved the fairy lights. I said to Jim, "They're taking it all in." '

'Lovely,' I say. Ickle wickle Theo and Toby have been 'taking it all in' since the nanosecond they were born. I'm already longing for the day one of them comes home shitfaced. Or sky high on glue. Audrey and Jim will be 'so disappointed'.

Of course, I realise that even by my reckoning, ickle wickle Theo and Toby's drinking days are a good fifteen years away.

So hopefully I'll miss their first night out on the Blue Nun. Surely to God I won't still be slogging my guts out for 10p a word at *Suki* by then. Something life-changing is bound to have happened to me before that.

I put down my raspberry latte and park my bum on my swivel chair, pondering the possibility of a sausage sandwich from the canteen downstairs. I've already had an industrial sized pain au chocolat, but there's something about work that makes me just want to jam food in my face all day.

'Hi, Katie.' Fat Claire's thick, cakey voice oozes out from behind the photocopier. 'Did you have a good holiday?'

'No,' I mutter, switching on my grape-coloured iMac. 'You?'

'Fantastic.' She smiles fatly. 'I found my Chi.'

'How lovely.' I grimace. 'Was it lurking at the bottom of a bag of chips?'

'What?' she wobbles.

'I said you must be fucking thrilled to bits.'

'Oh.' She looks surprised. 'I am. You really should try it. I feel so...so...'

'Well, that's lovely then.' I turn round purposefully and bury my head in a sheaf of papers.

God, this is depressing. I hate the hum of computers, the constantly shrilling phones, the irritating buzz of chatter. Actually, the chatting wouldn't be so bad if it weren't for the fact that everyone who works here is a complete Humour Eunuch. This place is about as much fun as AIDS. The only person who has ever laughed at a single one of my jokes is David. Gorgeous, sexy David. At ten thirty, he wanders in, positively ambrosial in a Daz-white T-shirt and a pair of faded Levi's, which cling seductively to his cute-as-a-cupcake bum. David gets away with being even later than me every day because he's a bloke. We haven't had a man in our office since Maurice the janitor left. A man as eminently bonkable as David has never before crossed our threshold, so there's no protocol regarding male lateness or couldn't give a toss-ness in general. Consequently, David could stub fags out on our editor's eyeballs and people would smile indulgently. Sometimes, if he's feeling especially tired, he puts a Post-it note on the back of his head which reads, 'Please wake at 2 o'clock.' Then he kips at his desk for the entire lunch hour. The rest of us think ourselves bloody lucky to *get* a lunch hour.

Watching him plonk down his caramel macchiato and his double chocolate muffin, I heave a gigantic sigh. Despite David's gorgeousness, I can't help feeling downright miserable at being back at work.

'Hi, David,' trills Melanie the Mouth.

'Hi.'

'Hello, David,' purrs Serena Bumlick, rewinding the tape in her dictaphone for some serious transcription.

'Hi,' he says politely, before turning his attention to me. I blush with pleasure, noticing that everyone else in the office, especially Serena and Mel, have turned the colour of mange-tout with envy.

'Good Christmas?' he asks me.

There's a collective intake of breath as I give everyone that smug 'Yes, he's asked Me a question' sort of look.

'The usual,' I reply. 'Crap weather, crap presents and crappier telly. If I hear the theme tune to *Only Fools And Horses* one more time I'll scream. What about you?'

'What's *Only Fools And Horses*?'

'Never mind. What about you?'

'The usual.' He grins, showing a neat row of sparkling white teeth. 'Gorgeous weather, great presents and no telly at all.'

'You haven't got a telly?' I'm incredulous.

'I was too busy sunbathing.'

'It was back to the land of barbies, beaches and brilliant sun-shine, was it?' I treat him to my flirtiest smile, secure in the knowledge that everyone else in the office is watching, jealous as hell. 'Thought you were looking sickeningly brown.'

'Just for a week.'

'Well, there's no need to get cocky,' I warn him. 'You might get all the nice weather over there, but just remember, you guys are responsible for giving us *Prisoner Cell Block H* and Rolf Harris. It can't be all good.'

We chat on about holidays for a few minutes then David's phone rings. Now, when this happens, I take it as my personal responsibility to ear-bog as much as I can. None of us have, as yet, managed to find out whether or not David has a girl-friend. But this time, disappointingly, he seems to be talking about work. And he's taking ages about it, so I bang off a couple of personal emails and resign myself to writing the article I was supposed to have handed in before Christmas. A piece on *crème brûlée*. It's my job to invent and test recipes for the Posh Nosh section at the back of the magazine. It's the least prestigious section, of course, next to all the celebrity interviews and the reportage. It's even lower down the ranks than the pages and pages of photos of spilt nail varnish and chopped-up lipstick, which pass for the Best Beauty Buys of the month. Actually, it's not what I thought I'd end up doing at all. I wanted to be a chef when I was at school. But when I left catering college, I didn't realise that if you wanted something badly you were supposed to go out and grab it, instead of waiting for it to land in your lap. So I drifted. And after months of temping, I ended up here.

Writing about food instead of cooking it.

'Concocting the perfect *crème brûlée* is rather like building the perfect relationship,' I type gloomily. 'If the luscious vanilla custard goo on the bottom is not strong enough to support the brittle, golden caramel crust, the whole structure will cave in on itself like a floppy, flaccid...'

God, now that makes me think of penises. Must concentrate.

On second thoughts—I look longingly at David—who cares?

I spent so long over the holidays testing recipes, I've got caramel oozing out of my ears. But I think I've got the ingredients and the timing right now. Unfortunately, relationships are a tad more complicated. If I had a foolproof recipe regarding that side of life, I'd be laughing all the way to Snatch West. But how could I? I can't even follow in the footsteps of parental example. My own father buggered off when I was fourteen. I wasn't surprised. The alarm bells of mid-life crisis had been ringing for months. It was 1984. He'd given up mowing the lawn at weekends and started wearing stretch jeans and leg-warmers instead. Howard Jones and Nik Kershaw records started to appear in our front room with alarming regularity. One Saturday, I arrived home from the cinema (*Ghostbusters*, if you're interested), to discover he'd disappeared while he and Mum were out looking at chest freezers. He'd vanished into the ether just north of Finsbury Park with a mail order Filipino. Mum was devastated. She prided herself on never having bought anything from a catalogue in her life.

I finish writing the introduction to my article then ring Janice.

She's depressed. Poor old Janice. She does work really, really hard. She lived in a shithole, went to school in a shithole and gritted her teeth through A levels so she could claw her way up and out to university. Where she met me. We got through our first year in halls together then shared an old Victorian house near Southsea seafront, where she really opened up to me about her past. Every week we'd have those silly girlie occasions, when we'd sit for hours, putting the world to rights with mudpacks on our faces, henna slathered over our hair and huge glasses of wine in our hands. Now, she's so glossy and polished, you'd never know she grew up on a council estate rougher than a badger's bum. And that's just the way she wants it to stay.

'If that wasp-bottomed sow whispers "you need some serum, sweetie" in my ear just one more time, I'm going to ram her precious Rolodex down her throat, the fucking flat-chested bitch.'

'We're not all lucky enough to have tits so versatile we can sling one over each shoulder and tie them together like a halterneck, you know.'

'Sorry.'

'Just try and be a bit more sensitive to those of us who ended up in the fried egg queue when they were giving out bosoms.' Hopefully a bit of flattery will cheer her up a bit.

'Well, I never asked to get any,' she snaps. 'You're welcome to mine.'

Oh dear. Wasp Bum, Janice's boss, has a terrible self-confidence problem. She has far too much of it. As do most of the other girls who work in her office. Janice won't admit it, but I think she constantly feels she has to prove herself because she thinks she isn't good enough.

'I thought you were doing fantastically at work.' I light a cigarette and deliberately waft the smoke in Fat Claire's face. 'You're always being promoted and getting cars and pay rises and stuff. Look at me. Still on ten pee a word. Compared to me, you're practically executive.'

'That's just the problem,' she grumbles. 'Being solely responsible for the anti-cellulite bum cream account isn't as glam as it's cracked up to be. Actually, it's really starting to get me down.'

'Why?'

'Well, it seems the more I'm paid, the more work I'm expected to do.'

'That's ridiculous,' I exclaim, shocked. 'Everyone knows that when you've climbed your way to the top, all you have to do is boss other people about. Why don't you just tell her to stick her serum where the sun don't shine and get the hell out?'

'I can't,' she says glumly. 'I've made certain lifestyle choices. Unlike you, I'm a homeowner. I've got a mortgage to pay. There's no way I can even think about giving it all up until I've found Filthy Rich. Then I'll tell her exactly where she can stick her precious job. Right up her wee hole.'

'Ouch.'

'Oh, Katie,' she groans. 'What am I going to do? My job gets right on my tits, and to top it all my mother wants me to go over for "tea" on Sunday. And she doesn't mean afternoon tea either. She means dinner. Which means I'll be expected to sit at the top of that rancid tower block and eat something over-cooked that comes with damp cabbage. And you know that makes me depressed.'

'Do you want me to come with you?'

'Nope. I'm going to try and get out of it if I can. Just look-ing at that cupboard I slept in for the first eighteen years of my life makes me want to slit my own throat.'

'Hmmm.'

Janice's mother—bless her—recently redecorated Janice's old bedroom. She found copies of *Elle Deco* and *Living Etc.* at a jum-ble sale, then splashed out on bright paint and touchy-feely cushions in an attempt to lure Janice home a bit more often. But now that Janice has escaped, it's going to take a bit more than a potful of Exotic Pink and a couple of sequin-sprinkled throws to drag her back to her roots. She's got her own place now; a little oasis of clean lines and calm and she ain't going back for no one. It's a bit sad, really.

'And that marriage agency I joined was a total disaster,' she goes on.

'Oh no.'

'Oh yes.' She sighs miserably. 'So far, I've done breakfast with Too Short, lunch with Too Sleazy—honestly, after the way he kept grabbing his crotch I couldn't even think of ordering the sausages—and dinner with Too Spotty.'

'Oh dear.'

'Then there was *Cats* with Too Poor—he made me go Dutch—and *Les Mis* with Too Married. Which just goes to show how thorough they are with their checking. I've wasted enough time and money on buying new outfits for that shower of losers. I'm thinking of moving on.'

'Good.'

'So will you come with me after work?'

'Where? To the marriage agency? But I don't want to get married.'

'No. Somewhere else. Tell you when we get there. Shall

Mina Ford

we say Balham tube at six thirty sharp? By Pigeon Poo cab rank.'

It's an order, not a question.

'Kay.'

I might as well. I don't have anything else to do. And now that my train of thought has been interrupted, I don't see myself getting much more work done this morning. I might as well go to the loo for a kip.

I nip into the Ladies, stealing a furtive glance right and left as I go in to make sure I haven't been seen, then enter a cubicle, flip down the lid, park myself firmly on top and rest my head against the cool plaster of the adjoining wall. Usually, I can stay like this for up to an hour, depending on how much traffic there is on any particular day. Sometimes, if there's an important editorial meeting, or if a celebrity chef or TV interior designer is visiting, you get a glut of people in here at once, all chatting, squirting hairspray, caking on mascara and re-doing lipliner in preparation, and it's almost impossible to get any shut-eye at all. But sometimes, it can be a full thirty minutes before anyone comes in and, even if someone does, I can usually manage to stay hidden. As long as I'm not snoring, of course. If I'm silent, people are lulled into a false sense of security. They think they're alone. And it can be comforting to hear board directors and such like come in, hooting out big trumps and then leaving without washing their hands.

Today, though, Melanie and Serena come clattering in before I've had time to nod off. Quickly, I scoot my feet up off the floor so they won't see me. You can learn a lot about office politics from hiding away in bogs.

'Did you see her?' Melanie starts to gob off, almost before the main door has swung shut.

'I did.' Serena's voice is slightly distorted from where she's puckering up her mouth to paint on more lipstick. 'She's so pathetic. Reckons she's well in there. As if he'd be interested in someone like her. He smiled at me in the canteen the other day.'

Canteen? What the buggery bollocks was she doing in the canteen? She doesn't do eating.

'He held the art room door open for me when I was carrying all those trannies,' Melanie says smugly. 'I think he fancies me.'

'It's not as though she's even good at her job.'

'I know. Rumour has it they're going to get rid of her.'

'When?'

'Soon.'

It doesn't take a fool to realise they're talking about David. After all, he is the only male in the office. Idly, I wonder who the 'she' who is going to be sacked is. It could be anyone. Everyone flirts with him, after all. And because he's so polite, everyone has, at one time or another, dared to hope that he fancies them back. The older women mother him and buy him cream buns, which he shares with me, and the younger ones just salivate over his arse. It might be Fat Claire. I know there's been some animosity because she's just had an undeserved pay rise.

But before I can glean any more info, the Flight of the Bumblebee warbles robotically from the depths of my bag at ever increasing volume. Shit. My bloody mobile. I delve in to switch off, but not before Serena and Melanie have fled, tottering on three-inch heels to the safety of their computer screens.

It's David.

'Thanks,' I tell him. 'I was just listening to some juicy office gossip then and you've gone and ruined it.'

'Where are you?'

'In the loo. I was having a bloody nap.'

He laughs. 'Come back. I'm trying to play Hangman. It's boring with one.'

'Can't,' I say firmly. 'I'm tired.'

'I've got a cherry bakewell in my top drawer.'

I scramble to my feet and leg it back to my desk where, after three games of Hangman, David gets back to work. He's still the New Boy, after all, so he has to at least look interested. The afternoon drags like buggery. George phones once, to ask me to go to his mother's birthday lunch in Kent with him in a couple of weeks. Apparently, she's asking 'when are you going to settle down?' type questions, which might all go away if he brings me over and nuzzles my shoulder every once in a while. I do love George's mum, especially when she makes apple crumble and custard, but I think she deserves the truth, so I refuse.

'Why don't you go on your own and tell her you're a raving homosexual?' I ask him. 'How hard can it be? She's pretty cool, you know, your mum.'

'I don't want to upset her.'

'You won't.'

'She's old. She might be shocked. She might just give up breathing or something. I can't exactly see her marching round Tunbridge Wells in an "I love my gay son" T-shirt. She hasn't got my dad any more either, remember?'

'I know.' I pick up a paperclip and start bending it into comedy shapes. 'But she's got People's Friend and Rich Tea. Not to mention endless cups of PG Tips. And, to be honest, I think it'll be a relief to her to find there's a reason for that appalling mauve coat you wear. She'll be fine.'

'I dunno.'

He then has one more go at persuading me to rent out my womb for a bit. It's only for nine months, he insists. He can't see what the problem is. Am I being deliberately obstructive, just to spite him? It's not even as though he'd be a sitting tenant. He'd be in and out before I knew it.

I hold firm. 'No. No and NO.' George can be very persuasive and I don't want to suddenly find myself agreeing accidentally.

'God, you're so selfish,' he rants. 'I sit here all day putting up with po' white trash who want to go on telly and all you can do is depress me. Do you know how hard this work lark is?'

'Er, yes actually.'

'Do you though? I have to interview raddled orange hags in slingbacks every day of my life, darling. People from chip pan families who say TOILET and LOUNGE. People who live in bungalows and think it's perfectly OK to do so.'

'Well...'

'Today I've had Linda from Dunstable all over the studio. Arse like a three-seater sofa. And Cherise from Romford who thought spaghetti hoops were—and I quote—"dead sophisticated".'

'Well, I'm very sorry about that but—'

'And Wayne from Luton who thought that baklava was something you pulled over your head to hold up your local Spar. Do you know—'

'George.'

'Yes?'

'Sod off.' I put the phone down. Work is bad enough without him ranting on about his own job all day. It's not even as though his work is very taxing. All he has to do is troll round the studio meeting people and yattering on to them, asking them questions about themselves to see if they're exciting enough to parade around on day-time TV. It's not exactly hard. It's not my fault he's such a sodding snob.

I spend the rest of the afternoon staring at my screen, willing my thoughts to unscramble themselves and transform themselves into clear, lucid prose. Occasionally, I pick up pieces of paper and put them back down again in an attempt to look busy. I make cups of tea. I tell myself I'll write today off and start with a clean slate tomorrow. I hack at a scab on my hand until it falls into the keyboard and no amount of poking with a paperclip will dislodge the bastard.

At five thirty on the dot, David scrapes his chair back, flips off his monitor and picks up his bag.

'Coming for a drink?'

He's talking to me.

I look round the office and am satisfied to see that Melanie is slack-gobbed with astonishment.

'OK,' I say. 'That'd be excellent.'

We go to the vodka bar around the corner. Lots of chrome and glass and huge pink squashy sofas. Feeling frivolous, I order a double straightaway. Jelly Baby flavour. David goes for black cherry, a choice I approve of wholeheartedly. At least he's not going to take the sparkle out of the evening by drinking lager all night like a blokey bloke would.

'So how are you enjoying it then?' I ask him. 'Work, I mean. What do you think of Imogen?'

Imogen is our editor.

'Fat ankles,' he says.

I'm delighted. A man who looks good *and* knows how to bitch his way out of a crisp packet. How refreshing.

'What about the others?' I ask, winding my legs round each other in what I hope is a vaguely sexy fashion. 'Melanie?'

'Wears too much acrylic.'

'Serena?'

'Face like a dog's bum.'

'Audrey?'

'Bit unsavoury, the way she comes into work with puke on her shoulder.'

I giggle delightedly. We're getting on so well. I don't know what I'm more excited about. The prospect of a shag, or the possibility of a bitching partner at work. Who knows where it might all lead? David might be my first hump and dump of the year.

Except that of course I'll have to be a bit nice about it. I won't be able to cruelly toss him aside, because I have to sit opposite him all day. Which is obviously a bit disappointing, but there are other ways of making sure a one-night stand doesn't go any further.

'Another drink?'

'Ooh yes.'

'Same again?'

'I'll have chocolate orange this time.'

'And I'll have lemon,' he says. 'Bit less sickly.'

I watch him swagger over to the bar. God, he's sexy. He's got one of those tanned, smooth, utterly male necks you find yourself wanting to bite into the back of. The only problem is, we've clicked so quickly that I almost forget that he's not actually my boyfriend. Therefore, I don't actually have licence to touch him or cuddle him. You see, I'm having so much fun that hugging him and draping myself all over him just seems like the natural thing to do.

'So where do you live?' I ask when he comes back with the drinks; chocolate orange like I ordered and a double blueberry to wash it down with. I'm already wondering about the logistics of the whole thing. Will I be able to nip home for a fresh set of clothes in the morning, for one thing? Gulping my blueberry vodka, I wonder hazily if he's trying to get me drunk. Probably. He's obviously been plucking up the courage to ask me out for a drink all through the holidays.

'Earl's Court.'

'I knew it.' I laugh, and down both drinks in quick succession, waving my arms around for a waiter. I need a waiter. I can't walk to the bar. My legs are already too wobbly, though whether it's the effect David is having on me or the vodka, bugger only knows.

'Don't tell me,' I slur. 'You share a house with ten other people. You have to sleep in shifts.'

'Sorry to disappoint you.' David laughs. 'But I live on my own.'

'How very unpatriotic of you.' I lurch over to the chalkboard and choose another flavour. 'We'll have two, no, four raspberry vodkas and a couple of butterscotch ones please.'

By eight o'clock, we're both off our tits. And we have so much in common that I decide I can really see us as a couple. I mean, obviously I don't want to rush things. I haven't got us moving in together, or purchasing joint electrical items yet. And I am supposed to be off monogamy this year. But you never know, do you? Perhaps the right man just hasn't come along before. Either that, or he did come along and he was George, and therefore unavailable to someone like me.

Perhaps David is the right one. Who knows?

Who cares, I think drunkenly, pouring more booze down my neck. This is funnnnn.

At half eight, my mobile rings. It's Janice.

'Where the fuck are you, you witless bee–atch?'

'In a bar,' I say gleefully. 'With vodka. Lotsha vodka. Why? Wanna come?'

'You were supposed to be meeting me,' she yells, clearly pissed off. 'I stood at the sodding tube station freezing my flaps off for an hour. You were supposed to come to the Evergreen Club with me.'

'The what?' I shout. 'Well, where is it? We'll come now.'

Drunkenly I decide that the thought of David and me dancing beneath an enormous glitterball in some tacky South London nightclub is the thing I'd most like to do in the whole world right now. And because I'm drunk, I can do exactly what I want. I'm cleverer, richer and more beautiful than anyone else in the bar. And I'll have anyone who dares to say otherwise.

I'm also probably a lot more shitfaced than anyone else here. But they...

'Don't be stupid,' Janice snaps. 'It's too late now. It's not a nightclub it's a social club.'

'Oh. Nemmind. Might be fun, doan'tcha think? Doesshit have a late lishensh? Isshit dead posh? You a member?'

'It's for the over-sixties, you dappy cow. I've been out sharking for Filthy Rich.'

'Well, be careful.' I laugh, the effect of the vodka causing circuit failure in my brain and a subsequent lack of any contrition whatsoever. 'You've heard of the dangers of getting pubes in yer teeth.'

'What?'

'Imagine what it's like to get teeth caught in your pubes.' I giggle as David brings something purple and noxious-looking to the table. 'Beware.'

I find that last 'beware' so hilarious that I start giggling. And then I can't stop. Janice flips her mobile off in disgust and I giggle some more. I'm having so much fun I don't care that she's pissed off with me.

'Shalright when iss her.' I grin at David, taking my purple drink and downing it in one. 'Ss muff before matesh every time when she's with a bloke she'shh shafting. Not that we are, you know, shagging.'

'No.' He looks grave. Probably a bit nervous. I give his leg a squeeze to put him at his ease.

'But we are having fun, aren't we?' I hiccup.

'We are.'

By the time the bar closes, I'm so pissed that David, bless him, worries that I won't be able to get home on my own. Perhaps, he says, looking concerned, I should stay at his.

'Aye aye,' I joke. 'I know your game.'

He laughs. It's nearer, he says. It'll save me rattling all the way home on the Northern Line. And it's easier to get into work in the morning from his. He walks it. Besides, he wants to prove to me that he doesn't have to share a bed with a hundred other antipodeans.

It's midnight by the time we arrive back at his. And before I slump into the elegant banana-coloured couch in his kitchen, I have time to notice that his pad is distinctly un-bloke-like. Lots of Alessi kitchen equipment. A shiny chrome Dualit toaster. A gleaming Waring blender...

'Nice shutff,' I slur as he hands me a cup of Lapsang.

'Thanks.'

We loll on the banana sofa for a while, then David, suddenly serious, looks at his watch.

'We've got an editorial meeting tomorrow,' he says. 'I think we should go to bed.'

Just as I thought. He's *gagging* for it.

I'm tingling with anticipation as he leads me up the stairs. He seems to spend an inordinate amount of time in the bathroom, brushing and flossing his teeth, but I tell myself it's nice to meet a man who takes care of his appearance, and concentrate on checking my own teeth for spinachy bits.

By the time he comes out, a tiny white towel wrapped round his delectable, nipped-in waist, I'm already in bed, my clothes in their usual crumply heap on the floor. Cursing myself for not wearing matching undies, I've taken my dirty grey bra off and hidden it under my shirt. I contemplated just leaving my purple bikini knicks on but then decided to be bold and let it all hang out. Under the sheets I'm starkers.

How bold is that?

He looks surprised.

'I was going to say you could have the spare room,' he says. 'But...'

'Oh, that's OK.' I grin boldly. After all, we both know why I'm here. 'Why dirty another lot of sheets? Not that I am, of course.'

'Not that you are what?'

'Dirty.' I laugh, leaning dangerously towards him as he sits on his side of the bed and pouting for all I'm worth.

'Katie, I...'

'What?' I lean so far forward that, in my pissed state, I collapse with my head in his lap.

'I...'

'Oooh,' I say, putting my hand on his penis and giggling. 'Is this a cucumber or are you just...Oh.'

Let's just say he's either hung like a grasshopper or he's in no state of excitement.

'Look,' he says firmly, removing my hand.

'It's OK,' I rush to reassure him. 'I'm not expecting marriage, you know.'

'Katie...'

'Is thish because you have to sit opposite me at work?' I try. 'Because we can completely forget about the whole thing in the morning, you know. You won't have to go out with me. Or buy me fancy goods of any sort whatsoever. I'll let you off scot-free. I won't tell a shoul.'

Although I might ask to borrow one of his T-shirts to wear into work, of course. One he's worn before. So that Melanie and Serena will know.

They'll be furious.

'No,' he says. 'It's not because of that.'

'Then what?' I'm stumped.

'Well...'

'Oh, I get it,' I say. 'You're married. You've got some Sheila baking you Lamingtons back at home. Well, you know what they say. What the eye doesn't see...'

God. I can't believe I'm being so flippant.

'It's because I'm gay.'

'I don't mind,' I say.

'Katie, I'm gay.' He takes my hands firmly. And suddenly I get it.

The beautiful kitchen. His immaculate appearance. His wonderfully bitchy sense of humour.

Of course he's sodding gay. Whenever was a straight guy that perfect?

Buggery buggery fuck.

Everything stops. I can hear traffic hooting outside but it all seems strangely far away. Has he just said what I think he's just said? It all feels surreal. Like some weird dream.

'It's not you,' he rushes to comfort me, seeing my look of horror.

How could I have made such a basic error?

Again.

'You can't be...' I make a quick salvage attempt. I've come this far, after all. I'm buggered if I'm letting him slip through my fingers.

'Why not?'

'You hate ABBA.'

'Y–yes...'

'Steps completely passed you by.'

'I'm Australian.'

'You don't even know the actions to "YMCA".' I'm sobbing now. 'I s–s–saw you at the Christmas party. You didn't have a clue.'

'Yes, but—'

'You're a fucking Australian, for fuck's fucking sake. You're supposed to be a sexist wanker. A slab of beefcake. A red-blooded fuck monkey. You don't mind drinking beer out of cans. And you actually like pork scratchings. I don't believe you. This is just an excuse not to shag me, isn't it? Well, let me tell you, I wouldn't shag you anyway. Not if the end of your excuse for a dick was covered in Ben & Jerry's. You're bound to be crap. So. So there.'

God. Now I'm making a complete tit of myself. Snot is coming out of my nose and everything and I don't even care.

Buggery, buggery bollocks.

Why does this sort of thing always, always happen to me?

I leap out of bed, acutely aware that all my bits are on display. My cheeks flame with humiliation. It seems absurd for him to be seeing me naked after what he's just told me.

'Look, Katie, come on, don't be like that,' he pleads as I pogo ridiculously round the room with one foot through the leg hole of my lurid violet knickers, trying to yank them up for all I'm worth.

'Look, if I were straight you'd be the first person I wanted to shag. Honestly.'

'Oh, spare me,' I beg. 'Please don't try to make me feel better. I've never been so embarrassed in my life. Look, I'm sorry. I'll leave my job. You'll never have to see me again.'

'You don't have to do that. Come on, let's have another cup of tea and—'

'No.' I pull on my pink shirt, which, after a night on the booze, is all scrunkled up in a teeny ball on the floor, before rushing down the stairs, out of the front door and into the street before he can utter another word.

I stagger towards the tube station, just managing to hail a taxi and telling the driver to take me to Balham.

Once inside, I stare moodily out of the window.

'Bastard,' I hiss.

'Are you referring to me, miss?' asks the taxi driver.

'Oh no, sorry,' I say. 'I've just found out that the bloke I thought I was shagging is gay. I was referring to him. Pretty understandable, don't you think?'

'Oh yes, love,' the taxi driver says. 'Nothing short of disgusting, what they get up to. Unnatural, I call it. I mean it's not what the Good Lord intended, is it, at the end of the day?'

Bile rises in my throat. It's the vodka, I think, though the awful hiccuppy crying hasn't helped. I swallow hard. I really don't want to have to park my lunch in a taxi. There's no handy receptacle. No bin. No scrumpled up Sainsbury's bag even. I could always use my jacket pocket, but I think that's going a bit far, even for me.

Luckily, I manage to hold on to my stomach contents until we finally pull up outside my front door, when the taxi driver looks at me so kindly I think I might be going to burst into tears again. 'Here you go, luvvie.' He smiles. 'You let yourself in and have a nice cuppa tea, eh?'

I wake up next morning feeling almost normal. Absolutely hanging, but not too embarrassed, considering. And then I realise two things.

Firstly, once again I've attempted to bag and shag yet another screaming great queen. George will have hysterics when he finds out I've made eyes at what he—and only he—would fondly term a 'cock jockey'.

And secondly, it's half nine. I was due at the office half an hour ago.

I dial my work number. It's obvious I can't go in. It's far too late, for starters, and I'd really rather not have to face up to the fact that I've actually made a complete twat of myself, thank you very much. I'll have to speak to Imogen and make some excuse.

I say I've got food poisoning. Not very original, I know, but the roof of my mouth honestly feels like a canary has just shat all over it and I really can't move without thinking I'm about to barf.

'I'm afraid you'll have to come in.' Imogen's voice seeps down the phone line like hydrochloric acid. 'We've an editorial meeting.'

'Yes, but—'

'Katie, just make sure you're here for once, will you?' she spits, and slams the phone down.

'She hung up,' I tell Graham and Shish Kebab in astonishment, before lugging my carcass out of bed and looking for some cleanish clothes to put on.

I hate the whole twatting lot of them.

How on earth am I going to face the world?

Chapter 4

I finally crawl into work at ten thirty-seven.

Marsha looks at me as though she knows something I don't.

'Imogen wants to see you immediately.' She looks pleased as punch. 'She's waiting in her office.'

'Is it about the *crème brûlée* piece?'

She shrugs. 'Search me.'

'Come in,' barks Imogen as I teeter on the threshold of her football pitch-sized office. I'm so nervous that I temporarily forget the shame of last night, which has been rollicking around in the pit of my stomach all the way here. Instead, I twiddle my fingers in terror. God, I'm hungover. The need to race to the loo for a big alcopoo is almost overwhelming. I feel absolutely rancid.

'You were late yesterday,' she snaps, swivelling her powder-blue chair round and narrowing her yellow eyes at me disconcertingly.

'Sorry.' I try to make light of it. 'The train came and I wasn't there.'

Imogen shoots me a look that leaves me in absolutely no

doubt that she finds me about as funny as liver failure, before motioning for me to sit down in one of the bevy of powder-blue suede chairs opposite her kidney-shaped desk. She's lowered mine, I note, by about four inches so she can enjoy looking down on me and watching me squirm.

'I won't bother offering you coffee,' she spits. 'I don't imagine you'll be staying long.'

'Die soon,' I mutter under my breath.

'Which do you want first?' she asks. 'The good news or the bad news?'

'Er...the good news?' I stammer. God. I hope she's going to be quick. I really, really need the loo.

'OK.' She pushes the sleeves of her immaculately cut black jacket up to her elbows and looks at me levelly. 'The good news is that I've been promoted. Again. To the board this time.'

'That's good,' I say, nearly adding, 'So you haven't worn away your tastebuds with arse-licking for nothing then.'

'Isn't it?' She screws up her nose with laughter. 'Of course I'll have to find a replacement for Audrey.'

'Audrey's leaving?'

'No.'

'Then?'

'She's left. Not ten minutes ago.'

'Why?'

'I fired her. She was becoming unreliable. Always racing home early to get back to those snotty brats. Falling asleep in meetings. And she was forever leaking milk over the boardroom table. When she damn well knows I'm allergic to dairy products.'

Any small flicker of maternal instinct is an indication of fatal weakness, in Imogen's opinion. According to her, it's on a par with quiche-eating in males.

So poor old Audrey getting the boot is the bad news. But why is she telling me? Unless... Of course. She's hoping I'll take on Audrey's job. As well as my own, no doubt. And probably for less money, knowing this bloody place.

But if I am doing two jobs, there'll have to be more money, won't there? And if there is more, I'll be able to afford somewhere nicer to live. Somewhere with a garden, perhaps. And a cat flap for Graham and Shish Kebab.

And if I am doing Audrey's job, I probably won't have to sit opposite David any more. Which'll be a major relief after last night.

'You're probably wondering what all this has got to do with you,' Imogen says matter-of-factly.

'Well, I was kind of wondering.'

'You'll be wanting the bad news, no doubt.'

'I thought...'

'What?' Her eyes gleam triumphantly. 'You thought that my sacking that lactating sap was the bad news? Oh no, darling, you don't know the half of it.'

She stretches lazily, like a cat in the sun, enjoying the fact that she's keeping me hanging like a fly in a web. I'm slightly put out. Not because I particularly care what she's got to say but because I'm desperate to get out of here and go for a wazz.

'The bad news,' she grins, 'is that you're fired as well.'

It takes a second for what she's just said to sink in. When it does, I feel winded.

'I would say I'm sorry,' she says, as I stare at her, mouth lolling in disbelief. 'But I'm not. And you know me. I don't mince my words.'

No indeed.

She gets straight down to business. 'If you have any personal belongings in the office, can I suggest you take them with you now, because I'll be giving strict instructions to Marsha that you are barred from the building with immediate effect. Got it?'

'B–but you can't.'

'I can, I'm afraid. I'm the big boss now.'

She's taking the piss.

'I could become a freelancer if it would help...'

'Freeloader, more like,' she scoffs. 'No thanks, love. This isn't a cost-saving exercise. I've already hired someone else on a higher salary to do your job. It's your attitude that's the problem.'

'You what?'

'You're about as reliable as a condom with a pin stuck through it. If it wasn't for your vast personal phone bill I'd be hard put to know whether you actually bothered to come into work at all.'

'But I won't have an income.'

'No, honey, you won't.' She treats me to a cyanide-dusted smile. 'But this is a profit-making organisation, not a charity. We don't think much of paupers in here, sweetcakes, so you'd better sling your hook before I call Security. Oh, and I'm off to the editorial meeting now. You can see yourself out.'

And with that, she spins on her heel, leaving me all alone in her office. I pull a lump of hour-old chewy out of my mouth and chuck it on her chair. That'll be a nice treat for the old bitch's Prada later on.

The first thought that crosses my mind as I step over the threshold of her top floor office and make my way to the lift is that at least I won't have to face David. The editorial meeting must have started by now, so he'll be safely ensconced in the boardroom.

And, much to my relief, he's not at his desk. As Melanie and Serena watch me pack up my highlighter collection and emergency Kit Kat supplies, I feel strangely detached. I'm upset, yes. Of course I'm upset. I've just lost my job. But a tiny part of me feels relieved. Relieved that the decision has been made for me. I don't have to decide to leave and find out what I really want to do. Now, I'm going to have to look for another job. I really don't have any choice in the matter.

I feel oddly elated as I leave the IBS building for the last time. Here I am, in the middle of the morning, with absolutely bugger all to do.

How fanbloodytastic is that?

Of course there's only one thing I can do.

Shop.

But first, I need to make a pit stop at McDonald's in the King's Road.

I'm walking past Whistles when I see David the Gay Homosexual strolling along past the Body Shop on the other side of the road. A hot wave of shame rolls over me and I duck into a shop so he won't see me. As I do so, a niggle of doubt gnaws away at my brain. Is he really gay?

Or was the thought of having to poke me so utterly repulsive that he had to pretend?

'Sod you,' I say out loud.

'Sorry? Can I help you?' asks the lemon-lipped shop assistant.

'No,' I say without thinking. 'You're a shop assistant, not a relationship counsellor. Frankly, I doubt it very much.'

I leave the shop without another word and trot towards the golden arches feeling glum. Bloody David. Who the hell does he think he is, strutting down the road, gayness unashamedly on display, completely spoiling my day of freedom?

The bastard.

I clatter into McDonald's and order a Filet-O-Fish and a Big Mac Meal. Who needs men when there's junk food to be had? Eh? After all, if brown can be the new black and staying in can be the new going out, who's to say that McDonald's can't be the new sex?

Huh?

'What drink would you like with that?' asks the acne-riddled assistant.

'Fanta. No. Coke.'

I forget all about David and losing my job and concentrate on the matter in hand: chuffing down my burger in double quick time. When I'm through, I turn my attention to retail therapy. I take a trip to Lush to drool over jewel-coloured slabs of soap, piled up like Lego bricks, and fizzy bath bombs, heaped on the counter like scoops of sorbet. I spend a fortune on bottles of violet-scented bath oil and orange juice flavour shower gel. I buy blue and white swirled cakes of bubble bath the size of bricks and cutely packaged talcum powder shakers. When I'm done there, I hotfoot it to Georgina von Etzdorf to choose a velvet scarf to see out the winter in. I can't decide between black and sugar-pink or black and mint-green so I buy both. I deserve it, after all. This is no time for economising. Then it's time for some more toiletry sniffing in Boots before selecting several CDs, scented candles, Whittard mugs, a jumper from Kookai and four complete sets of underwear.

It's not until I get home that I realise just how much I've spent. Totting it all up, I estimate that I've probably shelled out over six hundred quid on mere fripperies in an afternoon. All for the sake of cheering myself up.

And now I've lugged it all home, I suddenly don't feel quite so cheerful any more.

In fact, I'm downright miserable. I look at myself in the mirror, making my 'come to bed' face, just to see how pathetically sad I must have looked when I was trying to pull David last night.

Holy fuck.

Do I really look like that when I'm pouting?

The poor bastard must have thought I was constipated.

I call Janice's mobile. She's just leaving work.

'What's up?'

'I just lost my job.'

'You think that's bad,' she humphs. 'You should have seen the mothballed selection I was faced with at that sodding custard cream fest last night.'

'What?'

'At the Evergreen Club.' She sounds mildly irritated. 'Honestly, Katie, after standing me up I'd have thought you could at least pretend to be interested.'

'I lost my job.'

God, she can be so insensitive at times.

'So you said. But presumably you got laid last night to make up for it.'

'No, actually.'

'You didn't?' She brightens.

'No.'

'That's all right then. I mean I thought my evening was bad. I turned up expecting a few dashing war veterans and what did I get?'

'What?'

'Soggy Nice biscuits, dribble and card games.' She sounds disgusted. 'I'm going to have to think again.'

'Oh.'

'But at least I didn't lose my job,' she says. 'You must be really pissed off.'

'Thanks, Janice,' I say. 'I can always rely on you to make me feel better.'

'You're welcome.' All irony is lost on her. 'I have had a bit of good news, by the way.'

'Oh?'

'I just got put on a really prestigious account at work. For breakfast cereal.'

'Is that good?'

'Really good. This giraffe-legged no-burn called Thalia sucked off one of the client's sons and got found out. She was lobbed out faster than you can say fuckwit. And I got her job.'

'Great.'

'Means I'll have less time to look for a husband, of course. But maybe now you've got bugger all to do, you could look for me.'

'Oh, cheers.'

'Well, you could, couldn't you? Go to a few parties and pick someone up on my behalf. Or you could have a look on the internet. Anyway, gotta go. I really haven't got time to chat all day. I'm very busy and important now.'

And with that, she hangs up.

In the face of a distinct lack of sympathy from my girlfriend, I try the next best thing.

I ring George.

Unfortunately, he's ecstatic. He's in love. Lurve. The world has turned into a giant pink marshmallow in the space of an afternoon.

'I met someone.'

'Oh.' I bristle. I still can't help seething with jealousy whenever George declares himself to be in love. After all, David isn't the first gay man I've tried to bag in my lifetime. As I've already said, I've always had a thing for George. I've tried begging. Told him I wouldn't be offended if he wanted me to put a paper bag over my head and pretend I was Beppe from *EastEnders*. And he still declined.

Ungrateful bastard.

Luckily for me and my green-eyed monster, George's liaisons are nothing if not brief. He imagines himself to be in love at least twice a week, before realising that he has nothing whatsoever in common with the other person apart from sexual orientation. Consequently, he's had more brief flings than I've owned knickers. And then some.

'So have you done it yet?' I ask him.

'No.'

'No?' I echo. 'God. It must be serious.'

'I only met him at lunchtime. In the park.'

'Hasn't stopped you before.'

'Ooh,' George shrieks. 'Cutty sark. What's with you?'

'I met someone too,' I confess. 'At work.'

'Is he nice?'

'He's gay.'

'Oh, Katie,' he says sadly. 'You haven't gone and made a holy show of yourself again, have you?'

'I'm afraid I have,' I quaver. 'And now I've lost my job too.'

'Oh dear.' He sounds sympathetic. 'Well, that's all very sad but I'm afraid I can't stop to chat now. I've got a hot date to get ready for. He's taking me to Quaglinos for dinner.'

'Oh.'

I listen obediently for a good half an hour as George tells me just how great life is now that he's found that certain someone number four hundred and fifty-three. He's still talking as I put the phone down as gently as I can and turn to my last resort.

Sam.

Usually, I don't bother troubling Sam with my tales of torture. And I don't really know why I'm bothering now. He's bound to be out with one of the tampon-thin fuckwits he calls girlfriends. I wouldn't mind but they've always got such stupid, sugarpuff names like Coco and Indigo that they get right on my tits before I've even met them.

I'm pleasantly surprised. He's alone. 'Come round,' he says.

Sam lives four streets away, in Calbourne Road. He opens the door of his new house, looking scruffy and dishevelled. There's a paintbrush in his hand and the end of his nose and his fringe are coated in duck-egg blue paint. He looks so familiar and so...so ordinary and Charlie Brown-ish somehow, that I completely forget myself and burst into torrents of tears.

'TTFN?' he asks kindly.

TTFN stands for tea, toast and fags NOW.

'Or perhaps you'd prefer a pizza?'

I nod, miserably.

'Although you might want to wipe that blob of Big Mac sauce out of your fringe first.' He grins. 'And then you can help me paint my new office. I'm doing it blue.'

'Shut up.'

'I do believe I saw a smile. Just a small one. But it's a start.'

'Just ring for a pizza.' I grin despite myself and march into Sam's kitchen, where his precious collection of tube signs is stacked against one wall while he paints the other.

'I will.' He goes straight to the kettle. 'When you've told me what's wrong.'

'I tried to shag a homosexual.'

'Another one?'

I nod miserably. 'Stop fucking laughing.'

'Oh, Katie.' He cracks up. 'When will you ever learn?'

'Oh, take off your teacher's cap,' I strop, sitting down at the table and accepting the hot cup of tea he's offering me. 'You're not so cool, you know. Look at the pathetic excuses for humankind you go out with. Sorry, did I say go out? I meant hump and dump.'

'I don't mean to hump and dump them.' Sam looks moment-arily depressed. 'They just always end up being really boring, that's all.'

'Funny how you only notice that after you've slipped them a length, isn't it?' I tease him. 'After you've got them to give your pork sword a good battering?'

'That's not fair.'

'Yes it is. You're such a roll on, roll off, roll over and piss off merchant. Anyway, if they're all so boring, perhaps you should try a different type. Like one who is slightly more intelligent than your average jellyfish. There's always Janice. Want me to give her a call?'

Sam looks terrified.

'Don't worry,' I say. 'Janice was serious about changing her policy. She's after a capital injection not a hot-beef one right now so you should be safe for a bit.'

'You need to find yourself a proper boyfriend,' Sam tells me later. 'A straight one. Someone who'll take care of you. Then you can forget all this one-night stand nonsense and perhaps you'll actually be happy.'

'Men are pants,' I remind him.

'No they're not.' He flips over to the football.

'Channel flicking,' I say pointedly.

'You shouldn't be so harsh.' He laughs, flicking back to *East-Enders* for me. 'We're not all like Jake, you know. Some of us are actually quite nice.'

'Yes, and most of you are like periods,' I quip. 'Hang around like a bad smell when you're not wanted then when it actually comes to a matter of life or birth, you're off like a stripper's knickers. No thanks. I can do without you. All of you.'

When Sam finds out I've lost my job, he tries to make me tell Mum. After all, he says. I need all the support I can get. 'Or at least Dad then.'

'You're not telling Jeff,' I say firmly. 'No bloody way. He already thinks I'm crap. And he'll probably tell my mum. She'll be devastated if she knows I've been fired. Things like that don't happen in our family.'

Actually, that's the problem with my mother all round. She's so bloody nice. I can't tell you how much I've longed over the years for a mother like Janice's. One who wears Asda ski pants and can't even remember who the father of her children is. I'd even settle for one who went on at me all the time. You know the sort of thing. Nagging at me to lose weight, get a better job, more qualifications. Life would be so much easier. Just my luck to have it really hard. When I fuck up—through spending too much time in the Union bar and not enough in the library, for instance—I get a pat on the head and 'I'm sure you did your best' in reassuring tones. She has so much faith in me it hurts. I'm in a constant state of guilt.

Sam assures me that he won't tell Mum or his dad, as long as I agree to have a long, hard think about what I want to do for a living. Perhaps even go to a temping agency to get some other skills.

'So it's a toss-up between looking like a complete prat in a businessy type suit and women's tights and disappointing my mother, is it?'

'If you put it like that.'

I opt for the first. I promise to think about it.

And thinking about it is bloody well all I intend to do for the time being. After all I've been through, I think a good few weeks of lounging are thoroughly in order.

'So what do you think?' Sam looks at me expectantly.

'Sorry?'

'What do you think you'd like to do?' he asks me.

'You mean I have to think about it now?'

'Yes.'

'But I want to watch *Buffy*.'

'Well, you can't.' Sam takes the TV remote and firmly flips the off button. 'You're going to have to take control of your life, you know. The sooner the better. There must be something you'd like to do.'

'I can't think of anything,' I say honestly. 'But I don't want to work in a bloody office again. Your average tights and handbag environment is all just a bit bloody much for me. And being the new girl is horrid. No one bothers to show you where the toilets are and you always end up making your own tea because everyone else's tastes of fish and has a skin on top.'

Sam throws back his head and roars with laughter.

'What?'

'You're so funny.' He tweaks my ear. 'I can't believe you've come this far without having a clue what it is you want to do.'

'It's not funny.' I look glumly down into my teacup. 'What usually happens to people like me, Sam? Who helps them?'

'I'm very much afraid,' Sam pulls me towards him and gives me a brotherly hug, 'they generally find they have to help themselves.'

'That's what I was worried about.' I turn my attention to a copy of *GQ* on the coffee table. 'Bloody hell. Look at the state of her. More highlights than *Match Of The Day*.'

Sam gently takes the magazine away and looks at me.

'Come on, Simpson. There must be something you enjoy.'

'There isn't.' I shake my head sadly. 'The only things I'm good at are drinking, smoking and sleeping around. And I'm not even very good at that. Yet.'

'You're good at cooking.'

'Am I?' I look round in surprise.

'Course you are,' he says. 'That Malaysian curry you cooked on Janice's birthday was nothing short of stupendous.'

'Thanks.' I'm pleased. 'But where's that going to get me? I don't want to be a housewife.'

'You don't have to. Ever thought of being a chef, say? Or a caterer?'

'Yes,' I say honestly. 'But then I lounged around for too long and it just didn't happen.'

'Well, what about it?'

'I haven't got any experience,' I mope. I'm feeling really sorry for myself now. 'God, Sam, why is it all so bloody hard? It's not my fault I find it hard to apply myself. And no one consulted me before they dragged me into a world where I have to work for a bloody living. I think I'd have done far better in a trust fund type situation.'

'You could get some work experience in a restaurant for a few weeks,' Sam suggests, his face earnest. 'Ever thought about being a waitress for a bit? Just to earn some money and see what's around?'

'The only thing I've thought about waitressing is that it's a dreadful, menial, badly paid job,' I say. 'God, Sam, I've had more fun treating a vicious bout of cystitis.'

'What about setting up on your own?' Sam suddenly brightens.

'As what?'

'As a caterer.' He grins. 'I can even use you for some of my client launches.'

'I don't have the money to set up.'

'You could get a loan.'

'I'll think about it.'

'Well, do.' Sam gives me another bear hug. 'And so will I. Perhaps I can come up with a few ideas.'

Over the next few weeks I take to unemployment like a duck to water. One Friday, I meet Janice in the Exhibit for a bottle of wine and listen to all her work gossip. And that's when it strikes me that I have nothing to say in return. I mean, how interesting is the 'got up, dressed, bought a loaf' type scenario to your average advertising exec who is so busy from Monday to Friday she barely has time to wipe her own bum.

'What's wrong?'

'I'm bored,' I whinge. 'I've got nothing to look forward to.'

'Yes you have, hon.' She gives me a fag and lights one for herself. 'You're having a party.'

'I'm not.'

'You are. You're having a party for your thirtieth because I've met someone and I need an excuse to invite him out on a date.'

'Can't he invite you?'

'It's delicate.'

'Why? Does he melt if he goes outside?'

'No.'

'Where'd you meet him?'

'At a funeral.'

I immediately feel guilty. 'Oh God, Janice, I'm sorry. I had no idea someone had died.'

'They haven't.' She looks surprised. 'Oh, I see what you mean. Well, yes, they have. His wife actually. But I didn't know her from Adam so I'm hardly grief-stricken.'

'So what...?'

'Was I doing at the funeral? Well, I was getting nowhere fast with that bloody marriage agency, as you well know. And the Evergreen Club was a big no no. I mean I want old and rich but I'm not ready for incontinence just yet thanks. I want someone with a bit of get up and go. In case I have to take him anywhere public.'

'Right.'

'So I had a quick flick through the funeral notices in the *Tory-graph*. See if anyone interesting had carked it. Thought there might be a few eligible widowers knocking about. And this one looked promising. So I slipped into a little black suit, shrugged on some designer bins, got myself down to Waterloo and hopped on a train.'

'I see.'

'I stood at the back of the cathedral, of course. No point drawing attention to myself. It was easy-peasy. Afterwards, I shook his hand at the graveside. Said I was a friend of the wife. Told him we'd done charity work together.'

'Oh, right.'

About the nearest Janice has ever got to doing charity work was sucking off a sex-starved American sailor we met in the Mucky Duck pub in Portsmouth.

'I was glad I hadn't bothered to bone up beforehand,' she goes on, ignoring my shocked look. 'Because the vicar burbled on so much about what a wonderful woman she was, I felt as if I'd known her for years. I half expected him to start going on about what a great lay she was.'

'But...'

'Anyway, I went back to the house. Reassuringly large. And the champagne was good quality. None of your M&S cheap shite. And we got on like a house on fire. Afterwards, he kissed my hand and said he hoped I'd stay in touch. So I thought your birthday was the perfect excuse to cheer him up a bit.'

'And fuck your way to a fortune,' I say.

'Quite.'

'Was the death expected?' I ask.

'God, no. Totally out of the blue. Silly bitch skied into a tree. Completely ruined the holiday, as you can imagine. Poor bastard had to cut it short and come home. So selfish.'

'Janice!'

'What? What have you got to complain about? You're getting a birthday party out of this. And I'll invite lots of G 'n' T. For you, I mean. I'll probably have to go without.'

G 'n' T stand for Gorgeous 'n' Thick. It's a phrase reserved for decorative men with shit for brains.

'You'll have to,' I say. 'I certainly don't know any.'

'So that's a yes then?'

'Looks like it.'

'Oh, great,' she enthuses, pouring herself a last glass of wine. 'Now, which bag do you think I should use for the occasion? The pink Tocca or the black Gucci?'

'How old is he?'

'Sixty-nine.'

'Try the blue and white Tesco then.' I giggle. 'No, seriously, the only bag he'll be familiar with will be attached to his stomach with a plastic tube so he probably won't give a toss.'

She makes a wry face, downing the last of her wine and standing up to go.

'He's not THAT old,' she protests.

'He's Granddad age,' I point out. That's old enough for me. She pulls on a cardigan. 'I'll see you on Saturday then?'

'Will you?'

'Yes. For your party, duh.'

'Can't I have it on Friday? It's my actual birthday on Friday.'

'No, you can't.' She picks up her fags. 'He can't make it on Friday. He's got a meeting.'

'Golden oldies again?'

'Work,' she huffs. 'Anyway, you'll have to make it Saturday. Otherwise he can't come. And that's the whole point.'

'I thought it was my birthday party.'

'And that, obviously.'

'What about the invitations?'

'All taken care of.' She counts off on her fingers. 'I've invited all our friends. Plus a few of the No Bums from work. Gets me brownie points, you know.'

'Great.'

'And Poppy and Seb. Then we won't have to see them for a bit.'

'True.'

Poppy is our very worst duty friend. The college buddy we just can't seem to shake. She's so bloody nice there's nothing we can do to get rid of her.

'And George has invited a load of his friends. Didier's coming. And Sylvain. Christian. Fran the Tran. Felix and Oliver. Archie and Hugo. Fat Dexter. Colin and Huw. Sheena and Kath. And all of Sam's mates are coming. Oh, and George has invited his new man.'

'What's he like?'

'Dunno. Haven't met him yet. Anyway. Got to go. Got to ring Jasper.'

'Who's Jasper?'

'Funeral guy, dumbo. I've gotta tell him it's all on. Oh, and by the way, you'll have to do the catering. I'm tied to the fax machine by my Tampax string at the moment so I won't be able to help. Sozz.'

Chapter 5

For some reason, I'm so pissed off about having to do the catering for my own party, I almost cancel the whole blimming thing.

Until George offers to help me do all the shopping, that is.

'And pay for it?' I ask. 'I'm unemployed, don't forget.'

He clops round to my flat at nine o'clock on Saturday morning as arranged, just as I'm feeling weepy over the lovely birthday card Mum has sent me. There's one from Sam's dad, Jeff, as well. They're both so full of optimism for my 'bright' future that I just don't have the heart to tell them I'm a total failure.

I haven't even told them I've been sacked yet.

'Make me a cup of tea,' George demands, hurling himself melodramatically onto the sofa and lighting a fag. 'That's Earl Grey and not council house tea by the way. I'm not Dot frigging Cotton. Come on. Hurry up. I think I've got diphtheria. I've been shitting like a witch all morning and I'm severely dehydrated.'

'You're just hungover,' I tell him. 'And we haven't got time for tea, council house or otherwise.'

He wants to shop at the Italian deli, where he gleefully

squanders a small fortune each week on slivers of Parma ham, fat, glistening green olives, wodges of fruity taleggio and individual portions of panna cotta. I tell him that an out-of-town superstore, where we'll be able to peruse the on-pack promotions to our hearts' content, will be far more suitable. At ten o'clock, after Earl Grey and toast, we jump into the Rustbucket, which is really more of a shed on castors than an actual car, and head for Wandsworth town.

'What time's the cling film coming off?' he asks as I demonstrate how to put a pound in the slot to release the trolley.

'You should know,' I tell him. 'You organised this farce, not me. And I do hope you and Janice have thought to invite some potential shags for me. Because if I have to spend my party on my own while the two of you drag your arses round the cork flooring like bitches on heat, I'll quite happily whip out your small intestines with a crochet hook. Got it?'

'Absobloodylutely.' George takes the trolley off my hands. 'Now show me what we do. Can we smoke in here, or should I have brought patches?'

As we shop, I refuse to let him talk about his wonderful new man. Selfish, I may be, but the whole whimsy will only last a matter of weeks. George is as bad as Sam. They both ought to have revolving doors on their bedrooms.

'I hope people won't think we're *together* together,' he comments, lobbing a box of breadsticks into the trolley. 'You look like a right bush faggot since you lost your job and stopped brushing your hair.'

'Thanks.'

'People might think I'm responsible.' He examines a packet of meringue nests and turns his nose up. 'They'll think I've taken you home and rogered you senseless. And much as I love you, darling, and want you to have my basted baby, the thought of that whole carry-on makes me want to scrunch my bottom up rather.'

As George clacks happily round the store, amusing himself

with what he calls his 'common people impressions', yelling 'Winona, Kylie, Mazola. 'Old yer Nan's 'and while Mummay lights 'er fag', I escape to the crisps and snacks aisle, filling the trolley with as many cashew nuts, cheesy Wotsits and Twiglets I can get away with. Bowling round into the nappy section, I decide I'd better try and find him again, before he starts clucking over the breast pumps. I don't want him going on at me about the Womb To Let signs again. Not on my bloody birthday of all days.

As I wheel the wobbly trolley down the aisle, I start as my gaze hits upon someone familiar.

Frighteningly familiar.

Oh my God.

Isn't that...?

My bowels turn to liquid and my mouth fills with bile. I'm rooted to the spot.

It is.

Jake and Fishpants.

They're at the end of the aisle, cooing over the Postman Pat bibs. Which strikes me as odd. I'd have thought the Bacardi Breezers were more her style. Until I look down, of course, and realise that Fishpants is looking rather large. Which is putting it mildly. She's actually more than large. She's enormously, belly-button poppingly, titanically huge. Unless I'm very much mistaken, she's about to drop a sprog straight into the crotch of her white ski pants any minute now.

Which, again, is odd.

Seeing as Jake and I only split five months ago.

The bastard.

The packets of Farley's rusks stacked either side of me merge into a pink and blue blur as the room starts to spin. God. I have to get out of here before they spot me. I feel sick.

Too late. Before I can do a three-point turn and do a bunk, Jake sees me. And because it's all too obvious that I've seen him see me, there's no way we can avoid an encounter. Not without us both appearing rude. And that's not very nice, is it? So, despite the fact that we'd probably both rather drink the menstrual blood of a cow, we say hi. There's an uncomfortable silence as we both recall that the last time we clapped eyes on each other was when I caught him with Fishpants pranged on the end of his penis like a harpooned seal.

'Are you well?'

'Couldn't be better.' God. I wish I'd bothered to run a comb through my tatty hair. I bet I look as though I've really gone to pot. 'You?'

'Fine.' He tries a smile. 'We, er...' He pats Fishpant's tummy protectively and I decide that, yes, I really might be about to puke. Fathers-to-be shouldn't be allowed to be that damn attractive. He should be out cleaning the car, or mowing the lawn. Not strutting round the supermarket, getting in my face.

'So I see. Well, I'd better get going...' I drift uncomfortably. 'I've got a party to cook for.'

'I'm sure you have. Happy birthday, by the way.'

My stomach flick-flacks like an Olympic gymnast. He's remembered.

Fishpants looks as though she might be about to slap him.

'Thanks,' I say. 'Anyway. Better go. Good luck with the...you know. Child.'

'Thanks.' He smiles.

As I scuttle away, I tell myself that him remembering my birthday means nothing. I caught him shagging someone else, for fuck's sake. And he didn't exactly rush out and send me a card, did he?

I wander round in a daze, picking things up and slamming them into my trolley in arbitrary fashion. I don't even know what I'm buying. I'm just fingering a carton of orange juice when a sharp little voice behind me yells, 'Put that back. Immediately.'

I'm so confused I wonder if I might have been caught stealing. Then I spin round to see George hopping up and down like an angry pixie.

'We need orange juice for the Harvey Wallbangers,' I protest. 'Sam's bringing a load of Galliano.'

'It's got economy written all over it,' he points out. 'You can't buy that. Go and get us some of the reassuringly expensive kind.'

'What's the magic word?'

'Immediately.'

As we wait in the queue I tell him what I've just seen.

'They must have been at it for months before I found out,' I say miserably. 'What do you think?'

'I think,' he says joyfully, 'that I'd like to see her head on a stick. I hope she gets dental caries and all her teeth fall out. I hope she gets a horrible yeast infection.'

I cheer up slightly.

'And genital herpes,' I say happily.

'And burning wee,' he adds. 'For life.'

'And alopecia.'

'And I hope the baby has a hare lip,' George screeches.

'Oh no,' I plead. 'It's not the baby's fault if its father thinks with his dick and its mother's a brazen slag. Can't we just hope it has a big strawberry birthmark? On its back perhaps, so people only notice when it's changing for swimming.'

'If you want.' He chews his lip. 'But, God, you're too nice. That's why you let him treat you like poo in the first place, darling.'

Then seeing how miserable I am, he gives me a big hug. 'Come on,' he says. 'I'll pay for this lot then we'll have a lovely, faggotty clack round the shops.'

As we approach the till, the man in front of us hastily neatens his frozen lasagne, Fairy liquid and six-pack of Carlsberg into an anally retentive little pile so there's no chance of anything of ours getting mixed up with his and infecting it. I lob everything onto the belt. Scarlet cherry tomatoes. Ripe goat's cheese. Fragrant bunches of herbs. Spicy mango chutney. Bitter chocolate. Double cream. Plump prunes. Gooey Brie. Cheddar. Chicken. Steaks. A pineapple. The peroxide blonde on the till scans through the last of them and, setting her frosted peach lips into a hard line, tells us what we owe.

'Can we have a couple more bags, do you think?' I ask politely.

She sullenly slams down two more carriers and George hands over his Amex.

'Thank you so much, Jean,' he says, pointing at her badge. 'Pleasure doing business with you, I don't think.'

'I beg your—'

'I take it you can read?' he asks sternly. 'Even though you only work in a shop? So you'll know what that says.' He stabs a finger at the sign above her head.

Jean glances at it with a face that has forty Lambert and Butler a day stamped all over it.

'Says Service Till, does it not?' he prompts. 'Not Rudeness Till. And that badge you're wearing says "Here to help", not "Here to dish out the large". Perhaps you'd care to remember that in future.'

And with a final sneer he waltzes off with the trolley, clicking one last 'sour cow' in her direction.

I thank God I don't normally shop here and mentally cross it off my list for future patronage.

Chapter 6

George and I get a free sauna as I spend the rest of my big day slaving over a hot stove. I steam tiny Chinese pork dumplings over the stove and simmer hot and sour soup. Tumble juicy king prawns into coconut milk for fragrant green curry and sprinkle chunks of tender chicken into chopped fresh tomatoes for spicy balti. I chop mangoes. Simmer sugar. Find prawn crackers, fish sauce and chillies. I mix and mash, stir and steam. Make miniature Yorkshire puddings with cocktail sausages on top. As the room begins to fill with a medley of delicious aromas, I heave a sigh of satisfaction. Jamie and Delia, eat your bloody hearts out.

As I content myself in my kitchen, I suddenly realise I feel more relaxed than I have done for weeks. I'm upset about Jake. And that business with David. And losing my job, come to that. But it doesn't take much to realise that I'm definitely happiest when I'm cooking for other people. Perhaps I should look into actually using my qualifications instead of just having them.

While I cook, George fills the sitting room with fondant-pink peonies in chunky glass vases and covers the mantelpieces in every room with fat, waxy church candles. He hangs strings of tiny pink fairylights everywhere so they'll twinkle magically in the dusk. By the time we've both finished, the flat is party perfect.

'And now for the *pièce de résistance*.' George, grinning his head off, produces a large, flat box with a flourish.

'Open it then.'

I do. Inside, nestling among layers of tissue paper, is the most beautiful dress I've ever seen. The skirt is palest pink and gauzy, the bodice shocking pink, threaded with gold. It must have cost him the best part of five hundred quid.

But then he can afford it.

'It's gorgeous.' I hug him.

'Go and put it on then.' He hugs me back. 'I've got to put my slap on too.'

'Your slap?'

'Oh yes.' He nods. 'I'm coming in full drag.'

At seven o'clock, Janice's brand new plum-coloured Beetle mounts the kerb and she trips up to the door in a pair of four-inch stack heels and a crotch-skimming halter-necked frock that squashes her boobs together spectacularly.

'Happy birthday, my lovely.' She gives me a huge hug and hands over a bunch of my favourite marshmallow pink tulips and a bag filled with sweets and tiny presents wrapped in iridescent, rainbow-coloured paper. 'And fear not. I've invited a delicious selection of G 'n' Ts for you.'

'Ooh, goodie.' I smile. 'You look lovely, by the way.'

'So do you,' she says automatically, before realising I'm still in my Frank Bruno bathrobe. 'For a boxer,' she adds and we both collapse in giggles.

At seven thirty, Sam's convertible something or other pulls up outside and he waltzes in, putting down a huge box full of clinking bottles and giving me a whopping great kiss on the cheek.

'Happy birthday, old thing.'

'Not so much of the old, thanks.'

As all my friends greet each other, champagne corks pop and Janice, pouring me a glass full of bubbles, shoos me off to my room to put on the pink dress. I down my first drink in one, my stomach churning with a mixture of party excitement and secret misery at the thought of Jake and Fishpants and their bun, cooking happily away in her oven.

'So what's this man of yours like?' I ask Janice. 'Am I going to like him or am I going to wonder if you've had a taste lobotomy when I see him? Come on. Spill the beans. I've only got a name to go on. And judging by that, he sounds like a frigging labrador.'

'Let's just say he'll do nicely.'

'You make him sound like an American Express card.'

'Exactly.' She grins. 'And I'm banking on Voyage membership and an expense account at Harvey Nicks before the month's out. Now pucker up. You're going to look gorgeous when I'm done. Men will be falling over themselves to shag you.'

'As long as a shag's all they're after,' I joke. 'I'd rather stick broken bottles up my bum than go out with any of the men we know. And just between you and me, I feel, well...'

'What?'

'I feel a bit, you know, weird.'

'Why?'

'I saw Jake today.'

'Oh God. Oh hon. Are you OK?'

'Yup.' I swallow.

'Was he...'

'With her? Oh yes. She's only up the duff, isn't she?'

'Noooooooooooo way!'

'Way. About to have it, by the look of things. I'm really pissed off, to be honest.'

'I know,' she soothes, dusting glitter over my eyelids. 'You'll feel a lot better once you've shagged someone else. Honest.'

She gives me a comforting hug and gets back to work on

my face. By the time I get downstairs, the party is in full swing. Sam's on bar duty. He's set up a table in the corner and is pouring everyone decadent cocktails.

'Wow,' he says when he sees me in my new dress.

'Don't be a disgusting letch,' I admonish him. 'And give me a margarita. I love margaritas.'

'Oooh, so do I,' says a tapeworm in a see-through white dress. 'I'll have one of those too. My name's Kimberley, by the way,' she adds shyly, batting enormous eyelashes at Sam.

'Here we fucking go,' I mouth at him, saying, 'Just give me my drink and I'll leave you two to it.'

Sam is really excited tonight. But it's not just down to the prospect of pulling Kimberley, whoever she is. He's just persuaded one of his major clients to come with him when he starts up Freeman PR. Which is a huge coup. His boss'll be furious, but it means others will follow. And he'll be made. I only know this because my mum told me when she called me this afternoon to wish me a happy birthday.

'Jeff is pleased as punch,' she told me. 'He's just gone into his garden now to put some potatoes in, he's so pleased.'

'Great,' I said. God, the excitement of some people's lives. Couldn't he have hoofed back a double whisky in one go or something? Still, it did make me laugh to think of Jeff in the same garden Sam and I used to play in as kids, eating soil and making houses for worms. Sam's come a long way since then, I think now, seeing him, so easy and confident, happily mixing drinks for people he's never met before, safe in the knowledge that he has a shining career ahead of him and a father who's so proud of him he's taken to planting root vegetables in his honour. Meanwhile, what have I done?

Got the boot for being a lazy sow, that's what. Not much to be proud of there.

I glance round my sitting room. There's George, looking amazing in black leather hot pants, fishnets, six-inch stilettos and a long pillar-box red wig.

'You look lovely,' I tell him. 'Your new bloke is going to be blown away. When's he coming?'

'Sooner than he thinks,' George cackles. 'You're looking pretty bloody amazing yourself. I knew that dress was made for you.'

'Thanks.' I smile back, starting to enjoy myself. The room is filling up quickly. Good old Janice was right. There's tons of G 'n' T here. Who knows? I might even enjoy myself. Oh, and there's the doorbell again.

'Flowers for Miss Simpson.'

'That's me.'

A man hands me a huge bunch of sugar-pink roses.

I take them into the kitchen, ripping open the envelope on the little card and reading it. Who are they from?

Shagging fuck.

'Happy Birthday,' says the card. 'For Old Times' Sake.'

Inside is an all too familiar scrawl. 'Lovely to see you today. Have a good one. Love Jake.'

My stomach lurches. But there's no time to stop and think. Janice is nearly upon me, dragging the guy with the dead wife behind her. I chuck the roses into the corner of the room out of sight and prepare to meet her future husband.

'You OK?'

'Yep. Just getting some air, you know.'

'This is Jasper.'

'Hi.'

'Hi.' He grins.

Hmm. Not what I expected at all.

'You look...' I stop.

'Yes?'

'You don't look as sad as I expected.'

'I'm sorry?'

Well. His wife's dead, after all. He should have the decency to look a bit miserable, instead of blatantly undressing Janice with his eyes. And he's *far* too old for her. His combat pants and

T-shirt don't fool me. In fact, he looks faintly ridiculous. Just who is he trying to kid?

Janice, I suppose.

I mean it wouldn't be so bad if he wasn't so wrinkled. He's got a face like an apricot that's shrivelled in the sun.

Mutton dressed as pig.

Ram dressed as lamb.

The doorbell rings again and, gratefully, I excuse myself. I have no idea what to say to this strange creature. Janice will have to entertain him on her own.

I open the door.

And get the shock of my life.

'What the fuck are you doing here?' my party guest and I both screech at the same time.

'George invited me,' David stutters. 'I had no idea you'd be here.'

'I sodding well live here,' I bridle. 'It's my birthday. This is my party.'

And I'll cry if I sodding well want to.

'I tried to call you,' David says. 'After you left IBS. But you were always out.'

'I wasn't,' I reply. 'I just didn't want to talk to you.'

'Are you OK?'

'Never better. You?'

'Fine. Happy, actually. I've met this—'

'George,' I say. 'You already said.'

'You know him?'

'He's one of my best friends.'

'Oh God.'

'It's OK,' I tell him. 'To be honest, I'm a bit relieved to find out you are really gay. I thought you weren't a proper Marmite miner at all. You seemed so...well...so...'

'So what?'

'Straight, I suppose. I thought it might be just an excuse not to shag me.'

'So I'm forgiven?'

'I can't afford many more enemies at the moment.' I laugh. 'I've got one best friend desperately trying to marry that prune over there and another Velcroed to that creature over there in the see-through dress. Kimberley or something.'

'God,' he tuts. 'Terrible name. She sounds like a second-rate wine bar.'

'Doesn't she?' I giggle.

'Oh, it's so nice to see you.' He laughs, giving me a huge hug. 'And I'm sorry about your job. And, well, the other...'

'Forget about it.' I shrug. 'It's nice to see you too.'

And it is. I've sort of missed David, in a funny way. 'And I'm sorry I forced you to look at my minky.'

'Minky?' He grins. 'What minky?'

George greets David as though they've known each other for ever. Janice is flitting from room to room in her belt of a dress, finding cigars, drinks and nibbles for her prospective groom, and Sam and the Wine Bar are getting on famously.

I brush fag ash off my favourite saggy pink beanbag and flop, wondering if anyone's going to remember to talk to me. As the party progresses I watch from outside as my three best friends enjoy themselves with other people, drinking through the bar, smoking colourful fags and eating my food. I feel about as welcome at my own sodding party as a BLT at a Bar Mitzvah.

But hang on.

Isn't the room filling up with eligible men? And I do, after all, have a point to make. How dare Jake try to spoil my party by sending me flowers? Five months on and he's still playing mind games, the sod.

The shit was probably hoping they'd cause a wave of nostalgia so powerful I wouldn't be able to bring myself to bonk anyone else. Well, he can forget that idea for a start. Here I am. Young—well, thirty's not exactly old. Free. And raring to go. So it's decision time. Should I go all out for a nice bit of G 'n' T or should I play safe and Go Ugly Early?

I'm just deciding when George hands me a slippery witch. Janice taps me on the other shoulder and offers me another glass of champagne.

They haven't quite forgotten me then.

'Katie, this is Max.' Janice pulls some poor bloke over by the scruff of his neck. 'Max, Katie. Max and I work together.'

She's behaving so formally, I half expect her to fill in important personal details on my behalf, like 'Katie is unemployed and stuffs her face at every available opportunity. Max works very hard but his hobbies are panty-sniffing and reading the Yellow Pages.'

Except that he doesn't look like someone who might read the Yellow Pages for fun. Actually, he looks pretty good.

'You're very sparkly,' he says when Janice waltzes off to rejoin Filthy Rich.

'Thanks.' I check him out once more and mentally erase any thoughts of Going Ugly Early from my mind. Max is gorgeous. Beautiful eyes. A soft warm brown. Like melted Mars bars. No, wait. They're more like...

'And you have eyes like a cow,' I blurt.

Fuck. What made me say that?

'God, sorry.' I swig my drink. 'I'm not really used to flirting. I normally only fancy gay boys and bastards, you see. And seeing as you're obviously neither, I think it's only fair to inform you that you don't stand much of a chance.'

Bugger. And he seems so nice as well. Trust me to fuck up so early on in the proceedings.

Quickly, I remind myself that 'nice' is the sort of word people use to describe fairy cakes. I have no long-term use for this man, other than as my first Bag A Shag candidate. So why should I care what he thinks of me?

Still, it's probably just as well to be honest with him. Tell him that the most he can expect is a trip upstairs to my room, whereupon I'll bonk his brains out before offering him a post-coital Kit Kat from my knicker drawer.

Or perhaps it would be wiser to try the subtle approach.

Janice is right. I really am shit at shagging around. I have no idea what comes next.

Luckily, Max seems to know the form. Lips twitching with silent laughter, he asks me how I know he's not a complete bastard. 'I mean you're quite right,' he says. 'I'm not. But I'm sure we could probably put a daily beating clause into the pre-nuptial agreement if you wanted.'

'Huh?'

'That's a joke, by the way.'

'Oh...right.'

'Let's just take it one night at a time, shall we?' He grins. 'No need to plan the wedding just yet.'

It's the 'one night' that does it. Filled with relief, I realise his intentions are just as wicked as mine. He wants a quick shag. Which means he won't expect me to go out on a date afterwards. So I won't have to wear a glamorous golden dress and graze on lettuce leaves all night, when all I want to do is wear elasticated waists and splatter spag bol down my front. We can just get straight down to business.

Thank God I remembered to put clean sheets on the bed.

The rest of the evening is as sparkly as my dress. And despite the fact that I catch George and David snogging passionately more than once, and that Sam's hand is clamped to Wine Bar's boob like a piece of fuzzy felt, I don't mind. Because Max is brilliant fun. He's even better at dancing than George.

Which is saying something for a straight bloke.

'You are sure you're not gay, aren't you?' I double-check as we make our way to the 'bar'.

'I'm sure.' Max grins, mixing us both enormous Bellinis.

'How sure?'

'Very.'

'Sure?'

'Look,' he takes my hand in his, 'I'm very, very taken with you indeed. And if you'll only stop fart-arseing about with all this polite drinking and dancing, I'll bloody well take you up-stairs and show you just how un-gay I can be when it matters.'

I giggle. 'I thought you'd never ask.'

Thanking my lucky stars I've had my minky waxed, prop-erly this time, not *Blue Peter* fashion with a strip of sticky-backed plastic, I allow him to lead me to the bottom of the stairs as people dance, drink and fall drunkenly around us. We're halfway to my bedroom when Sam's voice comes floating up after us. He comes into the hall, swiftly followed by Wine Bar.

'Katie?'

'I'm going to bed.' I smile naughtily. 'And I'm not alone.'

'You sure you're OK?'

'Don't worry. I'm a big girl now. I can look after myself.'

I fling open the bedroom door, pushing Max towards the bed and pouncing on him like a lion. There's a squeal from under the bedclothes.

'Was that you?' He looks startled.

'Just the cat.' I nod, as Graham bolts, spiky with indignation, into the wardrobe.

Max's skin smells delicious. All sea salt and lemons. And he's so bloody gorgeous that his very proximity makes the edges of my teeth tingle. When he finally kisses me, a bolt of elec-tricity shoots from the top of my head to my groin and I melt against him, pressing myself to him with increasing urgency. And as I do so, I feel him pressing back. And I know how much he wants me.

Suddenly, I hold back.

What if he's after something more permanent?

Will I be able to say no?

Probably not. Max looks as if he might be kind of moreish. Dangerously moreish at that. Like chocolate.

And not your dodgy pretend chocolate either. I'm talking the dark, rich, exceptionally smooth kind.

One bite and you're hooked.

'What's wrong?'

'Nothing.'

'Don't you want to?'

Do I?

Oh sod it.

As I surrender myself completely, and Max slowly peels off George's gauzy pink dress, I rejoice that I've had the foresight to wear matching bra and knickers for a change.

I needn't have worried in any case. I'm soon rid of them.

As he frees himself from his boxers, a delicate operation involving trying to get them down without catching his stiffy in the fly, I'm more than pleased to note that he's in possession of the full box of tricks. He's got a good girth on him. I can't wait.

But I remember to be sensible. Tingling with anticipation, I help him roll on the condom. Then, with a silent 'up yours, Jake Carpenter', I lower myself onto his quivering cock.

Shit. It's been so long. It's amazing.

It's agony.

Ecstasy.

'Stop,' I pant. 'No, please don't stop. Don't ever stop.'

'You're gorgeous,' he moans, pulling on my hips and burying himself so deep inside me I can't tell where I end and he begins.

'Ooh, don't stop,' I pant again. 'Yes. Stop. Now. Fucking just stop. Max. I'm serious.'

'What?'

'Just getthefuckoffme. NOW. Something's wrong. Something's happened to my…AAAAAAAAAAAAAAAAAAAA AAAAGH.'

Afterwards, Janice said you could have heard my screams in Morden. I howled like a dog, apparently. Squealed like a pig on a stick. At any rate, it was enough to bring Sam, Janice, David and George (feather boa tangled around his legs in his haste) hurtling into my room, where Sam, thinking I was under some sort of attack, grabbed Max—actually grabbed him properly, like in a real fight—and told him to get the fuck out.

'At least let him put on his boxers,' George suggested, staring at Max in all his rapidly detumescing glory.

'No way,' Sam yelled. 'Get out of here now, you pervert, before I ram my fist down your throat.'

'Now hold on,' I managed to stutter. But to no avail. Sam was practically spitting with fury.

I can only imagine the poor guy must have waited until he got out into the street before removing the strawberry Jiffi, because it was still flobbering from the end of his willy when he ran from the room. And it wasn't until it was too late that I recovered the powers of speech and was able to indicate that he hadn't been trying to rape me. I was in agony. Unbearable, burning agony and I didn't know why. 'How can you be?' Janice hooted. 'You're not exactly a virgin.'

An ambulance was called nonetheless, and duly arrived, sirens blaring as the curtain twitchers across the road had a field day. Six grown men witnessed me writhing naked on the bed, a pillow pressed between my legs to try and numb the pain.

'What's wrong with her?' Sam shouted at them all, his face full of concern. 'Is there any blood?'

'I don't want Sam seeing my bum,' I sobbed, tears of shame pouring down my face as six strangers caught me full frontal. 'I know him.'

Mercifully, my examination is brief. Hospitalisation isn't necessary and I'm soon sitting in an ice-cold bath, still stinging, shivering with misery and howling at the four of them, who are sitting in a row along the edge of the bath smoking fags.

It's absolutely the last time I ever chop chillies then help roll on the condom.

'I'm so pathetic,' I hiccup. Snot streams down my face and blends into what's left of my lippy.

'You're not,' the four of them chorus dutifully.

'I am.' I shudder. 'I can't hold down a job and I can't even shag around when I want to without fucking it up. You lot are so lucky. Complete whores, the lot of you.'

'And damn good at it too,' George preens.

'Thanks,' huffs Janice.

'I'm the David Brent of sleeping around,' I whine.

'You're not.'

'I am. I'm a human bloody contraceptive.'

Sam looks as though he might be going to laugh, but Janice, bless her, silences him with a stiletto to the shin bone.

'You think you've got it bad,' she tells me. 'Think how I feel. Poppy told me tonight that she's getting bloody married. Before me and everything.'

'Well, she has got a boyfriend,' I tell her. 'That helps.'

'She's been with Seb for six years,' George points out. 'And they are the perfect couple.'

'Aren't they fucking just?' she says bitterly. 'And you haven't heard the worst of it.'

'What?'

'She's asked me to be her bridesmaid.'

'Oh God.'

'I know. Isn't it pathetic? I wouldn't even invite her to my wedding and she goes and asks me to be her bloody bridesmaid.'

'God,' I say again. 'Poor you.'

Then for some reason I burst into tears. Great, snotting, gulping tears.

Janice looks guilty.

'Come on, lovely,' she reassures me. 'Try not to cry. Shagging around will come much more easily with practice.'

'Well, she can practise on you if she likes but she's not having a go on me,' George pouts. 'I'm not a ruddy merry-go-round.'

'No,' I snipe. 'You're more like a short stay parking space.'

'She wouldn't want to have a go on you, would she?' Janice scoffs. 'You're a poo pusher, for fuck's sake. A mincing little fudge packer. Sorry, David. No offence.'

'None taken.'

'And you fancy Phillip Schofield,' I point out.

'You don't?' David looks as though he's going to laugh.

'She's making it up to get back at me,' George says. 'Because I can sleep with you and she can't.'

'I'll shag you if you like, Katie,' Sam says kindly.

'Don't be ridiculous,' I snap. 'I'd rather shag Neil Kinnock.'

Sam looks a bit hurt but soon bounces back.

'Who was that bloke anyway?'

'Friend of mine,' Janice says. 'From work.'

'Not any more,' David points out.

'Shit, you're right,' Janice realises. 'And he's on good terms with my boss. Bloody hell, Katie, you know how to pick them.'

'You introduced us.' I bristle with indignation. 'You picked him for me. Even though I told you not to try and matchmake.'

'You'll have to ring and apologise,' she bosses.

'I can't. How can I? He won't want to talk to me. Not after what happened. I'll be about as popular as a screening of *Deep Throat* at a royal wedding.'

'You can,' Janice says. 'And you will. You better bloody had, anyway. I'm not losing my job because of you.'

'Thanks, Janice,' I say. 'I'm choked.'

Chapter 7

Isn't it weird how something actually pretty OK can come out of such gloom and doom?

The smell of stale fags has barely left the living room when duty friend Poppy rings to say that the catering at my party was 'divine'. I'm surprised. I don't even remember Poppy actually being at my party, which shows a) just how rendered I was and b) how significant she is in my life. But she wants to know if I'd mind divulging the name of the firm. And when I tell her I did it all myself in an afternoon, her voice goes all wobbly and she suddenly bursts into tears.

'What?' I raise my eyes heavenward. For God's sake. It's me who is supposed to be upset, isn't it? I've got no job, no one to shag and a sore bum. Whereas Poppy has coins aplenty, courtesy of a rich, if slightly boring boyfriend, and a very small bum. Shouldn't I be the one grubbing for sympathy here?

'We've had a dizz...'

Cherrrist. Out with it, love. I haven't got all day.

Actually, I have, but it's not much fun listening to someone else blub down the phone.

'Dizzz. Dizzzarrster.'

'Oh dear,' I faux sympathise, hoping cruelly that Seb has up and dumped her from a truly great height. 'What is it? Anything I can do?'

'The ccccc...'

'Cunt?' I supply hopefully. God. He must have done something really horrible if Perfect Poppy is actually attempting to use the C word.

'NO.' She sounds shocked. 'Caterer. The caterer we were going to use for our wedding's gone bloody bust. Everything's ruined.'

'Is it?' I smile down the phone, hoping she can't hear it in my voice.

'I don't suppose...'

'What?'

'Don't suppose you fancy giving it a go, do you, Katie? I'd pay you, of course. It's just that we can't get anyone else at short notice. Mummy's tried everyone. She's even gone on the internet.'

'I don't know.' I hesitate. Frankly it all sounds a bit bloody much. I mean I know Sam says I'm a brilliant cook, but knocking up a bowlful of biryani or two for my mates—especially when it means I get to trough a good half of it—is one thing. Churning out miniature marzipan bridegrooms and serving teeny tomato tartlettes on silver platters to two hundred horsy strangers is quite another. Just how the fuck does one go about that sort of thing? What if I muck it all up? The happiest day of two people's lives will go skittering straight down the pan.

Buggering, buggering hell.

'I wouldn't worry too much,' Janice reassures me when I ring her. She's having a sunbed because she's just seen a photo of Jasper's permatanned dead wife. 'Half of them will be bloody bulimic anyway,' she adds. 'Lucky bitches. So they'll be barfing it all up again before you can say salmon-en-croute. You'll probably be able to do a second sitting with their leftovers.'

Sam, of course, persuades me it's a terrific idea.

'It's your perfect opportunity,' he enthuses. 'It's for someone you know, and there'll probably be loads of people there to impress. So you can make more contacts and—'

'OK, calm down,' I say. 'We don't all want to work in PR, you know.'

'But you'll do it?' he says eagerly. 'Go on, Simpson. Give it a go. You'll be brilliant. I know you will.'

'Well...'

'Well?' He tousles my hair.

'OK,' I say gingerly.

'Fantastic.'

I smile weakly. I don't really have any choice but to do this. My overdraft is snowballing. And I simply don't have a frugal mentality. If I want something, I convince myself I need it. So I buy it. Immediately. If I don't find a way of making money soon I'll be forced to put Graham and Shish Kebab on the streets.

Janice thinks it a great idea and magnanimously offers to let me cook a dinner party at hers as a sort of dry run. As usual she has a hidden agenda. I have to pretend she's done all the work herself. How else is Jasper going to be able to see what a suitable wife she'll make? Anyway, she huffs, when I point out that that would be false advertising (she's the only person I know who can chargrill a Pot Noodle), the offer is there. I can take it or I can bloody well leave it.

I take it. After all, I've got no one else to practise on. And Janice and Jasper are apparently getting on very well. They've done restaurant dates and the theatre. He's even taken her to the opera, where she betrayed her roots by falling fast asleep, bored to tears, and dribbling down the lapel of his suit. And she's holding out on the sex front. Doesn't want him to bugger off. So they've done breast touching, and even a bit of breast looking, but that's about it.

'I'm reeling him in gently.' She laughs. 'I'm being all mysterious. Anyway, I'll talk to you tomorrow. We'll decide what you're going to cook.'

George says I should at least go to a wedding beforehand. After all, it's been ages since I attended a reception. And, as luck would have it, he's been invited to one next weekend. He doesn't really want to go because it's rumoured that the bride is a money-grubbing, social-climbing, bottom-feeding bungalow dweller who's found herself a nice piece of rich, and is consequently getting ideas above her station, but now he thinks of it, David'll be away so why don't I go along with him. Save him having to go on his own.

'And it might give you some ideas,' Sam says enthusiastically.

I allow myself to be steamrollered into the whole thing. And the following Saturday, I pour myself into gold lamé and meet George in Bierodrome in Upper Street for cherry beer and chips with mayonnaise before stumbling down the Holloway Road where we buy him a pair of size eleven sparkly red mules and jump, giggly on beer bubbles, onto a tube bound for South Kensington.

The reception is being held in a large house off Eaton Square. Wobbling along the terrace of identical white mansions with squirly black numbers painted on wedding cake pillars outside, we identify the spiddly spoo strains of jazz filtering into the busy street and follow the sound up steps, through a front door, down a long panelled hallway and into a big, striped, tenty sort of thing attached to the back of number twelve. Girls in great pumpkins of ballgowns and chaps in DJs are twirling each other around in a blaze of flaming scarlet silk, soft emerald velvet and shimmering midnight-blue satin. Silver horseshoes and golden streamers are liberally scattered among the corks and coffee cups discarded on nearby tables and a girl with what George calls a common mouth and air hostess orange make-up is dressed as a giant pavlova and waltzing with someone's granddad over by the stage.

George seems to think introductions are superfluous to requirements.

'No point being polite,' he chirrups happily, lighting a banana-coloured fag and trolling over towards the booze. 'I already got all the delicious gossip. Groom's Zachary Faulkner.
Father's a zillionaire. This is his house. Or one of them, I
should say, darling. Bride's your average slapper in slingbacks.
It's the blessed union of Nice 'n' Rich and Cheap 'n' Nasty,
sweetie. Belgravia Boy and his Basildon Bride. Isn't it fantastic? His parents are furious. Look, over there. British Bulldog
smoking cigar, and Tweedy Stick Insect sucking lemon. Black
tie wedding theme was the bride's idea, of course. I mean who
does that these days, darling? So tacky. Oh, and that's the bride's
parents over there. Pink Liquorice Allsort Hat and Shiny
Brown Suit. See?'

I glance over to where a drab, sad-looking couple in their
fifties sit, bewildered and obviously leagues out of their depth.
No one's even bothering to talk to them. It seems so sad. It's
their own daughter's wedding.

George springs into action. Spotting a full, opened bottle of
champagne sitting unattended on a nearby table, he gleefully
points over at it. 'Are we having that or not?' he asks mischievously.

'Having it,' I reply as he swaggers over to swipe it, wrapping
his greedy little hands round the golden foil neck and joyfully
glugging straight from the bottle as he clacks over to a table
occupied by a solitary woman with a cleavage like a builder's
bum and a couple of pubescent bridesmaids, all pearlescent
pink ruffles and train-track braces. I follow, shuffling over in
ridiculous slut shoes that make my squashed feet feel like sides
of vacuum-packed ham. Feeling more than a tad silly, I con-
certina my gangly limbs into the spaghetti-sized gap between
tent pole and table.

Unfortunately, because I'm slightly uncomfortable, I drink.
A lot. And because I know I'm never likely to see any of these
people again in my life, things get out of hand pretty quickly.
Our stolen bottle of champagne is drained with Formula One
speed and I'm soon feeling as excited as a kid at a birthday party

as golden froth jostles and pops alongside bubbles of possibility in my brain. Perhaps I really can make a go of this catering lark.

It isn't long before I'm slurring my words, scanning the room for potential shags and drunkenly grabbing the disposable camera someone has thoughtfully left in the middle of the table. We finish the film taking silly snaps of each other flipping V signs and showing our pants, and it's not until I get up to find out where the Ladies is that I remember why I'm here. The caterers. I've got to talk to the caterers.

Shit-arama.

Where's the bloody kitchen?

'Stay,' I instruct George, who is far too busy downing the contents of every abandoned glass on our table to even notice I'm going anywhere.

The house is a mizz maze of passageways. Just how many rooms does Belgravia Boy's family need? In my search for the kitchen I totter into about ten living rooms alone, chocka with antiques and invitingly plump sofas, and decorated in every colour of the rainbow. Sweetshop pink. Emerald and gold. Soft candyfloss. Pure blue. Stinging yellow. Hot orange. This lot clearly take their lounging very seriously indeed.

I find a loo—all Regency striped wallpaper and lavatorial humour cartoons on the walls—and I've just about given up hope of ever locating the kitchen—perhaps Belgravia Boy and his family eat out every night—when I go over the heel of one of my sparkly slut shoes as I totter down the final twist in the back stairs. I end up in an enormous room filled with gleaming stainless steel. A tasty-looking bloke in head-to-toe Armani is huddled over the butcher's block, ruffled blond head in hands. Well, I think that's Armani he's wearing anyway. I've never been much of a one for recognising labels, unless you count the ingredients on the side of food packets, so I can't be absolutely sure. I'm one of those people who always reads captions in magazines which describe Gwyneth Paltrow as 'elegant, as ever, in charcoal Prada', or Madonna as 'radiant in shocking-pink Voyage' and wonder how the buggering hell the writer can tell, just by looking. I look at the adverts in glossy magazines and read Versace as Versass. So the expensive-looking suit could just as easily be a Paul Smith. Or a Hugo Boss. It could even be Man at sodding C&A. Who knows?

Who cares?

Still, it might do me good to have a talk to him. He may well have some useful tips. After all, catering a posh bash like this, he must be fairly experienced. And although I usually find net-working about as appealing as VD, I'm pissed enough not to care. So I go for it.

He glances up as I hoop-la, arse over tit, onto the gleaming floor, an ominous ripping sound coming from my crotch.

'Whoopsy.'

I bend down to check out the size of the hole.

Humungous.

Serves me right, I guess. What's a gangly great lummox like me thinking of, cramming myself into trews that make even my lanky lallies look like great jambons? 'I say,' I say, cursing myself the moment the words leave my mouth. Who actually says that? 'Finished for the day?' I garble, whipping cigarettes out of my trouser pocket and tearing off the cellophane in as seductive a manner as is possible for a person whose fingernails are en-crusted with chipped Barbie-pink polish and chewed to fat stumps. I'm more twelve-year-old than temptress but hey, I'm off my tits on champagne. Who gives a toss?

'Bloody well hope so.' He shrugs. 'I'm shagged out. And I'm still not even allowed to get pissed.'

'What?' I ask, shocked. If catering weddings doesn't involve a few free glasses of bubbly then perhaps I should seriously re-consider. Every job has its perks, doesn't it?

'Even though you've doled out all the grub and done the washing up? Surely they'll allow you to let your hair down for the last hour?' I say.

'You'd think so, wouldn't you?' He looks confused. I'm not surprised. I bet he's bloody knackered.

'I was thinking of starting up a catering business actually,' I admit, flopping down onto the bench beside him and offering him a fag. 'Any tips?'

He shrugs. 'Not really.'

Great. Clammed up like an oyster. Obviously isn't sharing any of his secrets so readily. Still, he's probably used to catering for all manner of glamorous dos. From the way he's dressed, he probably did Brad and Jennifer's wedding. He's probably bezzie mates with the Beckhams. The last thing he'll want is some up-start like me nicking his ideas off him.

Still, I could always get him drunk. He'd sing like a canary then.

Or I could shag him and get him to dish.

Better still, get him drunk and shag him. Then I can't fail.

Or is that a bit too sluttish for a beginner?

'Shall I nick you some champers?' I say wickedly. 'You could drink it in here. No one would know.'

He flashes me a lopsided grin. 'Go on then. But don't get caught. She'll murder me if she catches me boozing.'

'Tricky bride?' I say sympathetically.

Well, that's OK. There are bound to be a few difficult customers once in a while. I'd expect that.

'You could say that.' He winks.

I smile. Normally, I don't find men in suits attractive. For some reason, I've never been able to imagine a man in a suit possessing such a thing as a penis. Don't know why. It's always been the way with me. I imagine they'll be completely smooth underneath. But this chap is different. Not my usual type—he's blond, for one thing, whereas I usually prefer them dark and brooding. But he is male. And he looks as though he's got a pulse. And after the disaster with Max, who am I to play fussy?

I tiptoe back to the party, find a half drunk bottle of Moët on top of the grand piano, and sneak back to the kitchen with it, ruffling the back of my hair with my hand as I do so. I'm perfectly aware I can never look sleek and chic, so I try for sexy and tousled instead. Unfortunately, a piece of sausage roll pastry floats to the ground as I plonk myself down next to him, but I flap it away with my hand, as though I'm waving away smoke and I don't think he notices.

'So what are you doing here anyway?' he asks as I hand him the bottle.

'Sorry?'

Blimming heck. I've been rumbled, trying to worm trade secrets out of a pro.

'Bride or groom? And don't tell me you're neither. I know that perfectly well.'

'Oh.'

'Thing is,' he grabs the Moët bottle and takes a grateful glug, 'I don't think we've ever met before, have we?'

'Er. No.'

'Thought not.' He grins lazily. 'I'm sure I'd have remembered.'

He's flirting with me.

God, he's gorgeous. Well, no actually, not gorgeous exactly but he's averagely OK. Ish. Nice blue eyes. And a mischievous smile. A bit pink, perhaps—his face has that ruddy tinge of the terminally posh. Reminds me of a newborn rat. And his eyelashes are a bit on the sandy side which makes him look a bit squinty. I keep wanting to tell him he's got crusts of sleep in his eye.

And he is a bit posh for little old me, really. His name's probably Tarquin or Rupert. But drunken reasoning tells me it's just as well he's not perfect. If I'm out for a one-night stand, I don't want to start hankering after him tomorrow. That would defeat the object of humping and dumping altogether. The rules of Behaving Like a Bloke demand ruthlessness on a serious scale. I need to toughen up. Be as harsh as caustic soda. And it's therefore vitally important to remain totally and utterly emotionally detached from the whole thing.

So a faint lack of sexual attraction is undoubtedly a bonus.

'Well, to be honest,' I confess, quaffing another boozy great mouthful and leaning recklessly towards him, 'I wouldn't know either of them from Adam.'

'Really?'

'I mean I've seen the bride of course. That fucking awful big meringue sort of gave her away. But I wouldn't know the groom if he came up and slipped me a length from behind, so...'

He inches closer to my golden ham of a thigh and places one hand on it, perilously close to my minky.

Cue mental check for signs of arousal.

Nothing.

Absolutely zilch.

Dry as a goddamn bone. Not so much as a minge twinge. My nipples remain as flaccid as uncooked pancakes.

But I've started, so I may as well finish.

And being a top of the range caterer, he'll be an excellent contact for later.

Better make sure I'm good.

'And how exactly will you do that?' niggles an annoying voice in my brain. 'You're clueless at casual sex.'

I quash it.

He pulls me slightly towards him and moves in on me, running his tongue over my bottom lip.

And what do I do?

I giggle. And my mouth chooses that particular moment to go into overdrive.

'I don't normally make a habit of gatecrashing the weddings of complete strangers,' I gabble stupidly as he stands up, pulling me to my feet. He's slightly shorter than me, I notice, but that's no big deal. It means we can do it standing up.

'I came with George you see, he's downstairs, he's not my boyfriend you understand. He works with the groom.'

He puts a finger to his lips, taking me by the shoulders and leading me into a larder the size of my entire flat. He shuts the door firmly behind us, lifts me onto a chest freezer and kisses me.

I'm surprised it's so easy, getting men to sleep with you. So far, I haven't really had to do anything.

It's a sticky, Bakewell tarty sort of kiss that tastes of cherries and sweet dessert wine. Interesting. His hands move over my back, cupping my buttocks, as I wrap my thighs round his waist. Staring into my eyes, he peels off my trousers, unzipping his own in quick succession. I prop myself uncomfortably on one big toe for easy entry, at last feeling that familiar puppet string pull of excitement in my groin.

And then it hits me.

I'm about to have sex with a total stranger.

Because I can.

I don't even know what his name is.

How cool is that?

In the event, the sex is short, urgent and only Candarel sweet. He seems to think he's in a porn film, finding it necessary to keep up a running commentary throughout.

'What do you like?' he keeps asking me. 'What do you like?'

Seeing as though we've only just met, ordering him to stick his head between my legs and damn well stay there until I've finished doesn't quite seem the ticket, so instead I say, 'Oh, this is fine, thank you,' as though I'm praising a rather bland restaurant meal. It's just easier that way.

Besides, I'm too busy holding my stomach in, trying to keep my balance and leaning far enough forward to disguise my sticky-outty belly button to start quizzing him on his general knowledge of the Kamasutra. On the whole though, it goes pretty smoothly for my first time as a complete strumpet. And on the plus side, he doesn't have a dick like a chipolata. And no belly button fluff.

He doesn't even ask me to finish myself off and let him watch, which Janice has always assured me is pretty good going for a one-off.

OK, so I don't get Croissants, but then anyway that's an event usually as rare as a French beefburger in my limited experience.

Oh, and he produces a condom without my even having to ask, which is lucky, because in all the excitement of casual sex, I doubt it would have occurred to me to mention it. And this guy doesn't really have the cheekbones for sperm donation. If I was going to get pregnant accidentally on purpose, I think I'd probably rather have George's. And I'd go for someone with that extra bit of height.

When we're done and dusted, he actually looks more relieved than gutted when I push him away and yank up my knickers, pausing only to slip on my tarty slingbacks and throw one last withering glance at his rapidly deflating erection before legging it, but who cares? I'm empowered. I can do anything.

I swan downstairs on a powder puff of postcoital elation. George is going to be dead impressed. I'll get extra hardness points for doing it at a wedding. He spies me the moment I trip back into the ballroom.

'Where've you been?' he demands accusingly. 'I'm bloody miserable here without David, darling, and there you go and disappear on me.'

'Missing David, eh?' I tease him. 'That's a turn-up for the books. I wouldn't worry about him. He's probably off shagging some complete girl. He's dead flirty, you know. He's probably bi.'

'Darling, he's as camp as a row of pink tents with "Ooh knickers" scribbled on the side. And he seemed pretty interested in me, thank you very much, so I think we'll give him the benefit of the doubt before we condemn him to a life of football, Firkin pubs and fanny batter, don't you?'

'Whatever.'

'So where have you been?' he asks, slightly deflated, as I pause to poke in a sausage roll.

'Having sex,' I boast.

'No, seriously.'

'Just what I said.'

'Noooooooooo.'

'Yeeeeeeeees.'

'Oh my God, darling.' He slooshes wine around in his glass. 'I hope you've had a shower since. I mean I know that this is a real breakthrough for you and everything, what with you being practically hermetically sealed, but the bride's about to throw the boookay.'

'So?'

'We don't want you catching it with dribbly bits running down your legs, do we? We'll have the whole of SW1W smelling like a fleet of herring trawlers before you're done. Which just won't do. I mean, I've been to Hull Harbour, darling, and it isn't dainty. And I do hope you were selective, sweetie.'

'Sort of.'

'Oh look, come on, darling,' he urges, forgetting my conquest as though it were completely run of the mill. 'She's about to throw it now. Right nasty little scrubber she looks too. Real pram face. Come on, you're a girl. Up you go.'

'But...'

'No buts, darling, come on. Join in.'

And before I can protest, George, like a pushy mother at a ballet competition, has physically shoved me among the throng of girls in sparkly Cinderella dresses, all bobbing up and down expectantly at the side of the stage area, where Basildon Bride stands, brandishing a bouquet of salmon-pink roses, set off by billowing clouds of the nasty frothy white stuff you always get in service stations.

'One. Two. Three,' chorus the Cinders mob as the sorry-looking thing is launched spinning into the rabble.

Everyone scrabbles to get to it first. I get sucked into the crowd. My hand closes round a clump of stalks. Pulling away from the rest of the snatching hands, I hold my prize aloft, as two girls swoop down on me like angry seagulls and try to yank it back.

'I've gottit, Jo.'

'No, I've gottit.'

'Givvit back.'

'Leggo.'

'Ow.'

I give in gracefully, releasing my end before I lose an eye, and making my way back to George, who's grinning on the sidelines like a dad at School Sports Day. He's alone, I notice. Which is odd, seeing as the place should be filled with his colleagues. And I've met lots of George's work friends. So why are none of them here?

And then it hits me like a brick.

'George.'

'Yes?'

'You don't know a single sod here, do you?'

'No,' he admits. 'But this is one of the socialite weddings of the year, darling. It's going to be in *Hello!* and everything. I did it for you. Thought you'd feel better if you saw some real caterers in action. Be good experience for you.'

I'm touched, even if I do suspect that the real reason behind George's concern is that he had nothing better to do than gate-crash a smart wedding and he didn't want to do it alone.

'Thanks anyway.' I hug him. After all, I do absolutely love him to bits. And no one can say that life with George in it is boring.

We're still hugging several moments later when everything kicks off, so I'm totally unprepared for what happens next. One minute I'm cuddling George, holding on for just that bit too long as I surreptitiously inhale the delicious coconutty smell of his hair and try to suppress the weird butterflyish feeling I always get when we touch. The next, Basildon Bride is bearing down on me from nowhere like a UN tank, king-sized fag on the go in one hand and silver Nokia phone in the other.

'I don't fink we know you, do we?' She tosses her too tight perm and glares icily at George then me. She's pretty threatening. For a moment she's got me worried. But, buoyed up with a heady cocktail of champagne, shagging and George's blatant disrespect for this vision in slub silk, I stand my ground.

'Shouldn't think so,' I say bravely, taking a defiant swig of champagne from a glass on a nearby table. 'We don't know you.'

'I'm sorry.' George smiles, seeking to smooth ruffled feathers. 'You'd think she was dragged up in a terrace, wouldn't you? I'm George, by the way'—he pronounces it the French way for added sophistication—'and this is Katherine.'

'Hmm.' Basildon Bride looks unconvinced. Then she yells towards the other side of the hall. 'Oy, Zac, are these friends of yours or what?'

Now, I don't know Zac from King Kong, but I have a nasty feeling he's probably big and threatening. But, as luck would have it, I suddenly spot the caterer coming in my direction from the side of the room. Quick as a flash I run towards him, grabbing his arm and saying, 'Quick, pretend I'm with you. You can say I'm a waitress. I've been rumbled.'

'Can't,' he hisses, shaking me off violently and looking at me as though I'm some deluded trollop.

I'm furious. Livid. How dare he reject me? Treat me like a total lunatic? If there's any rejecting to be done I'll bloody well do it, thank you.

'All right, keep your pants on,' I say hotly. If he's going to be like that I'll make damn sure he doesn't work in this district again. 'If you can, that is,' I say. At the first sign of raised voices, a crowd has assembled. 'Oh yes,' I tell them. 'This man has the gall to pretend he's not with me when he was quite happily servicing me over the freezer not twenty minutes ago. What do you make of that?'

In a flash, the room is alive with whispers and murmurs, all writhing like maggots beneath the surface. I look at Basildon Bride. Basildon Bride looks at me. Then she looks at the caterer.

'Zac?' she demands, horrified. 'Is this true?'

Zac. Now where do I know that name from? It's oddly familiar.

Oh fuck.

Buggery bollocky fuck.

Zac is Belgravia Boy.

I've only gone and shagged the bloody bridegroom.

'Run,' I hiss at George, but he shakes his head, rooted to the spot.

'Can't. Want to see what happens next,' he whispers. 'This is better than *Brookside*.'

He soon gets his wish.

'Gettout!' Basildon Bride grabs my elbow in a vice-like grip and prepares to march me outside.

'Oooh, she's just like Jackie Dixon,' I hear George say.

'You're a fuckin' liar. And you're going down, you slag.'

Oh God.

Then she turns on George.

'And you,' she screeches. 'You've bloody gatecrashed as well, haven't you?'

''Fraid so, sweetie,' George agrees. 'But I really wouldn't be flattered. I'm not having a very nice time, I'm afraid. Actually, to be perfectly frank, this whole bash smacks rather of Asti Spumante. The guests are more egg and chips than gratin dauphinoise, darling, and talking of food, no one has had the common decency to offer me any more than a flaccid sausage roll since I got here.'

'Come on, George,' I hiss, preparing to make a run for it. The bride, for all her froth and frills, looks hard as frigging nails and I'm left in little doubt that she won't baulk at smashing a bottle over my head if she feels the need.

But George isn't to be deterred.

'This do has the class of the QVC Shopping Channel,' he spits. 'Belgravia? Huh. We might as well be in bloody Plaistow.'

That does it. George's venomous tongue is the final nail in my coffin. Tiara askew, Basildon Bride launches herself at me in a spitting, hissing flurry of dirty cream silk, grabbing me by the scruff of the neck and slopping rum and black all over my gold jacket, screeching that if we haven't got the fuck out of there by the time she's counted to ten, she's going to smash my fucking face to bits.

I believe her.

'Very elegant,' I counter bravely, administering a sharp kick to her shin and noticing with some satisfaction that I've made a whopping great rip in her tights. Well, that's one ladder that definitely isn't a stairway to heaven or why the hell did her husband of several hours feel the need to poke me, a ginger streak of piss from South London, on their wedding day?

'Just goes to show, darling,' George remarks spitefully. 'You can take the slag out of the council estate but you sure can't take the council estate out of the slag. I'd watch it if I were you, darling,' he comments to Zac, as I pray for the parquet to swallow us up. 'I wouldn't be at all surprised if her wedding lingerie turns out to be crotchless.'

Then, with a parting, 'Nasty dress, by the way,' he tugs on my hand and we stagger, cackling and hooting with deliciously bitchy laughter, into the night.

Chapter 8

The first grown-up dinner party Janice and I attended together was in Sixth Form. I smothered my hair in Sun-In and wore wraparound shades and a disgusting dress with a gingham puffball skirt. I thought I was the dog's bollocks. Janice hired a frock specially: a stunning fifties number, ink-black with a pinched-in waist, acres of gauzy netting and trillions of tiny jet beads. Then she shagged the school heartthrob, got sperm all over the dress and made me take it back to the shop while she sat outside in my mum's Austin Maxi with the engine running.

This time, she's adamant that everything's going to be perfect. Gone is the girl who changes her men as often as she changes her g-string. Jasper is the start of her grown-up life, and she's buggered if she's letting on she's really the type to go round dishing out blow jobs to sundry blokes with runaway egos.

If I'm honest, the thought of her giving all that up makes me depressed. It signals the taking on of responsibility. Adulthood. It reminds me I've got to do something with my life before it's too late.

Of course I don't have to. I could always opt out. I could open a sunbed centre or do a course in teaching aerobics. I wouldn't have to sit in an office then. I could dress permanently in sports wear and drive round in a Jeep. But before I really have a chance to decide whether or not I want to start my own catering business, Janice has organised her dinner party and sent out the invites. We meet in the Moon Under Water on Sunday to drink pints of shandy (doesn't really count as drinking as it's half lemonade and so entirely suitable for a school night) and discuss the menu.

'I thought carrot, coconut and cumin soup to start,' she announces bossily. 'Followed by roast rump of lamb with a minted polenta crust and seasonal vegetables and then a rich chocolate mousse cake with marscapone to follow. I got it all out of the Sugar Club cookbook. What d'you reck? Will that look as though it took me bastard ages?'

I don't know about that. But I do know that it's going to take me bastard ages. Any normal person would be happy to settle for pasta and pesto. Or spag bol at least. I'll give her flaming minted polenta crust.

'Oh, and look glam,' she warns me. 'I've invited quite a few other people as well. And I'm dressing up so you're going to have to at least stick a bit of slap and a frock on. I don't want to look as though I've made some sort of pathetic effort, do I? What I mean is, I want him to think I'm like that all the time.'

What she means is that she doesn't want me showing her up.

'Can't I just cook it?' I ask her. 'And then sod off? I could even do it all here and send it round to yours in a taxi in those little foil dishes you get down the Chinky.'

Apparently I can't. Janice won't hear of it. After all, I'm going to be cooking the food, she reminds me. So I can bloody well sit there and eat it if it damn well chokes me.

I'm pissed off, to put it mildly. A meal like that will take hours to prepare. I'll probably have to get going on Friday before the end of *Celebrity Ready Steady Cook*.

'But you'll do all the shopping, right?' I ask.

'Will I buggery,' she snorts, spraying me with lager top. 'I rather thought you'd be doing that, having sod all else to do except loll round the flat with your finger up your bum. I've got a fulltime job to hold down until I get married, remember?'

Well, that's just great, isn't it? I'll probably miss most of *Trisha* as well if I've got to whip round Sainsbury's first.

'I will leave some wine in the fridge though,' she says. 'So you can crack it open when you get there and I'll join you when I've finished shovelling shit for Wasp Bum. Not that I'll be much help, I'm afraid. I'm in for a busy week. I'll be pretty much shagged out come Friday.'

'Right you are then.'

'And Katie?'

'Yes?'

'I'm really sorreee but...'

'What?'

'You couldn't tidy the bathroom a bit and have a quick flick round with a duster, could you? I probably won't be home very much between now and then and the place is a bit of a sty.'

'Cheeky bitch,' George snorts, when I call him to tell him I'll have to miss our lunchtime bitching session in Café Flo because I'm going to have to plan the whole thing properly now I'm catering for loads of Jasper's friends.

'She's not a cheeky bitch,' I say.

'Oh?'

'She's a cheeky fucking bitch.'

'So she is. With knobs on.'

'She's so worried about showing Filthy Rich what a great executive wife she'll make that she couldn't give a toss about the rest of us. God knows why she's so taken with him. He's nearly seventy, for Christ's sake. He's got a face like a gnarled walnut.'

'Ooh yes,' George says delightedly. 'Like a badly griddled pancake, all screwed up.'

'All I can say is he must have a dick like a baby's arm clutching a grapefruit.'

'Oooh.'

'He's still working though. So he might not be that ancient. But I mean she doesn't even know what he does for a living. He could be a toilet cleaner for all she knows. Or a dustbin man. Nothing very executive about that. But from the way she goes on, you'd think he was Richard bloody Branson. She's so busy counting pound signs that she's forgotten all about me.'

'And she bleaches her hair.'

'Anything could be happening in my life right now and she wouldn't even notice. My boyfriend could be beating the shit out of me.'

'You don't have a boyfriend,' George points out. 'He dumped you months ago.'

'I dumped him actually. And only because he preferred dirty nylon knicker girls to normal girls like me.'

'Darling, if you're normal, I'm the Pope.'

'But hypothetically speaking, I could have a boyfriend, couldn't I?'

'I suppose you could, yes. If you did something with your hair.'

'And he *could* be beating the shit out of me.'

'He could be using your head as a dartboard,' George says gleefully.

'And my bum as a knife block.'

'Stubbing fags out on your arms,' he shouts happily.

'Exactly,' I say. 'And Little Miss Biddy Bonker wouldn't even notice. As a mate, I'm practically neglected. I could report her.'

'You could,' he agrees.

'She'll be laughing the other side of her lipliner when "luxury travel" means packing into some National Express biddy wagon for a day trip to Clacton,' I point out.

And that's not all, I think to myself, wearily dusting down my collection of recipe clippings. What's going to happen in ten years' time, when her carefully maintained home starts to stink of old people? All wee and boil-in-the-bag cod. I don't think she'll like that very much. She won't be able to redecorate in case the paintwork clashes with the stairlift.

Sometimes, I doubt whether she's actually thought about the future at all. To her, the wedding ceremony is the future. And after that—nothing! Janice is so wrapped up in her fantasy, she's yet to realise that marriage is, in all probability, very much like the female condom. Vastly overrated. If she actually stops to think further than the honeymoon, she'll realise that a girl who, until very recently, didn't even bother swapping first names before happily exchanging humungous quantities of bodily fluids, will probably find the challenge of coping with incontinence pants so early in life pretty hard to take.

On Friday, I stubbornly wait until *Trisha*'s finished, then strop round the supermarket in five minutes flat, grazing happily on Skips as I go. When I've bought everything I need, I waddle home to feed Graham and Shish Kebab. Graham winds himself around my legs, purring like a motorbike as I squidge a sachet of duck-flavoured slop into his bowl. Until recently, they've eaten out of tins, like every other moggy, but these sachet things are so convenient. The feline equivalent of an M&S lasagne for one.

When I've watched both furry bundles poke the lot down their greedy fat faces, I lug the shopping round to Janice's flat and unlock the door, catching a waft of her smell as I do so. It's weird. When we shared a flat together, I never noticed her 'other person' smell. But now I'm a visitor, I can't miss it. And 152 Calbourne Road smells of a mixture of CK One, Dettox, Elnett hairspray and fresh paint. It's so damn clean it screams 'One Careful Owner'. You see, whereas my rented hovel hasn't seen so much as a lick of paint since I've been there, Janice is constantly in decorating mode. In fact, when it comes to her flat, she's so anally retentive, she could probably do without a

Hoover. She could trot round the place sucking up crumbs through her bum instead. In the last six months, she's gone interior design mad. She's Anna Ryder Wotsit the second. Except she's a blonde version, with much bigger tits. She's forever painting this and varnishing that. Everything has to coordinate. She's been known to march into Homebase brandishing a violet resin ashtray someone at work bought her and demanding an entire colour scheme based on the bloody thing. The only item I've ever bought for my flat is my lovely squishy sofa. And that's only because Jake sprayed the last one with sperm as I gave him a post-prandial hand job—his last, as it turned out—and I couldn't so much as glance at the stain without getting rushes of nostalgia. Otherwise, I prefer to leave major purchases like that for when I grow up. Or when I actually manage to buy my own place. When that'll be, precisely, as I keep telling my mum, I'm not entirely sure. When a mortgage lands in my lap, I expect. I'm a Property Virgin, for God's sake. I don't have a clue how it all works. And don't get me wrong. I have tried. I asked George a few months back if he knew about mortgages. But he looked utterly horrified. 'Mortgage?' he screeched. 'What mortgage? Jesus Harriet Christ, sweetie, just what do you think I am? I live in Islington, I'll have you know. That's N bloody One, darling, not Albert flipping Square. I own that house outright.'

I dump the bags of shopping on Janice's kitchen table and have a quick snoop round. As usual, everything is cool, calm and elegant. Shortly after moving in, she had an attack of open plan-itis, knocking down certain walls and making egg-shaped holes in others. The floor is now an ice rink of highly polished beech and the whole place looks as though it has jumped straight from the pages of some glossy interiors magazine. I suppress a sigh of envy and tell myself she deserves to live somewhere beautiful, bless her nylon pop socks. She's worked bloody hard to escape the council estate in Walthamstow where she grew up, sitting in front of a one-bar fire with a packet of Garibaldi for her tea and an Asda ski-panted mother for company.

Wandering into the bathroom, with its fresh lilac walls, seamless stainless steel bath and pale mosaic floor, I pick up several clean outfits, unable to keep from smiling, as I envisage my best friend in the world trying them all on for a night out with Filthy Rich. I can see her in my mind's eye, twirling briefly in the full-length mirror by the door then casting each garment aside with mounting exasperation as she deems it highly unsuitable. I count four black tops, two white tops, an inviting little number in apricot lace and a slinky purple and pink spotted dress with a tantalisingly low back. Three bras, two thongs, four pairs of slingbacks and a pair of killer stilettos litter the floor by the mirror and I grab the whole jumble and shove it into her wardrobe, rescuing other assorted scraps of clothing, which are scattered across the landing like tickertape, as I go.

Then I stomp down to the kitchen to unpack the groceries and cook supper. I chop carrots and onions, simmer creamy coconut broth and tear up bunches of fragrant coriander. Whizz the whole lot through the blender and roll the most astronomically priced piece of lamb I've been able to find in freshly macerated mint. I boil potatoes then rough them up with a fork so they'll be deliciously crispy when I roast them in heaps of chopped rosemary and lashings of sizzling hot oil. Slice courgettes into razor-thin strips and pod peas. Melt prime quality chocolate over a saucepan and whip egg white into Everest-like peaks. As I do all this, a wave of contentment washes over me and I almost switch off from real life completely. I always feel like this when I'm cooking for friends. It soothes me, somehow. I used to love cooking for Jake. Every Friday night we'd have wonderful slap-up feasts, after which he always enjoyed nothing more than an evening of crap game shows rounded off with a blow job of distinction. I cooked that ungrateful sod everything under the sun. French. Italian. Indian. Thai. Chinese. Unfortunately, as it turned out, the only thing he really appre-

ciated in the end was Red Hot and Dutch, but it's some con-
solation to know that Fishpants Fraser is doing the cooking now.
Which means egg and chips will be about the limit. And it'll
doubtless be downhill from now on in. Soon, he'll be living off
carrot purée and Tubby custard.

And serve him bloody well right.

By the time Janice gets home from the office, stripping off
her suit jacket as she waltzes into the kitchen and declaring that
she needs a hot shower and a good half-hour of pampering,
everything is practically ready. The lamb is roasting to pink perfection in her sparkling Smeg and all that remains is for her to
stick the veg in boiling water for a few minutes when the guests
have arrived. Surely even she can manage that. As I wait for her
to come out of the shower, I slip into my own boring LBD,
pull on a sheer pair of black tights to conceal my corned beef
legs and flop down on her suede ottoman to neck a glass of
wine. She slaps on a bright blue face mask, exfoliates her legs,
douses herself in perfume and pours herself into a backless silver chainmail thing she's bought specially.

'TA-DAA.' She wafts down the stairs in a cloud of D&G and
gives me a quick twirl. 'What do you reck? Do I look gorgeous
or do I. Look. Gorgeous?'

'Erm...'

'It needs a bra, doesn't it?' she says irritably. 'Needs. A fucking. Bra. I knew it. And I don't have a sodding backless one.'
She practically hyperventilates. 'Shit piss fuck. What am I going
to do? Whywhywhy do I have to have tits like bloody balloons?'

I pass her a paper bag to breathe into. Luckily, I know just
how to deal with this particular crisis. Janice's big, bouncy boobs
are the bane of her life. She's simply too well-endowed to go
bra-free. For years now, she's aspired to a crop top, but to no
avail. No matter how much weight she loses, her boobs steadfastly refuse to shrink. I'm the total opposite. I don't have a
washboard stomach, I have a washboard chest. I've got a torso
like a xylophone. And she's jealous. Of me! The mad cow. I've

tried pointing out that my boobs are so small they practically poke inwards, like two piss holes in the snow, but she's having none of it. It means I can wear teeny vest tops and backless frocks to my heart's content if I want to, and that's what's so galling apparently. It's a classic case of 'grass is always greener'. I've yearned for boobs in the past. Great big udder-like boobs I'd be able to squash together to make a cleavage. One that looks like a huge bottom. Like the Edwardians had. I'd happily swap places with her any day.

In the end, the chainmail dress is discarded altogether, due to the fact that two boiled eggs in a handkerchief isn't a good look this season. Boobs, Janice assures me firmly, are out. She plumps for a flirty amethyst silk number instead and—I have to hand it to her—she does look absolutely stunning when she's eventually ready. She's used a gallon of straightener on her hair, which makes her appear at least five inches shorter than usual. Suddenly I realise my larger than life best friend has been transformed. She's a glossier, more sophisticated model. She's gone from tawdry Boy Racer Escort to sleek Alfa Romeo Spyder in minutes. Even her make-up is quieter. Gone is the sassy scarlet lipstick and thick black eyeliner. In its place, tasteful nude lipgloss and feather-light mascara. She almost doesn't look like Janice at all. If this is how it's going to be if she marries Filthy Rich, I'd rather she didn't bother. I'm already pining for her big hair and shouty make-up. I don't like the new Janice much. It feels as though I'm being fobbed off with a watered-down version.

Compared to Janice's sleek, elegant figure, I look putrid. I'm sure I've got scraps of potato peelings and bits of chopped mint in my hair. My hands absolutely reek of ingrained garlic. And I've already snagged my horrid 10 denier businesswoman's tights. When Janice has finished admiring herself, turning first to one side then the other, then baring her teeth in the mirror to check for stray lipgloss, she turns and looks at me in horror.

'At least put some lippy on,' she urges. 'You're as white as a blooming sheet.'

I've managed some natural gloss and a brushful or two of mascara, when the doorbell rings and Janice opens it to find Jasper hovering on the doorstep, bottle of champagne in one hand, enormous bouquet of rust-coloured roses in the other. She's not bothered about him, obviously, but she positively wilts with delight when she sees the expensive flowers. And when he picks her up and kisses the top of her forehead. I resign myself to an evening of feeling green and whiskery. Why the buggery fuck is she putting me through this anyway? Doesn't she want some privacy?

'I'll just stick these in a vase,' she tinkles, whisking her flowers into the kitchen in a sweep of sparkling purple. I hate the way she's changed her voice especially for him. She's also cultivated a way of sort of flitting from room to room instead of stomping about like she usually does. It really gets on my tits because I know it isn't the real her. All this flimflam is pure nonsense. And as she bashes pots and pans around in the kitchen, pretending to be putting last-minute touches to dinner, I'm left alone with the old bid. Embarrassed, I sort of shrug my shoulders and smile halfheartedly as I sit down, checking out his outfit as I do so. Plain blue shirt, open at the neck to reveal a veritable rug of chest hair. Navy chinos have replaced the ridiculous combat pants he wore to my birthday party. Even so, there's a worryingly large amount of gold jewellery on display. And is that a small medallion lurking in amongst the undergrowth?

Strewth.

This is going to be a bloody nightmare.

Jasper unwraps a Cuban cigar the size of a small gerbil as the doorbell goes again. And for the next twenty minutes, Janice flitter-flutters from kitchen to front door, leading a selection of chocolate-box party blondes and their assorted partners into the living room and handing them large gin and tonics. But when the bell rings for the last time, she's suddenly too busy to answer it. 'That'll be Colin,' she tinkles from the kitchen. 'Can you get that, Katie?'

Obediently, I turn to go into the hall, but Jasper jumps up instead. Why don't I sit down, there's a good girl? He'll see to the door. Then, placing both hands round my waist, he commits the cardinal sin. He physically moves me to one side, as though I'm nothing more than a piece of property. A shopping trolley obscuring the Jaffa Cakes in the supermarket! White-hot anger spurts like lava in my chest as he swaggers, puffing away on the gerbil cigar, to the front door. And suddenly, I'm itching to boot him through it and slam it in his face. Why is Janice putting up with such sexist claptrap? She's the girl who, on discovering an alien hand on her arse on the tube last year, grabbed the offending fingers in a vice-like grip and held them aloft for all to see, yelling, 'Whose hand is this, groping my bum?' at the top of her voice so everyone could hear. She'd rather have injected her thighs with pure cellulite than put up with this nonsense a year ago, so why is she indulging it now?

Actually, that's a stupid question. I know why she's indulging it now. She can hear the ringing of cash tills big time and nothing, but nothing, is getting in her way.

From the second Colin enters the room, I suspect he may well turn out to have 'Katie's Date' branded across his nether regions. Which is a crying shame, really. I might be trying not to have any morals when it comes to shagging around, but I sure as hell don't sleep with people called 'Colin'. It's such a stupid, slow, cornflakey kind of name. People name their coldsores Colin. If he'd been called anything else, like Luke or Will or even Giles—well, perhaps not Giles actually; it's a bit of a dopey public schoolboy name—I might have gone after him like shit off a shovel. Even given my track record when it comes to blokes in suits. But Colin?

It's a bit bloody estate agent, isn't it?

Did I say that Colin isn't particularly tall? Sorry. That's bollocks. Next to me, Colin is positively pygmy-esque. And he's forty-odd if he's a day. Which practically makes him Colin the Codger.

Hell's bells.

'What the heck do you think you're doing?' I hiss, as Janice attempts, not very successfully, to blanch the green beans.

'I'm doing beans.' She pokes a fork in.

'NO,' I almost shout.

'What? Bugger. Now look what you've made me do. I look as though I've pissed myself.'

'Why the fuck did you have to go and matchmake?'

'But he's a really nice chap,' she insists, going all wide-eyed. 'Got a lovely personality.'

And we all know what that means.

It means he's as ugly as sin.

'Don't look at me like that,' I hiss again. 'That butter wouldn't melt in your knickers look might cut the mustard with Medallion Man out there but you don't fool me. I'm not getting off with him and that's it.'

'That's a shame.' She shrugs. 'When he's got so much lovely dosh. All going to waste. He lives in a tiny flat and he's got no one to spend it on.'

'Why not?'

'Because he's single, stupid. And he's never been married, so he doesn't even have to pay alimony. He's loaded.'

'What's wrong with him?' I ask. 'Apart from being severely vertically challenged.'

'Nothing. He just hasn't met the right woman, I guess.'

That's utter rubbish, and well she knows it.

But Colin does have two points in his favour.

He's male.

And he's here.

His presence has involved no effort on my part whatsoever. He just turned up on the doorstep like a pizza delivery. A takeaway Shag Aloo. A McShag. And seeing as I'm going for a record number of one-night stands this year and—thus far—have managed a crappy total of one and a half (I figure Max only counts as half, seeing as Elvis left the building long before he was finished), I guess it's only polite to go for it.

After all, he's gone to the trouble of putting aftershave on and everything. Which is rather sweet really, when you think about it. And he's a lot more polite than the guys I'm used to; the kind who expect a full-on shag after they've coughed up for so much as a pint of lager and lime. So perhaps I can try to be polite too.

I can at least try to keep my hair out of the gravy and not say the 'C' word.

The dinner party is interminable. Janice and Jasper canoodle so much they completely put me off my lamb. Jasper blethers on about the new boat he hopes to buy in the summer. And the cinema he's having installed at the house in Winchester. And how he thinks it might be a good idea for Janice to learn how to ride, so he's getting another horse. A plodder. One she won't have any trouble with. Frankly, I find his attitude patronising. I can't believe Janice is grinning from ear to ear. She actually looks happy.

The rest of the party are so far back it's difficult to make out what they're saying. I push my food around my plate as, all around me, people boast about their children's prowess.

'We've put Liddy in for pre-school French,' a blonde with teeth like a hare brags. 'She's very, VERY advanced for her age.'

'Oh yars, yars,' a woman called Clarissa neighs. 'Felix and Elsie are so grown-up now we've left them at home on their own.'

'How old are they?' I ask politely, bored out of my mind.

'Three and a half and one.'

'But isn't that illegal?'

'Oh, don't worry.' She laughs. 'We've plugged in the baby monitor and given half to the nice couple over the road.'

'B-but...'

'Far cheaper than getting a babysitter, isn't it, Hugh?' She pats her husband.

'Far cheaper,' he blusters, pouring himself more wine. 'No harm done, eh?'

'Unless the house burns down, I guess,' I say. 'You can't really hear smoke, can you?'

But no one seems to care. And Janice shoots me a warning look. These are Jasper's awful friends. I am supposed to be being nice to them. But I'm fed up. And as the evening drags, I drift asleep and jerk awake again at least twice. I say the 'C' word three times before pudding and am even forced to nip to the loo after the starter for a quick relax just to stay sane. And Jasper is getting right on my tits. I've lost count of the number of arms he's 'brushed against' or the buttocks he's patted since he got here. He's such a sexist pig. If I so much as start speaking to him to be polite, he rests his hand in the small of my back, as if I'll collapse if I make conversation unsupported. I am, after all, only a girl. And his complexion is more like a Sunmaid raisin than ever. Plus, he seems to think that, because Janice and I are female, we have ears as delicate as spun sugar. Whenever one of the men utters so much as a measly 'bugger' or 'bastard' (tame by my standards), he instantly apologises, flicking his eyes towards us and saying, 'Sorry, ladies.' It really gets my back up. After the third time, I've had enough.

'Who are you calling a fucking lady?' I demand, looking him straight in the eye.

No one laughs. Janice deals me a vicious kick under the table. The only person who flickers so much as a smile is Colin. And in the end, I decide Colin is the only one in the room who seems vaguely human. So I have to talk to him. And to get through it, I drink. And drink. So much so in fact, that by the end of the evening, Colin is looking less and less like a Colin and more like a Paul. Or a Steve even. And by eleven o'clock, when the party blondes and their men have driven home to their various babysitters/baby monitors, the beer goggles are well and truly in place and I've forgotten to mind that Colin's main topic of conversation seems to be Charlie Dimmock's breasts. I don't even mind that he looks as though his flat might resemble the inside of a Travelodge. Or that he probably owns a Corby trouser press. I don't even give a toss about the eye bogie that's been wobbling away in the corner of his left eye since we finished pudding.

And when it's time to go home, I invite him to drive me back to mine.

Chapter 9

'Tell us again.' George rubs his hands together with glee. 'Tell us exactly what he was like.'

'Who?'

'Your biddy shag.'

Janice, George and I are sitting in Janice's kitchen, drinking frothy cappuccino from the new powder-blue machine Jasper bought her. It's the day before Poppy's wedding. In half an hour, we'll be legging it to Paddington to catch the train down to Bath. Everything is organised, down to the last silver sugared almond. The cake—a rich chocolate extravaganza the size of a mini roundabout—is baked, iced, and scattered with hundreds of Jelly Tots and parma violets at Poppy's request. Since Janice's dinner party, I've been working my fingers to the bone. I've been on the phone to Perfect Poppy and her mother day in, day out, planning menus, table decorations and suchlike, down to the last, teeniest, minutest detail. Which is great. It's helped me forget all about the whole Colin fiasco.

Or it would have done if Janice and George hadn't been in

such a complete hilarum over the whole sorry episode. They laughed so much, Janice nearly wet herself. And no matter how many times I've told the story of what happened when I took Comedy Colin back to mine, they always make me tell it all over again when a new person comes along.

I hold up my little finger.

'It was a widger,' I tell them for the umpteenth time. 'Called Alfred.'

'So you didn't go through with it?' George prods delightedly. 'You made your excuses and left.'

I shake my head. 'Do we have to go through all this again?'

They already know the story inside out. And a sorry one it is too. We went back to mine. I put on a Massive Attack CD and made coffee. We kissed. And I was surprised and somewhat delighted to discover that it was actually a very nice kiss. A kiss that was definitely leading somewhere. And I suddenly realised that I really, really wanted a shag. I didn't care, I told myself as I slipped my hand into his trousers, about silly, shallow things like the fact that he was shorter than me. Or older than me. I didn't even care about his greying chest hair. All I could see was the fact that he had sad, lonely eyes. And I wanted to make him feel better. So I didn't give a hoot that, being older, he probably had saggy bum skin like an elephant's. I thought I could cheer him up. I'd be a sort of SAGA holiday with a difference.

Oh, sod it. If I'm truly honest, what mattered—what really, really mattered at that blurry, heinously drunken moment in time, was that he had a lovely big...

Oh good giddy God.

'Acorn' was a word that immediately sprang to mind when I touched Colin's little willy.

'Meet Alfred.' He smiled, as I gaped in horror. Because, no matter what they say, size matters, doesn't it?

Of course it bloody well matters.

And I was worried. Poor old Alfred wasn't even going to touch the sides. It was going to be just like flinging a welly down the Holloway Road. Like waving a chipolata through the Channel Tunnel. Shagging Colin, I decided, as I allowed him to unfasten my bra, was going to be a lot like visiting the dentist. He might as well lay me down and say, 'Don't worry, you're not going to feel a thing.' God. Was this even going to count as a real shag? Could I justify another notch on the bedpost? Or would I still be Katie Eight and a Half Shags Simpson.

Eight and a half! Not very many really, is it?

So when Colin pulled out a ribbed Durex and announced, 'I think Alfred needs a hat on,' I braced myself for a mercy fuck of the first order.

I wouldn't have minded but he seemed pretty intent on staying the night. And did he have the decency to creep out while I was asleep like some shitty bastard? Not likely! Oh no, Colin was very much all there when I woke up. And Alfred was raring to go again. Fortunately, as I mentally prepared myself for another Wiener Invasion, the phone shrilled. It was Poppy, in a tremendous panic. She and her mother had had one almighty row over whether or not I should be wrapping bacon round the green beans. They really needed my opinion. So I was able to make my excuses and climb off.

I could've hugged Poppy. I've never been so pleased to hear from a duty friend in my life.

Now, sitting at Janice's kitchen table, gritting my teeth as the pair of them giggle at my woeful tale one more time, I run through a mental checklist. I can't help fussing, even though I know we've been through the wedding breakfast menu a dozen times. Everything is ready to go. Rosy slabs of salmon and oysters, glistening with seawater and heaped in crates, were flown in fresh from Dublin this morning. Sam, bless his billabong surf socks, has painstakingly packed them into his dad's refrigerator van, which he's driving down in later. But the fact that everything seems to be under control doesn't stop me from having bouts of nervous diarrhoea every five minutes.

I need something to take my mind off it.

'Hey, Janice, where's your bridesmaid's dress?' I wipe a blob of cappuccino froth off my nose and look round the kitchen. Janice turns moochy whenever her outfit is mentioned. Which is weird. Normally, she loves dressing up and being the centre of attention. Why isn't she dying to show me her finery?

'Upstairs.'

'Well, come on then. What are we waiting for?' I put down my cup and stand up. 'Show and tell.'

Wordlessly, Janice gets up and leads the way upstairs to her bedroom. She's actually still a bit pissy with me. I expect it's because I've been avoiding all Colin's postcoital telephone calls, thus depriving her of the cosy foursomes we might have shared. But the thought that she actually expects me to date a man with a baked bean for a penis for her sake is so gobsmackingly astounding that I completely forget to defend myself. There just doesn't seem to be anything to say.

The moment I enter her bedroom, it becomes obvious to any fool that my failure to appreciate Colin for his 'finer point', as it were, isn't the only reason for her puckered-up dog's bottom face. Janice's bridesmaid's dress is hanging on the back of the door, wrapped like a birthday present under layers of pink tissue and crinkly plastic. 'Look,' she says miserably.

'Ohhh,' George and I can't help exclaiming.

'Exactly.' Janice looks furious. 'About as sophisticated as a bottle of flipping Babycham.'

And once she's peeled off the layers of tissue paper, I have to admit I see her point. I can make 'It's a lovely colour, I'm sure it'll come in useful for something else' noises until the cows come home, but there's no disguising the fact that, whichever way you look at it, Janice is going to look like a misguided teenager on Prom night circa 1985.

'I can't wear it,' she whispers. 'I'm going to look putrid.'

I hate to say it, but putrid's not the word. A huge, squashy velvet number in deep crimson, the billowing bridesmaid's frock is as conspicuous among the elegant pale limewashed floorboards, the freshly starched linen sheets and the cool creams, earthy browns and mossy greens of Janice's calm bedroom as a gaudily decorated Christmas tree in a temple of Jehovah. It has bulbous, puffed out sleeves, a great beachball of a skirt with a hoop the size of the London Eye and a blimming great helicopter propeller of a bow on the bum. In fact, the whole ensemble is so enormous that I doubt very much whether she'll be able to actually wear it down the aisle tomorrow. She'll have to bloody well drive the thing. And there simply isn't time to get her HGV licence.

Now if Janice was still bonking one of her Driver Eating Yorkie types, she could have got them to swipe her a Wide Load sign from the depot. As it is though, she's going to have to hope that the aisle'll be relatively traffic-free.

'What the hell am I going to do?' she spits. 'When Jasper sees me in that he'll be off like shit through a goose. There'll be no wedding then. Not for me, at any rate.'

Her bottom lip trembles as she sees her gingerbread mansion of the future come crashing to the ground, no more than a few hastily held together crumbs after all.

The three of us gawp at the scarlet monstrosity in stunned silence.

Naturally, George finds his tongue first.

'Good God,' he ejaculates. 'She's not taking any chances, is she? Wants to make sure you look a complete dog all right. How much does one get paid for this bridesmaid lark? Whatever it is, it isn't worth it.'

'George,' I warn him.

Janice is on the verge of chucking a massive tantrum. Her face is thunderous. Any minute now, she's going to hurl herself, Scarlett O'Hara style, on the bed and start drumming her heels and howling.

'Try it on,' I soothe. 'Perhaps we can make a nip and a tuck here and there. Trim the bow down a bit.'

'No point,' George comments with all the subtlety of the

Hammersmith flyover. 'She's going to look like Ten Ton Tessie whatever you do to it. Christ Almighty, darling, Kate Moss would look like a block of bloody Trex in that get-up. Janice'll be able to get a part in the *Titanic* remake.'

'Oh, I don't know,' I say calmly. 'I think it's more nineteen eighty-two than nineteen twelve.'

'I meant a non-speaking part.' George can't help winking at me. 'As the bloody ship.'

'Come on,' I say sharply, before Janice actually bursts a blood vessel. 'It's the bride's prerogative to make the bridesmaids look dreadful. Poppy wouldn't want you upstaging her on her own wedding day, would she? It wouldn't be fair.'

'Darling, she couldn't upstage a pot-bellied pig in that dress,' George interjects.

'Thank you, George, for that,' I say. 'Come on, hon. Give it a go. It can't be that bad, can it? Actually,' I hold my breath— will she buy it or not?—'I think the colour really suits you. And it isn't physically possible for you to look that ugly. Not with your hair. And your gorgeous figure.'

Janice looks a bit happier.

'I have got better tits than her, haven't I?'

'Exactly. And no one can take those away from you. Just try it on,' I plead.

'You won't laugh?'

'We won't,' I say firmly. 'We promise. Don't we, George?'

'Yes,' he says in a small voice that means he's actually clamping his teeth shut to stop himself guffawing.

Janice steps gingerly into the gaudy creation and allows me to zip her up.

'OK,' I say, cringeing as I do so at my stupid children's TV presenter voice. 'Gissa twirl then.'

She obeys, for once.

'Ohmigod,' shrieks George. 'You look just like one of those loo roll holders.'

After George has delivered his last blow it takes a lot of coax-

ing and persuading for Janice even to get off the bed. In the
end, we miss our train at Paddington and have to wait an hour
for the next one. Janice sits miserably on the bench outside
Burger King, reading *Brides* magazine in preparation for her
own imaginary big day, stabbing her finger at pictures of al-
ternately gorgeous, flippy, flirty and sophisticated little numbers at intervals and saying bitterly, 'She could have let me wear
that. I'd look bloody gorgeous in that.' While she does that,
George bemoans the perils of public transport. I feel like a care-
worn mother dragging two ungrateful teenagers away on a day
trip. The way I feel, I'd make a damn good understudy for
Pauline Fowler. And I'm a bit blooming pissed off about it.
After all, I'm the one who needs pampering. I'm nervous. This
is my future career we're talking about. My reputation is riding on today.

'My greatest fear, darling, trains,' George whittles, looking
fearfully up at the departures board. 'Full of cheerful families
eating farty egg sandwiches and shouty people wearing baseball caps and Bermuda shorts.'

'There's no smoking here,' a woman opposite, eating a
Quarter Pounder with Cheese, points out, as George lights
himself a violet-coloured cigarette, crisscrosses his legs and exhales ostentatiously.

George glares at her. 'I don't object to your eating conveni-
ence food and wearing a purple shell suit, do I?' he demands.
'No. And do you see me wearing a "No dodgy home perms"
T-shirt? I think not. So I don't expect you to object to my
smoking. I'll smoke where I bloody well like, thank you. I certainly won't be dictated to by the likes of you.'

'I'm sorry,' I rush to apologise. 'He's dangerously schizo-
phrenic. We're taking him back to hospital now. You don't
know which platform the Bath train leaves from, by any
chance?'

'Platform three,' Purple Shell Suit informs me icily, picking
gherkin out of her Quarter Pounder and tossing it to the ground.

'What are you asking her for?' George can be heard bitching as we make our way towards our train. 'Probably never been further south than Morden in her life. Now are you going to carry my vanity case or not?'

'Not,' I say, marching off down the platform. I've had enough of Janice's sulking and George's tantrums. This is my big day. I have to make a success of this wedding or I'll be back in that tights and handbag environment before you can say Teeline.

Sometimes mates can be bastard selfish.

As the train draws out of the station, we strike up a 'Weddings I have known' type conversation, partly because none of us have thought to bring any reading matter—Janice's bridal porn excepted—partly to keep Janice's bottom lip from wobbling as her mind wanders back to the crimson monster stuffed out of sight in a squashy heap on top of the luggage rack and partly because I'm still positively squitty with nerves at the thought of all I have to do tomorrow.

'I hope it's not going to be a cash bar,' George frets. 'So vulgar.'

'Doubt it,' Janice ventures, cheering up slightly at the chance of a good bitch. 'Poppy's dad's a compulsive entertainer. Remember when he used to come down to see Poppy at college, Katie?'

'God, yes.' I laugh, trying not to slop coffee everywhere as the train rattles towards Reading. 'He should have been a member of Lunchers Anonymous. He used to take us to all those wonderfully smart places.'

'It was a bit pathetic, wasn't it, really?' she says suddenly. 'We didn't even like her much and it was always us she chose to take.'

'Mmm. Quite sad in a way.'

'Remember that Sarah-Jane's wedding in Leeds?' Janice asks me. 'Where it was a sit-down meal and they didn't put the wine bottles on the tables? They only filled our glasses about twice. We were gagging for a drink and we didn't have any money with us so we had to keep stealing other people's pints.'

'Mmm,' I remember. 'Mind you, fuck only knows why we were remotely surprised. Sarah-Jane was as tight as a gnat's chuff at college. She actually cried when I knocked over her Galliano and lime 'cos it cost her one pound twenty. Remember?'

'We all reckoned she was probably born with a fifty pee clenched between her bum cheeks.'

'Probably still there.'

'And we were really pissed off because of all the dosh we spent on actually going to the wedding.'

'I could have had a new bathroom installed with the money we spent on getting up there and paying for a hotel room.'

'That's right. So we took back the present. Remember? Swiped it off the hall table as we left and it was straight back to the shop with it for a refund. And we spent it on two vegetable biryanis and a couple of keema naans down the Punjab Paradise. Pass us a serviette, George. I've slopped coffee all over my boob.'

'Napkin.' He shudders. 'Napkin. And there wouldn't have been much point in you having a new bathroom installed, would there, Katie? Not with you still being in rented accommodation.'

I ignore him. Suddenly Janice is much cheerier. And I don't want to spoil it by fighting with George.

'You drank too many Bacardi Breezers and gave the best man a blow job under the top table,' I remind Janice. 'And then you blew chunks and passed out and we had to carry you back to the hotel room with bits of red wine sick in your hair.'

'Yesss.' Janice laughs. 'God, don't let me do that this time. Jasper would have a blue fit. He hates women who get shitfaced. Thinks it's unfeminine.'

'He would.'

'Pardon?'

'Nothing.'

'Oh,' she tosses her head, 'I know he's a sad old fart. And I'm probably going to have to boff him sooner or later if I want to get my hands on his wedge. But that's cricket for you.'

George and I exchange raised eyebrows and I swiftly change

the topic of conversation before one of us is forced to tell her that Jasper is a complete arsehole. Neither George nor I would actually choose to spend one millisecond with him for all the money in the world. But because she's my best friend and I love her to pieces, I feel the need to protect her from my caustic opinions so as not to hurt her.

'Don't forget I've booked a hotel for you tomorrow night,' I tell George. 'You're staying at Poppy's parents' house with me tonight to help me get everything ready.'

'A reassuringly expensive hotel, I hope?' George asks. 'I'm not staying in a damp B&B that smells of cat's piss and old people's cabbage and being forced to eat dodgy Grape Nuts for breakfast to get my bowels moving. I mean we have actually left London now, don't forget. They have different rules in the provinces, you know. "Sophisticated menu" means "next door but one to the Little Chef". We'll have to eat all our meals in those places where you're forever picking pubes out of your food.'

'We won't.'

'And the waitresses all wear sovereign rings and pink gingham smocks to match their eczema.'

'You're such a snob,' I accuse him.

'I am not.' He looks absolutely astounded at the very suggestion. 'I slept with someone from Sheffield once. And I've been to Leeds. They've got a Harvey Nicks there now, you know.'

'Bully for them.'

'And I had a very lengthy telephone conversation with a Welsh person only last week.'

'Good for you.'

'Well, I say conversation,' he adds. 'In the loosest sense of the word of course. I was the only one actually forming whole sentences. Do you know, when I picked up that phone I was convinced the woman was speaking another language? God only knows what the viewers are going to think. Still, it was a toss-up between her and some slack-titted bint from Solihull when it came down to it so...'

'So?'

'Solihull.' George looks at me as though I'm some kind of retard. 'Solihull in the West Midlands? As in "close proximity to Birmingham"? We can't go having Brummies on the show left, right and centre, darling. The accent makes people feel ill.'

The train dawdles through Didcot and chugs through Chippenham and, bored, Janice and I unpack the luxury Fortnum's hamper we've bought the happy couple as a wedding gift and start to work our way through a box of chocolate-covered macadamia nuts.

'They probably won't open them until they get back from honeymoon,' Janice reasons.

'Exactly.' I wedge in another one. 'And we can't risk them getting left by a radiator or something and going all squidgy, can we?'

At last, the solid tower of Bath Abbey looms into view. I hurriedly bunch shimmering gold cellophane around what's left of Poppy and Seb's gift and re-tie the white and gold ribbon.

'Think they'll notice?'

'Probably won't care.'

A watery sun warms the glowing clusters of butterscotch stone buildings on the surrounding hillsides as we pull into the station. Bath looks terribly pretty in the April sunshine. We jump in a taxi and watch, fascinated, as the car meanders through narrow cobbledy streets teeming with tourists. There are foreigners everywhere. Trendy Japanese with cameras slung round their necks like gas masks. Fat Americans in sparkling white trainers and lemon casualwear. And crocodiles of gabbling French schoolchildren with identical blue and white backpacks.

Poppy's parents live just outside the city, in an enormous pile built of Bath stone. As we arrive, festivities of some sort are already in full swing. Poppy's mother, a minuscule, elegant woman in an immaculate cream trouser suit, hands us a glass of mulled wine as we clomp through the door and greets us as though we're long lost friends.

'How marvellous.' She beams. 'The caterer and the brides-maid. Well, we won't have to worry about you turning up on time tomorrow, now will we? Of course you'll be wanting to unpack.'

'Not really,' I say at exactly the same time as George and Janice say, 'Oooh, yes please.'

Poppy's mother takes us up the grand staircase and shows us all to our rooms. Janice and Jasper get a bedroom at the front, while George and I get back bedrooms from which, she assures us, we'll be able to see the canal winding through the valley when we wake up tomorrow. Then it's downstairs with the lot of us to eat, drink and be merry.

'Are you having a marquee?' George asks as we wend our way downstairs, me trying, not very successfully, not to spill my wine all over the immaculate soft yellow carpet.

'No.' Poppy's mother shakes her head. 'The barn's plenty big enough. We thought we'd decorate that instead. That OK with you, Katie?'

'Erm.' I don't suppose I have any choice.

The house is chock-a-block with Poppy's relations, all drinking and laughing and patting each other on the back. And while Poppy races around the hall, decorating the place with bits of holly and ivy and generally panicking about every tiny little thing, Janice, George and I take advantage of the free pre-wedding champagne, gratefully golloping every drop that's being poured into our glasses at any given opportunity.

'So you're the caterer, are you?' asks a tall streak of nothing in a silvery dress. She's got white glitter around her eyes, which gives her an unearthly, angelic look. I can't help noticing that she's constantly looking over my shoulder for people to flirt with.

'Yes.' I hate her almost on sight. 'I'm also a person.'

'I'm sorry?'

'Never mind.'

'Oh.' She looks momentarily confused then taps a passing

waiter on the arm and bats her glitter-dusted eyelashes at him furiously. 'I don't suppose you'd like to get me a tiddly little canapé, would you?' she asks him.

'Yes, miss.'

'Thank you.' She smiles. Fluttering her lashes again. 'It's just that I'm terribly orally fixated at the moment. I really feel the need to put something in my mouth.'

'How's about my fist?' Janice, hearing her, mutters into my ear. 'That do you?'

But she doesn't hear. Instead, she extends a fragile hand towards mine, smiles with her teeth, not her eyes, and says, 'Pleased to meet you. I'm Persephone. Pussy for short.'

'Figures,' Janice says quietly.

When Pussy turns to speak to someone else, Janice exhales.

'Fucking hell. She's a man-eating bitch if ever I saw one. She'd better not try getting her claws into Jasper.'

'Don't worry,' I reassure her. 'She hasn't got a chance. No tits, for starters. Shit, she's coming back.'

'Those are quite nice.' She points at my favourite palest pink strides.

'Thanks,' I say, chuffed, despite myself. 'They're Jigsaw.'

'Thought so.' She turns up her pretty little nose. 'Last season, aren't they?'

'Cow,' mutters Janice.

I try to rise above bitchy comments, saying instead, 'So how do you fit in with all this? You a friend of Poppy's?'

'Cousin.' She tosses her head. 'Of sorts. Her mother's my father's cousin. That's my father over there. Talking to her other sister.'

'Which one?' I ask politely.

'Fat one,' she says coolly, lighting a cigarette and pointing in the direction of a largish woman wearing a hippyish creation in flowing lilac. 'Over there.'

'Oh.' I'm surprised at her frankness.

'Yes. Never married, that one. Still, you can see why, can't you?'

'I think she looks nice,' I say, hurt on the woman's behalf. 'She's got a lovely face.'

'Never goes anywhere without that little dog, poor cow,' the girl says unkindly. 'Oooh, look.' She suddenly bursts into gales of tinkling laughter that reminds me of silver bells. I can't help thinking what a pretty laugh she has for someone so transparently horrid. 'What?' I can't help turning my head.

'Will you look at that?' She's still pointing at the large woman. 'It's slobbered all over that dreadful skirt. She's covered, look. She hasn't even realised.'

'Someone should tell her,' I say, shocked at her outburst.

'I'm sorry.' She catches me staring at her and checks herself. 'I don't know whether I'm laughing so much at the dog drool or whether it's because she had the audacity to actually wear that dreadful outfit in the first place.'

I finally manage to get away from Pussy and fetch myself another drink. Or three. By half past eleven, I realise I'm absolutely knackered. Time for bed. I have a lot to do tomorrow and I really don't want to make a pig's ear of the whole thing. I make my way up to my room and flop straight into bed without cleaning my teeth.

I've probably been asleep for about forty minutes when I'm woken by someone getting into bed beside me.

'What the fuck?'

'Shhhh,' says a familiar voice. In the dark I can't quite make out his face.

'Sam?'

'Yes?'

'That you?'

'Well of course it's me.' He laughs. 'Who else would it be?'

'Johnny Depp?'

'Wishful thinking, Simpson,' he says and I can hear by his voice that he's grinning.

'Jesus, Sam, you frightened the life out of me. What the hell are you doing here? And get your hand off my bum.'

'Sorry.' He moves away. 'Didn't realise.'

'So?'

'So what?'

'Why are you here? You're not supposed to be arriving till tomorrow.'

'Bloody van broke down.'

'What?'

'Not the actual van. The fridge part. And I didn't want the food to go off. So I drove down here tonight. I've been outside with Poppy's dad filling bins with ice.'

'Oh, Sam.'

'What?'

'You're so sweet. Thank you.'

'I am not sweet. I'm a rugged, red-blooded male, thank you very much. And you're welcome.'

I bend to kiss the top of my friend's head. But because it's so dark, I miss and the kiss lands on his mouth instead.

'Sorry.'

'No problem.'

But he's grinning again. I can tell by his voice.

'You're laughing at me.'

'No more than usual.'

'Good.'

'Although you are rather funny.'

'Cheers.'

I smack him over the head with my pillow. And now that he's woken me up I can't go back to sleep. I'm too nervous about tomorrow.

'I suppose you'll have to sleep here,' I grumble. 'And just when I was looking forward to having this lovely big bed to myself.'

'Suppose so,' he says. 'Sorry.'

We pass the time till I'm able to nod off by talking about schooldays.

'Remember that dreadful felt jacket with the white leather sleeves you always wore?' I tease him.

'My baseball jacket?' he asks. 'I loved it.'

'It was awful.'

'Not as bad as that acid yellow ra-ra job you wore to the school disco.'

'True.' I laugh. 'You took the piss out of me for weeks.'

'No I didn't.'

'Did.'

'I didn't.' He sounds hurt. 'That was Mike McDonald. I stood up for you, I'll have you know. Said you couldn't help it. That you were stylistically challenged.'

'Ho ho.'

'And I said your legs weren't like a chicken's at all.'

'Ha ha.'

'Only joking. Actually I always thought you had rather nice legs.'

'Flatterer.'

But despite myself, I suddenly get the urge to kiss him. He's certainly close enough. But he's Sam. And that would just be stupid. It's just because I'm nervous. And he's so familiar.

'Remember when you had the top of your ear pierced?' I say hurriedly, as if to take my mind off the fact that he's lying so close. 'My mother said you were no better than vermin.'

'And when my dad caught us smoking in the shed...'

He's even nearer now.

'Do you remember when I broke your Culture Club album over your head 'cos you told everyone you'd read my diary?'

'Hmmm. Probably best place for it. I didn't read it, by the way.' He pinches my cheek affectionately.

'I know.' I push a bit of his hair off his face. 'You wouldn't be talking to me now if you had. You should see some of the things I wrote about you.'

'Oh yeah?' He laughs.

'Yeah.' I grin.

And suddenly, we're so close, our faces are almost touching. For one mad nanosecond, I think he's going to kiss me.

And then I remember.

This is Sam. My best mate. Not some dodgy notch on the bedpost.

And I haven't cleaned my teeth. Check me out. What the hell am I doing? I must stink of drink.

I jump away.

'Anyway,' I say.

'Right,' he says simultaneously.

Then we both look at each other.

'Sleep.'

Chapter 10

I wake up next morning with a jackhammer thumping in my temples from last night's champagne. Sam's side of the bed is empty. Groaning, I scuffle downstairs, where George, wearing nothing but white Jockey shorts and a pair of pink marabou-trimmed slippers, is standing in the kitchen stirring sugar into a big cup of coffee.

'All right?'

'Hanging.' He tosses his head back and points at his eyes to show how bloodshot they are. 'My breath's absolutely minging. Still, better show willing, I suppose, darling. Here you are.' He thrusts a glass of champers into my hand.

'God. Already?'

'Hair of the dog, darling. Hair of the goddamn dog. Ohmigod.' He suddenly gets up and stares out of the window. 'LOOK.'

'What?'

'He's here. The darling's only bloody well here.'

And with that, he runs out into the front yard in his undies and, slap bang in front of Poppy's mum and dad and other assembled guests, he gives a slightly bemused David a great big hello hug. And, somehow, much to my surprise, it all makes me feel a bit weird. A bit like I used to feel when Jake and I went to see some soppy film and it got to the end and I suddenly found I was sobbing my eyes out. And not because it was sad or even particularly happy or anything, but because I knew Jake and I simply weren't like that, and probably never would be.

Well, we certainly won't be now, so there's no point even thinking about that. But, as I watch David and George hugging and twirling each other around in the yard, it suddenly strikes me...

'He loves him,' I say out loud to myself. 'George really loves him.' It's a first. The only person George has ever loved until now is himself. And I can't help feeling a little bit jealous. I know it's childish but I know it means I'll get a lot less attention from George from now on. Of course, I pretend not to care, taking the piss out of them both and announcing how disgusting it is that they're so cheesily in love.

Janice gets up late. She's got a face like a smacked bum again. I expect it's the thought of wearing that terrible dress.

'Jasper not here yet?' I ask her.

'No.' She shakes her head. 'He's coming to the service. Had to work this morning, stuffy old bugger.'

'Your father, dear?' Poppy's mother hands her a cup of English Breakfast tea.

'Boyfriend,' Janice corrects her.

'Same age,' carps George.

'If you say so.' Janice throws him a look. 'I wouldn't know.'

'You said he was sixty-odd.'

'She means her father, stupid.' I glare. 'Not Jasper.'

There's a clamouring at the door as the little drooling dog from last night and a large golden retriever bark at someone coming in. It's Sam, of course. The minute I see him, my tummy flips over at the thought of our closeness last night. He made me feel safe. But then I notice that, following behind him, is the dreadful Pussy creature from last night.

Good old Sam. He'll never change.

'We've been for a walk,' a fresh-faced Pussy announces to the assembled company, smiling at Sam as though they've been best friends all their lives.

'Can she stop pouting?' David snipes and I laugh delightedly. Now I remember why I liked him so much in the first place. His ability to be sugar and spice and slugs and snails and puppy dogs' tails all at the same time is really rather charming. And suddenly, the fact that I so completely failed to bonk him really doesn't matter in the slightest. He's so nice, I'm finally able to forget my total humiliation.

I run around all morning making sure the food preparations are well and truly underway. Sam and David insist that I go to the church service, which is what Poppy wants. They'll keep everything ticking over until I'm back. George says he'll come to the church with me. He loves a good wedding, he says. Privately, I decide that this is because he wants to get out of doing any more of the work but he's already been such a help, in his own way, that I can't really forbid him from coming. Instead, I bite my lip and say nothing as he plonks his granny's jewel-encrusted tiara at a skewiff angle on top of his number two crop, straightens his shrimp-pink cravat and sticks a gerbera in his lapel. Then I hoick my tights out of my bum and we link arms, wandering past the canalside pub where lots of the guests are enjoying a pre-nuptial pint, and along the lane to the village church.

Poppy arrives fashionably late, setting my tummy off on its own peculiar spin cycle of nerves. What if Sam forgets to open the red wine? What if David doesn't put the oysters on ice so there's nothing for people to nibble on when they arrive? Will they remember to take the smoked salmon sandwiches out of the fridge in time? What if the puddings boil dry? What if I've forgotten something? What if...

'Calm down.' George puts a steadying hand on my arm.

The organist warbles through the opening bars of Handel and the bride and bridesmaids, a flotilla of strawberry and cream, sail down the aisle on a carpet of blood-red rose petals.

'Oooh.' George nudges me in the ribs. 'Will you look at Janice? Oozing all the glamour of a Robin Reliant.'

'Shhhh,' I hiss, as the woman in the pew in front, whiffing of mothballs and sporting a hat shaped like a Walnut Whip, turns round and glares at us with eyes like boiled sweets. I press my teeth together to quell the bubble of nervous laughter frolicking around in my windpipe and stare down at my toes, which peep, violet with cold and with chocolate-painted toenails, from ridiculous girlie heels. Oh for a pair of clumpy Timberland boots. I'm freezing my goddamn tits off in here. I have to keep tweaking my nips to make sure they're still on.

Seb is standing by the altar, a great big shit-eating grin on his face. As Poppy reaches his side, he takes one of her tiny hands in his, and the vicar tactfully motions for Janice to stand to one side because her bum bow is blocking everyone's view. Janice spends the rest of the ceremony with a face like a bulldog licking piss off a nettle, while George enjoys himself hugely, singing 'All Things Bright and Beautiful' in a stupid falsetto voice to get attention, sparking up a fag during 'Jerusalem' and stage-whispering 'Clunk! That was the sound of my tits dropping off through boredom,' at various intervals during the sermon.

Privately, I'm just glad I've come to my senses. Oh yes, it's all very romantic. And a year ago, I'd have probably been pea-green with envy as Seb, a tall, dark, handsome cliché in his top hat and tails, and Poppy, fragile, elegant and looking as though she's about to dance the Waltz of the Snowflakes in a simple sheath of pure white silk, dotted with thousands of tiny iridescent beads, sign the register as the choir choke their way through a dubious rendition of 'Pie Jesu'. I'd have probably been so swept up in the romance of the whole thing, I'd not even have noticed the cold, which is now turning my nips to Jelly Tots. I'd have been wishing fervently that this pomp and ceremony was all for my benefit. Fantasising that the two toddling flower girls, sweet rosebuds in ruby velvet dresses, and the older bridesmaids, skinny and plain as clothes pegs next to Janice's big hair and sweater girl curves, were here to support *me*. Dreaming of my own petal-strewn aisle and blizzard of heart-shaped pink confetti. And as the happy couple emerge into the churchyard, where crocuses the colour of creme egg yolks peep through the grass, I thank God I've realised marriage has all the appeal of a freshly whipped dog turd.

I mean buggery bollocks. It could have been me and Jake back there, signing our sanity away in a flourish of Bic biro.

Jake.

OK, so if I'm perfectly honest, I still get a fuzzy, feedbacky sort of feeling in my tummy whenever I think about Jake. Especially when I remember he's got a sprog on the way. That puts rather a different spin on things. If I did want him back—which of course I don't—there'd be a whole new person to consider.

At least I found out about the poisonous sod before it was too late. But Perfect Poppy and Seb are a different story. How can they be sure they'll be perfectly happy for the rest of their perfectly pristine lives? Sebastian, after all, is a bloke. He has a penis. So who's to say that, even while vowing publicly to keep himself—Sebastian Willoughby Gentle—only unto Poppy Cassandra Latimer as long as they both shall live, he hasn't got one hand in his pocket, fingers crossed as he adds silently, 'Until we get back from Aruba, or Antigua or Acabloodypulco, wherever it is she's decided we're going, when hopefully I'll have enough of a tan to talk that Monica from Accounts right out of her Janet Reger thong.'

I sneak away from the church as the bridal party pose for photos by the beribboned archway, poking my tongue out at Janice as I go in a clumsy attempt to make her laugh. I fail. She's as miserable as sin. Back at the house, I'm hugely relieved to find that, with George out of the way, David and Sam have done a brilliant job with the arrangements. The oysters I shucked seconds before I left for the ceremony are piled globbily onto silver trays, and platters of miniature smoked salmon and brown bread sandwiches with the crusts cut off have been placed, according to my instructions, at regular intervals around the barn. I reckoned that people would get less off their faces on fizz if they had something inside them before they drank too much. Sam, ever the PR man, has done me proud with the decorations. The barn is aglow with hundreds of flickering church candles, adorning every table and windowsill, casting romantic shadows across the old stone walls. In the centre of the room stands a stone pool, once used for cows' drinking water, now a mass of silver and gold floating candles and anemone heads in imperial purple and deep crimson. Thirty or so round tables cluster around the pool, each covered in a different coloured silk cloth; olive green, peacock blue, gold, silver, crimson, indigo, forest green. More candles, this time in wrought iron candelabra, stand in the centre of each table, lending a gothic atmosphere to the proceedings, and bowls of red roses, for love, their heads bunched tightly together to form a deep crimson mass, are on every surface. The plates and glasses, which Sam has somehow produced, like the shopkeeper in *Mr Benn*, as if by magic, provide the finishing touch. Iridescent and coloured like jewels in turquoise, emerald, ruby, sapphire and amber, they set everything off perfectly. Tiny silver and gold angels are entwined around the backs of wrought iron chairs and golden boxes of my homemade heart-shaped chocolates, silver sugared almonds and chocolate-covered ginger are on every guest's plate.

'It's perfect,' I breathe, a lump coming into my throat. 'Absolutely perfect. Thanks, Sam. And David. You've done wonders. Thank you both, so, so much.'

Cue hugs all round as I take in their penguin suits, worn specially for the occasion. They both look gorgeous and I'm relieved to find that Sam is acting completely normally. George, of course, refuses to change out of what he's already wearing. He might have to act like a waiter for the day but that doesn't mean he has to bloody well look like one. I slip into a simple black dress with spaghetti straps and pull my hair back into a fat orange plait to keep it out of the food.

'You're not wearing that.' Sam, fastening silver cufflinks, comes along the landing as I emerge from my room.

'What's wrong with it?'

'It's perfect. You'll upstage the bride.'

'Ha ha.'

'I mean it. You look great.'

'Do I?'

'You do.'

'I'm shitting myself.'

'You'll be fine.' He hugs me and, for a flash of a second, I feel all funny inside again. But when I pull away he's smiling at me. 'Good luck, Simpson.'

'Good luck yourself. You're the waiter. Oh, and if you accidentally slop soup into the ladies' laps, please try to restrain yourself from asking if you can lick it up. It's not quite the thing in polite circles.'

Sam slaps my back playfully. People begin to filter into the barn from their walk from the church. Ladies in flowery hats, swathed in head-to-foot crimplene. Men in suits, pinned to their wives' sides and looking as trapped as pockets of wind after dodgy vindaloos. Exhausted fathers. Elegant mothers. Eligible bachelors. And lots and lots of blondes. Busty blondes. Beaky blondes. Blondes in cream to outdo the bride and blondes with sunbed tans and hatfuls of dyed turquoise feathers, all filter in, greedily grabbing glasses of champagne and chattering like chaffinches. For the next hour, Sam, George and David, bristling with manic energy, flit from barn to kitchen and from kitchen to barn, pouring drinks, handing round oysters, sprinkling Tabasco, squeezing lemon wedges and doling out salmon sandwiches, while I panic and fret over the preparation of the starters.

'Christ, will you look at that.' George, coming back for more sandwiches, tuts loudly as a woman in her mid-thirties proudly hands round a fat, pink child of about six months for people to coo over. There are so many children around that the atmosphere is thick with the scent of follow-on milk, rather than the heady cocktail of pheromones I've been hoping for, but I can't afford to think about that now. I've got a meal to serve.

'Bloody breeders making a point,' George goes on. 'Yes, yes,' he scoffs. 'Isn't it lovely? What a shame we can't all have one. You know she really oughtn't to flash it around like that. Someone'll steal it if she's not careful.'

'It's a baby,' I point out, handing him another bottle of champagne and waving him in the direction of a crowd of rugger buggers with their drinking heads on. 'Not a Lotus Elan.'

'And the mother's common as cheap chocolate,' he snarls. 'She's got those horrible slag wellies on. Look.'

George has a thing about the wearers of knee-high boots. He can't bear to look at them. Thinks it says something about their personal hygiene. Or lack of it. God knows why.

Back in the kitchen I get trays of plump crab cakes out of the warming oven and arrange them quickly on plates with peppery rocket, purple lollo rosso and dollops of zingy tomato and chilli jam. There's just time to mop my sweaty top lip, then it's the veggies' turn. Goat's cheese and sundried tomatoes in crisp, filo pastry for them. As the boys serve them, I check on the lamb medallions slow-roasting with sprigs of rosemary and whole garlic cloves in Poppy's mum's Aga. I chop fresh mint, baste roast potatoes and toss cubes of pancetta and blobs of butter into green beans. Drizzle fat yellow peppers, red onions, fennel bulbs and garlic with generous lashings of oil. Flinch as a recently arrived Jasper, unseen by Janice (beaming now that she's shed her ladybird costume and is slinking around in a shimmering silvery-green party dress) flips me a wink, gives my arse a quick pinch and wishes me luck.

I stick thumbs up at Sam, George and David and smile as I catch snatches of conversation at tables. They're all here. The usual wedding guest Rolodex. The ones who've forgotten they left school ten years ago and still find the need to ask everyone else whether they were at Wellington or Gordonstoun, just to get the social measure of them. The ones who like to turn every conversation into a competition. Professional small talkers. Those who are under the mistaken impression that they are conducting a job interview and are asking everyone else at their table exactly where they see themselves in five years' time. Then there are those like me. Single, alone, out of place, like a headmistress on a Club Med holiday. Turning their attention to more important things like the downing of gratis gin and tonics and furtively looking around, dying for a cigarette but not wanting to make the social gaffe of being the first to light up. All the single girls have been placed, according to wedding etiquette, within crotch-sniffing distance of the rugger buggers' table.

As people tuck into the starter, slopping more and more wine into each other's glasses, an appreciative buzz hums round the barn and I actually catch murmurs of 'delicious', and 'wonderful' as crab cakes are chomped on and my special salad dressing is savoured. And quite right too. This is none of the usual school dinner-type crap you usually get at weddings. Perfect, stamped out rounds of lukewarm reconstituted turkey. Mash Get Smash potato, served with an ice-cream scoop. Chilly carrots. Lumpy gravy. Frozen peas. Oh no. My grub is Ritz standard, at the very least. When the main course has been cleared, there isn't a scrap on the plates. And, I have to admit, I'm quietly thrilled.

Time for my *pièce de résistance*. An adults' version of the old school favourite. Chocolate Toothpaste. Only my chocolate toothpaste is darker, richer, smoother and a thousand times more sinful than its predecessor, with a dollop of clotted cream on the top so thick it barely drips off the spoon. Or there are individual sticky toffee puddings, served with lashings of thick caramel sauce. Better than sex. And as we clear plates, bring coffee and chocolate mints, get more champagne, Poppy comes rushing, tripping over her fairy princess dress to congratulate me. I've made her day. It's been a success. I'm on my way. I'm a star.

But it's only when the speeches are finished that I finally allow myself to relax. And, as a divine-looking Poppy and Seb take the floor to the tune of 'My Funny Valentine', I spot Sam and Pussy talking together. She's looking up at him adoringly, just as she did to the assorted males who were prey to her charms last night. I almost can't bear to watch it.

'Bitch,' Janice, seeing me spying on the pair of them, says critically. 'Look at her. Why doesn't she just come straight out with it and say, "Oooh, Sam, I do think your face would look sooo much better with me sitting on it"?'

She can talk. She and Jasper spend the rest of the evening canoodling in the conservatory, which Sam and David have laced with scarlet Chinese lanterns and strings of red and green chilli pepper fairylights. I watch in fascinated disgust as they feed each other apricots and figs from the fruit bowl in some frenzied pre-coital ritual. Well, I say pre-coital. According to Janice, she still hasn't had to sleep with him yet. Only a few days ago she was describing the ten-inch kidney wiper attached to a nice bit o'rough she picked up over the free-range chickens in Sainsbury's in vein popping detail.

'It's not as if he's going to find out, is it?' she asked me. 'Jasper, I mean.'

'Guess not.' I sighed. 'Do you really find him that repulsive then? I mean, I know he's a lot older than us, but is he really that bad?'

'S'not that,' she said. 'It's just if I give in so soon he'll be off like a bride's nightie. So I have to get it elsewhere, if you know what I mean.'

I nodded. I knew all right. I could hardly expect a girl who's usually dropping her M&S specials before you can say 'doggy style' to go without sex for longer than a month.

So while Janice tries to wangle herself a place in Jasper's affections (and therefore wallet) with fruit and stolen kisses, I watch, stiff with boredom, as Pussy crosses one thigh the width of a strip of linguine over the other and throws back her golden mane, twittering with laughter at every tiny joke Sam makes. I'm saved by Poppy, coming over to talk to me again. I beam at her, mentally preparing myself for another gushing torrent of congratulations. This catering lark is all right. I'll have to think of a name for my new company. Neat Eats, perhaps? Not bad.

This time, though, it's not congratulations she's offering.

'Katie, thank God you're here. It's George.'

'George? Is he ill?'

'No. He's been accused of stealing by one of Seb's mum's friends.'

'Stealing? Stealing what?'

'A baby.'

Jesus H. Christ. Why me?

I look around for David, but he's nowhere to be seen. And Poppy is worried. Can I come? Now?

Buggery, buggery fuck.

I've got a feeling in my waters that everything just might be about to go tits up. Trust George to do his best to fuck up my big day.

Still, I can hardly be held responsible for George's behaviour, can I? I mean I'm only the cook, at the end of the day. So as long as I don't poison anyone, I'm all right, Jack. Aren't I?

Or did I automatically accept responsibility for Sam, George and David's behaviour when I asked them to help me out by being waiters for the day? If so, then it's all wrong. I'm not reliable enough to be responsible for anyone else. I can't even be relied upon to remember when to change my Tampax, for God's sake.

George is perched between the his 'n' hers marble basins in Poppy's mother's bathroom, shocking-pink fag in one hand, glittery tiara in the other. A woman with a big blonde pineapple hairdo, purple patent stilettos and a white satin frock coat with a Wonderbra and little else underneath is comforting a gross, snot-encrusted baby that is screaming so hard its mouth has turned into a perfect square. For a moment I forget all about George and am unable to stop myself from staring at it, wondering if its cheeks are going to burst open like overripe peaches. It really is horrid.

'There there.' She chucks it under the chin with a fake cerise talon. 'Poor little Chanel. Don't you worry, my lover. Mummy's got you now.'

'Chanel?' George wrinkles his nose in distaste. 'Methinks "Topshop" might be more appropriate. Poor little sod. I hardly think that outfit's what they call couture, darling. In fact, I doubt you could even term it off-the-peg. That's bargain bloody bin if ever I saw it. And it's stained.'

'I'm sorry,' I apologise. What the fuck is George doing? Does he want me to make a go of this business or not? I can't afford to have one of my waiters behave like this at my first gig. I'll never live the bloody thing down.

'Did you try to steal the baby?' I sigh, going hot and prickly behind the knees as I suddenly remember his New Year's request to rent my womb for a bit. Shit. Perhaps he was really serious about that. And now he's decided David is the best thing since ready-cooked polenta, he'll be feeling his lack of paternity all the more.

'Of course not,' he scoffs.

I breathe a sigh of relief.

'Look at it, for God's sake,' he spits. 'It's not even a very nice one. Bugger all bone structure. Weak chin, look.'

But Chanel's mother has other ideas.

'I caught him parading up and down with her in front of the mirror,' she accuses. 'Carrying her by the scruff of her neck, he was. As though she was a bleeding cat.'

Handbag's more like it.

Blimming heck.

'For the last time,' George raises his eyebrows to heaven, 'I wasn't stealing it. I was merely borrowing it.' He pouts. 'Wanted to see what it looked like with my cravat, darling. And it was entirely the wrong shade of pink so I went to put it back. Don't worry,' he assures the mother, 'it was nothing personal. If I'd known it was yours I wouldn't have touched it with a ten-foot pole. Oh, it was all very sweet lying in that bedroom, gurgling away on a Georgina Von Etzdorf throw, darling, but if I'd known where it came from I'd have throught twice about borrowing it, I can tell you.'

'George.'

'I mean the phrase "shallow end of gene pool" does spring to mind, I must admit. And lowest common denominator isn't a phrase that's far from tripping off the tongue either.'

'George. Stop.'

'And I think I'd like any daughter of mine to grow up know-ing the difference between dinner and lunch, thank you.'

Luckily, some bulimic bint in a wispy lavender dress chooses that precise moment to rush in and yack up her dinner, so in the rumpus that follows as everyone tries to leap out of the way of low-flying chunks of barf, I'm able to grab George by the cufflinks and slope off downstairs with him to find David. But not before some woman in the queue has looked at me, nod-ded towards the cubicle where the vomiting is taking place and muttered, 'It'll be them oysters, I bet.'

'*Those* oysters,' I say without thinking. 'And, no it won't. They're perfectly fresh.'

'Some people,' I say to George as I frogmarch him back to the barn. He grumbles all the way. It just isn't fair. Some peo-ple shouldn't be allowed to breed. That poor, chinless wonder upstairs is going to grow up thinking Black Tower and Match-makers are the height of sophistication. And when you think of the life he and David could have given it if it had been that little bit more attractive.

I can't be angry with him for long. After all, no damage has been done. And when he catches sight of David dancing along to Steps on his own and races over to give him a hug so that, for the second time that day, I get an enormous lump in my throat, I can forgive him anything.

Plus, people, even the Walnut Whip lady from the church, can't stop congratulating me on how wonderful the food has been. My very first venture has been a complete and utter success. I've given out countless business cards and already booked another two events. And, as I look in the mirror that night, too exhausted to bother taking my make-up off, I give my reflection a wink and a big grin.

'Katie Simpson,' I say, 'you've only gone and bloody done it.'

I get the train back to London on my own. I'm too excited to stay in Bath for long. I want to plan and think. Decide on a name for my business. Where to advertise, that sort of thing. And pretty soon, I'll probably need to rent an office. Find a house with a bigger kitchen.

I'm so excited I just can't wait.

I'm so pleased with myself that I almost fail to notice that the actual train journey is about as much fun in itself as salmonella. Young, sickeningly well-adjusted people who've been away for the weekend enjoying themselves fill the carriages with their cappuccinos, their Sunday papers and their irritatingly cheerful chatter. But I don't care. OK, so I have serious personal space issues with the guy sitting opposite, who seems to think it's perfectly reasonable to stretch his feet (deck shoe clad, I notice—nasty) out until they are wedged right under my seat. Where, precisely, does he think I'm going to put mine? Glaring at him while baring my teeth like a rabid dog proves totally ineffectual, so in the end I'm forced to twat him extremely hard in the shin with the heel of my Nike, while nonchalantly flipping through a magazine and pretending to be engrossed in an article on breast augmentation. And, when he jerks his feet back with a look of pain and surprise etched on his face, I'm right in there, making my legs as long as possible and stretching them out so quickly I almost get him in the nuts. Then I sit there, emptily triumphant and not daring to move again to so much as nip to the loo to shake a lettuce, in case I have to give up a single inch of my Fair Share Of Room.

Oh, and I keep getting those horrible fizzy pains in my feet every time I shift them. And I'm not exactly comfy because, thanks to the copious quantities of alcohol I consumed to celebrate my success last night, I keep feeling slightly nauseous, but even then I don't feel as bad as I normally would. I keep telling myself just how far I've come in so little time.

I get the tube back to Balham. Changing lines at Stockwell, I'm delighted to notice that, for the first time in about a year in my experience, a train pulls in within a minute. Brilliant. A good omen. Unfortunately, I'm not quite ready for it. Suddenly, I feel so sick I don't dare get on, in case I park a custard in the crowded carriage.

Which is bloody lucky, as it turns out, because the doors have only just whooshed shut when I get a funny saliva-ey feeling in my cheeks and I suddenly know—just know—I'm going to woof my cookies.

Shit, buggery, shit. What the hell am I going to do? I can hardly chuck up onto the platform in front of a train full of gawping passengers, can I?

Can I?

And then I have a brainwave. Sometimes, I tell myself, I can be a bloody genius. Thinking fast, I surreptitiously open my handbag and chunder straight into that instead. And, because, being mine, it isn't really a girlie handbag, but more like a capacious black rucksack, I'm completely hidden from view as I boke. And, as I quietly vom over my keys, mobile phone, chocolate stash and Filofax, I look for all the world as though I'm merely rummaging for a stray stick of chewing gum, or a packet of Tooty Frooties.

Of course, as the next train swooshes into the station and I realise I'm going to have to lug the whole stinking lot home so I can get to my keys at the bottom, I do spot a couple of flaws in my plan, but it's a little bit bastard late by then. Sticking my nose in the air for added confidence (what, puke in my bag? Me?) I gather my belongings and sweep onto the train, pushing two people out of my way in my determination to get to the only available seat and plonking myself firmly into it.

'Hi,' says the person sitting next to me. 'Katie, isn't it?'

I snap my head round, painfully aware of my sick breath and closing my bag quickly to avoid spattering the passengers opposite with a concoction of red wine sick and soggy chocolate.

Flipping heck.

It's Max.

Chapter 11

It's a big surprise to realise that Max seems to blame himself entirely for the sorry way my birthday bonk turned out. And, as we judder through Clapham Common, he confesses that he never actually got to find out why I found it necessary to scream the place down that night. He thought about asking Janice at work, but after she branded him a serial rapist at my party, he hasn't quite felt comfortable with her.

I giggle nervously.

As the train draws into Balham, there's an uncomfortable silence as we both realise that this is where I get off. One of us has to make a move now or we'll probably never see each other again. Which is a shame. Because from where I'm sitting, Max is still looking pretty fanciable. And now I've started, I sort of want to finish.

Well, it sure as hell ain't going to be me. I've made a complete lummox of myself once. I don't want to risk the possibility of rejection and the feeling of foolishness that would follow it.

'Bye.' I get up to go to the door, gripping the handles of my bag to avoid spillage.

'Look.' He pulls me back then, as the doors begin to close, thinks better of it and jumps out after me.

'Careful.' I grab my bag.

He looks a bit surprised but seems determined to carry on with what he's got to say. He seems nervous, which almost makes me despise him, but I wait to see what's on his mind.

'I don't suppose you fancy doing something, do you?'

'Like what?' I keep my cool, attempting to look vaguely bored, as if being asked out on a tube train by someone as gorgeous as Max is something that happens to me every day of my life.

'We could go to the Bedford. Have a pie and a pint. Sunday lunch. Whatever you fancy.'

'I'm not sure.' I bite my lip. It seems a bit of a waste of time to go through the rigmarole of polite small talk over a plate of roast beef and a bagful of sick, just so we can finish what we started. What if it turns out to be not worth finishing?

On the other hand, I am blimming starving.

And I suppose there's probably more than a morsel of truth in one of Janice's favourite sayings that suddenly comes to me as I stand on the platform, making up my mind: When in doubt, Get in, Get on, Get a present, Get out.

Sod it. Might as well get it where I can.

'Oh, OK then.' I grin. 'What the hell?'

As we come through the ticket barriers though, I check myself. What about my bagful of barf? I can hardly go out to eat with that sloshing jauntily at my side, can I? And what if one shag with Max isn't enough? After all, he is pretty delicious. Those eyes are edible.

But I do deserve sex, don't I? And, as far as I remember, Max has one of those willies that's actually pretty OK to look at. After Colin and his micro penis, a bunk up with Max will be a bit like treating myself to a nice chunky Mars bar after days of nibbling abstemiously on fruit.

On the downside, I haven't showered today. And there are a couple of grey minky hairs I really ought to pull out before I let anyone see me in the buff. And then there're my pits. I've been so busy with all the preparations for the wedding that they closely resemble the Epping Forest. Without the Essex accent, of course.

And with this hangover they probably smell like caramelised onions.

'We could have lunch at mine instead,' I say in a rush as we come out under Pigeonshit Bridge. 'I don't really feel like the pub and I've got some pumpkin soup in the freezer.'

'OK.' He smiles. I smile back. He really is rather saucy. How lucky that we ran into each other.

OK, so fortune might have waited until I didn't have a monster hangover, hairy legs and a handbag full of sick before waving her magic shag wand over my head, but this sort of thing doesn't really happen very often. It's being offered on a plate. It'd be rude not to help myself.

It's a bit tricky locating my key in front of Max. I don't really want him to see the contents of my bag, which I fully intend to dispose of the moment I've located and disinfected important items. When we eventually get inside the flat, there's no sign of Graham, but I sit Max in front of *EastEnders* while I busy myself with feeding Shish Kebab and making a big fuss of him in case he gets jealous. Then, on the pretext of unpacking my stuff, I dash upstairs and jump in the shower, hurriedly shaving my legs so I don't slice Max to pieces and slathering myself in lemon-scented body oil. Delicious. I know it's a bit obvious, smelling suspiciously fresh when I've just spent three hours travelling, but who cares. There's no point pretending. We both know what he's here for.

And it sure isn't homemade soup.

Anyway, sticking to one-night stands means I don't have to play stupid games any more. I can make it perfectly clear that I'm after a quick bunk up without fretting that it'll make him lose interest. The curse of the SOFA just doesn't apply any more.

I'm free.

Whoopee.

In the event, sex with Max is nice. Shadow play is completely unnecessary and I don't even feel the need to ask him to move his legs so I can rummage for the remote, either. His underwear is clean and white, not grey, tatty and Y-fronted, which I take as a good sign, particularly as we weren't expecting to see each other today, and so I couldn't reasonably have expected him to have come prepared. Of course it might mean that he's one of those superstitious types who always wears pristine grundies in case he gets mown down by a bus. Which probably means he's a complete Mummy's boy. But since I won't be seeing him again after today, who cares?

He goes straight for Croissants. What's more, he seems to know what to do. And he doesn't volley off a huge fart afterwards and then expect me to play Dutch Ovens, which I'm very grateful for. So all in all I have a nice time. Not wonderful, by any stretch of the imagination.

But nice. In the sort of way Madeira cake is nice. Pleasant.

It's only post-shag, while I'm still basking in that warm, tingly glow, that the alarm bells start clanging. You see, instead of stubbing out his fag and turning his back on me, as could only reasonably be expected of even the best one-night stand, Max props himself up on one elbow and pats the space on the bed next to him.

'What?' I eye him suspiciously. I mean, sorry to rain on his parade and all that, but I've got stuff to do. I've got to rake all that sick out of my spiral-bound address book before it starts to rust, for a start. What's he doing? Is he expecting me to congratulate him on his performance or what?

'Cuddle up.' He grins.

I gape at him in shock. Now I'm not much of a connoisseur re one-nighters, or even one-afternooners, come to that, but I do know this kind of behaviour isn't quite the ticket. I mean it's not normal, is it, expecting me to get slushy when all I want is a kip? Shouldn't he be fucking off out of it about now? Max smiles at me again, showing off a row of perfect pearly whites. Actually, I can't help noticing that they're starting to look a little too perfect. Like some cheesy toothpaste advert.

'I want to know everything about you.' He grins lazily, pulling my head down onto his chest in sloppy Mills & Boon fashion.

'You do?' I grit my teeth.

'Everything.' He seems to expect me to be pleased.

God, I hate it when people ask me to tell them about myself. I'm never quite sure how to answer. Or how much detail to go into. Does Max, for instance, need to know that I occasionally piss on people's toothbrushes when I'm annoyed with them? Or that I once used one of Sam's girlfriend's face flannels as loo roll at her birthday dinner because they'd run out and I hate having to drip dry. Or is that just too much information? Whatever I say, it's bad enough when it takes the form of self-congratulatory bullshit at some godawful dinner party. Talking about this stuff with someone who's just been nuzzling my nether regions really does seem rather *de trop*.

'What do you want to know?' I ask, more than a little perturbed as he searches for my icy feet under the duvet with his own warm ones. This is way too intimate for my liking. Couldn't we have just left it at the bunk up? Or the Croissants, even. But footsie? Forget it.

'Whatever you feel like telling me.' He grins again. I reluctantly tell him about the least interesting bits of my life in the hope that I'll actually bore him to death. Either that, or he'll feel claustrophobic and leave. Anything just to get the bed back to myself. All this attention is just plain freaky. I tell him about how I've been sacked, due to self-motivation issues. Which, I may add, I blame entirely on the exceptionally high standard of daytime TV these days.

Unfortunately, Max seems to find all this more amusing than offputting. And in the end, I'm actually quite flattered by him laughing at my jokes. So much so, in fact, that I even manage to find the energy for another quick shag. It's against my better judgement under the circumstances but what the hell?

I'm just stuffing the used condom into an empty black cherry yoghurt pot when I feel an odd, prickling sensation on the back of my neck. I turn round to find Max looking at me really intensely. I check myself. Do I have crusts of food round my mouth? Bits of orange kebab sauce under my nails?

Shit. Do I have a great big booga hanging out of my nose?

Whatever it is, I don't like him staring at me like this. The skin on the back of my neck feels as though I have a clutch of spider's eggs hatching underneath it. It's nothing short of disgusting.

'Aren't you supposed to roll over now and start snoring your head off?' I joke.

I'm only half-joking, actually. Surely any self-respecting bastard would have done just that? Shouldn't Max be waiting for me to fall asleep now so he can vanish, evaporating like a puff of amyl nitrate into the dusk? He should have started feeling trapped the second he heard the squelch of the condom coming off.

Shouldn't he?

Buggery bollocks.

He'll be getting so intimate he'll be going to the loo in front of me next.

'Not me.' He shakes his head and smiles at me. 'I'm not like that.'

Just my blimming luck then.

'I want to get to know you properly.' He beams. 'Spend time with you. Stuff like that.'

'What for?'

Flipping wonderful. I'm such a loser I can't even have a simple one-night stand without it all going tits up.

God, why is he gazing at me like that? There's obviously something very wrong with him.

'What?' I panic.

'Nothing, it's just...'

'What?' I ask a second time, a weird, uneasy feeling bubbling away like hot porridge in the pit of my stomach.

'You're just so...'

'Go on.'

'I think you're fantastic,' he bursts out.

'Oh.'

'I mean it.' He nods. 'You're funny, you're gorgeous. You're just...I can't believe...'

'Can't believe what?' I demand. Good God. Surely he isn't about to declare undying love for me, is he? That's not the idea at all.

I knew I should never have gone for that second shag. I've led him on. Allowed him to form an attachment. He seems to be expecting me to say something lovey-dovey back to him.

And 'love' is something I'm afraid I'm just not willing to get into right now. As far as I'm concerned, the L word means only one thing.

And that's 'Lack Of Vaginal Exercise'.

'I just can't believe you changed your mind.'

'About what?'

'About me.'

'I don't follow.'

'Well, after everything you said at your party. When we first met. About not wanting a boyfriend. I mean, I'm really not a bastard and I'm definitely not gay. So why did you change your mind? I just can't believe I'm your type.'

'You're not,' I tell him. 'I'm desperate.'

Of course it doesn't even occur to Max that I might actually be serious. He assumes I'm joking. God. Men can be so damn arrogant at times.

He stares at me adoringly for another ten minutes, gazing at me in bewildered awe and shaking his head in wonderment, as though I'm the star of ruddy Bethlehem, instead of plain old Katie Simpson, ginger spinster of Balham parish. And by the time I'm drifting in and out of uneasy slumber, I've decided that he's not even that good-looking. If he likes me that much, he clearly has big problems. Nope, I decide, staring at the silver mirrorball hanging by my window as I listen to the steady rhythm of his breathing. He's definitely not my type. The colour of his eyes is more mud than Mars bar. And, unless I'm very much mistaken, his head would probably look an awful lot better on the end of a stick.

Typical, isn't it? The minute I decide to live a single, blameless life, I've got blokes following me around like sick puppy dogs. I lie in the Sunday evening gloom feeling cheated. The only reason I was attracted to him in the first place was that I felt sure he had to be a complete and utter bastard. That cheeky grin. Those twinkly eyes. He had it written all over him. But I obviously misread the signs completely. Max has been masquerading as a bastard when he's really Mr Mills & Boon. He's the flipping Milk Tray Man in disguise. And I blooming well fell for it. Oh, he's pulled the wool over my eyes all right. Hoodwinked me good and proper. Now if I lived in America, I could sue him for reeling me in under false pretences.

He isn't what I ordered and I want my money back.

Finding out what Max is really like feels a lot like going into a restaurant and ordering what I believe to be lobster thermidor, only to discover when it arrives on my plate that I've actually asked for a grey lump of boil-in-the-bag cod and parsley sauce.

Bugger it.

I have to pretend I'm going to visit my granny in order to get rid of him. And when he's finally gone, grinning and loping off down the street like a loon, I flop onto the sofa to think and plan. And then I see it...

A spider the size of a saucer is making its way spikily across the sitting-room rug.

Flipping wonderful.

I haven't a hope in hell of getting a wink of sleep now. And I can't even escape round the corner to Janice's, because I know full well she's staying at Jasper's this evening. She told me so this morning. She might even have to bonk him, she said. She's been telling porkies for weeks now. According to her, the reds have been playing at home for a month and a half and Jasper's starting to think she's on an everlasting period.

In desperation, I call Sam.

'What are you doing?'

'Watching TV.'

'In bed?'

'Yep.'

'Oh.'

'Why?'

'Feel like coming over?' I try to keep the edge of panic from creeping into my voice. I can still see the spider. It's crouching disgustingly in the middle of the carpet. Sodding thing has the gall to enter my flat and plonk itself in front of Channel 5. I have to keep it in sight, no matter how traumatic, because if it hides before I can get rid of it, I'll never be able to set foot in the flat again.

'Now?' He sounds surprised. 'At half past eleven?'

'Uh huh.' I inch back as the revolting creature flexes a spindly leg.

'Any particular reason?'

'Oh,' I try to sound as flippant as possible, 'thought you might want to hang out for a bit. Share a bottle of wine. I've got some Pinot Grigio chilling nicely in the fridge.'

'But it's a school night. And I'm knackered after all that splendid maître d' stuff I did last night.'

'God,' I scoff. 'You're so square.'

'I am not.'

He is, actually. He never goes out in the middle of the week any more. He's so busy with Freeman PR he doesn't have time for hangovers.

'We could watch *Donnie Brasco*.'

'But I've got a really important meeting in the morning.'

'How important?'

'Very. I'm pitching. It's a really big client.'

'Are you going to have to be all bumlicky and everything?'

'And everything,' he says firmly. 'So I'll have to give Al Pacino a miss this time, I'm afraid.'

'Spoilsport.'

'You OK, Simpson?'

'Yes.'

'No you're not. You sound all shaky.'

'I'm fine,' I say firmly.

'You don't sound fine. This isn't about us watching a video at all, is it?'

'No.'

'So you've finally decided you want my body.' He laughs. 'Is that it?'

'In yer dreams, Sam Freeman.'

'Then I guess there's only one thing it can be,' he says.

'Guess so.'

'OK.' He sighs, and I hear crinkly, crunkly sounds as he pulls back the duvet and hauls himself out of bed. I imagine him reaching for his jeans, which will probably be strewn across the back of the sofa in his bedroom. Pulling a white T-shirt from the pile by the door over his tanned chest.

'How big is it this time?' he asks.

'What?' I snap my head up. God, what am I doing, thinking about Sam's chest like that? Haven't I learnt anything from Max? Christ, Simpson, have some sense. Back away.

'The spider.' I can tell he's trying to keep from laughing. 'I assume that's what all this is about.'

'Massive,' I whimper. 'Can you hurry up?'

'How massive?' he asks, a chuckle bouncing about somewhere in the back of his throat.

'The size of a dinner plate.'

'Not a tractor wheel this time then.' He laughs. 'Don't worry. Chuck a yoghurt pot over it or something and I'll see you in ten.'

I do as he says, grabbing the yoghurt pot from beside my bed, dashing downstairs with it before the spider scuttles away and gingerly placing it over the top of the hunched form. Then I curl up on my squishy sofa awaiting rescue. By the time Sam actually lets himself in, I've fallen fast asleep.

'Great.' He pokes me in the ribs. 'You're asleep after all. I needn't have bothered.'

'Yes you had.'

'So where's the culprit?'

'There,' I quake, pointing a finger in the direction of the yoghurt pot. 'And if you say it's more scared of me than I am of it, I'll punch your lights out. Check me out. I'm shaking like a jelly. My legs have turned to sponge fingers.'

Sam shakes his head, pretending to be serious. 'And I thought this was no trifling matter.'

'Oh God. Spare me your Dad jokes,' I grumble. And I'm not being funny but I do feel all wobbly. It's a relief when Sam, casual as you like in jogging bottoms and a faded red T-shirt, saunters back in through the kitchen door, shaking his head at me and grinning.

'All gone,' he says. 'Condom and all.'

'Oh God...'

'So who was he?' he teases. 'One of those hundreds of one-night stands you've been planning, I suppose.'

'None of your business,' I snap.

'Well, at least you're having safe sex,' he says.

'You're not my dad,' I tell him. 'It's nothing to do with you.'

'OK, OK.' Sam holds up his hands in defeat. 'I won't ask. Now are you making me a cup of tea or not?'

'Not,' I say. But I make it anyway and bring it over to the sofa where he's crashed out upside down, head on my best chocolate-coloured cushion and bare feet slung over the back.

'So d'you think I did OK yesterday then?' I ask. Now that revolting Max and the horrible spider have both gone, I can think about yesterday's achievements. The food was pretty damn good. Everyone said so. I'm actually feeling quite proud. Perhaps I'm not such a non-achiever after all.

'You know you did.' He rumples my hair affectionately. 'You did brilliant.'

'I've got another two lined up, you know,' I say proudly. 'Just from last night.'

'That's excellent.'

'Thing is,' I say, 'that wedding cost me a fortune. When can I send them the bill?'

A chuckle starts rollicking around in Sam's chest and bubbles quickly to the surface.

'God, you really are crap at the real world, aren't you?' He guffaws. 'Do you know how businesses work or not?'

'Not,' I say decidedly. 'I really haven't a clue. You'll have to help me with all that book balancing and stuff.'

'Send the bill now,' Sam says. 'Then you'll at least get paid in sixty days.'

'What?' I shriek. 'But I need the money now. Otherwise I can't even buy a loaf, let alone all the stuff I need for this christening I've got to do. It's in three weeks. Shit, Sam. How can I make some money quickly?'

He looks me up and down. 'Topless model?'

'Have to get implants first.'

'True. Lottery?'

'Too touch and go.'

'*Millionaire* then.' He smiles, pulling me towards him and giving me a sympathetic hug. 'Charm the pants off Chris Tarrant and win yourself a cool million. The questions are easy.'

'No they're not,' I say gloomily. 'Not for someone like me they aren't.'

'You're bright.'

'But I don't have any general knowledge,' I mooch. 'I only know the answers to questions like "What's the price of Rimmel nail varnish in Superdrug?" and "How many colourways do Nike Air Max trainers come in?" That's not going to be much help, is it?'

'Possibly not,' he says. 'What about a loan? A small business loan. All you need is a clear business and marketing plan and you're home and dry. That's how I've managed to start up Freeman PR.'

'God,' I groan. 'You sad bastard. Why do you have to be so bloody sensible?'

'One of us has to be. And it's never going to be you, is it?'

'Guess not. Anyway, I haven't got a clue how to go about doing one of those plan things. The only thing I ever plan is what I'm having for dinner. Can't *you* do it while *I'm* watching *Coronation Street*?'

'No.'

'Thanks,' I grump. 'Fat lot of use you are. This whole catering thing was your idea, you know.'

'Calm down.' Sam pats my shoulder and takes a noisy gulp of tea. 'I didn't say I wouldn't help you. I just said I wouldn't do it for you. You have to learn, otherwise you'll have no idea how it's all supposed to work.'

'You'll help then?' I brighten.

'Course.' He hugs me quickly before standing up and draining his tea in one last gulp. 'You might be sodding useless but you're practically my sister. Look, give me a ring in the week and we'll sort it out.'

'Thanks,' I say, seeing him to the door. 'Oh, and Sam?'

'Yes?' He spins round, an odd look on his face. It's the same look I saw through the darkness when we shared a bed at Poppy's mum and dad's and for a second I feel distinctly funny inside. I'm not sure I like it.

'Thanks for getting rid of that spider.'

'Any time, Simpson.' He shrugs, rummaging for his car keys.

Chapter 12

I bet Max is a complete Mummy's boy. Over the next few weeks, as I try to plan menus for my next two bookings, he calls me no less than fourteen times. Honestly! It's enough to make you spit. Still, I call-dodge quite successfully, until one Thursday when I completely forget myself and snatch up the phone. Sam lent me enough money to tide me over, so I could provide the food for the christening of Baby Ellis of Lewishan and I expect this is Mrs Ellis calling to confirm her views on the cake.

'Katie?'

It's him.

'No,' I almost shout, slamming down the phone. Then I ring Janice at her office. If the line's busy he'll have no chance of getting through again. I'm going to have to be more careful in future.

'I saw Max today,' she announces, when she hears it's me. 'In a planning meeting.'

'That's nice for you.'

'Why are you screening his calls?'

'He said that?'

'Yes. So why? And don't lie.'

'Dunno. Because I can?'

'You're mad.'

'I suppose he told you I bonked him?'

'No, actually. But he does seem pretty keen. Shit. Everyone at work's going to be so jealous when I tell them.'

'They can have him if they like. I'm done.'

'But he's gorgeous.'

'You have him then.'

'I wish.' She laughs. 'I'm afraid I'm spoken for, rather.'

'You shagged him then? Jasper, I mean. No more treating yourself to nice bits of rough?'

'Had to,' she announces. 'Honestly, Katie, you should have seen him. He was so grateful it was pathetic.'

'Leave him then.'

'Can't,' she says firmly. 'I nicked a bank statement from the hall as I left this morning.'

'You did what?'

'A girl needs to know,' she defends herself.

'Did you open it?'

'Oh yes. And it's all fine. He's wadded.'

'God. Wish I was. My Switch was refused in Safeway last night when I was trying to buy a tin of macaroni cheese. I don't even have sixty-eight pence. God only knows how I'm going to be able to afford to smoke fags and buy expensive toiletry items. Sam's loan has pretty much run out.'

'You think that's bad,' she says unsympathetically. 'I've got another pitch coming up and I'm here till ten o'clock every night as it is. I'll never get a wedding sorted out at this rate.'

'You're getting married?' I gasp. Christ Almighty. She's kept that quiet.

'Of course. Why else do you think I'm boffing the silly old sod.'

'Well, when's the wedding?'

'Oh, he doesn't actually know about it yet,' Janice says. 'But he will. He has to. Check me out. I'm a catch.'

I'm impressed at her optimism. 'And when he does ask, will you have the full works? The big meringue and the marquee and stuff?'

'Will I fuck,' she booms, almost perforating my eardrum. 'God, if I start inviting loads of people along I'm going to have to ask my mother too, aren't I?'

'Oh Janice,' I say. 'She is your mother.'

'Katie, she'd turn up in head-to-foot floral crimplene and smoke Raffles all night. She'd make a holy show of me. I can't take the risk.'

'But—'

'But nothing. Sorry, Katie, but I can't afford to have her showing me up, complaining that the gazpacho is cold and asking where the "toilet" is in a loud voice. Anyway. Face it. The poor cow just hasn't got the wardrobe so she'll have to stay at home. Nope. When we get married it'll be on some beach somewhere hot. Bastard hot. And I'll be wearing a white bikini and pink flowers in my hair. No guests.'

'Oh.'

'Well, you can come, I suppose,' she adds generously. 'Seeing as you're my best mate.'

'Thanks.' I feel better.

'As long as you can afford it, of course. Flights to Hawaii don't come cheap.'

'Oh.'

'At least I won't have to worry about you showing me up.'

'That's good.'

'I mean, I won't have to worry about you having better hair than me or anything, for a start.'

Good old Janice. She always knows how to make me feel better.

'And you don't have a hope in hell of getting a better tan than me, either.'

'Mmm.'

'Your legs will still be like two milk bottles when we get back.'

'Thanks,' I say miserably.

'Oh, cheer up, Katie,' she says irritably. 'Whatever's the matter? You should be happy for me. I think you're being a bit selfish.'

'I told you. I'm skint. And that's not a "can't afford to buy that Jigsaw white dress" kind of skint. It's the "can I afford that Tesco's white sliced?" sort.' Suddenly, the fizz has gone out of my great success at Poppy's wedding and reality has started to kick in. What if I can't afford to start up a business at all? What if this christening I'm catering for all goes to the wall and I've wasted a fortune on enough sugar to ice the Millennium Dome?

'Well,' she says importantly, 'I just might have something that'll cheer you up.'

'What?' Frankly I doubt that anything she can say is going to make me feel any better. Janice's efforts at cheering me up usually involve spending lots of time in hideously expensive shops, followed by a long sesh in a bar where the drinks are six quid a throw. And the chances of the bank seeing its way clear to financing that one are slimmer than Ally McBeal, so it looks as though I'll have to wallow in poverty for a bit longer yet.

'Well,' she begins. 'You know I told you Jasper had that flat in Paris?'

'Mmmm?' I pick at my big toenail and inspect it carefully. Perhaps I might manage to cheer up after all. A long weekend away before I have to knuckle down and sort out my finances and really get to work on my new business is just what I need. I haven't been on holiday for ages. It'd be great just to kick back for a couple of weeks. After all, I won't be able to go for years once I'm running my own catering conglomerate, will I?

For a second, I allow myself to get excited. Gay Paree with Janice, eh? We'll have a great laugh. And how lovely of her to think of me like that. She's been spending so much time with Jasper over the past few weeks that I can't help feeling a bit bereft. Especially as George and David are so cheesily in love as well. Honestly, it's enough to make you boke.

And if I'm honest, I have been a bit worried that now she's in pursuit of a signed and sealed marriage certificate, we'll drift apart and end up not even knowing where the other lives. But I needn't have been concerned. Janice is my absolute best mate. I might have known she wouldn't forget about me.

God. Paris. It'll be just like the old times. Girlie shopping trips in Galeries Lafayette. Lazy, gossipy afternoons drinking big creamy coffees in pavement cafés. Gorging ourselves silly on huge pains au chocolat and generous slabs of tarte au citron. Glimpsing the view from the top of the Eiffel Tower. Bohemian Montmartre. Les Tuileries. The Sacré Coeur...

'And guess what?'

'What?' I ask, getting so carried away with my imaginings that I'm hardly bothering to listen to what she's saying. We might even take a boat trip down the Seine. Have a game of boules. And we'll get slowly plastered on pastis before noshing on snails and steak frites in a lovely, garlicky little restaurant somewhere.

'He's taking me there for a romantic weekend. Isn't it fantastic?'

I come crashing down to earth with a bump. How stupid. Of course she didn't mean for me to go with her. And I should know by now that Janice's mind works in mysterious ways. Quite how the prospect of the weekend of biddy sex she's letting herself in for is supposed to cheer me up, I'll never know, but that's Janice for you.

Self-centred to the core.

'Of course I'm going to have to shag him again, I expect,' she bubbles. 'But he's bound to propose. Isn't he? I mean this is Paris we're talking about, mate. Who wouldn't want to get engaged in Paris. Sooooo romantic.'

God, she's cracked.

'Janice, you practically have to prop up his willy with a lolly stick.'

'But he's rich.'

'And Jake took me to Paris,' I remind her. 'He didn't propose.'

'He didn't take you,' she points out. 'He made you pay for yourself.'

That's true. He did. The disappointment was piercing. I was going through a prolonged period of yearning pathetically after mini breaks at the time. I thought sex would be more exciting somewhere new. And I'd imagined us jetting off from Heathrow to Charles de Gaulle, where we'd jump into a limo and head for the Georges V. We'd have an opulent four-poster, where Jake would do unspeakably erotic things to me with chilled champagne bottles. And it'd be the best holiday I'd ever had. Ever.

In reality, of course, we headed for the Eurostar terminal, where he bought his own ticket then waved me forward to pay for my own. He took me to a Travelodge equivalent near the Bois de Boulogne. Full of prozzies and miles from anywhere. Anywhere nice, anyway. I kept expecting Alan Partridge to leap out of the chipboard closet, brandishing his big plate. We got drunk on halves of lager because the hotel bar didn't serve pints and the sex that followed was so pathetically mediocre that I actually fell asleep, mid thrust. I only know this because, being somewhat pissed, I cannoned off a couple of huge snores that actually woke me up, only to find that my being deep in slumber hadn't deterred Jake from his single-minded pursuit of orgasm in the least. I left him to it, drifting off into gentle dreams of rushing waterfalls, flowing rivers and tempestous oceans before coming to in the small hours to the realisation that water was actually dripping on to me.

And, calm as you like, Jake was standing over me treating me to a quality golden shower.

Quite frankly, if I'd wanted watersports, I'd have gone to the Algarve.

'Jake,' I yelled, scrabbling around to escape.

'On the toilet,' he yelled back, clearly fast asleep. 'Out in a minute.'

Even though I know that Janice's Paris weekend probably won't be much more romantic than my own, I can't help feeling a bit cheesed off at my own state of affairs in comparison to hers. I can't even afford a day trip to Bognor. And I don't have a clue what the hell I'm going to do about it. So when I've put the phone down, I fashion myself a rough cheese, chilli and peanut butter sandwich and tune into *Trisha* to watch women in polyester leggings discuss wayward teenage daughters and dysfunctional acne-riddled sons.

Sam is as good as his word though. On Saturday morning, he calls me to make sure I get up, then he loafs round in his new Levi's Twisted jeans, a grey V-neck T-shirt and a New York Yankees baseball cap to explain how grown-ups apply for loans.

'Looking good.' I tweak the hat. 'Like the weekend outfit. Very Father of Two.'

'Not looking so bad yourself.' He gives me a hug and laughs at the fact that I'm still in my pink and white stripy pyjamas, all muzzy with sleep. 'Come on, bed breath. Let's sort out this mess.'

And bless him. He spends the whole of the morning and most of the afternoon helping me define my objectives. Actually, he practically has to tell me what my objectives are, but he's a great help. By four o'clock, I have what he tells me is a sound business plan. And I'm feeling so optimistic that I offer to cook him dinner tonight as a sort of thank you.

'It'll have to be beans on toast, mind,' I tell him. 'Unless you want to pay for it.'

'Oh, I'm sorry.' He looks kind of embarrassed.

'Why?' I can't help asking him, even though it's none of my business really.

'Well, I've got a date.'

'I see.' For some reason I'm completely pissed off. It's not often Sam turns down my dinner invitations. He'd rather bite off his foot at the ankle and throw it to the dogs than miss one of my slap-up feasts.

'With Pussy. The girl from the wedding. She phoned me a while ago. We're going to some trendy new club in the West End.'

'Oh,' I say dismissively. 'Sniffing after Slinky Malinky No Boobs, eh? But you hate clubbing.'

'I don't.'

'With me you do. You always refuse to come.'

'Because you and George always make me go to gay clubs. And I always get hit on.'

'Don't be such a homophobe.'

'I'm not. I just—'

'Anyway.' I shrug. 'Thanks for your help.'

'But I don't have to go now.'

'You might as well,' I say, finding it necessary to add, 'I'm probably busy anyway. Very busy actually. Many thanks, though, for all your help.'

'But—'

'Bye.'

When he's gone I flop onto my bed, looking up at my big silver glitterball and wondering what the hell made me behave like that. I'm just a bit pissed off that he must have known about this date for a whole week. And he hasn't bothered to tell me. I tell him everything. Well, almost everything, And I'm feeling protective, I suppose. I don't like Pussy. I suspect she's really not a very nice person. And Sam's like a big brother. I don't want him to get dumped on.

Even though he's usually the one who does the dumping.

The bank schedules my appointment for next Wednesday. And when the day comes, I pull on my smartest trouser suit. There's a small chicken madras stain on the left thigh, but if I keep the jacket on it won't show.

After all, this loan is really my last chance. A chance to make Mum proud of me. It's the least she deserves, after all. God knows, since Dad left, she's made enough sacrifices for me. The least she can hope for is a daughter who doesn't lounge around the house watching hospital soaps all day.

Mind you, life would have been a hell of a lot easier for me if she had just bloody well given up on me. I could have been a complete failure in peace then. Damn her. Why couldn't she have rejected me at birth? Held up her hand and announced to the midwife, 'I'm sorry, I just can't bond. Put it up for adoption.' Or left me in a bin bag in a phone box outside St Pancras. Why does she have to be so bloody, irritatingly supportive all the time? She's no idea of the pressure it puts on me.

At the bank I have to wait for a good hour outside the Loans Adviser's office. I'm just thinking about sodding right off out of there and lying to Sam about it when the door opens and a man pokes his head out.

'Ms Faulkner will see you now.'

Bugger.

'Sorry.' He rubs his forehead. 'It's not Faulkner any more. It's back to Brisco now. Keep forgetting, you know?'

'Right.' I shrug, picking up my rucksack, not feeling businesslike in the slightest. I have absolutely no idea what he's talking about. But Faulkner. The name rings a bell. Why? I wonder.

Shit. It's not some friend of my mother's, is it?

'Sit down.' The manager indicates an orange plastic chair in front of her desk. Classy.

I look up expectantly. Who starts first? I have no idea what to expect. But buggery fuck. Where have I seen that face before? At least it's not one of my mother's friends. She's too young for that. She's tall, extremely smart and with hair drawn into a tidy French pleat. Perhaps she used to work in Safeway's. Or Victoria Wine. That'll be it.

'Hello, Ms…?'

'Simpson,' I remind her. God. She could have at least bothered to do her research. 'As in Edward and Mrs.'

'And you want a loan for?'

'I want to start up my own business.'

She looks at me derisively, as though I've just told her I want it for Bacardi and Cokes and stocking up on blue mascara.

'Well, yes.' She picks up a pencil. 'That is usually the idea.'

'And I really want to make it work,' I sputter.

'Don't they all?'

I ignore her. Because the moment I've said it, I realise that I really, really do. I want to make a go of this, come hell or high water.

She looks back at me and chews on the end of her pencil. Then she looks at me again, looks away and looks back, startled.

'I think we know each other, don't we?'

'I thought so, yes,' I gabble, pleased. Perhaps this will give me some sort of advantage over the other loan seekers. 'Were we at college—?'

'Oh no,' she interrupts. 'I think it's a little more recent than that.'

'I'm sorry, I don't...'

'Oh yes. I'd recognise your face anywhere,' she sneers.

'I'm sorry?'

'I only have to look through my wedding photos to see you and your friend flashing your pants at all and sundry.'

And then it clicks. Of course. I know exactly who this is.

Buggery fuck.

It's Basildon Bride.

'Nice souvenir of my wedding, that was,' she snarls. 'The only one, as it turns out.'

'Oh right,' I sputter. 'And how is your...er...husband?'

'Ex-husband,' she spits. 'We're getting divorced. I caught him humping one of the bridesmaids not three days after we got back from honeymoon. I'm going for half of everything, of course.'

'Of course.'

'So what was it like?' she asks me.

'Your honeymoon? How should I know?'

'Fucking my husband?'

How the fuck she expects me to know that, I don't know. I was rendered. Completely off my face. So I don't respond. Instead I stand up, pulling my jacket down to cover the curry stain and feeling my cheeks burn.

'I think I should go.'

'You got that right.'

As I get to the door, I decide it's worth one last-ditch attempt at least.

'I don't suppose there's any chance of a loan then?'

'You got that right too,' she says. 'Now fuck off.'

Chapter 13

When I tell Sam I didn't get the loan, he's sympathetic.

Ish.

'Come on, you.' He gives me a hug. He's just been playing football and he smells of outside.

'I'm a failure.'

'You're not.'

'I am. I didn't get the loan.'

'I'm sorry.' He looks worried. 'Was it...?'

'Don't worry,' I reassure him. 'It wasn't your business plan. Just my luck, I'm afraid, that the loans adviser was that woman from the wedding.'

'Poppy's wedding?'

'Nope. The woman whose wedding I gatecrashed. Whose husband I boffed.'

'Oh dear.'

'Don't look as though you're trying not to laugh.'

'Oh. OK.'

'You're still doing it.'

'I can't help it.' Sam's wide grin explodes onto his face once more. 'Only you could fuck up something like that so professionally, Simpson. And with such style.'

'Thanks.'

'Sorry.' He smirks. 'But it is funny. Would you like some tea?'

'I'd prefer a pizza,' I confess.

'Things must be bad.'

I pull a face. It's OK for him. He's good at anything he turns his hand to. People get sucked in by his enthusiasm for everything so they can't help making life easy for him. All I can muster enthusiasm for is cake. And curry. And crisps. Sam's natural aptitude for brown-nosing and agreeing with people—he sits there like a nodding dog even when he just wants to punch someone's lights out—stands him in good stead when it comes to his career. But then he could decide to go into catering tomorrow and he'd make a damn sight better job of it than I ever could. Even though I'm definitely the better cook.

Sam rifles through the pile of junk mail in the knife and fork drawer until he finds a Speedy Pizza menu. Switching the phone to speakerphone, he dials the number.

'Hello,' he says, 'I'd like to order a pizza, please.'

Despite my dark mood, I stifle a giggle. It's so funny the way people always say that. As though the guy in the pizza shop might be expecting you to tell him you've broken down on the M25 and require emergency assistance. Or that you need a taxi to the maternity ward of St George's Hospital within the next five minutes or else your wife is going to bugger up the soft furnishings good and proper.

'Oh, large, definitely,' Sam is saying to the man on the end of the phone. 'Absolutely whopping if you've got it. You have? Marvellous. Well, we'll have an extra large cheese and tomato then...'

'Thin crust,' I remind him.

'Thin crust, please. With...'

'Anchovies.'

'Did you get that?' he asks Mr Speedy Pizza. 'We'll have some of your finest anchovies for the lady and perhaps some pineapple chunks to go with them.'

We've played the pizza game since we were about twelve, each coming up with the most outlandish toppings we could think of and daring the other to order it. And because I'm miserable, I get to do all the choosing. Those are the rules.

'And chillies,' I demand, digging at a new ingrowing hair on my knee.

'Chilles as well, please,' Sam instructs. 'And perhaps you could lob on a couple of artichoke hearts for the sophisticated touch.'

'Parma ham.' I laugh, setting to work on my other leg. 'And peppersan'onionsan'extracheese. And capers.'

'Are you writing all this down?' Sam asks the pizza guy. 'No, no, it isn't a joke. I've just got one very hungry young lady here, that's all. A very hungry young lady indeed. She's been thinking about working for a living a lot this morning and she's absolutely worn out.'

'Fuck off.' I giggle, forgetting that the pizza guy can hear me.

'No, that's me she's telling to fuck off,' Sam says. 'Not you.'

'Peas,' I interrupt. 'I love peas on pizza. And in curry.'

'Curry? Oh, no, sorry, not curry on the pizza, but we will have some peas, please. And some tuna and some mushrooms.'

'And goat's cheese,' I say. 'Ask if they've got goat's cheese.'

'Goat's cheese then. And some fine tiger prawns sprinkled over the top?'

'I hate prawns,' I remind him. 'Nasty pink commas that taste of sewage.'

'Right, sorry, hold the prawns. No just rewind a bit and whack those prawns on half of it.'

And so on, until we've ordered about twenty different toppings each and the pizza guy is telling us firmly that yes, actually, they do draw the line at bananas and chocolate and that no, we can't have Smarties sprinkled all over the damn thing.

'How come I can never do this with any of my girlfriends?' Sam asks me later, as we munch and slurp our way through the pizza, which, when it finally arrives, is the size of a dustbin lid.

'Because you always plump—if you'll excuse the expression—for the anorexic ones,' I inform him coolly, taking a rogue prawn off my fourth slice of pizza and lobbing it back into the box. 'Like that Pussy creature. You can be so thick sometimes, you know. Did you think they all naturally had thighs the width of skipping ropes?'

'Well, you do.' Sam brushes his sandy mop into his baseball cap and looks at my legs. 'The amount you put away you ought to be the size of a tower block by now.'

'Well, now you come to mention it, I don't hear the talking scales at the supermarket yelling "No coach parties please", when I step on them, no.' I laugh, looking down at my thighs.

'Or "One at a time please" ' Sam joins in, laughing.

'But I'm not that skinny,' I say defensively. 'I mean I haven't got BHS.'

'Huh?'

'BHS. Big Head Syndrome. I mean, I don't look like a football perched on a javelin, do I?'

'No-o.'

'Well, there you are then,' I say. 'Dieting's boring, Sam. Counting fat units is even less exciting than watching Des O'Connor tonight. So I just don't bother with it. I do treacle roll and Kettle chips instead.'

'God.' Sam rolls over on the floor and grins at me. 'Why can't all girls be like you? The ones I take out to dinner gnaw on one tiny asparagus spear then say they're full. Costs me a fortune in wasted food.'

'And when you think of all those poor starving Africans,' I say, 'it's criminal. Well, I hate seeing things go to waste.'

'You do?'

'Absolutely.' I grin, feeling a lot better now. 'Which is why I'm having the last bit of pizza.'

'You think so, do you?' Sam's head snaps towards the box where the last slice is waiting temptingly, oozing with cheese and smelling of fried onions.

'Oh yes,' I tell him. 'That's mine. S'got my name on it.'

'You sure?'

'Absolutely,' I say. 'I'm having it.'

'Not if I get there first.'

We both jump to it and fight to snaffle the last slice until I slip on Sam's polished floor and flip, arse over tit, ending up on my back on top of the pizza box. On my way down, I grab the front of Sam's sweatshirt and end up taking him down with me. For a split second we find ourselves on top of each other in some kind of farcical clinch.

Quickly, I sit up, shoving him to the floor.

'Gerroff. Your hair's tickling my nose.'

He pulls away, laughing.

'Oh dear.'

'What?'

'I don't think either of us will be eating that pizza now. Most of it's stuck to the back of your head.'

'Yuck.'

As I pick the worst of it off, Sam looks really thoughtful, as though some amazing idea has suddenly occurred to him.

'What?' I ask him. 'Don't tell me you've found the answer to all my problems in the bottom of a pizza box.'

'No,' he says slowly. 'But I have got an idea.'

'What?'

'Why don't you move in here?'

'And why the buggery bollocks would I want to do that?'

'Not as in move in, move in,' he rushes to reassure me. 'Not unless you want to, of course.'

'You what?'

'I'm joking,' he says hurriedly. 'But you could have the spare room, couldn't you? It would save you paying rent on your flat while you get started. You could even use the study as an office.'

'I can do it myself, thank you.'

'Simpson, don't be so stubborn.' Sam starts to clear away hunks of mozzarella from the floor. 'You've just told me you have no money. And I can't lend you anymore 'cos it's all tied up in my house. And the business. But I can share my house with you so you don't have so many outgoings. Come on, Simpson. There's not much alternative. Not unless you want to go back to working for someone else. And you know you don't want to do that.'

'And who are you to say what I want, exactly?' I say through gritted teeth. This is typical of Sam, trying to control me like this. He's done it ever since my dad disappeared with that oriental temptress.

'Well, I...' He looks surprised at my tone of voice.

'Well what?'

'I just thought it was best.'

'There you go again,' I snap. 'Thinking you're my dad. Well, I'm several months older than you, Sam Freeman, and don't you forget it.'

'Don't be flippant.'

'Don't be a twat then.'

I know I sound ungrateful. But I don't want to give up my independence. I can't actually think of anything worse than living in someone else's flat, cooking my dinner in shifts, creeping around so as not to get in the way and having to miss *EastEnders* because his mates are playing Grand Theft Auto on the PlayStation 2. And the problem with Sam is that he just won't leave well alone. He'll take it upon himself to meddle in every aspect of my life, 'just making sure I'm OK'. And if I want to set up my own business, I need to feel that I can do things alone. Without some father figure always looking out for me.

And it's not just that, of course. There's the Pussy factor. If My Little Pony started spending any time here, I'd have to give up breathing or something.

'So you think I should give up my flat?' I ask him coldly.

'If you have to, yes.'

'Well, for your information, I don't "have" to do anything. I can do what I want. I'm thirty years of age.'

'Start acting it then.'

'Piss off,' I say. 'On second thoughts, I'll piss off. It is your house, after all.'

'Stay.'

I calm down a bit after Sam gives me a fag. I can't really afford to buy my own these days. And I suppose it was nice of him to offer. He was only trying to help, after all. It's just that I can't bear to acknowledge that I need help. After all I went through with Jake bloody Carpenter, I need to believe I can do all this on my own.

'That better?' he asks, as I take a deep drag.

'Yep.'

'Good.' He grins, obviously relieved to see I'm calmer. 'Shall I give you some to take home with you? I don't suppose you can afford such luxuries these days.'

Suddenly, a white flash of fury erupts in my chest, surprising even me.

'I've had enough of this.' I jump up, throwing my lit cigarette onto the floor and pulling on my jacket.

'Don't do that.'

'Why not?' I nod towards the cigarette end. 'I have no further use for it.'

'I mean,' Sam picks up the burning end and throws it into the ashtray, 'don't go home. Let's sort things out properly.'

'I don't need to sort things out, thank you,' I say. 'Especially not with you. I'm not staying round here to be treated like some sort of bloody charity case. Do you see me wandering around outside Woollies, shaking a little tin and giving out stickers?'

'No, but...I just thought...'

'Trouble is,' I stab a finger at his chest, 'you didn't just think, did you? Otherwise you'd realise you've just made me feel about this big.' I hold my forefinger and thumb about half an inch apart.

'I was trying to help,' he protests as I open the front door and step outside into the early summer sunshine.

'I don't need your help.'

'Then what, exactly, do you intend to do? Go home to your mother? You can't afford to live in that flat without a job. You know that. The rent's extortionate for one person as it is.'

'Well, I didn't exactly force Janice to move out, now did I?'

'You didn't exactly try very hard to find someone else to replace her, did you?'

'Fuck off, Sam.' I'm shouting now. 'I don't have to replace her if I don't want to. I can do what I want.'

'Oh, grow up,' I hear him say just before I slam the door in his face. I open up the letterbox.

'Grow up yourself,' I shriek through it, then stomp off down the path, almost ending up in the privet hedge. When I get to the street I turn round. He's standing at the window, an odd look—contempt, perhaps—on his face. 'And don't call me Simpson,' I bellow at the top of my voice.

I steam down Hearnville Road in a foul temper. Me, grow up? Who the hell does he think he is? Just because he bestows that horrible game show host's smile on every female who has the misfortune to cross his path, and gets away with murder. Well, it isn't going to work on me. It just annoys me. And another thing that really blimming well bugs me, I tell myself, passing a couple of middle-aged men enjoying the sunshine on the Common, is that the minute the sun comes out, people all over the capital decide it's OK to behave as though they've undergone some sort of dreadful taste lobotomy. Why do blokes who have short, hairy, sausagey legs think it's perfectly OK to wear shorts at all hours of the day just because it's gone above seventy?

I unlock my front door, still fuming. Who cares if I haven't got a job? It just means I can spend the rest of the afternoon jamming down oversalted instant noodles and watching shit telly. And that's exactly what I do.

A couple of hours later, I'm engrossed in some shallow fly-on-the-wall documentary when the phone shrills and, probably because I'm sick to the molars of my own company and am feeling restless and sort of squinchly after my row with Sam, I decide to answer the damn thing for a change, even though common sense tells me I should be avoiding all calls for the immediate future until Max gets it into his thick head that I don't want anything more to do with him.

It isn't Max. It's George, calling to demand my immediate presence in the posh end of Islington.

'Can't,' I mutter, glancing down at the grey jogging bottoms and ancient Wham! 'Choose Life' T-shirt I'm unashamedly slobbing about in. 'Can't leave the house until I find out whether the Harris family from Weston Super-Mare are going to miss their flight or not, I'm afraid. Mr Harris has got half an hour to get back to the airport with little Callum's passport and if he doesn't make it they'll lose their holiday to Magaluf. A whole year's savings down the drain. I'm on the edge of my seat here.'

'Please?' George sounds anxious. 'It's important.'

'So's the Harrises' holiday to Majorca,' I joke. 'For them, anyway. They've never been able to afford to go abroad before.'

'Pretty please?' he wheedles. 'With hundreds and thousands on top?'

Bloody hell. It isn't normally like George to say please once during a conversation. Twice is unthinkable. Something dreadful must have happened. 'OK. Keep your designer stubble on. Oh, look at that. He's back.'

'Who?'

'Mr Harris. Made it by the seat of his shell suit. Thank goodness for that. Now all I have to do is wait and see if bubbly Denise Mason, nineteen, from Hertford gets her standby flight and we're home and dry.'

'Katie...'

'Sorry. Are you going to tell me what's happened?'

'I can't say over the phone.' George goes all mysterious. 'Just say you'll come, darling. I need your help.'

Well, that's a different matter. No one has needed my help for ages. Not even Mum. For some reason even she hasn't bothered to call for almost a fortnight. And I have to admit to being a teensy bit curious. George can't usually keep his mouth shut for one second. So the fact that he's refused to tell me over the phone about whatever it is that's bothering him holds my interest for longer than your average episode of *Dawson's Creek*. Perhaps it's something exciting and illegal.

God, I hope so. Anything to brighten things up a bit.

'Where shall I meet you?'

'The Italian café in Upper Street. That's the one we do like, with the expensive menu and the swarthy waiters, as opposed to the one we don't like, with the nasty red checked tablecloths and the candles in bottles.'

'And is that the royal we?'

'Certainly,' he says cockily. 'Well, it's me and David at any rate. See you there, darling. And look glam. I don't want you turning up looking like a bloody woolly mammoth on acid again. This is important.'

After he's gone I look down at my worn-in comfies. So I can't really go out looking like a rag 'n' bone man then. And, more importantly, do I actually have the raw materials to do anything about it? Knickers are scarce. Clean knickers are out of the ruddy question. I think I used the last nice pair up on Max. It really is time I did some laundry but there's so much else to think about at the moment. Dislodging Shish Kebab from where he's soaking in blissful slumber in my knicker drawer, I rummage through a dismal pile of grizzly grey buckets and a selection of dingy bras. In the end, I decide that an ancient, slightly see-through pink and white striped swimsuit is probably a damn sight more respectable than my grungiest period pants. I cover it with a stinging-pink linen shirt I find scrumpled up at the foot of the bed. I sniff it gingerly for the scent of takeaway biryani or worse, but instead get a whiff of Comfort, which means it's only creased because I haven't bothered to hang it up after wash day. I add a pair of black moleskin combat pants from the floor, sponging off a teeny spattering of ketchup and checking to see that there are no socks or knicks tucked inside, waiting to creep like slugs from the ankle holes the moment I hit the crowded tube. Shuffling to the mirror, I untangle a worm of supernoodle out of my hair and twist my curls into a topknot with a bright green scrunchie, leaving just a couple of coppery tendrils loose. My skin is clammy and grey, so I dust pinky gold blusher over my cheekbones, slick on a bit of neutral lippie and, before I know it, I'm on autopilot.

Eventually, I emerge from Angel station, turn right onto Islington High Street and make for George's favourite Italian on Upper Street.

'I came as quickly as I could.' I scuttle over to the corner of the sunny courtyard where George and David are sitting gossiping, a half-drunk bottle of Pinot Grigio and a dishful of glossy Queen olives between them.

'Story of my life, darling,' George giggles. 'Oooh, God.' He looks me up and down with the derision only a professional snob can summon. 'Christ, you look as rough as a dog's tits, sweetie. Doesn't she, David? What happened?'

'Hectic weekend,' I lie, taking the extra glass they've laid out for me and glugging copious quantities of wine into it.

'Yeah, right.' George looks sceptical.

'Well,' I admit, 'I just haven't been used to getting out much, that's all. No dosh, you see. And I'm feeling a bit pissy today.'

'Figures,' George says. 'You've got a face like a bloody slapped bum again. What's up?'

'I've argued with Sam.'

'When are you just going to admit you fancy each other and shag each other stupid?' George asks. 'Get the whole damn thing out of your system?'

'But I don't fancy him,' I say. 'He thinks he's my bloody father, for one thing. And now he's really pissed me off. He's only gone and asked me to move in with him.'

'Told you,' George hisses. 'He lurves you.'

'Not like that, you dope.' I shrug. 'He just wants to keep an eye on me because he thinks I'm poor.'

'Have some more wine,' David offers kindly, picking up the bottle and sloshing more into my glass 'And some nibbly bits. Are you an olivey person? I don't remember? There's a marinated anchovy if you prefer.'

I relax, tipping my head back to enjoy the sunshine warming my face.

'Don't overdo it,' George warns. 'The boiled lobster look is so unattractive.'

In the opposite corner of the courtyard, a delicious waiter is seating a tall, slim girl in a raspberry linen shift dress next to the honeysuckle-covered wall. Her hair, hanging in a glossy sheet down her back, is the colour of golden treacle and she's groomed to perfection. Something about her makes me watch her, and I can't help playing a game with myself, imagining who it is she's waiting for. Someone special, from the way she keeps checking her lipgloss and looking at her watch.

That's absolutely the best thing about having no boyfriend. At least I don't have to torture myself with the hidden fear that it's him she's re-applying her make-up for.

George refills my wine glass for the second time, and in the split second it takes me to look down at it and take a sip, Raspberry Dress's suitor has arrived and is bending to kiss her cheek.

He looks very familiar somehow.

Startlingly familiar, in fact.

As he turns to wave the waiter over, I catch a glimpse of his face in profile.

And with a jolt of recognition, I almost call out.

It's Jasper.

Buggerfuck!

'Right, come on, ladies, tell all,' I urge, before the boys notice him. I can't risk them clocking him. If anyone's going to inform Janice of this little rendezvous, it should surely be me.

And of course it might not even be him. After all, I've only seen him in profile. And even if it is him, Raspberry Dress isn't necessarily his bit on the side. She could be his daughter, for all I know. So it wouldn't do to go jumping to conclusions. I mean, so far I've spotted them kissing but there definitely weren't any tongues. So it could all be perfectly innocent.

Or not.

Still, I definitely don't want him to see me, so I studiously avoid looking directly at him, inching myself down in my seat so I get backache and asking the boys why they've dragged me halfway across London on a lazy Sunday afternoon, when I could have been doing something far more productive like waxing my minky.

'Well, go on then,' George urges. David quickly stuffs an anchovy in his mouth so he doesn't have to do the talking.

'Oh bloody buggery hell.' George runs his hands over his velvety black crop and tries to look serious. It doesn't suit him. 'We've got a proposition for you.'

'I'm not doing a threesome,' I say quickly.

At least I don't think I am. Even though it could reasonably be said that I do quite fancy them both, it does seem a tiny bit sordid.

On the other hand, it would add considerably to this year's measly score. But I'm not really that kind of girl.

'God, no.' George looks shocked.

Well, that's that then.

'Do we look remotely as though we might want to involve ourselves in all that?' he asks. 'No. Sorry, lovey, but I don't think we're ready for rug munching just yet. No, what we wanted to say was...'

'Yes?' I encourage. 'It's not that Rent My Womb thing again, is it? Because I've given you my opinion on that score.' George takes a deep breath.

'Katie,' he says, and it takes a gargantuan effort for me not to wee myself with laughter at the expression on his face. 'Will you marry us?'

I laugh. 'Oh George. That's the most romantic thing anyone's ever said to me in my life.'

And it is. You see, I'm naive enough to think he means it metaphorically. The idea of the three of us being friends. Together all the time. Being there for each other. Exactly how a marriage should be, but rarely ever is in this day and age.

Which, of course, is precisely why I'm not bothering. So the prospect of having a friendship pact with David and George is the most attractive I've been offered in a long time. It cheers me up immensely. I don't even mind if I'm not included in the actual sex part. After all, plenty of people are married in the true, forsaking all others sense of the word. And they never have sex.

Well, not with each other, anyway.

It certainly doesn't cross my mind for a minute that George means it literally. As in the full-on, slip into big frou-frou dress, stick ridiculous spangly crown on head and waltz up aisle feeling like complete twat to sign life away on dotted line type scenario.

Of course, he doesn't actually want me to marry both of them, he explains later after they've rammed a plate of angel hair squid-ink pasta, rocket and Parmesan salad, cappuccino and marscapone ice cream and a bottle of fizz laced with a generous dash of Smirnoff down me to butter me up. He did mean that bit metaphorically. Well, sort of. It's just that, despite the tonsil-tickling-in-vodka-bar incident, David doesn't actually feel he knows me well enough to ask me something so ginormously huge, and he's a teensy bit scared. So George said he'd do the actual asking part. After all, he knows me well enough to understand that it's completely necessary to soften the blow with alcohol and lard.

The crux of the matter is that David's visa runs out in a few weeks' time.

Which is where, normal circumstances prevailing, he buggers off back to the land of Kylie, koalas and kangaroos. But, of course, there's no way George is having that. Not with a regular bunk up on tap. So a secret marriage has been arranged. David is due to marry Jemima, George's cousin, an eminent Edinburgh doctor. But she's inconveniently found someone to fall in love with at the very last minute and, quite understandably, wants to marry him instead.

'Selfish bitch,' George mutters, glugging back more wine.

'It's not really her fault though, is it?' David says kindly. 'But you see, Katie, it does leave us up fanny alley rather.'

I can quite see that it does, but playing for time to cover my surprise, I suggest that we shouldn't do anything rash. Perhaps George could go back to Oz with David? After all, he hates English weather. He's Britain's number one sun worshipper. He'd love Australia, wouldn't he?

All that sea and sunshine. All those glorious beaches.

'All those queer-bashers?' he points out. 'All those open spaces? Miles and miles of nothing? Nowhere to shop, darling? And nowhere to get one's hair done to one's satisfaction?'

'He has a point.' David shrugs. 'It can all get rather heterosexual over there. All brawn and no brain, as it were. And we had rather planned to stay in London for now.'

'Yes, we sodding well had,' George says bitterly. 'We've just spent a fortune on a new love seat for the garden. It's symbloodybolic, darling. We can hardly cart that halfway across the world, now can we? So what do you think? I mean it's not as though you're going to want to go marrying anyone else a few years down the line, is it? You've said so yourself.'

'Absolutely,' David agrees, putting one hand on George's knee and downing an Amaretto with ice in one. 'I wouldn't even be asking you if I thought it'd mean you giving up your freedom. And there's the small matter of fringe benefits.'

'What?'

'You tell her,' he urges George.

'Fifty grand,' George bursts out. 'I come into some money from the trust when I hit thirty. You can have fifty grand if you'll marry David so we can stay together. Say you'll think about it. You can even come and live in my house if you want. Rent free.'

'And we'll let you bring your shags back,' David adds.

'Yes.' George nods vigorously. 'Can't say fairer than that, now can we? Not many husbands let their wives fornicate with total strangers under their own roof.'

I light one of George's fags while I think about it for a moment. Fifty grand would mean I could have another go at the catering. Properly. Budgets, cash flow projections, hedging, fencing, whatever they are. And George and David are right. I don't want to get married. Not in the true sense of the word, anyway. And if I'm already married, I can't be tempted any time in the future, can I?

But I love these guys to bits. Both of them. Even if David won't sleep with me. I can't take their money.

Can I?

Can I buffalo.

'I'm sorry,' I tell them. 'I can't accept.'

'Oh?' David looks disappointed.

'I mean, I can't accept the money.' I hesitate. 'But I would like to come and live with you. It would help me out no end.'

OK, so I've refused charity from Sam. But this is different. With George and David, I'm actually doing something in return. Without rent to pay it'll be much easier to fund my existing venture. And, knowing George and David, they won't be down my throat about book-keeping and doing the right thing all the time. Hopefully, they'll actively encourage me to be as irresponsible as I damn well like.

'And the wedding thing?' George asks.

'Well,' I begin, 'you're right. I don't want to get married.'

'Oh.' George is crestfallen.

'So I'll do it.'

'You will?'

'Sure.'

For a second, I do wonder if I've just gone completely dool-lally. Round the twist. Loop the bloody loo. We could all get into lots of trouble, for starters. I mean, this whole carry-on ain't exactly legal, as far as I know. What the hell have I just agreed to?

Then I catch sight of their grins. Like huge slices of water-melon, splitting both their faces in half.

'Oh, Katie.' George, delighted, throws himself at me and gives me a squeeze so tight I can hardly breathe. 'You're the best friend ever.'

'Thanks, Katie.' David pats my shoulder. 'You're a star.'

'I know.' I grin. 'But I'm expecting a big do, mind. I'm not your average "dap me in the dunny then march me to the nearest registry office 'cos I'm up the duff" sorta Sheila.'

'Vol-au-vents and everything,' they both promise.

'Right.' I shrug my shoulders and smile at my friends. 'So when do I move in?'

Chapter 14

I drop round to Janice's to tell her the news first. With her weekend in Paris looming, she's just been out on a severe shopping bender. Her cool white and sludge-green bedroom is awash with the latest fashions.

'Thought you were supposed to wait till you were actually in Paris before you splurged on clothes.' I help myself to a fag and plonk myself down on her bed, immediately creasing the white linen duvet cover.

'No point putting myself through retail denial, is there?' she says firmly, showing me piles of brand new lingerie. And these aren't your understated Marks 'n' Sparks jobs either. She's bought enough pants to keep Agent Provocateur in business for the next decade and more. Stunning, gauzy creations in ice-cream colours. Soft blackberry, palest sugar-almond pink and scrumptious strawberry scraps of satin have been duly purchased, slipped into tiny glossy pink bags, promptly removed and piled on her bed for scrutiny. Everything, but everything, she assures me, as she throws black bin bags full of grey bucket pants out of her bedroom window onto the porch below, has to be brand, spanking new before they actually get there, so he thinks she's a stylish kind of chick and not some throwaway old slap. And it's not only the underwear. She's bought glitzy dresses, glam nighties and a pair of shoes with transparent heels and shiny straps the colour of the foil on a Quality Street noisette triangle.

'Imagine, Katie.' She grins, showing me a white sequinned top the size of a handkerchief. 'In six months' time I'll be Mrs Jasper.'

I decide not to tell her about the girl in the raspberry dress. After all, she might not be a serious contender at all. And anyway, Janice probably won't believe me. And I can't afford to argue with another one of my friends. So instead I try to tell her about George and David's proposal.

'I think George is in love,' I begin.

'Yeah, right,' she scoffs. 'With himself, you mean?'

'No,' I protest. 'With David.'

'Nooooo.'

'Well, they've been together for a while now,' I say. 'And I think George is even managing to stay faithful. He certainly isn't the Meat Seeking Missile he was a few weeks ago.'

'Still,' Janice examines a scrap of pistachio-coloured lace that in her eyes passes for a pair of pants, 'it's easy for them, isn't it?'

'What?'

'Well,' she says, 'a pair of Marmite miners like them don't have to burden themselves with all that crippling anxiety and inse-curity over other people, do they?'

'Sorry?'

'What I mean is, they're more likely to know what's going on in each other's heads than you and Jake did, say.'

'What about me and Jake?' I'm suddenly defensive.

'Well, they probably fancy the same people. Sleep with the same people even, if that's what they want.'

'But I really think they love each other,' I protest. 'I saw them at Poppy's wedding. Couldn't get enough of each other.'

'Oh, bollocks,' Janice scoffs. 'Do you honestly believe in all that rubbish?'

'Well, no, I mean...'

'We've been through all this, haven't we? Blokes these days just don't want to commit,' she carries on, packing a damson-coloured teddy into her suitcase. 'I mean, look at Sam. His flings never last much longer than your average feature film. You won't find him welding himself to some silly girly like a bit of fuzzy felt. You've said so yourself. Even you don't want a relationship any more. Which is why you shat all over poor Max from such a great height when he was totally in love with you. I'm still having to live that down at work, by the way.'

I decide to wait until I can get hold of Sam before I tell Janice I'm going to marry David. She can't be bothered to listen to me anyway and after what she's just said, I don't really see why she should get to know first, even if Sam is being totally infuriating at the moment. So I call Sam and arrange for us both to go over to his later on. And George and David promise to meet me there so they can explain if I get it all wrong.

Sam opens the door straightaway. And any worries I had over the possibility of any nasty vibes hanging around vanish like a puff of smoke. He's grinning from ear to ear like a Cheshire cat.

'You've had your hair cut,' I say as he hugs me. I take in his newly shorn self. His floppy fringe has disappeared and his head, when I stroke it, feels all soft and fuzzy. 'I like it.'

'You do?' He looks pleased.

'Yep.' I grin. I should've known Sam wouldn't let some silly disagreement over my living arrangements spoil our friendship. 'It's lovely to see you.'

'You too, Simpson.' He smiles. 'You look the same as ever.'

'Meaning?'

'Meaning it's good to see you still don't bother running a brush through that hair.'

'Ha ha.'

Inside, Sam's flat, with its newly snow-white painted walls, its swathes of film mags stacked everywhere and the goldfish orange, egg-yolk yellow and Matisse blue splotches he refers to as 'art' all over the walls is looking great.

'I like it,' I tell him. 'You've made it look really good.'

'Of course it's mainly down to me,' a voice filters into the room and Janice and I look up to see Pussy, stick-thin in a tiny black vest, a weeny scarlet and white skirt and a pair of sexy black mules, emerge from the kitchen.

'God,' hisses Janice. 'It's that orally fixated slapper from the wedding.'

'We chose the colours together, didn't we?' She gazes up at Sam.

Sam looks momentarily embarrassed at being discovered wallowing in domestic togetherness. And so he should. The two of them have only been seeing each other a matter of weeks.

'Er...'

'Have you moved in then?' Janice probes.

'Well—'

'She's just helping me decorate,' Sam says quickly. 'She chose the blue wall over there.'

Pussy looks pissy for a second then, pulling herself together, snipes, 'That's an unusual outfit, Kylie.'

'Katie,' I say.

'Oh, I'm sorry.' She looks not at all sorry. 'Of course. You were the caterer at my cousin's wedding. You know, you need some jewellery with that top. To draw the eye away from the dodgy waistline.'

I wait until George and David have arrived, bursting through Sam's front door in a blur of Habitat catalogues and Heals carriers, before I tell Sam and Janice my news.

'We're here,' they chorus.

'God, sweetie, don't look so worried.' George, about six foot four in his Cuban-heeled boots, practically rips his white PVC trousers as he bends down to air kiss my cheeks. 'You look knackered, doesn't she, David?'

'Well...'

'Oh, come off it, darling, her eyebags are rouched.' George starts stabbing numbers excitedly into his mobile phone. ''Scuse I, darling. Just got to ring Aria to order some new bedlinen for your room.'

'Her room?' Sam asks suspiciously.

'Never mind that.' I wave him away and throw George a meaningful look.

'Sorry, darling.' George throws his hand to his mouth. 'You haven't told them then?'

'Told us what?'

'Yes,' Pussy purrs. 'Told us what?'

'Nothing,' I say.

'Jesus Christ.' George bangs his phone on the table in exasperation and looks straight at Pussy. 'That bloody network goes down more often than you do, love.'

'George...' Sam warns, as Pussy turns her pretty little nose up. I don't know why he's bothering. I'm not even sure she's understood.

When George has calmed down, I eventually manage to break the news of my forthcoming nuptials to the others. When I'm done, there's a hideous silence, followed by a sharp intake of breath from Janice and Sam as their jaws crash to the floor. I suppose I can't exactly blame them for being so shocked. After all, it's not every day a girl who's more single than a one-way bus ticket decides to get spliced on a whim, even if the reasoning behind it isn't exactly fairytale stuff. Of course, I don't tell them the full story. Not at first, anyway. I don't let slip exactly who it is I'm marrying until I've let them stew a bit. As it is, the only person who looks remotely pleased for me is the odious Pussy. And that's probably only because she's relieved because she thinks it means I won't be hanging around Sam like a rat round a rubbish bin. She looks the type to be jealous of platonic friends.

As the news sinks in, Sam wanders around making hot, sweet

tea as though we've just been through some kind of emergency, and Janice just stands there looking blatantly bloody furious. Her face wears exactly the same expression it did when Johnny Martin, who she was only with because it was rumoured he had a twelve-inch kidney wiper, snogged her then vommed in her mouth. She's absolutely horrified. She simply can't believe I've beaten her to it. I'll be waltzing up that aisle before her. And her with her new underwear and all. But then she always has been very competitive as far as I'm concerned. To her, this is just like the time I pipped her to the post in the 100 m charity butterfly at college. She refused to share her fags with me for a month after that.

'You will be my bridesmaid, won't you?' I tease, enjoying my moment of glory. Janice is so jealous she's turned the colour of Swarfega. 'Bet you didn't think in a million years I'd be marching up that aisle before you. Isn't it going to be weird, being able to say "my husband this" and "my husband that"?'

'But...' she stammers, looking aghast. 'How? Who? And when?'

'And why? Why didn't you tell us?' Sam blurts out.

'I am telling you.'

'But we didn't even know you were seeing anyone. Is it someone we know? Are you pregnant?'

'Don't be stupid.'

'Because if you are, we'll support you. You don't have to rush into anything, you know. Ouch!' he yelps, as a pissed-off Pussy digs him in the ribs.

'Who is he?' Pussy asks. 'Is he successful?'

'I should bloody say so,' George interrupts, throwing her one of his 'looks'. I'm delighted he obviously hates her as much as I do.

'You already knew about this?' Sam starts to look cross.

'Course, darling.' George winces as David, almost imperceptibly, steps on his toe.

'You can't have met someone,' Janice spits. 'You never even go out. And you said you were happy being single. You said...'

God. I feel as though I've promised her sweets at the check-out, then changed my mind at the last minute.

'What's going on?' Sam eyes George with all the affection one usually reserves for a rabid dog.

'I mean,' Janice carries on, 'you were the one who said you wanted to be single for ever. I thought you'd be like those women in Sainsburys with the purple holey tights and the knitted berets. I thought, I honestly thought you'd end up living in your car or taking over from that woman who stands on Trinity Road roundabout and flashes her bum at cars.'

'It's not Jake, is it?' Sam interrupts, a worried expression flickering across his face.

'Who?' I ask. 'The woman on Trinity Road roundabout? I don't think so. I mean I know Jake is kind of fond of flashing his arse around, but I don't think even an old slutbucket like him would want every Tom, Dick and Harry in Wandsworth bogging at his bum.'

'You know full well what I mean.'

'I didn't really want to tell you all yet,' I tease. 'Not until I'd told my mum. But...'

Like buggery I'm telling my mum. She'll have a hairy baby if she so much as catches an inkling of what I'm planning to do. After all, we're talking wedding fake here, not wedding cake. This isn't exactly what she planned for me when she scrimped and saved on her schoolteacher's salary to put me through university. Somehow, I can't exactly see her dusting down the hatbox and talking royal icing. And I can't bear to hurt her feelings by playing the 'no grandchildren' card again. So as far as she's concerned, I'm keeping well and truly schtum. After all, what the eye doesn't see and all that.

'Well.' I shrug. 'You're my best friends in the world.'

'With the exception of her.' George points at Pussy.

I ignore him. I can see Sam's furious already.

'So of course it would mean an awful lot to me if you could

all be there for my big day. We were hoping for the Fourth of July...'

'Independence Day,' says Sam, not without a touch of irony. I ignore him too.

'But everything was booked up so we're going for early September instead. So don't say I don't give you plenty of notice.'

Janice is silent. In fact, she's too busy hyperventilating to say anything at all. Considering the possibility of slapping her face on the pretext of calming her down, I reject it in case it's construed as an attempt on my part at taking the piss.

'There's just so much to sort out,' I flap, waving my hands about and thoroughly enjoying playing the part of blushing bride-to-be. 'Guest list. Flowers. Food. And of course the cake's going to have to be the complete dog's bollocks, what with me being a cook and all. How am I ever going to find the time?' Actually, I can't care less about the cake. Granted, I dreamed of a big white wedding when I was a little girl, joining in with the excited chitter-chatter of princesses, plaits, ponies and pink marquees as we sucked on sherbet dib dabs and swirled red liquorice bootlaces round our wedding fingers. But now, I can't see why we don't just have the reception down the Punjab Paradise or the Peking Palace. Especially with the circumstances regarding the love stuff being what they are. And, as for the guest list, I rather think we'll be keeping it small.

'I can't wait to go dress shopping,' I add.

Janice looks so disappointed, as though she's just started a new job and someone has asked her to scrub out the lav, that I can't resist one final tease. 'I can just see you in lilac. With puffed sleeves.'

The relief on her face when I finally admit it's only David I'm marrying is a picture. I haven't beaten her to it after all. Well, not really.

Unfortunately, as far as Sam is concerned, the whole idea goes down like a Brussels sprout down a toddler.

'I can't think of anything worse than marrying someone you don't love,' he says quietly.

Personally, I think that's pretty rich, coming from him. But his friendship, and therefore his approval, means a lot to me. I love Sam to bits. I can't bear for him to be annoyed with me.

'Oooh, can't you?' George says. 'I can.'

'So can I,' I say cheerfully, trying to smooth things over.

'Lots and lots of things,' George carries on wittering. 'Silk flower arrangements, for one. Lambrusco, there's another. Anything grape-based in a screw-topped bottle, come to think of it. Erm...'

'People who say doofer. And doobrey,' adds David.

'And malarkey,' Janice agrees.

'Menthol fags' (George again).

'Being fat' (Pussy).

'Being poor' (Janice).

'You do know they'll ask you the colour of his toothbrush, don't you?' Pussy pulls on a teensy-weensy angora sweater and shivers prettily. 'I saw it on *Green Card.*'

I'm tempted to whack her one round the face but I don't want her running to the Home Office or something ridiculous and spoiling everything, so I simply explain that we'll cross that bridge when we come to it.

'And it's all going to be fine,' I assure them.

'For George and David, yes,' Sam mutters 'What about you?'

'What about me?' I ask. 'Don't ask me if I'm sure I love him, for God's sake. It's not like we're getting married for real, anyway.'

'You are getting married for real, you silly girl.'

'Only on paper. And it's not like I'm going into this with my eyes shut. I know exactly what I'm doing.'

'Are they paying you?' I can practically see the pound signs going Kerching! across Janice's eyeballs.

'No,' I say. 'But it is a mutual arrangement. I get to benefit too.'

'Well, I hope you're not going to be wearing that.' Pussy looks at my outfit in distaste. 'I hope one of these boys is going to take you in hand and get you something decent to wear.'

'She can get her own clothes, thank you,' George snaps. 'And I certainly don't think she needs advice from the likes of you, love. You with your prissy little name and your little dolly clothes. I bet your mother's called something really common like Cheryl.'

Pussy's bottom lip starts to wobble. George, as usual, has obviously hit the nail right on the head.

I rush to appease Sam, who is looking furious.

'No.' Sam holds up both his hands and I can't help noticing how huge they are. Big, safe hands. 'What was that you were saying about you getting to benefit as well?'

'Well,' I say slowly, 'I'm going to be moving house. It makes sense, anyway, for me to be living with David if we're going to be married. It'll look more realistic.'

'I thought you didn't want to move out of your flat,' he says coldly. 'What was it? You didn't want to "lose your independence". Well, I hate to say it, Simpson, but I think you've bloody well gone and done that now. So George's pad is good enough for you, is it? But not mine.'

'Oh Sam, please try and understand.' I go to hug him but he pulls away.

'Understand what? That you're making the biggest mistake of your life? You do realise you'll end up regretting this, don't you?'

'Of course I won't. And if I do, this is the twenty-first century. There is such a thing as divorce now. We don't have to stay together until we cark it.'

'That's the general idea, isn't it?' Sam points out. 'I mean this isn't exactly what you'd call romantic, is it?'

'And what would you know?' I ask him. 'Your idea of romance is bringing home a takeaway and asking your girlfriend to warm it through.'

'I'll come,' Janice offers. 'I'll be there for you, hon.'

'Thanks, mate.'

'As long as I can bring Jasper.'

'OK.'

'I'll come too if you like,' Pussy says. 'If Kirsty—'

'Katie.'

'Sorry.' She flashes me a smile that's about as genuine as a moody Vuitton bag. 'If Katie here wants to get married then we should surely all go along to support her. And I love weddings.' She looks at Sam petulantly.

'I bet you do,' George says. 'Let's face it, love. Nice wedding on a Saturday's probably your equivalent of a weekly whip round Sainsbury's. Who knows what you might pick up? Or who, to be more exact.'

'That's not fair, George,' Sam says quietly. I shiver. I hate Sam's quiet voice. It means he's internally combusting. I think we should go before he explodes. He does this very rarely, but when he does he goes up like Sydney Harbour on Millennium Eve.

'Oh, come off it,' George says. 'The little cow's in it for all she can get. Her mother's probably been waiting forever to palm her off onto some successful blokey like yourself. And she won't stop at you. Do you think for a minute she'd be hanging round you if Richard Branson glanced twice in her direction? Oh no, darling. She'd be off like Linda Lusardi's bra.'

'Right.' Sam's lips are white with fury. 'Get out.'

Then he turns to me.

'And as for you,' he says in the disappointed tone of voice my mother reserves for occasions when she wants to make me feel extra guilty, 'I'd have thought you'd have had more sense. I just hope you realise how selfish these two are being before it's too late.'

'The whole point is that she's being completely unselfish.' Janice tries, not very successfully, to back me up. Unfortunately her attempt cuts no ice with Sam. He ignores her completely, stabbing a finger at me instead.

'It's rude to point,' I say childishly.

'Don't be facetious.'

'Don't pretend you're my dad then.'

'You haven't thought this through at all, have you, Simpson?' he lectures me. 'What happens in five years' time when you suddenly decide you want children before it's too late and you're married to a Jaffa?'

'A what?' George booms.

'A Jaffa,' I explain. 'You know, seedless.'

'Oooh,' George spits. 'There's nothing wrong with the quality of David's seed, thank you very much. My God. I never had you down for a homophobe, darling. Still, you know what they say. He who doth protest too much and all that. Takes one to know one.'

'Look, if I ever do change my mind about having children, I'll come to you, Sam, for a sample of your quality heterosexual semen, OK? So there really is no need for you to worry. I'll be OK. Really.'

'I think you'll live to regret it.' He looks at me sadly.

'I don't think so,' I say. 'And you'll probably understand when you've had time to think about it. I told you already. I don't want to get married. Ever. So I'm really not losing out.'

'Aren't you?'

'What?'

'Leave her alone.' George pulls on my arm. 'Come on, Katie darling, let's go. Why do you have to try and spoil everything, Sam? Just because you have no idea what it's like to be in love.'

'Oh, but I do,' Sam says quietly, as Pussy gazes up at him besottedly. 'I know perfectly well, thank you.'

'Being in love with yourself doesn't count.' I flounce off without turning back to look at him, so I won't see the hurt look I know will cross his face as he shuts the door in mine.

Chapter 15

I hump the flotsam and jetsam of my life round to George and David's in dribs and drabs. The following Saturday, I wave an excited Janice off to Paris before chucking Rollerblades, clothes, CDs, ghettoblaster, espresso machine, books, a jumble of mismatched crockery and—last but not least—Graham and Shish Kebab, who are both yowling with outrage in their baskets, into the Rustbucket. Then I throw one last look towards my flat before we pootle northwards, leaving Balham for good.

'Onwards and upwards, eh boys?' I crank up the volume on my ancient car stereo and smile as we turn onto the Balham High Road and drive north towards Clapham Common.

George has obviously been awaiting our arrival. Clad in his favourite violet shaggy coat and a pair of enormous black boots, he clops out through the front door the moment I putter to a halt by the kerb. He's waving and signalling hysterically. I have no idea what he's after so I merely shrug my shoulders and switch off the ignition. He motions for me to wind down the window.

'Park a bit further up,' he hisses.

'Why? I'm not in anyone's way.'

'We don't want that sodding wheelie bin right outside the front door, darling. What'll the neighbours think?'

I ignore him, clambering out of the passenger door and opening the back to let Graham and Shish Kebab out.

'You haven't brought *them*?' George looks horrified.

'Of course I have.' I put Graham's basket down on the pavement and hand Shish Kebab to George. He shrinks away and the cat, sensing a possible rival, mewls indignantly.

'What did you think I was going to do with them?' I say, hurt. 'Put them up for adoption?'

'You can sling them in the Finsbury Park reservoir for all I care.' George picks up my ghettoblaster and walks, wiggling his hips in exaggerated disdain, towards the house. 'You do realise I'm dangerously allergic, don't you? I could go into anaphylactic shock in seconds with these little buggers around. I just hope they're toilet trained. I don't want them spraying the soft furnishings.'

'Of course they are.' I bend to stroke Graham's nose through the bars of his travel basket and jump back as he goes to scratch me.

'Vicious little bastard as well, that one, isn't he?' George tuts.

'He's just upset,' I protest. 'He's been squashed up for too long.'

'God, you sad bitch.' George puts the cat basket down in the hall, making absolutely no attempt to free its occupant. 'You'll be thinking the little bags of shite are your own children next.'

Despite the fact that they are most unwelcome, Graham and Shish Kebab seem to like their new home. And I can't really complain. My new bedroom is twice the size of my old one. Plus, I get to use all the latest mod cons in the kitchen.

My first week is taken up with preparing for the christening in Lewisham and for the wedding of some ghastly girl called Marina who I met at Poppy's bash. But then I'm free to spend the next week happily painting my new office a rather delicious shade of dark pink. And when it's finished I decide I love it so much I could live in it. David generously lends me his laptop so I don't have to use my ancient Mac any more and I place advertisements in all the local papers, next to ads for comedy nights and articles on the threatened closure of local nurseries, which have indignant Hermès-clad mothers leaping out of Mercedes people carriers all over Canonbury to waggle clipboards and petitions in the faces of perfectly innocent passers-by. Then I sit back in my lovely pink office and wait.

The first caller on my new business line is—quite predictably—my mother.

'Why didn't you tell me?' she asks, hurt.

'I was going to tell you when I'd settled in,' I sigh, ripping the paper off a Pepperami with my teeth and jamming the end in my mouth. 'I only moved in a week ago.'

'You've *moved*?' she screeches.

'Yes,' I tell her. 'I assumed that's what you meant.'

'Katherine Simpson, you're not telling me you've moved house and not even thought to mention it to your own mother?'

'I'm sorry, Mum, I—'

'You know Jeff was right,' she huffs into the receiver.

'What's Jeff got to do with it?' I raise my eyes to the ceiling and chew off another bit of sausage.

'We had Sam coming round the other day, all upset about some row or other you've had, the pair of you. Honestly, you're worse than you were as kids. And don't think I don't know what you did to him with that spade. If I've told you once I've told you a thousand times. I've got eyes in the back of my head.'

'I was four.'

'Old enough to know better.'

'Did he say what the row was about?' I'm suspicious. Bugger Sam. If he's mentioned the wedding I'll bloody well rip his balls off.

'Refused, apparently,' Mum says. 'It was the girlfriend, I think.

Nice little thing. Lovely manners. Yes, it was she who brought the whole thing up in the first place.'

'Along with most of her dinner, I bet,' I say.

'What?'

'Nothing.' I sigh. 'It's just all really silly. Anyway, Mum, I'm living at George's to save some money so I can start up my catering business properly. I'm going to make a real go of it this time.'

Obviously, I don't tell her about my end of the bargain. That's going to have to be a closely guarded secret. But I'm much better off now I'm not paying rent, and Poppy's dad, bless him, has paid my invoice early, so I'm hoping I won't let anyone down.

'Good for you, darling.' She sounds delighted. 'I know you'll make a success of it.'

Christ Almighty. There she goes again, with her bloody care and support.

Now I'm going to sodding well *have* to make a success of it, aren't I? Otherwise I'll be had up for cruelty to menopausal old women. I'm lining her up for disappointment, of course. It'll be even worse when she *is* disappointed and tries really hard not to show it. Cue guilt trip from hell.

Bloody hell. Why on earth can't she just laugh in my face like her mate Gloria would? Tell me no daughter of hers is swaddling herself in overalls and rolling out pastry for a living, no better than a common kitchen maid.

Still, two days after the free papers containing my ad have been pushed through letterboxes all over London, the phone calls start for real. I can't believe how easy it is. A woman in Totteridge wants to know if I can make red food for her ruby wedding anniversary. A TV gardener needs a 'green finger' buffet when he opens the grounds of his manor in Hertfordshire to the public for charity. And a Sloane Ranger from Battersea (only, needless to say, she pronounces it Batterseaar) wants me to 'do' her hen night.

I suppose I'd better not let on about my record for doing husbands as well.

Slowly, with each booking, my confidence, along with my contacts book, starts to grow. And during the next few weeks, I'm so busy, sitting in my pink office planning menus and seating arrangements, that I don't even have time to think about the wedding. Even Sam's disapproval over the whole affair pales into insignificance when I think about how much I have to do. I'm spending every single minute cooking. Baking mini banoffee pies and tiny tiramisus, designed to be scoffed in one mouthful for Mr TV Gardener. Making podgy pink babies out of marzipan for a christening cake in Nappy Valley. Or strawberry flans the size of paddling pools for Mr and Mrs Ruby Wedding. One afternoon, I'm slaving over phallic vodka jellies for Battersear's hen night when the doorbell rings. I put down the Smirnoff bottle. It'll be the lard-arse from the bakery, delivering the basket of fresh hereby focaccia, the fat loaves of olive ciabatta and the sundried tomato bread I've ordered. I open the front door.

Blimey oh Reilly!

It isn't lardy at all. It's a new chap altogether. And let's just say that the last time I saw thighs like those, I was gawping at an advert for Calvin Klein pants. Before they got those bag-o'-bones Jarvis Cocker lookalikes to drape themselves all over the show likes great big strings of snot, that is.

Oh yes. This one's what Janice would call a 'nice bit of rough'.

Not quite her Driver Eating Yorkie type, of course, but close. Cyclist eating Curly Wurly, say.

He's younger than me, probably around twenty-five. He wears an ageing, possibly cheesy, pair of Adidas old school trainers and has eyes the colour of espresso. And a quick glance at his skin-tight cycling shorts reveals that his thighs aren't the only attractive bulge he possesses. I wouldn't kick him out of bed for farting, that's for sure.

I rootle through my purse. On a normal day, I'd have taken one look at a bloke in cycling shorts and thought, 'Ew, all sweaty,' and moved on. But there's something about today that makes me think twice. Perhaps it's the fact that it's such a beautiful day. I can practically smell the pheromones bouncing around in the air. Or perhaps it's just the way his browny gold hair is knotted into deliciously scruffy dreads. Or the way he drapes himself languidly against the doorframe, looking so utterly carefree.

Or perhaps I just need a good shag.

Call it chemistry, call it desperation, whatever it is, I suddenly feel totally compelled to come on to him. I'm getting married soon, for God's sake. I need to get it while I still can.

OK, so Max is still calling my mobile. Which means I could just shag him and save myself the bother. But Max is *nice*. And nice just gets on my nerves. If Max wanted some kind of relationship when we got it together that day I saw him on the tube, he should have got it from me in writing. I didn't make him any promises. I am a single, independent woman. I have nothing whatsoever to feel guilty about.

'I don't seem to have any money in here.' I smile, cupping my hand round the crisp tenner I've just found and taking a step backwards into George's immaculate cream-painted hall. 'Do you mind coming in a moment while I find some upstairs?'

He smiles, a slow, sexy, slightly stupid smile that might or might not be interpreted as open to suggestion. Which is fine, obviously. Stupid is good. I have absolutely no problem with stupid whatsoever. The chances of a reasonably intelligent—albeit slightly ginger—girl like me forming a lasting relationship with anyone who's thicker than two short planks are verging on nil, so I can drag this chap upstairs right now if I feel like it, without giving a flying fuck about the consequences.

'Sure.' He lopes after me into the hall. 'Whatevva.'

Of course by the time I've rolled the note I've just found in my purse into my palm, gone upstairs with it and come back down again, waving it between forefinger and thumb, I suddenly realise that I have absolutely no idea how to pull.

Do I just go straight for it and say huskily, 'Come in, Notch Number Nine and a half, your time is up'? Should I just slip him my phone number and have done with it? Or would that look a bit Bored Housewife? Then again, I don't live in my own house, I don't even live in the dumpy, clarty flat any more either. I live in a house that's so effortlessly pristine and minimalist it can only be inhabited by gay guys. So I can't reasonably be mistaken for Mrs Two Point Four Children.

I'm just deciding to sod it and hand him the cash, when I notice he's glancing into the kitchen, looking vaguely amused. I follow his gaze, to where the first batch of pink jelly willies stand turned out of their moulds, proud and erect—if ever so slightly wibbly—on the kitchen worktop. Buggeroo. He's probably thinking I'm some sort of pervert serial killer who lures delivery boys into the house so I can have my wicked way with them before boshing them over the head and stashing them in the freezer to do things to with jelly later. I know if I were in his shoes—or even just his skanky trainers—I'd be a smidgen concerned for my personal safety right now.

'It's not what you think,' I stutter. 'I'm doing them for a hen party, see. Just for fun. I mean I'm not into anything kinky. I'm more M&S than S&M, honest. You can't beat them for knickers.'

'Shame.' He treats me to another lazy, sexy grin, which turns my knees to a wobbling mass of blancmange. Is he laughing at me or not?

'You're a chef?' he asks.

'Caterer,' I reply. 'Weddings and stuff, mainly. Just getting started.'

He grins. 'And does the caterer get to test the canapés?' He nods towards the pink willies, which now seem so downright ridiculous, I have an absurd compulsion to get rid of him as quickly as possible.

'Not really,' I say.

'What about the delivery boy?' His grin widens. 'Does he get to have a taste?'

'He might.' I can't help laughing at the mischievous expression on his face. 'Just the one, mind. These have to be at a party in Battersear tomorrow.'

I should really have known better. I should know that my capacity for alcohol generally tends to exceed the 'just the one' that's good for me. Nick, as his name turns out to be, pronounces my jelly willies so delicious that he has to have another. And I just think sod it and jam in a couple for myself. And after I've eaten nine, or thereabouts, I tell myself that not only is he probably the most fanciable, un-uphimself male I've seen since I came to live in Islington, I decide he's also one of the most scintillating I've ever met.

And we're getting on so well.

'Sheriously,' he says, finishing off the last jelly and beginning to slur his words just ever so slightly. 'I might be looking for shomeone like you. I'm a DJ, shee? I'll be famoush this time next year.'

'Really?' I'm impressed. 'How faschinating.'

I'm so drunk by this time that I'm pouring what's left of the vodka into shot glasses and liberally tipping it down my neck. It doesn't really occur to me to wonder why, if he's such a famous DJ, he's delivering bread all over North London on a crappy pushbike. And, to be honest, I don't really care.

'Me mate'sh organising a party shoon. He needs shomeone to do the food and shit. How 'bout I give him your number?'

In my drunken state, I decide this is a definite attempt on his part at trying to pull me. And, when I scribble my mobile number on the corner of a crumpled-up copy of *Attitude* and he closes his hand over mine as I hand it to him, I just know I'm IN THERE.

With barely any effort whatesoever.

Two seconds later, he's kissing me passionately, and a second after that, he's explaining drunkenly that he can't go back to his

shift in the state he's in, so we might as well go to bed. I don't
care that he's being presumptuous. I don't even care that he
probably does this all the time. In fact, it just makes him ideal
one-off material.

What I do care about, however, is that I've been so into work
all day that I haven't even bothered to shower. Consequently,
I'm still stewing in the sour pants I slept in. I can't let him see
me like this, regardless of the fact that afterwards I never want
to see him again.

'Wait here.' I pull away from his searching tongue.

'Wh–wha?'

'Telly'sh there. Wait five minutes. I'll be back in a...'

I dash upstairs with the intention of jumping in the shower
for literally two seconds. But the enormous walk-in shower
in George and David's bedroom is out of bounds, so I decide, out of loyalty to the pair of them, to use my en-suite
bath instead.

Turning on the taps, I stumble around drunkenly, finding
lavender-scented soap, bubble bath and a fresh towel, before eas-
ing myself into the deliciously hot, scented water and inhaling
the fragrant steam. There's something so utterly decadent about
having a bath when shitfaced that I relax my body totally. And,
come to think of it, I've had a hard day. Exhausting, in fact. Actually, now you mention it, I'm really, really...

Shit.

I've no idea how much time has passed by the time I eventually come to. All I do know is that I'm freezing my tits off
and my fingers are all pruny. Shivering, I pull a white, fluffy
towel around me and gingerly tiptoe through my bedroom and
onto the landing. Seconds later, I hear the front door bang. I
rush to the window, hoping to stop him from leaving. But
there's no one outside. And then I realise why. It's not him leaving, it's someone coming in.

'Hello?'

David.

'Oh, hi.' I pad down the stairs feeling sheepish. God. My head. 'How's things?'

'Good, thanks. I've just got some freelance work on a new magazine. Brilliant money as well.'

'Good for you. I don't suppose...'

'Hmmm?'

'Is anyone else there?'

'Where? In here? I don't think...' David peers into the kitchen, the sitting room then every other room in turn. 'No. No one.'

'Bollocks.'

'What?'

'Nothing.'

Trust me to miss out on a shag. But I really can't have been up there that long. The impatient sod. It can only have been three o'clock when I went for my bath.

'What time is it?' I ask David, as nonchalantly as I can.

He glances at his watch. 'Five thirty. Bloody hell, Katie, it's a bit of a mess in here.'

'You wha'?'

'Five thirty.' He looks at me. 'Don't tell me you've been abducted by aliens and you've totally lost the last two hours.'

'Something like that,' I say. 'Shit, David, I have to meet Janice in half an hour. She's coming back from Paris. I don't suppose if I paid you you'd clear up all that vodka shite from the kitchen before George gets back and goes totally mentalist, would you?'

'Go on.' David grins at me. 'I mean you've shown me your bum at least once and you're going to be my wife in a couple of months' time so the least I can do is mop up a bit of vodka. What the bloody hell have you been doing in here anyway?'

'Tell you another time.' I hug him. 'Thanks, mate. Janice is going to have my tits for earmuffs if I'm late. She'll be dying to tell me all the goss.'

* * *

Janice, when I eventually meet her in Soho, is thunderous. Plonking her turquoise baguette on the table, she orders a large margarita, lights two cigarettes at once and pronounces the whole Paris thing a 'total washout'.

Actually, it doesn't sound like much of a washout to me. Days of glorious sunshine, clothes purchased by the glossy designer bagful, courtesy of Jasper's platinum credit card. Dinner at the Ritz, which she couldn't really take pleasure in because the sheer sumptuousness of the menu meant that she was forced to break her wedding diet completely, even to the extent of having a pudding. And every time she took another forkful, she got palpitations, because she felt certain that this was the night he was going to pop the question, and she didn't want to have to tell their grandchildren that she had her mouth full when she said, 'I do'.

There was also the additional worry that he'd hidden the ring in her pot au chocolat and there was nothing remotely romantic about the Heimlich manoeuvre.

On their last evening in Paris, they sat on the wrought iron balcony of his apartment drinking a bottle of extremely mellow red wine, while the noise and the hubbub of the Champs Elysées at night buzzed way below them. Janice was getting desperate. It was, after all, the last night of the holiday.

Jasper's last chance to propose.

And as she describes their conversation in minute detail, my mind keeps rewinding like videotape, back to an event that, in the whole whirlwind of my fake engagement, I've totally forgotten. The restaurant on Upper Street and the girl in the raspberry dress. Should I tell her what I saw?

But if I *do* tell her, and it turns out to be something completely innocuous, then I'll look like a stirring old witch.

But what if I *don't* tell her and he's been stringing her along the entire time? What happens then? She'll be having charity biddy sex for nothing when she could be bonking half of London Irish instead.

'And so I've just given up altogether,' Janice is sipping her third margarita and looking at me curiously, 'when he says…' She gulps.

'Ye-es?'

Thank God for that! He's proposed after all. Phew. I'm saved! I don't have to mention Raspberry Dress. After all, as long as she gets the marriage certificate and the bank account, she's hardly going to be concerned about a smidgen of infidelity, now is she?

'He says, "I've got something for you",' she finishes. 'And he brings out this Tiffany box. I know it's Tiffany, right, because I recognise the colour, you know, it's the same as the walls in my kitchen.'

I nod eagerly. 'Go on.'

'Well, of course I'm getting really excited by this time, because I know, I just know, it's a solitaire diamond and that this is It and I'm sure he must have popped out and bought it that morning while I had a lie-in and he went to fetch fresh croissants…'

'Croissants too.' I snigger. 'Lucky girl. So you didn't have any problems with the false zoobies then?'

'Don't be stupid.' She shoots me a look. 'His back won't take that kind of bending. No, I mean real croissants. And those nice, sticky pains au raisins you get from the boulangerie. Well, I don't mind telling you I wolfed down three, because I'd just about given up hope of there being any wedding to speak of so there wasn't any point in slimming any more. So there we are,' she continues, talking faster and faster to get out exactly what she has to say, 'in the most romantic city in the world, and he's giving me the famous turquoise box and I'm just kicking myself for eating three pastries for breakfast, because the moment has finally arrived. And I just know, Katie, I just know that this is when my life is going to change for the better and I'm finally going to get rich, so I delay opening the box because there's a tiny little part of me that's worried he's picked one I'll hate and I won't know what expression to have on my face if that happens. But then I can't wait to see it, because I can't wait to know and so I open the box and…and…'

'And...' I breathe, urging her on. God, even I'm getting excited. I must be going soft.

'And it's a fucking locket,' she spits. 'Imagine, Katie. A silver Tiffany locket. And there I am, wanting to go to the bathroom and cry my eyes out with the disappointment of it all, and there he is, slinking up behind me and expecting me to be thrilled to bits, saying, "Shall I put it on for you?" The smarmy old git.'

'Oh dear,' I say sympathetically.

'Oh dear is fucking right,' she says bitterly, a fat tear rolling down her cheek. 'You see, I was so sure that this was it that I let him boff me every night. Imagine!'

'Yuck.'

'And you know what's worse?'

'What?' I signal for more drinks. I think we need them.

'I gave him a blow job and everything. Yes, a blow job,' she shouts, as the whole of the next table, and the one after that look on, open-mouthed. 'And I swallowed. And this is the thanks I get. A poxy fucking locket and a gutful of fogie sperm. And then, when we get back to London, I have to get the sodding tube here on my own. No limo. No car. Not even a shitty black cab. Nothing.'

'Why? Where'd he go?'

'No idea.' She shrugs. 'Work, I expect. He's a workafucking-holic, that man.'

I decide I *have* to tell her about Raspberry Dress. At least then she won't have to have sex with the old fart for nothing. She can find herself a nice G 'n' T to have sex with instead.

'Janice,' I begin.

'What?'

'If he was having an affair, would you want to know?'

'He's not having an affair,' she snaps. 'He's old, for God's sake. Who'd want to shag him?'

'You?'

'I don't particularly *want* to shag him.' She takes a drag of her fag and looks at me sympathetically. 'I *have* to.'

'OK...'

'Why do you ask, anyway?' She knocks back her margarita in two big gulps and signals for another. 'Do you know something I don't?'

'Well.' I hesitate. 'You know I told you George and David proposed over lunch?'

'Mmmm?'

'Well, Jasper was there.'

'Having lunch with you?' she asks innocently. 'Well, that's fine. Why didn't you just say? Having lunch with him's hardly having an *affair* with him, is it? I trust you. And we don't have to tell each other every little thing.'

'He wasn't exactly having lunch with me,' I say. 'He was having lunch with a woman.'

'A woman?' She snaps her head back. 'What sort of a woman?'

'Just a woman,' I say. I don't think she needs to know that the woman concerned was so, well, sexual that I was staring at her even before I knew she was with Jasper. If I can just get Janice to knock this nonsense on the head now...

'Well, it could have been his sister then, couldn't it?'

'I doubt it,' I say kindly. 'She couldn't have been more than twenty-five.'

'His daughter then?'

'Well, that's what I thought,' I say, relieved. 'Has he *got* a daughter?'

'No idea.'

'Well then.'

'And how do you know they were having an affair?' she demands. 'Did they get right up on the table and go for it hammer and tongs there and then? Huh?'

'Well, no...'

'So?' she snarls. 'She could have been anyone. Someone from work even. You know what your problem is, Katie? You're just jealous.'

'No I'm not,' I say, surprised at her tone of voice.

'You're a sad, jealous bitch. No one wants to shag you, let alone have a relationship with you. You've got to marry a bum bandit 'cos no one else will have you and you just can't bear to see anyone else happy, can you?'

'That's just it,' I say bravely, even though inside I'm quaking. I haven't even had a chance to mourn my missed shag with her. We could have had a good old giggle over it, at least. 'If you *were* happy, it wouldn't be so bad. But you're not, are you? You spent this whole holiday hoping and praying for something that just didn't happen. You didn't even enjoy the good bits, like the gratis shopping and, well, the fucking.'

'He fucks like a warthog,' she points out. 'Not even *you* would enjoy that.'

I decide to ignore her. 'You can't enjoy anything any more because you're so on edge about getting married. I don't call that happy.'

'Oh, what would you know?' she says so harshly that I can't help wondering if anything else is wrong. And with that, she turns on her heel and storms out of the pub.

Chapter 16

With every booking I get for Neat Eats, my confidence, as well as my bank balance, soars. The breakthrough comes one morning when I realise I'm far happier pounding red peppers into mayonnaise and shredding potatoes for shoestring chips than I ever was slumped in front of daytime TV, watching fat people biff the shit out of each other. And with my newfound confidence in my career comes a healthier attitude towards men.

I decide to assume they all fancy me, unless they expressly tell me otherwise.

In writing.

Which means, of course, that by rights I can quite reasonably expect Johnny Depp, Nicholas Cage and Finn from *Hollyoaks* to be baying at my door on various occasions in the near future. I mean, none of them have actually contacted me to tell me I'm a complete munter, have they?

OK, so I missed out on a goodie the day I let that bakery chap slip through my fingers, snoring my head off in the bath like that instead of slinking down the stairs, slippery with baby oil and smelling so delicious that he was compelled to rip my clothes off there and then. But nobody's bloody perfect.

And then, of course, the diminutive Colin was no great catch either. But we'll gloss over that one. There's no point in thinking negatively. In future, I decide, pummelling a big wedge of pizza dough into submission, I can do and *have* exactly what— and who—I want.

I, Katie Simpson, am going to be a success.

On Saturday night, I'm flicking through recipes for a Bar Mitzvah in Hampstead Garden Suburb, when my mobile shrills.

'Yep?' I casually toss my curls off my face with a flick of my hand. Flour showers all over George and David's brand new heather-coloured carpet. Fuck.

'It's Max.'

'Oh.'

See what I mean? I've got them lining up. But buggery. I thought I was safe from Max. It's been *weeks* since I heard from him, I really thought he'd got the message. What's he doing, still hanging around like a sour, eggy trump?

'I just wondered...'

'Yes, yes?' I snap irritably, slopping into the kitchen, checking the sell-by date on a tub of sour cream and spooning a dollop straight into my mouth.

'Well, do you fancy going out tonight?'

It's Saturday. What the flipping heck does he think he's playing at? Any chick worth her weight in chocolate has her Saturday nights planned *well* in advance.

Well, not me, exactly. Janice still isn't talking to me so I've planned an evening in front of the telly with a bowlful of lumpfish caviare, a mile-high stack of blinis and a bucket of sour cream. Purely for research purposes, mind.

'Or are you busy?' He sounds doubtful.

'Yes,' I tell him, gazing at all my lovely shiny cooking paraphernalia. ''Fraid so.'

'Doing what?'

'Staying in,' I tell him firmly, pressing the 'end call' button.

God, if that doesn't convince him he's nothing more than a one-night stand, I don't know what will. If he keeps up this level of harassment I'm going to have to pay Janice to seduce him and shag him so I can burst in on them and pretend to be all upset.

Almost immediately it rings again.

'WHAT?'

But it's not Moony Max. In fact, I don't know who the hell it is. I sort of recognise the voice but I can't quite place it.

'It's Nick.'

'Nick?' I say quickly. 'Nick who?'

Quite a reasonable question, under the circumstances. It could, after all, be Nick the Dick. Or Nick O'Teen. A single girl, even one who is getting married in a few months, has to be on her guard.

'I just wanted to make sure you was OK,' the voice says.

'I'm fine.' I sexily scoop caviare into my mouth with my little finger. 'Why wouldn't I be?'

'I delivered some stuff to yours about a week ago and you disappeared while we was chattin'. I thought I might 'ave frightened you. Innit.'

'Isn't what?' I ask, before the penny drops.

Holy cow.

It's the delicious bakery guy. Quickly, even though he can't see me, I check my reflection in the hall mirror. I look terrible. There's pizza flour all over my nose and my hair is clagged with something that looks a lot like raw egg. Nice.

'Oh, I'm fine,' I say hurriedly, aware that my voice has gone all shaky.

'Then do you feel like dinner tonight to make up? Nuffin' fancy, like.'

Now in my experience, when a guy says 'nothing fancy', he usually means full-on five-course slap-up job, followed by quick bunk up, followed by expert disappearing act. He'll be off faster than you can say 'Mine's the wet patch'. Well, not this time, sunshine, I think, picking a piece of spinach from between my front teeth. *I'll* be the one doing the postcoital buggering off, thank you very much.

'OK.' I manage to sound bored, disguising the fact that my heart is thumping like billyo in my chest. At least this one's *highly* unsuitable. Which means I probably won't have any qualms about dumping him.

'I'll pick you up at seven.'

'No problem.'

I check my watch. It's five thirty already. Jesus. Talk about cutting it fine. Perhaps I'm his second choice. Some glossy-haired bimbette has probably let him down at the last minute. Oh well, her loss, my gain I suppose. I'm not really bothered whether he thinks I'm special or not. In double-quick time I shave my toes, bleach my tache and trim my minky, then spend a good twenty minutes trying on underwear. I pull on my fave plum silk bra and knickers, change them for a black lycra crop top and little fifties-style shorts, change those for a simple white cotton ensemble for understated sexiness, then go straight back to the original plum again. Then, remembering the canapés I made, in true *Blue Peter* fashion, earlier on in the day, which have to be in a maisonette in Saint Reetham (that's Streatham to you and me), by six thirty, I jump into a taxi, drop them off and tell the driver to race back to Islington. By seven o three I've managed a quick shower and I've changed into tight black jeans and a sexy black vest. Not quite suitable for the night of filthy sex I have in mind, but it'll do. I only hope he won't turn up in anything remotely smart. Perhaps I should have warned him beforehand that I find it nigh on impossible to think dirty thoughts about anyone in a two-piece. And if it's a three-piece—waistcoat and all—he can forget it.

Worse still, what if he turns out to be the perfect gentleman? What if he wants to take me on more than one date before flip-

ping me over and shagging me stupid? What the buggery bollocks do I do then?

Still, at least he's not called anything awful like Derek. Or
Nigel. I could never let a Nigel near my bits.

And he'd better bloody well take me somewhere nice. I quite
fancy Thai. Or we could go to George and David's nice Italian. The one with the swarthy waiters, where David—or rather
George on his behalf—proposed.

Wherever it is we're going, he's late.

Bastard late, as it goes.

At eight, the phone rings and I answer it, feeling butterflyish.
OK, so I know I'm not in love with the guy or anything like
that. In fact I couldn't care less one way or the other, but I've
put lipstick on and everything and I'll feel a bit foolish if he
blows me out. But hey ho. I definitely don't love him. In fact
I'm not even that sure I *fancy* him.

So why am I going on this date in the first place?

I suppose there's only one answer to that.

Because I can.

But it's not Nick blowing me out. It's Max. Again.

'What is it now?' I ask him sternly.

'If you're busy tonight...' he ventures.

'I said I was, didn't I?'

'Well, what about tomorrow then?' He hesitates. 'We could
go to the cinema. Or something.'

God. He's making himself look pathetic now. Does the guy
have no pride whatsoever? All this hoo-ha over me. He must
definitely have something wrong with him.

'I'm afraid it'll have to be the "or something",' I say flippantly.
'I'm busy.'

'Some other time then,' he says. 'You see, the thing is...'

'Yes?' I'm impatient now. 'You'll have to be quick, I'm afraid.
I'm due somewhere in ten minutes.'

I'll be blooming lucky. But then he doesn't know that,
does he?

'You see, the thing is,' he goes on, 'I like you.'

'Thank you.'

Well, let's face it. The poor guy's only human.

'I like you a lot.'

'Good for you.'

'And I'd really like you to be my girlfriend.'

'What?'

'I said—'

'It's OK.' I wave my hands around to stop him even though he can't see me. 'I heard.'

'Well then?'

God. What is it with blokes? I've been avoiding his calls for weeks and he still thinks he stands a prozzie's chances in King's Cross of getting another bunk up. Any self-respecting girlie on the receiving end of such call-dodging would have hung up her fuck-me heels for good. She'd have been sat at home, rocking backwards and forwards and blubbering into a vodka bottle every night for the past three weeks.

'Is there no one else you can ask?' I say.

'But I want *you*,' he whines, sounding like a petulant child.

'Well, I'm afraid I'm going to have to rely on a parental cliché in answer to that one,' I tell him firmly, lighting a fag and wincing slightly as sparks from my lighter fly all over the sheepskin on the sofa.

'Sorry?'

'I want doesn't get,' I say, switching off my mobile as the doorbell rings.

I'm relieved to see that Nick, even if he is an hour and a half late, looks most acceptable, in scruffy jeans and sloppy T-shirt. The latter has ridden up ever so slightly to reveal a tantalising glimpse of six-pack. Hmmm.

Hopefully I'll be getting to grips with that later.

'Can I leave me bike in yer hall?'

I bite back surprise. Nipping round on your pushbike is not quite my idea of 'picking someone up for a date'. But it doesn't really matter, does it? I'm not in this for the long term, after all. Anyway, it's quite pleasant, walking from George's house down Upper Street, watching people sitting outside on the pavement, tucking into delicious-looking food. It's still warm outside, and I keep catching wafts of barbecued steak on the wind as we wander past Islington Green and down towards Highbury Corner.

I'm slightly disappointed when Nick finally reveals the setting for our date. But then I pull myself up by my bootstraps and tell myself to cheer up. After all, filthy sex is filthy sex, whatever you get to eat beforehand. And I've always fancied there's something distinctly sensual about eating chips straight from the wrapper, what with all the finger licking and lip smacking that goes on. And then of course there's the pickled egg thing. Nick steams on in there and orders one as though it were the most natural thing in the world. Secretly, I'm delighted. I've always wondered about them, lurking pale and enormous in their glass jars, reminding me of the biology labs at school. But I've never met anyone who's eaten one. And no one I know can ever be persuaded to try. So when Nick asks for his, I order one too.

And I'm not disappointed.

We sit on Highbury Fields, tucking into cod and chips and breathing in the scent of fresh cut grass, watching as the light fades and the kids all pack up their games of football to head home to bed—or to mug old ladies or whatever else they cite as their activity of choice when it starts to get dark. As we eat, it doesn't take long to dawn on me that Nick and I have precious little in common. In fact, it could safely be said that we have precisely bugger all in common. But that just makes the thought of having sex with him all the more exciting. And he *is* gorgeous. All that cycling outside has given him the lean, sun-kissed body of a Greek god.

And those espresso eyes are nothing short of delectable.

I make an attempt at conversation. Something tells me there's no point talking about art or books or interiors. So I try asking him questions about himself as he wodges in a last mouthful of chips and wipes at a dribble of grease on his chiselled jaw.

'It must be so great doing your job,' I blurt. 'Not tied down to a desk all day. Outside, getting all that fresh air.'

'Oxford Street air ain't exactly fresh, innit?' he points out.

'Still, you know what I mean.' I quiver with delight at his turn of phrase. 'Sun on your back and all that.'

'Yeah.' He nods, scrumpling up his fish and chip wrapper and lobbing it over by a patch of trees. I feel slightly self-conscious about a) having jammed mine down way before he was finished and b) responsibly screwing my paper up and popping it into my bag till I find a bin.

'Gets bloody cold in winter though. Goes right through you. Still I don't 'ave to go in at all if I don't want to. It's like being that thing. You know. Wotsit.'

'Wotsit?'

'Hacks do it. And the paparrattzy. Working for yerself and gettin' uvver people to pay you.'

'Freelance?'

God, he's even thicker than I thought. Which is fine by me. At least he's decorative. It's what's inside his trousers, not his head, that interests me.

'Thassit. Pedal Power's a bit like that.'

'So you don't actually work for the bakery then?'

'Nah. S'an agency. And if I don't wanna go in, I work extra next day. And the money ain't bad. Danger money, I s'pose. Fuckin' take yer life into yer own 'ands when you take to them streets on a pushbike.'

I laugh, telling him the last time I rode a bike, I slammed on the wrong brake when a fly went into my eye. I flew over the handlebars like shit off a spade, bruising my chin on the kerb and putting my tooth through my lip into the bargain. It's a funny story now, although of course it wasn't remotely amusing at the time, even though Sam nearly wet himself laughing once he'd made sure I wasn't concussed. But Nick doesn't seem to really be listening. In fact he doesn't seem to want to talk much at all. Instead, he starts rubbing rather urgently at my leg, very much in the manner of a teenager on a first date. This is all a bit quick, even for me, so I still find the need to gabble like a goose.

'What about when you start work?' I ask, even though I really couldn't care less. 'Do you have to turn up at an office to begin with or what?'

'Nah.' Nick lets go of my thigh for a second, pushes a matted lump of hair behind his ear, puts his can of Stella to his pouty lips and shrugs. 'I just radio control with me call sign when I'm ready to start. You know.' He puts an imaginary radio to his mouth and crackles, '"One six, one six. I've 'ad me flakes and I'm ready to go." That sorter thing. Then they tell me where my first pick-up is.'

OK, so it's not as glamorous as being a celebrity PA or working in TV, but having such freedom is great. Which is why I just have to cross my fingers and hope Neat Eats works out. I'm already, I realise, enjoying working for myself immensely. It's so much better than having to sit in an office being nice to people I'd never so much as share air with in a lift if I had the choice, and having to pretend I never say the 'C' word or fart.

'It ain't bad,' Nick says. 'Me dad wanted me to join 'im in the trade.'

'In the City?'

'Nah. Buildin' trade. They was both really young when they met, me mum and dad. Dead wild. But he buckled down and set up a buildin' business. Made a fuckin' mint.'

'Good for him.' I swig at my own can of Stella and cringe as I realise how ridiculously 'jolly hockey sticks' I sound.

'Yeah.' He shrugs. ''E's still really pissed off I couldn't do it.'

'You didn't want to?' I pat his arm as it traces another route up my thigh. After all, I don't want him to think I'm respectable. He might stop. And that would never do.

'Nah,' he says. 'I did wanner. I 'ad a bloody good go attit, as it goes. But, like I say, I just couldn't seem to get it. The first wall I done collapsed.'

'Oh dear.'

'Onto a coupla teenagers.'

'Shit.'

'Yeah. They got out all right, but me 'eart weren't in it after that.'

'I see.' I lean against him for a second. He looks so sweet when he frowns. Like a little lost child. 'Were you very upset?' I lean on him some more, just to get the ball rolling, and he turns quickly away.

'Sorry.' I feel foolish.

'S'orwight. You was kind of squashing me though.'

God. Great big lummox crushes sylph boy to death on common. I can just see the headline.

But I needn't have worried. As I move quickly away, Nick pulls me back towards him, turning his face to mine and putting his first two fingers under my chin, tilting my face towards his until his gorgeous, sultry, pouty lips are about half an inch away from mine. And now, I decide, I really, *really* fancy him. And, as his lips brush mine, a tingle of electricity shoots down my spine and the tops of my bum cheeks fizz in anticipation.

'There's something else I gotta tell ya,' he says, his tongue slowly teasing its way along my bottom lip until I think I might actually be going to *scream* with lust.

'What?' I almost snap. At this precise moment, he could tell me he's the love child of Fred West and Myra Hindley and I really wouldn't give a flying fuck. The only information I require at the moment is re the size of his...

Unless, of course, what he's going to tell me is that he hasn't *got* one. Which *would* be a bit of a setback, I have to admit.

Other than that, he could tell me anything he wants and I'd still happily grab the back of his head, pull his face onto mine and snog the life out of him.

'You're not gay, are you?'

'Oh no.' He squeezes the top of my thigh. 'It's just...my name's not really Nick.'

Oh God. He really *is* the love child of Fred West.

'You're not the Mardi Gras bomber, are you?' I joke lamely.

'It's Dudley.'

'Dudley?' I can't help giggling. 'Isn't that in the West Midlands?'

'S'after Dudley Moore. I was conceived in the back of a cinema,' he explains, his breath coming in shallow gasps as I run my finger up the back of his neck. 'Me parents went to see *Arthur*.'

'Oh.'

'You don't wanna snog me now, do you?'

'On the contrary.' I grin, grabbing a handful of his hair and lowering his mouth onto mine. The fact that we're doing this outside makes me feel totally wanton and vampish. And, as kissers go, Nick—or Dudley—is a pretty good one. I can't exactly run my fingers lustfully and dreamily through his hair, like he's doing to mine, because it's all matted. But I do clasp my hands round his neck and go at it hell for leather until he finally pulls away.

'Can't breathe.'

'Sorry.'

We jump into a taxi back to his, snogging like teenagers on the back seat as the driver stares at the road and pretends not to notice. 'You're fuckin' beautiful,' Nick tells me. 'I mean, I know I dropped an E and that before I come out...'

'You did?' That would account for the frantic thigh touching then. Perhaps he doesn't fancy me as much as I thought. Bloody great. I could be just anyone. In fact he probably only called me in the first place because he was feeling all touchy-feely.

'Yeah. But you are bloody lovely.'

Oh sod it. He's male, isn't he? And he's here.

'You are weird-lookin' mind,' he adds.

'I am?' I catch sight of the driver's expression in the mirror. His lips are wobbling at the corners, as though he's trying not to laugh.

'But fuckin' lovely.' Nick/Dudley finishes his monologue. 'Like that Karen Elson.'

'Who?'

'Tall ginger supermodel. Looks kinda other worldly.'

'*Thanks.*'

'A total space babe. You remind me of 'er.'

I'm still confused as to whether or not this is a compliment when the taxi draws to a halt outside a tall town house in Notting Hill. After forking out six pounds twenty for our fish, chips and Stella, Nick hasn't got any money left so, telling myself I don't really mind, I get out my glittery purse and pay the driver while Nick goes to unlock the door.

As the taxi speeds away from the kerb, I take a step back and look at the house. It's enormous. Presumably, a guy like him doesn't live in the whole pile. I expect I'll get inside to discover that he's dragged me to some grotty bedsit with a fan heater and cold spaghetti hoops burnt onto the stove. And he'll have a bed that's supposed to turn into a sofa during the day but which, like a typical bloke, he won't have bothered to fold away, so it'll still be covered with a rucked-up sheet—just why *is* it that single blokes always have navy or bottle green sheets that so readily show up bodily fluids?—and a duvet with no cover.

I couldn't have been more wrong. Nick lives in the whole house. Which is as immense as I thought. And it's beautifully decorated. The hall alone is the size of my old Balham flat. The floor is carpeted in silky buttermilk and every room is stuffed full of objects that look as though they've been lovingly collected over years of travelling. Indian rugs and saris are draped in a stunning jewel-pink sitting room just off the kitchen. African wood carvings fill the study. In the downstairs loo are several large Chinese papier-mâché heads and a Nepalese prayer flag. And there are photos in silver frames everywhere. A couple I assume to be his parents. And several endearing kids, one of which has to be him. Licking an ice lolly, petting sheep at the children's zoo, riding a tractor. In all of them, he's got the same coffee-coloured eyes and cheeky, lopsided grin.

'Ahh.' I pick up one of him on a beach. He must be about seven in this one. His smile is all gappy and he's sat on a fat, black donkey, eating an ice cream with a flake stuck in the top. 'Little Dudley at the seaside.'

'Stop it,' he begs, laughing and grabbing me by the wrist. 'Come upstairs. There ain't no embarrassin' piccies up there.'

'Now hold one just one minute.' I spin round, catching him unawares as I slap the photo back on the silver leaf fireplace. 'What do you think I am? Some easy lay?'

Nick/Dudley looks horrified.

'I'm sorry,' he stutters. 'I didn't mean. We don't 'ave to...you know. I just fort...'

'I'm joking, you daft sod.' I giggle, pulling him in the direction of the stairs and allowing him to lead me up them. 'In fact I thought you'd never bloody ask.'

This is *excellent*. OK, so we have nothing in common, apart from drinking and shagging, but we don't have to talk, do we? Anyway, he's gagging for it and I'm stone cold sober. I'm going to have a completely meaningless shag and I'm not even shiftfaced.

I don't even feel guilty.

Nick's bedroom is as stunning as the rest of the house. A huge French sleigh bed dominates the middle of the room. Crisp, white sheets, covered with a soft grape-coloured throw. Not very bachelor-like. Something's not really right here. I can't help hearing the faintest ding-a-ling of alarm bells somewhere at the back of my mind. He's a *bike courier*, for flip's sake. And not a very bright one at that. You'd expect someone like him to live in a right bugger's muddle. Not this vast showpiece.

I think back to when the taxi drew up outside. He *did* have a key, didn't he?

I mean we haven't just broken into a total stranger's home... Have we?

Buggery fuck. I've had an entirely different sort of break and enter situation in mind all evening.

I decide to test him.

'Where's the bathroom?'

He jerks his head towards a door which opens straight off the bedroom. Of course. An en-suite. Well, that doesn't mean he lives here. Anyone—well, anyone apart from me, obviously— might reasonably have expected a house like this to have such a luxury. And this bathroom is luxurious. Everything is polished, expensive and has something of the feminine touch about it. Bottles of Ralph Lauren Romance products line the sink. There's even a tube of Immac in the bathroom cabinet. This last, of course, can mean one of only two things.

Hairy Back.

Or Live-In Girlfriend.

I sincerely hope it's the latter.

Nick insists on showering before coming to bed, thus allay- ing any fears I might have had personal hygiene-wise. I notice he doesn't use the en-suite. Which is weird. As if from habit, he goes into another bathroom just off the landing. Which seems really odd. When he comes back, scrubbed clean and smelling, not of expensive French cologne, as you'd have ex- pected of the owner of this stylish palace, but of Pine Fresh Flash—or perhaps it's Toilet Duck—I'm relieved to notice his back is rug-free.

It must be Live-In Girlfriend then. Unless the Immac has worked wonders. After all, this is the house of one, or even two, very wealthy professionals. Nick can't possibly live here by him- self. He's quite clearly a Kept Man. This is very obviously a case of Absent Girlfriend Syndrome.

Well, I certainly don't have a problem with that. In fact, if I'm brutally honest, it only adds to the thrill. I'm about to have sex in a strange girl's bed. Hope she doesn't mind me rumpling her sheets, I think, giggling as Nick undoes the zip on my jeans, pulls off my vest in one swift movement and pushes me down on the bed, covering me with kisses and running his hands under my buttocks. His movements are urgent, almost like those of a teenager having sex for the first time. Which makes me laugh. I wonder if he's like this with his girlfriend, the rich cow.

Still, the fact that he has a girlfriend already certainly makes life a lot easier for me. It reduces any chances of him wanting a repeat performance to virtually zero. So the chances of him phone-stalking me like that bloody drip Max are also pretty much nil.

I've only gone and done it.

I've achieved the perfect String-Free Shag. I'll be able to creep off before he wakes up and he won't even care. He'll probably be pleased, because it'll give him time to wash, dry and replace the sheets in time to avoid suspicion.

In the event, we don't actually go to sleep because Nick (well, it's a lot sexier than 'Dudley' isn't it?) seems to be able to go like a train all night. We do it five times, to be exact. And, at seven o'clock, as he treats me to a third helping of Croissants for Breakfast, I decide it might be harder than I thought to sneak out because he's still up for more and I don't actually think I'm going to be able to walk, when a car pulls up outside and Nick jumps as though he's been shot in the gonads.

'Shhhhh.'

Bugger. Not his girlfriend already? And just when I was about to have the kind of orgasm that makes your ears ring too. How selfish can you get? Resignedly—even though I'm shitting myself at the thought of a showdown—I take out both earrings. There's nothing less attractive than an earlobe torn in two and I'd better prepare for the worst.

Seconds later, the inevitable key rattles in the door and Nick is racing round the room like a headless chicken, still with an erection you could hang a coat on, but picking up my knickers, jeans and vest and chucking them all at me.

'Quick,' he yelps, wincing in agony as he catches the end of his willy on the open wardrobe door. I silently convulse with laughter. His girlfriend might have put the kibosh on my chances of one last orgasm but she can damn well forget any thoughts she might have had on the subject of Hide the Sausage for a while yet. Nick's dick will be more like a black pudding by teatime.

'Quick,' he hisses again. 'Go and hide in my bedroom.'

Pardon me?

'*Your* bedroom?' I gulp. 'But isn't this...?'

Without explanation, he opens the bedroom door, shoves me—still completely starkers, mind—across the landing and into a single bedroom, plastered with *Baywatch*, Jordan and Man. United posters. Slamming the door behind us, he breathes a sigh of relief as, dazed, confused, and ever so slightly pee'd off, I sink onto a Star Trek Next Generation duvet and await further instructions, torn between feeling annoyed and wishing he'd damn well stick his head between my legs and stay there until I'm done.

'In the wardrobe,' he hisses quickly as we hear the pad of footsteps on the stairs and a woman's voice calls his name.

I crunch up like a dead spider, cursing him as a baseball glove digs into my bare bum. I'm busting for a wee and I have no idea how long I'm expected to stay here. After what seems like half an hour, I dare to emerge. The room is empty so, with the idea of having a quick widdle before looking for my clothes and making a dash for it, I tiptoe across to the door and open it.

The coast is clear. I can go for a wazz in complete safety. But hang on a mo. This is an old house. The floorboards are pretty creaky up here. One false step and I'm a prime candidate for a bitch slap across the chops and no mistake. And I'm not much of a fighter. In fact, when it comes to violence, I'm a bit of a weed. I make a split second evaluation of the situation. And, in a flash of pure genius, I know exactly what to do.

I roll.

Yep, you got it. I lie down on the floor and I roll like a suet pudding towards the bathroom. And I'm almost there when my right boob hits something.

A polished court shoe.

And in the court shoe is a foot.

Shit.

Ever so slowly, I roll onto my back, open my eyes and look, cold with dread, into the twinkling eyes of a middle-aged woman, who has just been rummaging in the airing cupboard.

'Hello, duck.' She smiles, apparently unfazed by the fact that I'm completely starkers. 'You must be a bit chilly.'

'Erm. A bit,' I admit.

'Put these on,' she says helpfully, chucking me a horrid floral blouse and a pair of what can only be described as slacks. And beige slacks to boot. I have no idea who this woman is but, if she lives here, her taste in clothes is nothing like her taste in interior decor. Reluctantly I stand up, pulling on the blouse to cover my boobs and hastily stepping into the nasty slacks. 'That's better.' The woman smiles brightly. 'And you are?'

'Katie,' I say, stupidly holding out my hand in introduction. 'Katie Simpson.'

'God, why don't you give her your full address and phone number as well, you ludicrous bat?' a voice inside my head mocks, as I take in the full idiocy of the situation.

'Mrs Black,' says the woman, shaking my hand in return.

'Hi.'

Well, I'm still none the bloody wiser, am I? Who is this? The cleaner? And if so, is she a nice cleaner? Is she likely to tell Nick's girlfriend that her bloke is a lying, cheating, adulterous bastard? Or have we got away with it?

'I'm Dudley's mum,' says the woman helpfully, spotting my confusion.

I gape like a goldfish. His *mum*?

'Now, duck, you must be hungry. Come downstairs. There's plenty of fresh coffee and I can put some more bacon under if you'd fancy it.'

And without another word she bustles me downstairs and into the kitchen where Nick—sorry, Dudley—a little girl of about twelve and a burly middle-aged geezer in overalls are all having breakfast.

I stare at the manky turquoise polish on my tootsies. This is truly excruciating.

'Well, come in, duck,' booms the man in the overalls, who is obviously Nick's dad. 'Let's 'ave a look at yer.'

I step inside, feeling ridiculous in my mumsy outfit. The whole ensemble would be bad enough in itself, but unfortunately I'm so damn lanky that the slacks barely reach mid-calf.

'Well, she's a girl all right, in't she, Ma?' He laughs, scooping up egg yolk and brown sauce with a hunk of white sliced. 'You know, love, 'e's 'ad us right worried. Thought 'e was a poofter, we did. 'E's never 'ad a girl back 'ere as long as we can re-member, 'as 'e, Ma?'

'Nope.' Nick's mum shakes her head. 'Eighteen 'e is now and not a single girlfriend to speak of.'

Pardon me?

Eighteen?

God. That practically makes me a pervert. A flipping kiddie fiddler.

I tussle with my conscience all the way home on the tube. After I'd rammed down my bacon and fled, Nick followed me to the door, an anxious expression on his face. And it was suddenly ob-vious how much younger he was. God, I can be dappy at times.

'Can I see you again?'

Oh God. Not the lovesick pup act.

'Fuck off,' said my head.

'OK,' said my treacherous, humungously large gob. 'Call me. Anytime.'

Now I'm actually on my way home, I curse myself for my complete inability to pull off a successful one-night stand.

Mind you, just because I've *said* he can call me, doesn't mean he's actually going to bother, does it? That's blokes for you.

Completely unreliable. After all, isn't that the whole point of my not wanting one?

I'm a bundled up bunch of frustration all the way home. The Croissantus Interruptus I experienced earlier means I feel all unfulfilled and weird. I try leaning against the metal pole in the middle of the carriage, remembering the time Janice gleefully informed me she got a surprise orgasm from the vibrations.

Nothing.

Not a sausage.

And people are staring at me, wondering why the hell I'm standing up when the train is half empty. I shrug and make my way to a seat. Perhaps Janice was on a different line when it happened to her.

Anyway, it's nothing a couple of Jaffa Cakes and a minute or two with the shower head won't sort out the minute I get home.

When I eventually shuffle through the front gate, I'm surprised to see a figure hunched on George and David's front steps. I'm not quite sure who it is, but from the way George is standing at the top window, peering over the scarlet geraniums in their window box and chucking the odd missile, I assume it's someone who isn't very popular.

And then I recognise the T-shirt he's wearing.

It's one of mine.

Which, I might add, I wouldn't have minded getting back.

Yep. You've guessed it.

It's only bloody Jake.

'What do you want?'

My insides are doing back flips faster than an Olympic gymnast and my heart is using my tongue as a trampoline but I dodge the cherry tomato George lobs down at him and manage to appear cool as a cucumber.

Until Jake stands up, that is, and I realise he's still as tall and handsome as ever. That unruly dark hair is so sexy it takes my breath away and I involuntarily take a step backwards, losing my footing as I do so and ending up straight on my arse.

Nice one, Katie. Real slick.

'How did you find me?'

'Your mum told me where you were.'

'She did?'

What the bloody hell is *she* playing at? Mind you, she always did have a bit of a thing for Jake. He was such a smarmball whenever she was around, she never could quite understand why I 'dropped' him, as she put it. Of course I was too ashamed to fill her in on all the extra details, like my catching him with old Fishpants Fraser, so she didn't really get the gist of it at all. She's probably at home right now, gleefully planning all manner of savoury vol-au-vents for our forthcoming nuptials.

George is still at the upstairs window, torn between trying not to piss himself laughing at my slapstick fall and looking absolutely horrified that I might actually be about to let Jake into his house.

Which, of course, I am. I mean I'm not stupid. I know I really shouldn't forgive him. But I would quite like to hear what he's got to say. And, I have to admit, there's a tiny part of me that's hoping he's going to admit he made a mistake.

Of course if he does, I have no idea what I'll do, but let's just see, shall we?

I smile nervously at him and rummage for my key. As I do so, a sort of whooping scream comes from the upstairs window.

'What are you doing, you ridiculous hag?'

'Fuck off, George,' I tell him shortly. 'I'll deal with this.'

And the truth is, I just can't resist Jake. His twinkling green eyes are as mischievous as ever. To be honest, it would have been quite a coup if he'd lost some of his sparkle. If his emerald eyes had turned sludge green with the stress of losing me and then having to cope with a slutbucket girlfriend and her devil spawn. I mean, there's nothing nicer than bumping into someone who's dumped you and realising that you've come off better, is there?

I let him in. Smile at him as he smiles at me. Motion for him to take a seat in George's immaculate white sitting room. Once he's sat down, I realise I don't have a clue what to do next, so I check my reflection in the Venetian glass mirror above the fireplace and am horrified to notice I look like a panda on smack. Great dark circles of eyeliner have slurred their way halfway down my cheeks and I look dreadful. My Damart-type outfit definitely isn't helping. I might have thought to get my own clothes back before making a beeline for the exit.

Graham, fat ginger traitor that he is, jumps onto Jake's knee, purring like an engine. Bugger. He shouldn't be in here either. George will have a pink fit if he sees him.

'Oh, Katie,' Jake sighs, stroking between Graham's ears so gently that I start wishing it was me on his lap and not the cat at all. 'Isn't life strange?'

'What do you mean?'

'I just feel...'

'Yes?'

'I mean, don't get me wrong...'

'Go on.'

'I feel as though I've made a terrible mistake,' he finishes eventually.

'Oh.'

Is that re shagging Fishpants or losing me? I wonder.

'I mean having a baby isn't all it's cracked up to be,' he says. George, coming down the stairs, catches the tail end of the conversation.

'I'll take it if you like. How much do you want for it?' he asks bluntly. 'Unless it has 666 stamped across its forehead, of course.'

'I'm sorry?'

'I can probably take the thing off your hands. Depending on facial features, of course. It's not a fat one, is it?'

'She's fine,' Jake says. 'She's beautiful, in fact. And she's not that much trouble. I—I mean we certainly don't want to sell her.'

'Oh.' George looks disappointed. 'OK. Well, if you change your mind, you know where we are. Bye, darling.' He kisses me on both cheeks, whispering as he does so, 'Don't do anything silly, darling. I don't want the place reeking of muff when I come back.'

'Where are you going?' I run after him in a panic, suddenly not sure that I want to be left on my own with Jake.

'Dinner with Mother. And get that ball of ginger fluff out of my drawing room before I get back.'

'Can I come?'

'No.' George laughs. 'You can sodding well stay here and sort out that fucking infidel. Make sure he's gone by the time I get home. And don't worry. I won't forget your toffee.'

I laugh. Good old George's mum was knocking forty by the time her only son was born. Four years later, George's dad died. She's been on her own ever since, as George is always at pains to point out whenever I try to get him to talk to her about his gayness. You see, George, despite the frantic clubbing and cottaging of his Life Before David, has always been a dutiful son, dashing down to visit her in her tiny cottage in Kent whenever he can. Quite often, he's dragged me down there with him. And his mum, bless her, never lets us leave without some sugary treat. A Penguin biscuit, perhaps, or a Creamline toffee. Personally, I wouldn't mind betting that she's perfectly well aware of the situation re his sexuality and just doesn't give two hoots. I wouldn't be at all surprised if her questioning about his pseudo single state was merely a wind-up. She's a wise old bird, is George's mum. There's not much she doesn't know. I'm just hoping one of them decides to get it out into the open before it's too late. It would be a shame if she never got to know how happy George is with David.

'Actually,' Jake says when George has slammed the door behind him, 'Tallulah's the reason I'm here.'

'Tallulah?' I ask him. 'Who the hell's Tallulah?'

'The baby.'

'Oh, of course, sorry.'

'You did the food for the wedding of some friends of mine. In Hampton Court.'

'The ones with the swimming pool, where everyone ended up pissed off their tits?'

'Marina and Giles, yes.'

'They can't be very good friends if they didn't invite you,' I crack, quick as a whip.

'They did actually.' He smiles. 'We couldn't get a babysitter.'

'Well, if you're thinking of asking me, don't bother,' I tell him shortly. 'I really don't think I owe you any favours. And I don't do shit-caked nappies.'

'No, silly.' He grins, and I'm reminded of how he used to be with me when we met. He used to smile at me indulgently all the time. And even though I knew it was ever so slightly patronising, it made me feel wanted. Janice and Sam used to say he was trying to make me look stupid but I didn't care.

I was in *love*, for God's sake.

'I wondered if you'd do her christening,' he finishes, smiling as though he's just done me a great big favour. He's got a bloody cheek, to be honest. If he really thinks I'm going to run around serving cucumber butties to all his friends (who, incidentally, used to be *our* friends), he's got another think coming.

But hang on a sec. Jake, after all, is absolutely brilliant at networking. He knows *loads* of cool people.

'What sort of thing did you have in mind?' I ask him.

Business is business, after all. And as long as I don't shag him, what harm can it do?

Chapter 17

'So does this mean we can have casual sex on a regular basis?' Jake wipes his willy on my duvet cover and shrugs his faded 501s over his neat little bum.

OK, OK, so I should be feeling pretty stupid right now. And soiled. And probably a tiny bit used. And George is due back any minute, and if he catches Jake still here he's going to go mad.

And I suppose it was a bit cruel, letting Jake go down on me so soon after shagging Nick. But then I didn't know how things were going to work out, did I? And I was feeling all frustrated.

Of course, you could probably say I'm a bit dim for jumping into bed with Jake, just because he ladled it on thick about how since the baby arrived they haven't had sex once. Fishpants is too busy calling for posset cloths or doing pelvic floor exercises to pay much attention to him. Apparently, she's afraid that if she doesn't keep doing the exercises, her bottom might actually fall out into her leggings as she whips round Somerfield.

The sight of her with her legs in stirrups and her nether regions doing a pretty good impression of a car crash hadn't done much for his libido either, he said, stroking my cheek and saying how much he'd missed me. Not as far as she was concerned, anyway.

I lapped it all up like a puppy.

In fact, I was enjoying the attention so much I forgot to be caustic and say I never understood what on earth a sexy, intelligent man like Jake saw in a woman who has the class of your average pound shop. The fact that he's finally seen sense is enough for me.

I'm delighted.

In fact, I'm more than delighted. Suddenly, I realise that I actually wouldn't mind having Jake back in my life. Not seriously, of course. I'm not a complete idiot. I know I could never trust him again. But what if I take his offer of frequent casual sex seriously? Would it *really* do any harm?

After all, I won't be adding any notches to my bedpost. I've already been there, seen that, bought the T-shirt. And, in the very unlikely event that I *do* suddenly start to fall in love with him all over again, I won't be able to do anything about it. I certainly won't be able to dream of marriage.

Because I'll already *be* married. To David.

And, of course, there's the Revenge Factor. While Fishpants is at home, mopping up baby sick and mashing up Weetabix, Jake and I will be having sordid, extramarital sex behind her back. OK, so I can't avoid a slight twinge of guilt. There's a baby involved here, after all. And it really isn't the poor beggar's fault its parents are so horribly dysfunctional. But then I tell myself I'm not really risking little Tallulah's happiness in the slightest. After all, I certainly don't want Jake to leave Fishpants and take up with me. She need never know that Daddy's a philanderer.

So I conveniently gloss over the memory of sex with Jake pre-split. I forget that, most of the time, the sex was actually so dull I had to ask to go on my front so I didn't miss *Holby City*. Because having sex with Jake just now felt so natural, so comfortably familiar, that I suddenly realise, with a stab of nostalgia, that this is what I want. To be with him again, no matter how infrequently. I want to feel safe.

I've missed him.

Over the next few weeks we meet on Saturdays, mainly. George and David usually go clubbing on Saturdays. And it's easy for Jake to get away. It's not so easy, however, for me to lie to Nick/Dudley who, against all the odds, has proved himself to be bum-numbingly reliable. Which is a bit of a shame. He really *did* have bastard potential. Finding out someone so utterly unsuitable is completely in love with me is rather like getting a really tasteful Valentine card and then discovering it's from Mum.

Still, I decide that it's probably just as well to keep him on side. After all, it's one in the eye for Jake. It's nice to feel I'm sort of cheating on him, just as he cheated on me. Even if he doesn't know about it yet. Janice would understand. Except I can't talk to her about it because she's gone off on a Rich Bitch weekend in Ipswich without even telling me. I have to hear all about it from George.

'*Are* there any rich bitches in Ipswich?' I ask him doubtfully, as we sit in his kitchen (I still can't quite think of it as my home too) eating raspberry yoghurt with dollops of honey.

'Well, that's what I wondered,' he says. 'They must bus them in specially.'

'And what happens, precisely, on this rich bitch wotsit?'

'It's run by vapid, cocksucking whores with gold-digging habits,' he assures me. 'They tell you exactly how to dress and behave in order to bag a rich man. They tell you how to get out of cars at premieres without showing your pants. You know the sort of thing. And if you talk like Bianca from *EastEnders*, they teach you to either learn to talk posh or keep your mouth shut. She's learning to be a proper lady so Jasper will marry her.'

'Why didn't she say she was going?' I whinge.

'She did.' George licks the back of his spoon. 'She just couldn't tell you because you're too busy. And she's still upset about you making up that story about Jasper and some other woman.'

'But I *did* see him with another woman,' I insist.

'But *I* didn't,' he says. 'And I think it's better to stay out of it really, darling. Don't you?'

'Oh.'

I suppose I *have* been rather busy lately, what with Neat Eats doing so well. Word of mouth, it seems, spreads like wildfire and I'm getting bookings for parties up and down the country now.

Tallulah's christening, for which I provide a huge T-shaped cake, covered in palest pink icing and tiny fresh blueberries, goes like a dream. Jake and I even manage a guilty bunk up in the bathroom when nobody's looking. Well, *I* feel guilty. I don't think he's even aware that he's doing anything wrong. And then I can never see my friends on Saturday nights because I'm usually seeing Jake. Apparently, it's much easier for him to sneak out then because Saturday night is always a good night for engineering an argument. All Fishpants wants to do then is spend quality time together when the baby's in bed. This evidently involves watching shit TV together and eating takeaways. 'As if she can afford to eat takeaways,' he grumbles one night. 'She's the size of the bloody Hindenberg as it is.'

Even *I* have to feel a bit sorry for her when I hear poor old Fishpants being denied a decent calorie intake.

Apparently, on a normal Saturday, the eating of the takeaway is followed by the implementation of a cunning device that, Jake assures me, is typical of 'all blokes'. He lets Fishpants choose the video, then sits down to watch it. And then he waits. And waits. Until she demands the remote control to herself for a change. Or talks over an important bit of the film. And then he storms out and comes round to mine. Where *we* watch shit TV together and eat takeaways. And then have sex.

It's as easy-peasy as that.

The sly fox.

Still, Fishpants made her bed (nasty frilly sheets and a horrid valance, no doubt), when the pair of them played hide the salami behind my back, so she can sodding well lie in it as far as I'm concerned. After all, it's hardly my fault if Jake seems to be labouring under the impression that monogamy is a low-fat spread, is it?

Nick, of course, is a different kettle of fish altogether. And the more I see him, the more I realise we really do have nothing in common at all. He was born in the eighties, for God's sake. To him, a Snickers has always been a Snickers. A Texan is someone who comes from a particular part of America. 'Watch Out, There's a Humphrey About' means nothing to him at all. He was about four when Culture Club belted out 'Karma Chameleon'. He never spent his holidays giggling as Irish children made 'fillums' on *Why Don't Yew*? And he's never eaten Pacers, Spangles or Star Bars in his life.

Still, with no common reference points, I don't really have to bother talking to him at all. We can get straight down to the sex. Which, I might add, can get pretty exciting. Sex with Nick is very much of the sordid, shag-me-up-a-back-alley variety. He loves doing it outside, which means we spend little time in bed and lots behind skips, on park benches and in other people's back gardens. Still, it keeps things interesting, or so I tell myself with a sigh one evening, as the back door of a pebbledashed semi opens and a fat woman in a peach candlewick dressing gown screams abuse in our general direction, before hurling a bucket of cold water over us.

Now though, as George tells me bluntly that even Janice, Mrs Muff Before Mates herself, feels I have no time for her any more, I feel suddenly depressed. I remember that I haven't even bothered to make up with Sam after the row we had about my moving into George's. And it suddenly becomes clear to me that, whatever might or might not have been said in the heat of the moment, Sam and Janice are my best friends. And I can't afford to lose them. Besides, in the back of my mind I've known all along that I've got something very, very important I need to ask Sam. So, feeling ridiculously nervous, I call him to apologise. And then I ask him if I can take him out for dinner tonight to make up.

'Course you can, Simpson.' I can hear Sam's grin down the phone and I love him for it. 'Always happy to take your money.'

'I'll be round at eight,' I tell him, feeling relieved.

It's one of those beautiful, balmy June evenings. The pavements around every pub I walk past on my way to Angel tube are thronging with girls in short, flippy dresses drinking vodka and clean-cut city blokes oozing the scent of lemony aftershave and freshly laundered shirt. The air is thick with the smell of sexual promise and, as I emerge from the tube and wander up to Sam's house, newly painted and with every windowsill over-spilling with glorious purple and orange pansies, I realise I'm really, really nervous and I don't know why. Surely it can't be because I fancy Sam, of all people. Besides, even if I did, I've got quite enough on my plate with Jake and Nick. I really haven't got the time to rack up a third.

Nevertheless, when Pussy answers the door, flicking around a lot of glossy blonde hair and shrugging a delicate lilac cardie over her sticky-outty collarbones, I can't help feeling more than a tad annoyed.

'Oh,' I say involuntarily as she narrows her eyes at me.

'We're almost ready,' she says, with lots of emphasis on the 'we'. She's definitely hostile. But the minute she hears Sam's footsteps behind her, she flips expertly from arch mother cat to fluffy Persian kitten. In fact, she reminds me so much of a cat, I keep expecting her to bend over and start licking her bum.

Sam bounces up behind her, pulling his favourite scruffy tan suede jacket over his shoulders. 'Simpson, you ol' slapper.' He grins, looking really pleased to see me after all this time. 'It's great to see you.'

'You too.' I smile back, enjoying the sour look on Pussy's face as he gives me a huge smacker on either cheek.

'I've got vodka,' he says. 'We can make cosmopolitans before we go.'

Pussy and I sit in silence as he lopes into the kitchen to mix the drinks. The moment he's out of earshot, she turns to me.

'Are you actually going to *wear* that?'

I look down at my blue shirt dress in surprise.

'Yes,' I say. 'What else would I be wearing?'

'Nothing.' She looks at me benignly. 'I just thought...'

'Thought what?'

'Well,' she says, 'I mean it's like your mum said, isn't it?'

'You've met my mother?' I say in surprise. 'When?'

'Lots of times,' she says, innocently. 'When we visit Sam's dad she's usually there. She despairs of you getting yourself a man, you know. We've discussed it in full.'

I suddenly have a vague recollection of Mum mentioning something about lovely manners. I bet the snide little cow's been stirring all shades of shit round that dinner table.

'Not that she'd say it to you, of course.'

'I know.'

I think I know my own mother better than she does actually.

'But it's just like she says, isn't it?' Pussy picks at a stray bit of fluff on her girlie cardie and looks at me innocently with her big blue eyes. 'I mean, if you will loaf around wearing baggy clothes and great big clodhopping shoes, no bloke within a mile is going to fancy you. I mean, she was almost in tears because she thought you'd never wear anything feminine or get married. I can tell you, Sam and I had trouble keeping our mouths shut about your wedding. It seems such a shame she won't be there to see you get married. So selfish of you.'

'*What?*'

But before the nasty cow can say anything else, Sam breezes back into the room with our cocktails. Pussy's expression changes, as if at the flick of a switch, from bitch to blameless bimbo as he comes in, and all I can do is sit there seething. And it's not only because, even in skintight white trousers, she's managed to overcome the curse of VPL. It's because I know what a manipulative little bitch she is. She's managed to make me feel uncomfortable about my outfit in two seconds flat. And she's made me worry for my mum. Sam, obviously is none the wiser. He has absolutely no idea. He can't help it, of course; it's partly because, being a bloke, he has the handicap of only having a penis to think through. But she's pulled the wool over his eyes good and proper. She's all sweetness and light now he's in the room. Only I, with my feminine intuition, can tell that every time she turns to me, pretending to be interested in what I'm saying, her 'barely there' tinted moisturiser is cracking under the strain.

How the hell am I going to ask him what I've got to ask him with her in my way?

'We should go, Sam.' I look at my watch. 'The table's booked for nine and it's ten to now.'

'Kay.' Sam stands up and grabs his jacket.

We both look at Pussy. It's time for her to do the decent thing and butt out.

'Great.' She stands up, pulling her cardigan round her shoulders as if to protect herself from my glare. 'Where're we going? Somewhere you can eat your body weight in fattening food, eh, Katie?' She slaps me on the shoulder a little too hard. 'Sam's told me what a great big foodie you are, you fat bloater.'

Sam laughs, unaware of how spitefully she intends this. I, however, can see straight through her. She's as transparent as gin and tonic. And if he's surprised at her inviting herself along to dinner, he's too much of a gentleman to show it. I, on the other hand, am spitting fire. If I'd wanted her to come, I'd bloody well have invited her, wouldn't I? And now I'm going to have to pay for both of them. I can't be seen to be a complete skinflint.

Especially not by her.

Still, at least my money situation has improved somewhat,

what with the round of weddings and christenings I've been doing of late. I'm almost in the black again, thank goodness.

But it doesn't stop me feeling the need to get my own back.

'Can I just use the bathroom quickly before we go?' I ask Sam.

'Go ahead.'

You can learn a lot about people from their bathrooms. Locking the door behind me, I have a quick wazz before rootling through Pussy's stuff. I might have known she'd already have tried to wangle her way into his flat. And there's evidence of her everywhere.

Two toothbrushes. One black, and one made of transparent plastic, with lots of tiny pink lovehearts floating around inside the handle. And the toothbrush isn't the only sign of Pussy's gradual takeover of Sam's house. Bottles of expensive shampoo and conditioner, Trésor perfume, 2000 calorie mascara—frankly I'm surprised she hasn't chucked this one out on the pretext that it'll make her eyelashes look fat—and lipstick line the shelf above the basin. And the cupboard above the loo is stuffed full of Tampax, Immac and girlie pink razors. Quick as a flash, before I really have time to think about the consequences, I grab the Immac and squeeze a huge dollop into her conditioner. Then, spinning on my heel and refusing to feel guilty, I unlock the door and trip lightly down the stairs.

'Sorry,' I tell them. 'I was busting. Shall we go?'

Pussy manages half a venison sausage before putting her knife and fork down with a clatter and declaring herself 'full to bursting'. 'Ew,' she says, patting her concave stomach. 'That filled me right up. I suppose that would just have been a tiny snack for you, Katie.'

Sam laughs indulgently at both of us, totally unaware that she means to make me feel small. I beam back at her.

'May all your children have webbed feet.' And port wine stains over their entire heads, I almost add. But, worried that might be taking it a bit far in front of Sam, I keep my trap shut.

'Katie,' Sam says, shocked. 'Pussy was only joking, weren't you, Pussy?'

'Of course.' She smiles sweetly, eyeing me over the top of his head as he ruffles her hair. 'I'm just feeling terribly full up.'

'Well, mind you don't choke on a fur ball.'

'Pussy's only got a tiny little appetite,' Sam fawns. 'She can't eat as much as you do.'

'No,' Pussy purrs, 'I can't fill my face like you can.'

'In that case,' I can't resist saying, 'I'll be only too happy to assist you by putting my fist through it if you like.'

'*Katie*,' Sam says again. 'Don't be nasty.'

'Sorry.' I bite my cheek. There's no point incurring the wrath of Sam now. Not when I've got something so completely major to ask him. When, oh when, is the silly cow going to at least go to the bog to throw up so I can get him on his own?

'Have some more water.' I pour Pussy a glass. If she's only got a 'tiny little tummy', it can only be a matter of time until she has to dash to the lav to break her seal.

Eventually, she goes to put on more lipgloss and I have Sam all to myself. He's looking particularly groovy tonight. Sort of smart but casual all at the same time. And suddenly, I realise what it is I most admire about him. It's his confidence. He knows how to dress, act and behave himself at any occasion. You could, quite literally, take him anywhere.

'I'm sorry about all the things I said when I left yours,' I tell him. 'When I told you about the wedding. I was upset.'

'It's OK.' He rumples my hair affectionately. 'And so was I. I felt rejected because you planned to live at George's but you didn't want to live at mine. And I asked you first.'

'I'm sorry.' I rest my head on his shoulder. 'It just would have felt like charity, staying at yours.'

'You're staying at George's…'

'But that's OK,' I say. 'I'm doing them a favour in return. Marrying David, I mean.'

'Of course.'

'You see, I started off this year so sure I was going to make a go of things. Not rely on a man again.'

'I know.'

'And now I've gone and mucked it all up.' I want to confess all about Jake. And Nick. Suddenly, sleeping around doesn't seem so big or clever any more. And, despite the fact that I live with two of my best friends, I feel kind of lonely.

'But Neat Eats is going so well.' He strokes my hair again. 'I'm really proud of what you've done.'

'Thanks. And I couldn't have done it without you, you know.'

'You're more than welcome, Simpson.' He turns to face me, suddenly serious. 'You know that.'

'Or George, or David, of course,' I say hurriedly. For some reason then I felt like he was going to kiss me. More to the point, I sort of wanted him to. Which is, of course, ridiculous. I mean this is *Sam*, for God's sake. My oldest bud. Plus, I'm seeing Jake again. Well, sort of. And Nick. I've got two on the go, so I shouldn't be feeling lonely, should I?

'About this wedding,' he says tentatively.

'You're not going to have another go at me, are you?' I beg. 'I really don't think I can bear that. You know, you're a huge part of my life, Sam. You always have been.'

'And you mine,' he says, stroking my cheek.

'In fact,' I sit up and look at him seriously, 'I've got something I need to ask you.'

'Me too,' he says.

'You have?'

'Sam?' A voice suddenly pierces the intimacy of the moment. 'I'm tired. Can we go now?'

Pussy, back from the loo.

Bugger.

Chapter 18

It seems as though I'm never going to be able to get Sam on his own to ask him to give me away at the wedding. You see, even though I know he doesn't really approve, it means a hell of a lot to me to have his blessing. Plus, George has insisted that we need to make it look as real as possible. In case the Home Office turn up. And I can't very well ask my own father, can I, seeing as I have absolutely no bloody idea where he is.

On Sunday morning I wake early with worries about Sam and the whole giving away thing rolling around inside my head. I wander through to the bright kitchen, where George, in his favourite pink slippers, drinks fresh coffee at the table and pecks out text messages to someone in his office about the contestants they've got for tomorrow's show. David, naked apart from a pair of flappy billabong shorts, is sat opposite him with his feet on the table, chattering excitedly on the telephone to his sister Nettie in Australia. From what I can gather, he's telling her all about our wedding, as though it's the most normal thing in the world. Obviously no secrets there.

'Are you inviting your mum to our wedding?' I ask George, when the beeping of his phone has ceased, signalling an end to the frantic volley of text messages.

'I don't know.' He looks miserable. 'I really want to. I mean, it'd be nice for her to be able to dress up and have somewhere to go. But I just can't imagine having to explain it all to her.'

'She's tougher than you think, you know, George.' I fetch a purple mug from the cupboard and pour myself a coffee. 'Why don't you try her? I think she'd be pleased for you.'

'Really?'

'Really.'

'I might.' He sounds a bit forlorn. Then, looking at me, he's back to his old self again. 'God, darling. You look totally RAF.'

'What's that?' David finishes telling his sister all about the article he's writing on the contents of Posh Spice's make-up bag and puts the phone down. 'Oooh. Coffee. Yummy.'

'Katie,' George jerks his head towards me as if I'm not there, 'looks terrible. What's the matter, darling? Business gone under already? You look as though you haven't slept for weeks.'

'God, yes.' David sips coffee and looks apologetic. 'Sorry, love, but you do look a bit shit. You could carry all of George's lotions and potions around for months in those eyebags.'

'I can't sleep,' I say honestly. 'I'm nervous about the wedding. And I don't know what to do about Jake.'

'Are you in love with him?'

'I don't think so.' I shake my head. 'And then there's Nick. You know the bike guy?'

'Yes,' they chorus, excited at the thought of gossip. 'We know the bike guy.'

'I'm still sleeping with him.'

'Ooooh,' George says with evident relish. 'Utterly slutterly. Do tell.'

'Well, he seems to like me,' I say. 'But he's eighteen. And we have nothing in common.'

'So?' George shrugs.

'So I'm starting to realise that meaningless sex isn't all it's cracked up to be.'

'Fine, fine,' George says dismissively. 'I mean, sorry to seem callous but as long as none of them are actually hurting your feelings, can we get on to more important matters? Like the wedding? Now, the theme is NCP.'

'You want to hold the wedding in a multi-storey car park?' I ask in surprise.

'Don't be thick, darling.' George looks at me. 'I mean No Common People. Although I suppose we can let Janice come, even though she's been dipped in the peasant pot more than once. She is your best friend, after all. After me, of course.'

'That's if she's still talking to me,' I reason. 'After what I said about Jasper.'

'Of course she is.' George sips coffee.

'Don't forget the surprise.' David nudges George.

'Oh.' George waves his hands around excitedly. 'The surprise. Of course. Oh, Katie. You'll never guess what we've planned for you.'

Of course I can't guess. And George can't help telling me before I can even try. And when he does, I'm gobsmacked.

'A *hen weekend*?' I ask, just to be sure I've heard him right.

'Yes.' George looks so pleased with himself you'd have thought he'd just invented the wheel.

'It was Nettie's idea.' David looks proud. 'She says if she can't come to the wedding, the least she can do is contribute some ideas.'

'She can come if she wants. I don't mind having your family there.'

'She can't.' David shakes his head. 'For a start, she'll call me Davo in front of everybody and they'll all think I'm some straight Australian wide boy.'

'You're supposed to be straight,' I point out. 'For one day, at least.'

'I know.' David laughs. 'She can't come anyway. She can't take Iris and Isabella out of school. Shame really. I'd love to see them.'

'All very sad.' George gets on to more important business. 'Now. Your hen weekend.'

'But—'

'Now don't be ungrateful.' George wags his finger at me. 'We just thought you'd like a little holiday, sweetie. After all, you won't be able to come on the actual honeymoon. You do know that, don't you? Three's a bit of a crowd, darling, if you know what I mean.'

'But there's just so much to do,' I worry. 'There's Neat Eats, for a start. It won't run itself, you know. I've got three weddings and a christening booked in for August alone. That's a lot of smoked salmon and fruit cake. And there's paperwork.'

'But we've booked it now. For five. So you have to come.'

'You can't have,' I point out. 'David's only just spoken to his sister.'

'Well, it's in our heads now.' George pours himself more coffee. 'So it's as good as.'

'And five?' I ask. 'Why five?'

George counts off on his fingers.

'Us three, Janice and Sam. No partners.'

'Good,' I say. 'I don't want any skinny bitches who stink of raw vegetables on board, thank you.'

'So you'll come then?' David looks delighted.

'I'll think about it.'

And I will. After all, I could do with some sun. And perhaps Mum would like the challenge of coping with Neat Eats for a weekend. It is only a weekend, after all. She'll probably enjoy the company of all the customers and stuff. It must get lonely for her sometimes. 'Where're we going, anyway?'

'The Canaries.' George looks gleeful.

'Isn't that a bit...'

'Chip fat?' George shivers and pulls on a T-shirt with 'Some Don't. Some Might. I probably Will' stamped across the chest in pink glitter. 'That's the whole idea. It's ironic, darling. Total Tacksville. We're off to the land of egg, chips and Union Jack beach towels for a whole weekend. I'm so excited I just can't wait.'

'And I'm promised thousand decibel re-runs of *Only Fools and Horses* every five minutes.' David laughs.

'We'll be out on the razzle-dazzle in those dreadful discos, darling.' George is thrilled. 'Where your feet are practically glued to the floor and they've tied an ugly stick to all the ceiling fans. Won't it be great?'

'Well...'

'Such a refreshing change not to have to mix with glittering success stories like myself all the time.' George lights a fag and inhales deeply. 'Think how refreshing it'll be to be with people whose idea of job satisfaction is merely waving a tin in the air and yelling "Price check on baked beans".'

'I don't want to go.'

'You do,' George tells me firmly. 'You'll love it. And we'll all get gorgeous tans in time for the wedding.'

'I doubt it. The only time I look remotely brown is when my freckles join up.'

'You'll still look great next to all those tangerine women on the beach,' George says. 'With their arses full of cellulite and their cheaply done tattoos plastered across their great teats.'

'*You've* got a tattoo,' David points out.

'Darling, there's a world of difference between a tasteful tortoise, carefully positioned to enhance an already deliciously pert buttock, and a whopping great tiger's head on some flabby proletarian udder,' George informs him. 'Especially when it's an udder that started out the size of an egg cup but ballooned to a dinner plate thanks to one night too many on the pies.'

David laughs so much his purple flip-flops slap up and down on the flagstones.

'Can you try not to turn completely into George before the wedding?' I beg him. 'You used to be so lovely and un-gay as well.'

'So lovely and un-gay you decided you'd give him a go your-self,' George chortles.

'Ha ha,' I scoff. 'I just don't want the whole thing to look too gay.'

'Don't say you're getting nervy?' George asks.

'Well,' I bristle, 'you do realise that what we're doing is a crime, don't you?'

'Oh, come on.' George shakes me by the shoulder. 'Lighten up, sweetie. Of course we know. That's why we want to repay you by luring you into the bowels of slapperdom so you can stand next to red-faced skinheads on day release from Broad-moor as they belt out "Alice, Alice, who the fuck is Alice?"'

'What about the food?' I ask. 'I'm a food snob. I like waiters to greet me with "May I take your jacket please?" Not "Have you ever been to a Harvester before?" Anyway, you used to re-fuse to go to places like the Canaries. You said the government should ban common people from going abroad 'cos they spoiled it for everybody else.'

'Well, that's partly true,' George admits. 'I mean, we will be mixing with the kind of people who win the lottery. The ones who don't actually know what to do with the money when they get it because they already subscribe to Sky Sports and they don't have the nous to switch to a decent brand of ciggie.'

'The ones who spend it on vulgar mock-Tudor mansions and fill them with swirly red carpets and gold mixer taps?' David asks.

'The very ones.' George squeezes his hand.

'So which particular Canary are we visiting?' I sigh. 'Lanza-grotty or Tenegrief.'

'Fuerteventura,' George says. 'You're coming, and there's an end on it.'

I imagine myself lying on a beach with absolutely bugger all to do.

Beer and chips for brekky.

Fat, trashy novels, thick as bricks and smudged with co-conutty fingerprints.

Hot sunshine, prickling the backs of my knees. The smell of fresh ginger cake on my skin as the sun warms it.

'Sod it,' I tell them. 'I'm in. As long as the others come too. I'm not playing gooseberry to you two all weekend.'

I invite Sam first. I figure he's probably feeling a bit guilty about letting Pussy gatecrash our nice dinner, so he owes me one.

I'm right.

'Look,' he says, as soon as he hears my voice, 'I'm sorry about our dinner the other night. About Pussy coming along, I mean. I honestly had no idea she thought she was invited.'

'She didn't,' I say.

'What?'

'Never mind,' I tell him. 'It's OK.'

'Well, I'm sorry. I just didn't think it was worth making a big thing of it, you know. She's a bit, well, insecure sometimes, and I didn't want a scene.'

'Right.'

Hrrmph. As long as *she's* OK then...

'But at least we're friends again,' he says. 'You and I, I mean. That has to be worth it, eh, Simpson?'

'Course,' I tell him. 'I need a favour, actually.'

'Oh?'

'Well, two favours.'

'Is this what you wanted to ask me the other night?'

'Well, one is.'

'Go on.' He sounds eager.

'I want you to give me away.'

'Oh.' He sounds cold.

'Sam?'

'I'm here.'

'So will you?'

'Well,' he says carefully, 'you know how I feel about that. I don't really think you should be doing this at all. You should be marrying someone who really loves you for you. And I don't mean Jake bloody Carpenter. Or that twelve-year-old you've been seeing. Don't think I don't know about that. George has got a gob the size of the Blackwall Tunnel. I saw him in Cuba Libre the other night. He'd spout any old shite after a couple of Bellinis.'

'You won't then?' My heart sinks. Somehow, for no reason on earth I can think of, I've built this whole thing up into an event of such importance that, if he says no, I don't know if I can go through with the wedding at all. If I'm honest, I'm so nervous about the whole thing, I just need to feel someone's on my side. There's no one else in the world I can ask.

There's a long silence. Then...

'I'm not saying I *won't*,' he says eventually. 'I'm saying I'll have to think about it.'

'Thanks, Sam,' I gush.

'But you have to return the favour.'

'Of course,' I say. 'Whatever you want.'

'Oh really, Simpson?' he says, flirting playfully so I know everything is going to be all right. '*Whatever* I want?'

'You know what I mean.' I laugh. 'What is it?'

'It's my birthday next week,' he says. 'I thought I might have a bit of a barbie if the weather's nice. Have the boys over. Kick a football around and stuff.'

'You and football,' I tease him. 'So what's the plan?'

'You do the food?' he asks. 'I'll pay you of course.'

'How 'bout I give you a discount?' I'm pink with pleasure at him asking me to do it. 'You just pay for the grub. I mean I'm not as poor as I was, but I still can't really do it for free.'

'Done.'

'Is that what you were going to ask me the other night? When I bought you a lovely expensive dinner and you were dragged home early?'

'Er, yes,' he says. 'Of course it was. And sorry about that, by the way.'

'So when do you want to do this barbie?'

'Next Saturday?'

'Kay.'

'What was that other thing you wanted to ask me, Simpson?'

'Oh God,' I groan. 'It's this sodding holiday the boys have planned. A sort of hen weekend in the Canaries. In lieu of a honeymoon for me. Will you come?'

'Well...'

'Please.'

'Calm down, Simpson. Course I will,' he says, and I can hear the smile in his voice. 'A holiday'd be great. Course I'll come. I wouldn't miss it for the world.'

I put the phone down feeling happier than I have in ages. I can handle Jake and Nick too, knowing I've got my oldest friend back on side. I've hated arguing with him over something as simple as where I live. And, I think charitably, he can't help the fact that his girlfriend is a toxic slut who enjoys nothing better than watching me squirm under the magnifying glass of her pale blue eyes.

When I've finished talking to Sam I call Janice.

'What've you been up to?' I ask her. 'It's been yonks.'

'I know, hon,' she says, surprising me with her friendliness. 'I've been so busy with work. I've got this new account. For a mobile phone company. Massive budget and everything. I'm knackered. And then I've been trying to make more of an effort to see my mum.'

'Oh that's nice,' I say. And I mean it. Janice's poor mum does get a bit neglected.

'Yeah,' Janice continues. 'I mean, all she's got to do all day is watch telly. And listen to bloody Cliff Richard, of course. Mind you, she has done a bit of decorating. Painted the kitchen. That sort of thing. The place isn't quite so grim as it was. Anyway, I popped round a few times for a chat. Thought she might be able to tell me a bit more about my dad. Thought I might try and track him down. In case I need him to give me away.'

'Oh.'

'Unless he's something awful, like a dustbin man or a drunk. Then I thought about asking Sam. What do you think?'

What do I think? I think she's just reminded me of my own dilemma. Anyhow, Sam's MY friend. Call me childish, but if he's giving anyone away, it ought to be me. I don't say anything, though. Instead I ask her what she thinks about coming away on holiday.

'I dunno, Katie,' she grumbles. 'What if Jasper comes over all romantic and I'm on the other bloody side of the world? I mean, according to you, he's already having an affair, so I can't really afford to leave him, can I?'

God, she's making this hard. I've been fretting all the time over how to apologise re this whole Jasper and 'other woman' thingy. And all she's worried about is herself. Mind you. I'm determined to say my piece. So I do.

'Oh that,' she says, when I'm finished. 'I'm really not that bothered whether he was or wasn't with anyone else. He's got a dick like a turkey's neck, so I doubt he's putting it about that much. Nope. I was just feeling a bit pissy about that whole Paris thing, y'know? I really thought he was going to get me a ring and everything.'

'I know. So we're friends again?'

'Course,' she says. 'In fact, let's have a drink. We haven't got pissed together for ages. Sorry about that, by the way. I would have visited you at George's before but I have to keep on at bloody giblet dick. Let's face it, he's getting on a bit. He could cark it any day now during sex.'

'He could slump down on top of you?' I gasp.

'Yep. And I'd have to stay there until the cleaner arrived. I might not even have the TV remote to hand so it could all get very boring indeed. Especially if she starts skiving off again to visit her son in prison.'

'Oh.'

'Oh, Katie, do you think he's going to pop the question soon? It's been absolutely yonks.'

'It certainly has,' I agree. 'So long, in fact, that if I were you I'd be worried that the only question he's likely to pop is "Mind if I flip you over and do you from behind?"'

'God, I shudder to think. Nope. Hasn't got it in him, for all his combat pants and his young dressing. I just wish he'd hurry up and get this proposal out of the way. I'm in a constant state of nerves.'

'Come on holiday then,' I urge her. 'You know what they say about absence making the heart grow fonder and all.'

'You reckon?'

'I reckon,' I say firmly. 'He'll be begging you to marry him when you come back. With a tan and everything.'

'You know, Katie, you're right. Bugger it. I'll come.'

'Great.'

'But only if we can go shopping first. For a whole lot of gorgeous stuff to wear on the beach.'

'We're only going for the weekend. And we need to get you a bridesmaid's dress first.'

'Just make sure you steer well clear of the London bus look this time.'

We both cackle with laughter.

We celebrate by going out. Like we used to. Just the two of us. Jasper's gone to a conference in the West Midlands, so Janice doesn't feel she needs to put in any groundwork tonight.

'Are you really OK about this wedding?' she asks me, as we queue for Long Island iced teas at the bar.

'Of course.'

'Really?'

'No,' I reply. 'I'm fucking shitting myself, to tell you the truth.'

'You're not upset that you'll never have the whole pavlova thing? With the apartment-block cake and all?'

'Not really. I mean blokes are all the bloody same at the end of the day, aren't they?'

'They certainly are.' She raises her glass to mine. 'Here's to our fake weddings then. *Both* of them. Yours and mine, eh?'

'Cheers.'

'Oh sod it,' she says. 'Let's get pissed.'

We drink shedloads. And we flirt with men to get gratis drinks, although we can perfectly well afford to buy our own. Even me. And we're not exactly polite to the men who do buy us drinks. In fact, once they've given in, we lose all respect for them.

'Sorry,' Janice tells one bloke with a Jimmy Hill chin when he asks her to dance. 'I'm a fully paid up member of ANAL.'

'Uh?'

'Anti Nauseating Arseholes League. So bugger off.'

'And I've just joined WART,' I join in. 'Women Against Randy Tossers.'

It feels good to be letting off steam with my best mate after working so hard to get Neat Eats off the ground. It's almost like being back at college again. Of course then I'd be shagging guys like these, just so I didn't cause offence. And I'd go out with them afterwards to avoid upsetting them further. Which would make me so miserable I'd howl with self-pity as Janice and the rest of my housemates brought me cups of hot chocolate with marshmallows and sat on the end of my bed, partly to make me feel better, but mainly because they hugely enjoyed the whole cabaret atmosphere of it all.

'God,' I laugh later, as we step into the loo to re-apply lipstick and untwist gussets. 'I'm choking on the smell of Lynx in there and I still can't see anyone I fancy. When I took up this whole being single business I thought it was going to be so exciting, you know? A new man every day and all that? No strings attached.'

'A Daily Male.' Janice giggles drunkenly.

'Exactly.' I laugh. 'With a Male on Sunday for weekends. Extra thick and full of useless information.'

'Too right.'

'But all I seem to have ended up with is one ex-boyfriend

and a twelve-year-old I have nothing in common with.' I frown. 'Where did I go wrong, Janice?'

She hugs me warmly. 'I don't know, mate,' she says. 'I just don't know.'

On Friday morning, I drop Nick off at college so he can resit his maths GCSE and wang over to Sam's house in Balham. He's taken the morning off work to plan the menu for his birthday barbie with me.

'Did you like the invitations?' he asks me.

'I didn't get one.' I look up from my notebook in surprise.

'What?' He runs his hands through his hair, confused. 'But Pussy posted them ages ago.'

'Did the postbox she put mine into have Keep Britain Tidy on it?' I laugh.

'Don't be silly, Simpson. Pussy likes you. She's always saying how great you are.'

To *you*, yes, I think, chewing the end of my pencil.

He frowns. 'Though I think she did want to help with the food at my birthday.'

'You should have let her then,' I lie. 'I wouldn't have minded.'

Though actually, I realise, I would have minded like buggery. It occurs to me that I'm actually jealous of what Pussy and Sam have. He looks after her so well. I don't have that kind of security. Jake's always too busy rushing back to look after Fishpants and the baby, and with Nick, it's me doing the looking after. He's a big kid, after all.

'It's OK, Simpson.' Sam grins at me. He's actually very good-looking when he smiles. I guess I can't really blame Pussy for wanting me out of the way. Even though there's nothing whatsoever going on between us. 'You haven't seen her cooking.'

'That bad, eh?'

I'm ridiculously pleased to hear him criticise her.

'Put it this way, she cooked me one of those ready-made

cheeseburgers once. You know the kind you get in a box. With the bun and everything.'

'Ugh.' I shudder. 'Disgusting.'

'Exactly.' He grins. 'Well, the cheese looked suspiciously shiny...'

'Was it the plastic kind?'

'Oh yes. But it wasn't just that. She'd actually forgotten to take the plastic off. I nearly threw up.'

We both wheeze with laughter at the thought of Sam ingesting mouthfuls of cellophane.

'You will make those pork and mango thingummyjigs, won't you?' he asks me, suddenly serious. 'The ones on the skewers?'

'As long as your girlfriend doesn't eat them then chuck them back up again in one great multicolour yawn.'

'Don't be mean.'

'Sorry. No. I'll do them, on one condition.'

'Anything. I'd sell my own grandmother for pork and mango wotsits.'

'I've got to buy a wedding dress tomorrow,' I say. 'Janice is coming with me but I could do with a male opinion.'

'Why? Your husband-to-be isn't going to give a toss what you look like.'

'No, but *I* will.' I whack him round the head with a sheep-skin cushion. 'I don't want to trip up the aisle looking like a turd in taffeta, do I? *Please*, Sam.'

'I'm supposed to be having lunch with Pussy's mother.'

'Pretty please.'

'Erm...'

'Pork and mango skewers...' I play my trump card.

'Done,' he says. 'I'll say I've got to work. Anyway, it might even give me the chance to talk you out of this completely insane idea. Honestly, Simpson, you do get yourself in some scrapes.'

'That's me for you.' I help myself to an olive from the bowl on the table. 'Like to fly by the seat of my pants.'

'Really?' He pretends to lift up my denim skirt for a look.

'You must show me sometime. Oh, and there's just one more favour I'd like to ask while we're at it.'

'What?'

'I've got to take Lucy to the park while Sal goes for a job interview.'

Two months ago, Sal, Sam's sister—three years older than us and bloody scary when we were growing up, thank you very much—was ceremoniously dumped by her City Wanker husband. He moved into a flat in the Barbican to 'find himself' and she's found herself looking after a four-year-old child and a dramatically reduced income.

'Ye-es,' I say cautiously. 'When?'

'Two weeks on Thursday. Will you come?'

'This isn't a date, is it?' I laugh.

'Ha ha. I just thought it would be fun if you came. And Lucy would like it.'

I bet she would. Last time I babysat, she squealed like a guinea pig until I bought her Hula Hoops then insisted on trying out all my make-up, ruining every Ruby & Millie face gloss and Stila lip glaze under the sun in the process. But I'm pleased to have been asked. So I say yes.

On Saturday morning, I'm flat out making nibbly bits for a wanky luncheon in Fulham. Chock-a-block with vacant little ant women who'll sip Chardonnay and pick at my pickled herrings on rye before rushing to the loos to yack it all up again. Since David did a piece on Neat Eats in the July edition of *Suki*, the bookings have been pouring in like cheap Sangria. And Sam, bless him, has helped out too. He's booked me for the launch of Nikerzoff cucumber vodka, a client he's managed to claw from the clutches of his old company. Quite a coup for a start-up company, I'm told. So my caviare and cocktails will soon be savoured by the elite of London's mee-jah bods.

Soon, I'm going to have to think about taking on extra staff. Things couldn't be better.

Sam, fresh-faced from playing football, comes round at half

one, and at two o'clock Janice picks me up, mounting the kerb in an enormous four-wheel drive, squashing a big dog turd on the pavement and nearly mowing me down in the process.

'Car's gone in for a service,' she explains. 'Jasper's lent me this bastard for the day. Can't seem to get the hang of the clutch.'

We make for Bulimic Brides, or whatever the blimming heck this pre-nuptial haven is called, in Covent Garden. A hush descends on the room as we enter and a woman with electric-blue eyeliner, frosted pink lipstick and cheeks like a blood-hound's pads over, her neat court shoes sinking into the deep pile of the cream carpet.

Sam squeezes my hand. 'You OK?'

'Yep,' I gulp, even though every nerve in my body is scream-ing, 'Run, Simpson, run.'

Janice, of course, hardly notices my nervousness. She's too busy fingering taffeta and lace, silk and satin in every shade of white, cream and off-white.

'Well, well, well,' beams the Bloodhound Lady, showing much more plaque than is strictly necessary for two thirty on a Sat-urday afternoon. Or any afternoon, come to that.

'Who's the lucky lady then?'

'I am,' I say, feeling as though I'm in some kind of panto-mime. Any minute now, Sam or Janice is going to shout, 'Oh no, she's not.'

'What a lovely couple you'll make.' She beams even more. 'Although I'm afraid I'm going to have to ask you to wait out-side, sir.' She takes Sam by his broad shoulders, firmly turns him round and shows him the door.

'Look behind you,' I want to shout.

'Why does he have to wait out there?' I demand.

'We can't have the groom seeing the bride before the big day, now can we?'

'Oh, no, he's not...' I begin, stuttering and mumbling to try and get the words out.

'I'm not the lucky man, I'm afraid.' Sam booms with laughter. 'That's someone else altogether.'

I smile at him gratefully. I seem to have lost all power of speech.

He winks back, a lovely friendly wink that calms me down and makes me feel all gooey inside at the same time. Jesus. What's happening to me? Surely I can't be wishing I was marrying Sam? No. I'm getting confused. It's just nerves, I tell myself. Just nerves. I'll be OK when we get out of this clotted-cream-coloured hellhole.

'OK,' trills the Bloodhound, moving briskly towards a rail at the far side of the room and whisking a couple of frocks off it. 'When's the big day?'

'Soon,' I tell her.

'Well, obviously, dear.' She looks at me as though I'm retarded. 'But when, exactly? We need to get some idea of what the weather's going to be like so we can dress you properly, don't we?'

'Janice?' I prompt. I'm so jumpy, I've actually completely forgotten when this fake wedding I'm having's going to be held.

'Beginning of September,' Janice supplies helpfully, fingering a creation in antique rose silk.

'September?' The Bloodhound looks absolutely horrified. 'But this is couture.' She pronounces it koooootewer. 'I'm afraid that's going to be impossible. It's July already. We need six months' notice at least. We don't knock them up just like that, you know.'

She manages to look at me so disdainfully I feel as though I'm the one who's knocked up.

'You know what?' Janice has an idea. 'You should just try some of these on to get an idea of what you like and then we'll get that fat ponce Didier to copy it for you. He's really good at stuff like that.'

Of course. George's friend Didier. Why didn't I think of that before? It'd be a darn sight cheaper for David too. After all, he's insisting on paying for my dress.

'I'm afraid that won't be possible,' sneers the Bloodhound. 'I can't let you try any of these on if you aren't intending to buy.'

'Oh.' I'm crestfallen. Now what?

'Excuse me.' Sam takes charge, squeezing my hand again and staring the Bloodhound straight in the eye. 'The young lady said she'd like to try on some of these dresses and so that's what she'll do. This other young lady happens to be getting married... what...at some point next year?' He looks at Janice.

'Oh, yes, definitely.' She nods back. 'Very early next year.'

'And I don't imagine there's much call for wedding gowns in January, is there?' Sam asks.

'Er, well, no, not...' stutters the Bloodhound.

'Just as I thought.' Sam grins at me and winks again. 'So you'll be polite to us now and then maybe, just maybe, if we get the full service today, we'll be back. But that very much depends on you.'

'Of course,' mutters the Bloodhound, racing off and coming back with piles of utterly gorgeous dresses. We get peach bellinis in celebration of my forthcoming wedding and from the way she's acting you'd have thought I was bloody Princess Di.

Or Fergie at the very least.

'What about this one?' she asks me. 'White chocolate, we call this.'

'It's bloody cream,' Janice mutters in my ear. 'Same as all the others.'

'Have you got anything *not* in cream?' I'm starting to enjoy myself now.

'Well,' the woman says, 'like I said. This is white chocolate.'

'I was thinking oyster pink,' I tell her. 'I'm not really having anything traditional, you see.'

'Are you *sure*, dear?' she asks. 'Pink? With *your* hair...'

Then she catches Sam's expression and bustles off towards the back of the shop.

'*Here* we are.' She pulls out the most stunning creation in palest rose, threaded with shots of gold. 'And I thought this, to go with it.' She holds up a beautiful tiara, fashioned in rose quartz and crystal. It's so pretty I want it. Wedding or no wedding.

'Try it on,' urges Sam.

So I do.

The dress fits like a glove. It clings to every part of my body, giving even *me* the most glorious curves. I pop on the tiara, open the curtain of the fitting room and...

DA-NAAAAAAAH.

I twirl round and round, secure in the knowledge that I look about as good as is possible—for me, anyway.

There's silence from Janice and Sam.

'Don't you like it?' I look down aghast. 'Have I got the back tucked into my knicks or something?'

'It's perfect, hon.' Janice looks delighted.

'You look beautiful.' Sam appears to have tears in his eyes. Taking my hand he leads me to the mirror on the far wall. 'Look at you. You look amazing.'

I look at myself. Next to him. And, even though I'm tall, he's still a good four or five inches taller. We look good together.

Suddenly, I realise that I fancy him.

Only a tiny bit.

But those lustful feelings are there.

Buggery. And with me just about to tie the knot, too. How inconvenient.

'Amazing,' he says again, looking at himself next to me and back at himself again.

Janice breaks the spell.

'Stunning,' she says. 'And seeing as it fits her so well, can she buy it now?'

'Well, like I said,' the Bloodhound explains, 'we haven't got time to have it specially made.'

'Can she not take this one?' Janice wants to know. 'Fits her, doesn't it?'

'I'm afraid not, dear. This is the only sample we have.'

'Oh.' I'm crestfallen.

'You could take the tiara though,' says the Bloodhound, ever in sales mode. 'Only five hundred pounds.'

'Oh yes, Katie.' Janice is excited. 'Gettit. It's lush.'

'I can't,' I hiss. 'I really can't justify spending all that money on fripperies for a wedding that isn't really real. It's stupid.'

'It's fine.' Sam whips out a Visa card. 'Stick it on that. My treat, Simpson. Call it my blessing. In lieu of my giving you away.'

'So you won't...?'

'We'll just see, shall we?'

'But what about the dress?' Janice wants to know.

'It's OK.' I shake my head. 'I guess I'll just get Didier to make me one that looks the same. I'll go and change.'

'One minute then.' Sam stops me, pulling something out of his jacket pocket. A camera.

'I take it you don't mind if I take a photo?' he asks. 'Seeing as she looks so beautiful in it.'

'Well,' the Bloodhound bites her flabby lip, 'we don't usually...'

'I suppose there's always that shop down the road you liked.' Sam looks pointedly at Janice.

'OK, OK.' The Bloodhound raises her hands in defeat. 'Take a photo if you must.'

'Say Cheezels.' Sam snaps me. 'Lovely.'

'I wasn't ready,' I grumble later, sitting in the car, gleefully clutching my sparkling new tiara. 'I'm going to look horrid.'

'Oh well,' Sam hugs me, 'doesn't really matter. The dress looked fantastic.'

'It can bloody get married without me then.'

'Seriously though, Simpson, at least now Didier will know what it looks like so he'll be able to copy it.'

'Thanks.' I hug him.

He looks pleased, though he won't come and drink celebratory cocktails with Janice and me afterwards, saying he has to meet Joff in the Bedford to talk about the Arsenal/Leeds United match. Janice and I drop him home and Janice says if we're not going for cocktails she might as well take the Jeep back to Jasper's. I go along for the ride.

'We can even get him to mix us cocktails if he's back,' Janice says. 'He makes a wicked martini.'

'Excellent.'

We wait forever for a silver Mondeo to vacate a parking space outside Jasper's luxury waterside apartment (his City residence) then, just as we're about to back in, some flash knobhead in a dark blue Porsche appears from nowhere, zooming up behind us and zapping into the space before Janice's reverse lights have even come on.

'I had my fucking blinker on,' she yells at me. 'Can you believe the fucking fucker's nerve?'

I tell her that no, the fucking fucker has surprised even me with his arrogance.

Fucking fucker hops out, strutting like the cock of the rock, flipping a pair of pathetically trendy sunglasses from the top of his head and onto his nose.

'There you go, love.' He grins cockily. 'That's what you can do when you can drive.'

Janice's face turns thunderous. For a split second I'm scared that she might be considering doing some damage to his face with the car key. But I needn't have worried. She has something far more spectacular in mind. Before I have time to fully understand what's happening, she slams her foot to the floor and wrenches the steering wheel hard left, just missing a parking meter and slamming expertly into the front of the Porsche. The Porsche caves in completely, folding itself around the back of the virtually undamaged Jeep like uncooked pastry round a Cornish pasty.

'Sorry,' she says to me, worried I may have suffered injury as my head snapped forward and hit the dashboard with a thunk. 'Had to go nuclear.'

'No problem whatsoever,' I say shakily, checking that all my bones are still in place.

Janice winds down the window and bats her eyelids oh so

sweetly at the Porsche driver, who is staring in mortification at the remains of his precious understudy penis.

'There *you* go, love,' she says sweetly. 'That's what you can do when you've got money.'

Then she puts the four-wheel drive into first and calmly cruises the pavement, looking for another place to park.

'Fucking lezzers,' the man shouts after us. And then, pointing at me, 'Bit tall for a girl, aren't you? Ever been mistaken for a man?'

I lean across Janice and poke my head out of the window.

'Never.' I waggle my little finger at him. 'Have you?'

We cackle all the way to Jasper's flat, whereupon, on pressing the buzzer and receiving no reply, we assume he must be out.

'I'll just leave the keys to the Jeep inside.' Janice unlocks the front door. 'And we can nick a couple of bottles of wine while we're there. Have a bit of a celebration round mine. In honour of your tiara.'

'OK.'

Inside, Jasper's apartment is beautiful. All open plan, with lots of pale wood and white walls everywhere.

'That's weird.' Janice looks at the key and back at the lock.

'What?'

'S'not deadlocked. Usually when he goes away he dead-locks it. Doddering old fool. He'd forget his head if it wasn't screwed on.'

As we go inside, though, something else strikes me as weird.

'What's that noise?' I lift my head towards the ceiling.

'What?'

'That plinky plonky noise.'

She listens. 'It's Nina Simone. Stupid old buffer's favourite.'

'It's loud though,' I say. 'Sounds like he's having a party or something.'

'He'd better not be. Not without inviting me.'

'Do you think he's OK?' I say. 'I mean, he might have fallen over. Slipped on a banana skin or something while waltzing with himself, all lonely and sad.'

'He's got a cleaner,' she reminds me. 'And he's not *that* old.'

I hold my hands to my heart in mock horror. 'He could have been felled by a heart attack as he tried to open a simple tin of mushy peas,' I say. 'The poor sod.'

'Don't.' She looks as though she's going to burst out laughing.

'He could have gassed himself as he put his last fifty pence into the meter, just to keep warm,' I say. 'Or choked on a custard cream...'

'Stop.' She holds her sides. 'Come on. Let's go and see where the party is. It's probably the neighbours upstairs. They're pretty wild.'

The party is in full swing, it seems. And it would appear that it's in Jasper's flat after all. As we round the bend in the spiral staircase we discover that the music is coming from his study. Popping our heads round the door, there's nothing stopping us from coming face to hairy arse with all the glory of Jasper's slack backside. He's stark bollock naked, erection in one hand, camera in the other. And, sitting on his desk with a notebook and pen in one hand and with her legs so far apart we can see what she had for breakfast, is a hussy with a huge diamond stud in her nose and tits that stand up on their own.

'Fuck,' we both say at the same time.

Hearing us, Jasper swings round.

'*Darling,*' he says to Janice. 'I didn't hear...'

'Clearly,' she says coldly, grabbing my hand and pulling me back downstairs.

'Are you OK?' I ask her as we get outside.

'Yes,' she says slowly. She's as white as a sheet. 'Although I think I'm going to throw up.'

I hand her a tissue as she chucks all over my shoes.

'Try not to worry,' I say comfortingly. 'I mean you did only want him for his cash, didn't you?'

'Well, yes,' she says. 'Of course. Although I *am* a bit shocked. I didn't think the stupid old buffer had it in him.'

Something's wrong. She's strangely calm.

So why is she being sick? She's not even that upset.

'Bang goes my country house in Winchester then,' she says bitterly. 'And you know, Katie, I've given him five blow jobs. It wasn't exactly fun.'

'I'm sure,' I soothe.

'I even swallowed twice,' she says. 'Think how bloody daft I feel now.'

I tell her that I know she feels daft. But at least she's not crying. I was worried she might start volleying off bucketfuls of tears. I thought there might be snot everywhere. But no, it's only money. It clearly isn't that bad.

'Actually, Katie,' she looks me straight in the eye, 'it *is* that bad.'

'Why?' I ask her. 'You aren't in debt, are you?'

'No.'

'What then?'

Something about the way she's looking at me gives me a very bad feeling about this.

A very bad feeling indeed.

'Well, I was so fed up of waiting for him to pop the question I tried a new tactic,' she says, her bottom lip wobbling just ever so slightly.

'Oh.'

'Yes,' she says. 'I plumped for Plan B. And plump is about bloody right.'

'Oh, come on, Janice, you aren't fat. Would I have asked you to be my bridesmaid if you were a great tub of lard?'

'I don't mean *now*.' She looks at me derisively. 'I mean in a few months' time. *Six* months to be exact. In six months, I'll be the size of a house.'

'What?'

'I'm up the stick. Got a mouse in the chimney. A bun in the oven. I'm up the bloody duff.'

'But how?'

'Shagging.' She looks at me seriously. 'That's how. Oh fuck, Katie. What am I going to do?'

'Have a baby?' I say weakly.

'Well, it's a bit late for anything else now,' she says. 'Talk about history bloody repeating itself. I'm my bloody mother all over again. The poor, poor cow.'

'But you've got a good job,' I tell her.

'Which I hate.'

'You'll be able to afford to look after it at least,' I say. 'You'll be a great mother. Just make sure you don't sell it to George.'

She manages a weak smile. 'You think I should chuck in my job and go on the social?' she says. 'Isn't that what single mothers do?'

'You could get a nanny.'

'Oh God.' She ignores me. 'Me. A single mother. Of course I'll have to get the poor little sod's ears pierced, even if it's a boy. And I'll have to wear cheap and nasty shoes and paint purple blotches on my legs so the other single mums won't think I'm up myself.'

'Try to cheer up.' I can't think of much else to say. 'The labour won't hurt much.'

'Katie, it's supposed to be like shitting a melon through the eye of a needle.'

'Don't worry, Jasper's will probably get a chauffeur to drive it out. It'll probably already have cruise control and everything. It'll come out at eighty miles an hour with a cigar the size of a dog poo in its gob. You probably won't even have to push.'

Janice manages another small smile. 'God, he was a twat, wasn't he?' She giggles. 'So totally nouve.'

'Completely.' I laugh, walking towards the Jeep and putting my hand on the door. 'You still got the keys?'

Janice feels in her pockets. 'Yep.'

'C'mon then,' I say. 'Might as well have it. Call it child support.'

'It's about the only support I'll be getting from him.'

'You aren't going to tell him, then?'

'No way. You saw him, Katie. I don't want the baby to end up with a father like that.'

'How will you sting him for cash then?'

'I'll just have to manage on my own, won't I?'

'Fair play.' I open the door of the Jeep. 'All the more reason to half-inch this then. I'll drive it back to yours, shall I, while you take your car?'

Suddenly, Janice grins. 'Katie?'

'Yep?'

'I fucking love you to bits.'

Chapter 19

On Sam's birthday, I arrive at his house just before the first guest arrives. Pussy's there already of course. And while I faff about with marinades and salad dressings, she drapes herself across Sam's blue velvet ottoman and taunts me with her teeny tiny loveliness. Only one thing seems to have changed. I look more closely. It's her hair. Her glossy blonde mane has been chopped short. It doesn't suit her.

'Gone gamine, have we?' I tease, sloping into the kitchen to finish the food.

As the guests congregate in the courtyard garden, Sam serves tall glasses of Pimms, brimming with strawberries, cucumber and mint. I take the food outside and start laying the long, low table by the wall. The bright sun on the whitewashed walls of Sam's little patio hurts my eyes after the relative gloom of the kitchen so I don't really get the chance to bog at who the guests are. It feels kind of weird serving food at my best friend's birthday party. By rights, of course, I should be with all the others, getting nicely drunk on gin.

'Looks brilliant.' Sam comes out of the house and puts an arm across my shoulders as I put bowls of my special potato salad and trays of halloumi cheese and red onion kebabs on the table.

'Thanks.' I hug him back. He smells lovely. All sort of clean and freshly laundered. 'Happy birthday.'

As more and more Pimms is quaffed, I start to relax. The guests seem to be enjoying themselves and once I've prepared all the food, there really isn't very much else to do. Jeff, Sam's dad, is firing up the actual barbecue, so luckily I don't have any worries on that score. I even get a chance to have a few nibbles myself, finding a seat next to Janice on the garden wall and admiring the terracotta pots, tumbling with jewel-bright flowers and the sugar candy coloured sweet peas that rest against a sunny wall. I even spot Bertie, Sam's tortoise, munching on a piece of cucumber in a patch of grass. Sam's had him for years.

'I'd forgotten all about him,' I say to Janice.

'What?' Janice is munching on a rollmop. She's been craving them for the past week. Disgusting.

But I don't have time to point out Bertie because we're interrupted by a shrill voice. Pussy, swanning over in a red and white gingham bikini top.

'Ooooh,' she says spitefully. 'Look at you, Katie, golloping all that food down.'

'I'm sorry?' I look her straight in the eye.

'Well, it isn't really done, is it, the caterer scoffing everything in sight. I mean, shouldn't you be below stairs, as it were. At the very least you should be in the kitchen, clearing away.'

'Bitch,' clucks Janice under her breath.

'It's a bit different though, isn't it?' I say, determined to remain grown-up about it. 'A bit more relaxed. It's not as if Sam's paying me or anything. I wouldn't dream of it. He's my best friend.'

'You'd think, wouldn't you?' she says in a horrid 'I know something you don't' sort of voice.

'I'm sorry?'

'Well, if you two are such good friends, you'd have thought you wouldn't have any secrets,' she says brightly as Sam saunters towards us. He looks, I'm surprised to find myself thinking, very handsome.

'What secrets?'

'Oh, nothing,' she says. 'Hello, darling.'

'Hi.' Sam looks confused.

'What secrets?' I repeat.

'Oh, it doesn't matter,' Pussy says. 'Oh look, Katie, there's your mum. I must go over and say hi.'

And with that she wafts away, leaving Sam and me looking at each other.

'What's the matter?'

'Nothing,' I say. It's all a bit strange.

I soon find out what Pussy means. Later on, when Sam's blown out the candles on his cake, my mother, who I've barely had the chance to talk to all day, takes me by the hand and says she's got a little announcement.

'What?' I say.

'Let's find Jeff first, shall we?' She leads me towards the kitchen door, where Jeff is standing, smoking a celebratory cigar and smiling at my mum in a way that's way too intimate for my liking.

'*Tell* me then,' I say.

'Well,' my mother begins, turning round to smile at Sam and Pussy, who have stumbled up beside me. Pussy's smiling so hard she's practically smacking her chops with relish.

'What?' I say, starting to feel worried. 'I haven't got all day.'

'I've asked your mother for her hand,' Jeff says eventually.

'What?' I'm stunned.

'I've asked her for her hand,' he repeats.

'What about the rest of her?' I snap suddenly. 'That not good enough for you?'

I don't understand. I know I'm being childish but I cannot see how my mother could be so gullible as to fall for Sam's

dad's charms. It's always been just her and me. How could she
even think of getting married again after what my father did
to her?

What hurts even more is that Sam and Pussy already knew.
She's told them first. And Pussy bloody loves the fact. The bitch.
She's sucking up to my mother like a ruddy Dyson.

'You'll get used to the idea, love.' Jeff pats my shoulder.

'Will I?' I sulk. Somehow I doubt it. What's worse is that I
can't stop thinking how handsome Sam looks today. And now
he's going to be my brother.

It's perverted.

'It'll be company for me, love,' says Mum.

'Right.'

'And your mother's got a lovely garden,' Jeff pipes up. 'There'll
be more room for my tomatoes.'

'Oh well, that's all right then, isn't it?' I spit. 'S'long as your
tomatoes are going to be OK.'

I'm about to make a run for it to try and sort out my head
when Pussy slimes her way into the conversation.

'We've got a little announcement of our own to make,
haven't we, darling?' She yanks Sam forward, as though he's a
small child, slightly shy of being made to speak up.

'We have?'

I'm not sure if it's a statement or a question, but Sam is
clearly as confused as I am.

'We're getting engaged too.' She beams.

'Oh, fucking great,' I huff.

'Katie.' Sam grabs my hand.

'Fuck off.'

'What's wrong with you?'

'I don't know.'

And it's true. I don't really. All I know is that nothing is going
right. I can't cope with this. Two wedding announcements in
one day. And I can't even tell my mother about my own.

Buggery.

'I'm going home,' I say. 'To George's.'

'But...'

'No buts. I'm off.'

I'm halfway out of the house, midway between tears and hysterical laughter at the absurdity of it all when Sam catches me.

'What's wrong?'

I look at his face, all handsome and concerned.

'How can you marry that little cow?' I say.

'What?'

'You heard. She's a bitch. She went round telling everyone she'd made all the food. I heard her.'

That's true actually. I did hear Joff congratulating her on the wonderful tenderness of his chicken kebab. And she just batted her eyelashes and thanked him. I wanted to pick her up by her hair and use her as a fly swat but decided to rise above it at the time.

And where did that bloody get me?

'She wouldn't.'

'Oh yes she bloody well would. I caught her doctoring the marinade as well.'

That bit's a lie but I wouldn't put it past her.

'You're just being ridiculous now,' Sam says, his face suddenly changing.

'What?'

'Ridiculous and childish.'

'Then you won't be wanting to speak to me, will you?' I spit. 'So fuck off.'

'OK then, I will. Ring me when you've grown-up,' he says. 'And when you've decided not to put us all through this ridiculous charade of a wedding you're having.'

And without another word, he turns and storms back into the house.

'Ditto,' I yell back at him. 'Fucking ditto, you bastard.'

Then I turn and storm towards the tube station.

Bugger it. Now I've gone and lost my best mate. And with

my mum getting married and all I've been through, I could really do with him. What with George and David being so cheesily in love all the time and Janice's hormones all over the place now she'll soon be using her tummy as a shelf for her cup of tea.

And the very worst thing is, I think I sort of fancy Sam.

And he's going to be my brother.

And he hates me.

Bollocks.

Before my dress fitting, I worry myself stupid over whether or not Didier will be able to make the dress look right. Sam gave me the photo as soon as he'd got it out of Boots and George gave it to Didier in plenty of time. But I'd hate to think that after finding the perfect dress, the whole thing'll be down the pan like a dodgy prawn vindaloo.

'And I want Sam to think I look nice,' I whine at Janice. 'After all the effort he's been to.'

'Sam probably won't even *come* to the wedding.' She pats her stomach absent-mindedly.

'How do you know he won't come?' I accuse her. 'He might.'

'Well, *you* don't know, do you?' she bellows. 'So *I* sure as buggery don't have a clue. In a few months' time I'll be a single mother, for God's sake. Which damned well gives me licence to not have a clue about anything. All I'll be fit for is hooning round town with a shoulder caked in sick and a sodding buggy. And I'm *bound* to get post-natal depression.'

'Don't,' I say.

'S'OK.' She shrugs, cutting herself a wedge of stinky Stilton and slathering it with mango chutney and peanut butter. 'I'll be able to rob things from shops and get away with it.'

And then, as has happened a handful of times over the past couple of days, it suddenly hits her again that she's actually having a real, live baby.

'Fuuuuuuck,' she yells at the top of her voice. 'What the effing hell am I going to do with the poor little sod when it comes out?'

I wince, putting my hands over my ears. 'You'll give the poor thing tinnitus. And Tourette's. And you've got mango chutney all over your yap. Wipe it off.'

I wait until George gets home from work before asking him when Didier's coming over. He's slightly concerned over the E-coli poisoning he may have sustained after consuming a ropy chicken chausseur in the work canteen so I figure now is as good a time is any. He wasn't exactly delighted about asking Didier to make the dress because he once slept with him in a moment of weakness and is terrified of people finding out. But eventually he agreed.

'Well, I don't want you having to slop to Top Shop like some strumpet from Sydenham and buying something rubbish,' he tutted. 'So I suppose having him using our fridge as a nosebag and dragging his fat arse across our soft furnishings for one day will be just about bearable.'

Didier's visit is fixed for a Sunday morning. And on the day, I chuck Nick out before the damp patch has dried and schlep downstairs, where George is having pre-wedding nerves. He's making tea like it's going out of fashion and pacing up and down the hall like an expectant father. All that's missing is the cigar.

'He's been at it all morning,' David frets, when I plonk myself on the sofa. I'm hot, grubby and reeking of sweaty hangover sex. Not exactly your typical blushing bride. 'Anyone would think he was getting cold feet.'

'Anyone would think he was the bloody *bride*,' I say firmly, chugging my feet out of the scrofulous black trainers I've worn downstairs and wincing as Didier, who has arrived already and is looking absolutely colossal today in a mauve three-piece suit, complete with apricot-coloured tie, grabs me, tells me to stand on the coffee table and cuts my circulation off somewhere around mid-thigh with his tape measure.

'Careful,' he worrits, smoothing the lapels of his mauve shirt and frowning. 'You'll stick your great clodhopping foot straight through the fabric.' He layers great swathes of shimmering pinky-gold material around me, nipping and tucking with small, neat movements as David supplies us with gallons of hot tea and thick bacon sandwiches, dripping in ketchup. 'This is the right sort of colour, I take it?'

I'm forced to admit that yes, Didier is a bloody genius. It's *exactly* the right colour.

He smiles fatly, his cheeks puce with pleasure. George winces, presumably at the thought of that ill-fated night when they shared a bed.

'Thank you.' He does a silly little bow. 'And may I just say what a treat it is to work with someone who has absolutely no suggestion of any bosom whatsoever.'

'It is?' I yelp, as another pin jabs into the flesh of my thigh.

'Oh yes.' He nods. 'You've got the perfect figure for this lark. Tits like gnat bites.'

'I have?'

'Yes. Nothing better than a golf club to hang clothes on. Ever thought of modelling?'

'I'd rather piss blood, thanks.'

'Oh.'

'Sorry,' I shake my head, 'but I haven't got the time to sit around worrying about how cottage cheesy my arse is going to get or how I'm going to persuade my hair to lie stick straight,' I explain. 'I've got better things to think about.'

'Some of these blushing brides-to-be come to you expecting miracles, don't they, Did?' George says.

'They do.'

'Actually square-shaped, some of them, you know, Katie,' George goes on. 'They come podging in looking like ruddy Rubik's cubes. All wringing their porky little fingers in pathetic pre-nuptial excitement. And you can't come straight out with it and tell them it just isn't possible to stuff six pounds of sausagemeat into a one-pound skin. Can you?'

'No.' Didier yanks at my shoulder straps, almost choking me. 'Breathe in then, love. No, you're quite right, Georgie. My talents may be considerable but one has to draw the line somewhere. One can't make a Pucci bag out of a pig's arsehole, no matter how hard one tries.'

I stand, bored out of my brains, as Didier pins and tucks, stitches and bitches around me. My mind's on other things. I can't help worrying about the coffee cake and other fancies I'm supposed to be making for some do or other in Lavender Hill. Just when am I going to find the time to do it all?

'Isn't this fantastic?' George is helping Didier and patting my hair excitedly. 'Like having our very own Girls' World. Where's that tiara you got?'

'In my room.' George obediently trots upstairs to get it and brings it back down and plonks it straight on my head. I preen in the mirror, thoroughly delighted at the sparkliness of it all.

'It's funny, isn't it, really?' I say, as George, David and I take time out for about our tenth cup of tea. 'I mean, what the buggery bollocks does it matter how I look if the guests amount to diddly squat and no one's going to see me? I could just wear my comfy combat pants and my Timberlands, couldn't I?'

'No one?' George ejaculates.

'No one?' Didier echoes.

'I wouldn't exactly call Marcel *no one*, would you, darling?' screeches George. 'He's done flowers for Fergie more than once.'

'*And* Davina McCall,' says Didier. 'And she's *very* now.'

'And that Dorien from *Birds of a Feather*, come to that,' adds David. 'Did her some lovely delphiniums, he did. She's lovely in real life, apparently. Not a complete slapper at all.'

'And there's Fran the Tran and Ermintrude,' George says. 'Just because they've had their bits chopped off doesn't mean they're no one either, darling. They'd be terribly hurt to hear you say that.'

'*They're* coming?' I ask.

'We said they could be the Confetti Bettys,' David admits. 'They felt a bit left out so they're going to give out rose petals by the front door when you come down the steps. And we've got Prosper and Rex ushing.'

'Ushing what?' I ask sharply.

George raises his eyebrows to heaven. Actually, it's just the one eyebrow he raises. He currently only has one. A monobrow. Usually, he plucks the tufty in-between bits to death. But his head has been too full of hysterical puffy pink wedding thoughts of late. He simply hasn't the time to attend to personal grooming.

'What do *you* think?' he says tiredly. 'Whatever needs to be ushed, of course. Guests, children, small dogs. *I* don't know.'

'But we aren't *having* any guests,' I protest. 'Apart from Janice and Sam, of course.'

Actually, after our argument, I still don't know if Sam is coming. But I can't worry about that right now. I have to think positive thoughts.

'Of *course* he'll come,' George says, reading my thoughts. 'And of *course* we're having guests. We've invited everyone we can think of.'

'But I thought we agreed...'

'Oh, *bugger* what we agreed, darling,' George scoffs. 'I'm bloody well paying for the whole shebang so I'll have what I want, if that's all right by you.'

'Isn't it all going to look a bit gay?' I ask. 'What with half of Madame Jo Jo's turning up? What if the Home Office decide to investigate? Aren't they going to get a tad suspicious when the wedding guests all resemble the Village People?'

'Sam'll be there,' David reassures me. '*He's* not gay.'

'Sad but true,' George says.

They both giggle.

'Great,' I say. 'Sam and Pussy. Sport Billy and a strip of linguine hardly count as representatives of the Heterosexual London Members Club.'

'And *you'll* be there,' David says. 'In your girlie pink dress and your glitzy shoes. Now if we were dressing you as a dirty great diesel dyke, then I could understand your concern.'

'Yes,' George says. 'And you can't try telling me you're a rug muncher now, darling. Not with you out trapping cock all over the shop.'

'*Don't* make us cancel,' David begs.

'No, don't,' George pleads. 'It's *our* day, after all.'

I suppose I can't really disagree with that. *I* might be the one signing the piece of paper but it's George and David who are really making the commitment. After all, they love the bones of each other, don't they?

Don't they?

Of course they do. Or, at least, I bloody well hope so. Or why am I putting myself through all this?

'Perhaps you're running away from something,' niggles a little voice inside my head.

'Oh yeah,' I challenge it. 'Like what?'

'Perhaps you're afraid of getting hurt again?' it nags.

'Yeah, right,' I tell it, more firmly this time. 'I think I've got my own back on Jake Carpenter, thank you. This time, I'm in control. So who's the daddy now? Eh?'

But something's still niggling at me. And, as I think about it, a picture of Sam comes into my head.

Isn't that weird?

Not Jake. Not Nick. Not even Moony Max, total letdown and Mr Mills & Boon in disguise. Sam. Simple as that.

Not that I *want* him, obviously. I mean I wasn't interested in him when he was single, was I? When he was running around with every teensy weensy blonde bit of fluff in London? Of *course* I didn't. I'd have eaten fibreglass for brekky before I'd have settled for Sam in the old days.

So what's changed?

'You *do* want him,' a voice in my head informs me.

'No I bloody don't,' I protest.

'Oh yes you do,' says the voice.

'Oh sod off,' I tell it. 'This isn't a bloody pantomime.'

'You want him,' insists the voice. 'Because you can't have him.'

'Bollocks,' I say. But I have to admit, I always have been a bit like that. Always wanting the impossible. Like when I was two and I wanted my bath towel to be dry immediately. A new one just wouldn't do. It was well before the days of tumble dryers and my parents tried to explain that it just wasn't on. But I wouldn't have it. I screamed until I was maroon in the face and had to be pacified with a chocolate Homewheat.

But Sam is different. Of course I don't want him. Not in that way. But I am supposed to be seeing him soon, so we can take Lucy to the park. And I don't really want to let him down. We'd already arranged it before we rowed. Now I just don't know whether I should turn up or not. George is still twittering when I snap out of my reverie. Something about shelling out for the wedding. How much it's all going to cost and everything.

'I'll be an official poor person after I've paid for this lot,' he threatens. 'I'll probably have to give up my lovely mews house and go out East. I'll end up in Stoke Newington. Probably. Or Barking. I might even have to go 0208.'

'Yeah, right.' I flinch as Didier, quick as a whippet, stabs a hand down my bra to hoick up one of my nipples. They aren't on straight apparently, and it's spoiling the line of the frock.

'S'true, darling,' George tells me. 'We'll be in market jumpers come winter. We'll be forced to buy a deep fat fryer and a set-top box and live at the top of a tower block. A really rank one that smells of wee. You know, like they have on *The Bill*. All our neighbours will look like Pauline Quirke in *Birds of a Feather*, darling, and we'll be afraid to go out in case we get queer-bashed, so we'll have to stay in every Saturday night on our orange Dralon sofa watching *Wheel of Fortune* with the volume up and eating Pot Noodle.'

He's clearly conveniently forgotten he has a trust fund the size of the Third World debt.

Chapter 20

Sam and Lucy, wearing matching navy baseball caps, are waiting for me by the bridge, just as Sam said they'd be. As I shamble over, Sam grins and Lucy, in glittery jeans and pink trainers that light up when they hit the pavement, runs over to give me a hug.

'Mum says you're going to be my Auntie Katie now. Are you and my Uncle Sam getting married?'

I laugh. 'No. My mum is marrying your granddad. Which sort of makes me your mum and Sam's new sister.'

'Oh.' Lucy looks a bit confused but cheers up almost immediately. 'I've gotta kite. Are you going to help me fly it?'

'OK.' I raise my eyebrows at Sam. 'But only if we can have cake first.'

'OK.'

We troop to the café. I'm still a bit worried that Sam'll be off with me after our row so I offer to buy the tea and cake. Normally, I wouldn't pay under any circumstances but I feel the need. And when Lucy has chomped her way through a hunk of ginger cake and got a sugar rush from a huge glass of Coke, she runs onto the grass to tie herself up in knots with the kite and I tell Sam how sorry I am.

'S'OK.' He shakes his head and gulps his tea. 'It was all a bit of a shock, I suppose.'

'I felt bad that you knew about Mum and Jeff before I did.' I look at the crumbs on my plate. 'And Pussy. And she's not even family. Well, not yet anyway.'

'No.' Sam gazes into the distance, watching Lucy tearing around in a blur of glitter and flashing light.

'So?' I say, not really knowing what to say next.

'So?'

'So have you thought about a date?'

'A date?' He looks confused. 'Who with?'

'For your wedding, doh. Or had you forgotten?'

'God.' He wedges in more banana loaf. 'I'm so busy with the company at the moment I can't really think about that now. I'm doing the launch of a new restaurant in the City next week. It's really high-profile.'

'That's great, Sam.' I'm pleased.

'So I think,' he finishes the last of his tea, 'that we should talk about *your* wedding. Don't you? I mean you're getting married way before I am.'

'I guess,' I admit, watching as two girls, all long legs and tiny vests, eye Sam appreciatively. 'But it's boring. I mean it's not really real, is it? No passion or romance or anything.'

'I thought you didn't believe in all that claptrap.' Sam ruffles my hair.

'I don't. That's why I'm having a pretend wedding instead.'

'You mad hoon.' He grins, just as an indignant voice pipes up from somewhere in the distance.

'Uncle *Sam*.'

'Here we go,' he sighs. 'Playground duty. You coming?'

'Think I might just have another bit of cake, thanks.'

'Typical,' he snorts, dashing off to help Lucy untangle her kite from a nearby bench. A yappy Jack Russell has somehow become involved and I almost choke on cake as I watch Sam get in a terrible 'mess with string, while the dog barks at his heels and Lucy squeals delightedly. Privately, I think that nasty, scratty little creatures like that just shouldn't be allowed but then it becomes apparent that its owner is sitting at the table next to ours. Winking at me, the lady adjusts her strange floppy hat and whistles to the dog, who comes trotting obediently over to stick its head in my crotch. I have to pat it and pretend I think it's sweet, then she twinkles at me and nods in Sam and Lucy's direction.

'Like her dad, isn't she?'

'Who?' I look up sharply.

'Your little girl.'

'Oh, no.' I laugh. 'He's not, I mean, she's not ours. We're just borrowing her.'

'A-ha.' The woman twinkles again. 'Practising, are we?'

Not sodding likely. Nevertheless, the fact that the doggy lady thought Sam and I were together cheers me up immensely for some ridiculous reason. And the thought of babies and children makes me think of Janice, who is probably sitting at home on her own, knitting bootees. Or drinking gin and rocking, knowing her. So, after another hour of cheek-chapping kite antics, I nip over to Janice's flat. She looks delighted to see me because I've interrupted the work she's doing on a pitch for a new brand of fizzy drink.

'Since you've made the effort to come over, it'd be damn rude to send you away, wouldn't it?' She grins, patting her tummy.

'Damn rude.' I flop on her immaculate sofa and immediately crinkle up three velvet cushions. Janice makes a 'what am I going to do with you' face and decrees that we need to go shopping.

'What for?'

'Holiday.' She stands up. 'That's what. Come on. You need a new swimsuit. You don't want Sam to think you look rancid, do you?'

'Why would I care what Sam thinks?'

'Oh, come on. You look suspiciously rosy for someone who's been lumbered with a small child all day.'

'It's windy.'

'And you've got a bit of a soft spot.'

'Haven't.'

'Have. It's written all over your chops. Now come on, let's shop.'

Janice's theory is that if she's going to look like a poached egg on toast on this holiday, she might as well have some luxury items to do it in. Personally, I can't even see a bump yet but, as we flick through rails of clothes, she looks as happy as a pig in muck.

'This is just what we need.' She flicks through the rack of Kookai dresses we're examining. 'Shopping always makes me feel better.'

'What's wrong with you then? I thought you'd come to terms with the baby.'

'I have. Sort of. But I've still got to tell my mother she's going to be a grandma. I'm dreading it.'

'You think she'll be angry?'

'*Christ* no.' She shakes her head. 'Quite the flaming opposite. She'll be over the bloody moon. I just dread to think of the clothes she'll buy the poor little sod. One of those ghastly furry hats with ears, probably. Why do some people dress their kids up as dogs and bears and imagine it's cute, Katie?'

'I don't know.'

'And she'll insist it calls her Nan, or something horrid like that.'

'So?'

'Sod it.' She lets go of the stunning shell-pink halterneck she's checking out and shrugs. 'None of these are going to fit me in a few months' time. Still, just because I'm going to look like a juggernaut in the holiday photos doesn't mean *you* have to. You won't want shot after shot of you in the same threadbare cozzie with your thighs all pink and stuck to a deck chair with sweat and your head jammed in a Jackie Collins, will you? What you need is a whole new wardrobe. A new bikini for every day.'

'You don't look like a juggernaut. And we're only going for the weekend,' I point out. 'But *you* have to buy new stuff as well,' I say. 'For the future. You're up the duff, don't forget.'

'I am, aren't I?' she says wistfully, looking down at her boobs, which will soon resemble a pair of barrage balloons. 'I'm *right* up that duff. I couldn't be more up the duff if I tried.'

'When does your belly button turn inside out?' I want to know.

'Not sure.' She grins. 'I'm quite looking forward to that part. It really freaks blokes out.'

'You're not going to fill your wardrobe with those horrible clothes that have baggy kangaroo pouches at the front for your enormous stomach, are you?' I ask.

'God, no. I'm going to wear bikinis and let it all hang out. Like Madonna. And Posh. And I'm not going to let myself go *completely*. While we're in Spain, I'm going to swim all the time. And just eat salads.'

'I'm not,' I say. 'I'm going to lard it. Lager for breakfast, pina colada for lunch and chips with everything. I can't wait.'

And I *am* looking forward to it, funnily enough, although I'm still surprised by George's decision to go completely bargain basement, holiday-wise. Generally, his idea of a package is something he takes home from Harrods Food Hall, filled with chunks of smoked venison and slivers of wild salmon.

Doesn't he *know* charter flights only have one class?

If you can call it class.

How's he going to cope?

Unfortunately, shopping for new clothes doesn't really make me feel better for very long. When I get home, George and David have gone out, leaving a note that they've gone to see a rom com at the Screen on the Green, and I suddenly feel all lonely and scared stiff about my wedding. I'm currently sleeping in a room full of David's pants in case the Home Office decide to drop by at seven o'clock of a morning and catch us unawares, and I'm not at all sure I've done the right thing, agreeing to this madness.

Except I've *seen* George and David together. And, although they're professionally flippant, I know they love each other hugely. So I really can't back out now, can I? Not without sending David scarpering off back to Oz and handily ruining two lives in the process. Anyway, even if my plans to marry David aren't exactly conventional, at least I'm making two other people happy. So when Sam's sister Sally and I meet for coffee to talk about Mum and Jeff's wedding reception and she asks me if I'm sure I'm not going to regret it, I'm able to say with absolute certainty that I know I'm doing the right thing.

'Don't worry on my account, Sal. I don't need to see sense. I've seen it already. And it's dull, dull, dull.'

'You know, I'm not just saying all this for the sake of it.' She frowns. 'It's for your own good.'

Privately, I doubt that. When someone tells you something is for your own good, you know you are going to find it about as pleasant as colonic irrigation.

'To be honest, Sal,' I explain, 'I really can't be arsed with the whole love and marriage thing. In my experience, blokes really only seem to be good for shagging and leaving and not very much else.'

The day of our departure looms and I decide not to bother telling Jake or Nick I'm off to sunny Spain (well, sort of Spain) for the weekend. Let them figure it out for themselves. Janice comes over first thing to check over my packing.

'Olay, olay,' she yells, bursting through the front door on heels you could spike a salmon on, teamed with a tiny lipstick-pink vest and crisp white cotton shorts. 'Feelin' hot hot hot,' she carries on. 'Look, check this out.' She flashes me a lemon-yellow scrap of not very much. 'My new cozzie. And this silver boob tube. I mean, I may have a mouse in the chimney but I don't have an arseful of cellulite quite yet so I might as well whore it up one last time before I get great bunches of grapes dangling out of my bum. What do you reckon?'

'Oh, Janice.' I shake my head in mock pity.

'What?'

'Nothing.' I hug her. 'I just bloody love you to pieces.'

'You too, hon.' She hugs me back. 'So come on. Show us yer cozzie.'

'Here.' I hold up a chunky one-piece. Practically polo-necked, it's the only thing I'll be seen dead on the beach in. Short of full body armour, that is.

'What the fuck is that?' she hoots.

'Everything else made me look like a member of Legs and Co,' I explain.

'That's, like, the point.' She grins. 'You nutter. I still think you should have bought that powder-blue jobby with the fluffy bits on the boobs. You looked great in that.'

I shrug. 'I don't really see it matters what the hell I look like. I have it on very good authority that my fiancé's a screaming poof. It's going to take a lot more than a scrap of lycra and a couple of banana daiquiris to get him to play tame the trouser snake with me.'

She laughs. 'True.'

'And believe me,' I can't help giggling, 'I've tried.'

Janice throws back her head and roars.

'It's not exactly sexy though, is it?' she protests when she's recovered from the giggles. 'Your cozzie, I mean, not your fiancé. Who is, as it happens, very sexy.'

'*Very*,' I agree.

'It's the kind of thing you see on middle-aged women in the swimming pool. The ones who wear flowery rubber swimming caps and keep their heads above water so their eyeshadow doesn't wash off.'

'Whatever.'

'Have you got your factor fifty sunblock?'

'I've got factor five.' I look at the bottle. 'Will that do?'

'Katie, you *know* you can't tan,' she admonishes me. 'And freckles are *so* last year. I read it in *Marie Claire*. Do you really want to turn up to your fake wedding with a face you can play join the dots on?'

'I'll buy some at the airport.'

'What about trashy novels for the beach?' she asks. 'I've got *Appassionata* by Jilly Cooper and the new Penny Vincenzi.'

'I've got *Bugger Me Backwards* by Fawn Starr and *Fuck Me Pink* by Regina De Vine.'

'Really?'

'No.'

'What *have* you got then?'

'I've got *Captain Corelli's Mandolin* and *Memoirs of a Geisha*,' I say.

'I said "trashy",' she protests. 'What you need is a good shopping and fucking extravaganza the size of a brick. I'll lend you one. Now, moving on swiftly. Beach towel?'

I pull out a threadbare orange and purple thing I used to have for swimming at school. My name tag is still sewn along one edge.

'Er. OK. Insect repellent?'

'*Pleb* repellent's what we need.' George struts in from the sitting room with three huge glasses of Sex on the Beach and an orange juice for Janice. 'God, if someone came up with a handy pocket-sized spray that kept white socks and acne at bay, they'd stand to make a fucking fortune.'

We hoover back cocktails to get us in the holiday mood, then hop in a taxi bound for Gatwick. The airport is buzzing with families, all looking forward to taking off for a couple of weeks in the sun. George wrinkles up his nose.

'Been saving all year, probably, most of these people,' he says. 'I mean, I could afford to go and come back then turn round and go again if I wanted.'

'Snob,' I tell him.

'It's exciting though, isn't it?' He rubs his hands together with glee. 'I keep expecting that nice satsuma-skinned Easyjet lady to come clipping over to ask if we need help with our bags.'

Surprisingly, we manage to find the airline desk without mishap, then George declares he can't possibly check in until he's had a fag, so we all obediently trot over to the smoking area and sit there until he's had his nicotine fix.

'Where's Sam?' I look round, worried. He should be here by now.

'Dunno.' George inhales. 'Tell you what,' he grins lecherously at David, 'can't wait till we get on the plane. I love the bit when the pilot says. "Cabin crew, positions for take-off, please."'

'Why?' I'm stumped.

'They always have those gorgeous "come to bed" voices, don't they?' He titters. 'Is it part of the training, do you reckon, to learn to speak silkily?'

'I suppose it must be.' I think about it and decide he's probably right. 'I mean, you never get Geordie pilots, do you?'

'Exactly.' He nods. 'Or ones with Brookie accents. When did you ever hear a flight captain saying, "Haway, man, let's gan tae the canny Canaries then"?'

'They're always Milk Tray Men,' Janice agrees.

David laughs. 'They could have back-up careers as understudy for the man who does the voiceovers on cinema trailers.'

'If he hadn't got there first,' I point out.

'Obviously.'

'They're always tall, dark and handsome as well, aren't they?' Janice looks excited.

'Oh, please don't shag the pilot,' I beg.

'Hardly.' She prods her still-flat stomach. 'This is kinda going to get in the way, don't you think?'

'I know what you mean though,' David says suddenly. 'I suppose they must weed out the blond ones.'

'Doesn't go so well with the uniform,' George points out.

'Must be tricky if you work for KLM though,' Janice says. 'Or Finn Air. They must be a bit short on brunettes.'

'Probably have to take on a few blonds just to make up the numbers,' George says.

Everyone starts laughing. I laugh too, although inside I'm panicking like mad. Where's Sam? He should be here by now. I mean, I know he's really busy with work. And Pussy's probably furious at him for coming on holiday without her, but he promised. The holiday won't be the same without him.

'Soddim.' George hands our passports to the nice lady behind the airline desk and tells her that, yes, he did pack his bag himself, though if he could have sodding well afforded it, he'd have got a personal valet to do it for him. She starts looking pale under her tangerine-tinted moisturiser.

George insists we can't wait out here for Sam any more. He needs to go into the Duty Free to buy products. We're just choosing ciggies to last us the weekend when my mobile rings. Typically, it's wedged at the very bottom of my tote bag.

'Bugger.' I rummage, trying to get to the damn thing before it stops. 'If that's my sodding mother ringing to tell me to be careful...'

'Why shouldn't she?' David defends her.

'Well, what does she think I'm going to do?' I demand, still rummaging. 'Go out of my way to *not* be careful. Throw myself out of the plane on the way over? Deliberately catch malaria?'

'They don't have malaria in Tenerife,' Janice points out.

'We're not going to Tenerife, thickie,' George reminds her.

'As good as.' She shrugs.

'Or perhaps she thinks I'll go off and shag some bloke who carries a flick knife.'

'Wouldn't put it past you,' Janice sniggers.

'Sod off.' I shoot her a look, finally finding my phone. 'Hello?'

'Katie?'

Shit.

Sam.

My heart spins in my chest at the mere sound of his voice. I shake myself. What's *wrong* with me? Sam's just a mate. But what if he's ringing to say he can't make it? I think I'll be too depressed to last out the weekend if my oldest friend isn't there.

'Where are you?' he asks.

'I'm at the airport,' I say. 'Where did you think I was?'

'Shit,' he says. 'You mean the holiday's now? As in today?'

'Well, yes, obviously,' I say. 'I mean, I haven't come here to watch planes take off all day. And I'm not making a television documentary about aeroplane food, either. It's the real thing all right. I'm off to the Canaries in roughly an hour and a half.'

'Bugger.'

The line goes dead.

'Who was it?' Janice catches sight of my confused expression.

'Sam.'

'What did he want?'

'Fuck knows.' I stare at the handset as though it holds all the answers. 'He didn't exactly say.'

'Didn't say he loved you then?' She grins.

'Sod off.'

For some reason, we both find this hilarious.

'Is he on his way?'

'I don't know.' I look at my mobile, depressed.

At twelve thirty-five, just as our flight is due to be called, an announcement comes over the tannoy.

'*Would Miss Katherine Simpson please come to the Britannia Airways information desk immediately.*'

'Shit.' I look at my watch. 'We'll miss the flight.'

'You'd better go, hon,' Janice says. 'It might be urgent.'

'It's probably your bloody mother ringing to tell you to be careful.' George laughs.

'More than likely.' I stick my passport in my bag and flounce off in the direction of the information desk. Trust my mother to almost make me miss the one holiday I've had in about fifteen years.

'Miss Simpson?'

'Yes?'

'Telephone call for you.'

It *is* my sodding mother.

'Hello?'

'Miss Simpson?'

'*Yes.*'

Shit. How many more times?

'Check-in here. I have a Mr Freeman at the desk. He says you have his ticket.'

'Mr...?'

'Freeman.'

Oh God.

Sam.

He's *here*.

He's coming.

We're going to have a brilliant time, after all.

But, hang on. *Have* I got his ticket? Did I bring it with me? Oh soddit, soddit. SOD it.

Wherethefuckisit?

I haven't got it.

Yes I have. Here it is.

No. That's a receipt for a black skirt from Oasis. Shit.

Wait a minute. Yes. That's it.

Yesssssss.

'It's here,' I tell the man on the other end of the phone.

Sam is standing, flushed, gorgeous, by the entrance to departures. His hair is sticking up all over the place and his T-shirt is rucked up around his waist. As I approach I can hear our names being called for our flight.

'What are you doing here?' I ask as he comes through the gate and gives me a hug. He's all hot and sweaty. Lovely.

'Coming on holiday.' He grins. 'What does it look like?'

'We've got two minutes to catch the plane. I thought you weren't coming.'

'I'm sorry. I've been so busy at work. I got the dates mixed up. I knew I had to be somewhere today but I thought it was the restaurant. And then when I got there and they told me that was a week away, I remembered I was going on holiday.'

'Nutter.'

'Nutter yourself, Simpson.' He grabs my hand and we make a run for it.

As we board, just in time, I suddenly feel ridiculously happy. My best buddy is here. For some insane reason, at this crazy, confused moment in my life, that simple fact means the world to me.

Chapter 21

I settle into my tiny aeroplane seat and tell Sam that now he's actually remembered to come along on my hen weekend, perhaps he can try not to flirt with any of the air hostesses as they trot past with the trolley.

'There'll be hell to pay if one of them gets all worked up and lets the brake off by accident. We don't want the perfume and fags careening off into the toilets.'

George and David both laugh, but Sam isn't listening. He's too busy trying to look out of the window to see if the wings are in the correct position. And he's turned the colour of guacamole.

'What's the matter?'

'Do you know that planes sometimes come within a hundred yards of each other?' He looks worried. 'And the passengers aren't even told?'

'Hardly ever.' I pat his knee, remembering that he's absolutely terrified of flying. When he goes away on business he has to take tranquillisers. But he's putting up with it. For me.

Bless.

'What was that bump?'

'It's the wheels coming up, you silly sod.' I laugh. 'Are you really that scared?'

'Yes.' He gives me a withering look. 'I won't even be able to eat my aeroplane food when they bring it.'

'Oh?'

'No. But don't think I'm giving it to you. It can stay in the wrapper.'

Still scared out of his wits, Sam rests his head on my shoulder. I smell his hair and restrain myself from wanting to either lick him or snog the face off him, while the rest of our party take out sweets and magazines and prepare for the four-hour flight.

'This is going to be terrible,' Sam groans.

'Don't worry. We'll have fun when we get there.'

'True.'

'As long as you don't spoil it by making us all do loads of sport.' I kind of like the way his fear is making him nuzzle against me. 'The only exercise I'm doing this holiday is lifting a pint glass.'

'Or snogging a Greek waiter.' Janice looks up from *Marie Claire*.

'We're going to the Canaries,' George points out.

'So?'

'It's about as Greek as you are, retard,' he clicks. 'They speak Spanish.'

'Whatever.'

I sit back and enjoy the flight, relishing Sam's nearness. It's probably just me, but I feel as though there's a tiny electric current between us, crackling away in the air. He's so terrified of the plane crashing I take complete advantage, pulling him closer to me and thinking of all the things I'd like to do to him.

God. It's a good job I'm not a bloke. I'd have a hard-on by now.

Actually, I've never understood people who are afraid of flying. I love everything about it, from the important feeling I get when they ask if I've packed my bag myself to the special orangey-red lippy the air hostesses wear.

After all, people in real life never wear that colour, do they?

I even love the plastic food they dish out. In fact, the only time I do get a bit fluttery during the flight is when the trolley comes out. And that's only because I'm terrified they'll miss me out. How does everyone else stay so calm, leaving their tables up and reading until the last minute? I'm quite the opposite, whipping my head round faster than Darcy Bussell in mid-pirouette, the moment I smell that telltale waft of school dinners.

'Can I have your pretzels if you don't want them?'

Sam silently hands over the packet.

'I don't know why you're bothering to look at that safety card,' George cuts in.

'*George,*' I warn.

'Well,' he pouts, 'you know what Fran said.'

'Who's Fran?' Sam looks worried.

'No one.' I hug him.

'Fran the Tran,' George says. 'You know.'

'Oh. Yes.'

Fran is the only woman I know with facial stubble and an Adam's apple bigger than Nicholas Lyndhurst's. Still, she managed to get a job as a trolley dolly before the airline in question clamped down one day and discovered her to be in possession of a bagful of stolen fags and a penis.

Actually, even when they found out about the penis they were prepared to keep her on because she fulfilled the height requirements and she didn't spit into the food when the passengers got tricky. But she refused to tone down the make-up and wear the slacks instead of the skirt, so they said she'd have to go.

And go she did.

'What did Fran the Tran say?' Sam looks terrified.

'Well...'

'George, no,' I say.

Too late.

'When they were training,' George begins, cattily.

'Yes?'

'Well, they were told that all this palaver with the oxygen

masks and the escape chutes and the life jackets is just complete bollocks to put the passengers at ease. You see, basically...'

'Go on.'

'Basically, the general rule of thumb is, if you're thirty thousand feet above the Atlantic and both your engines are fucked, then so are you.'

Despite Sam's fears, we land safely at Fuerteventura airport, to be met by a peroxide blonde wearing the regulation Top Rank Holidays uniform. She's bright tangerine in colour and has huge calf muscles. Her feet are stuffed into navy plastic court shoes.

She smiles. 'Welcome to your Top Rank Holiday.' Except she doesn't exactly say 'Rank' because she has an unfortunate wet R. Janice and I stifle giggles as she herds us into a bus that looks as though it's held together with string and we proceed to rattle and joggle through miles of barren scrubland until we reach our 'resort'.

If I've been expecting to be surrounded by a bunch of shiny, happy people all ready for Sun, Sea, Sand and maybe a smidgen of Sex, it looks as though I'm sadly mistaken. Judging by the state of our fellow passengers, it seems that in mid-August, Snotty kids, Sweaty pits and Slingbacks are what we're in for. Still, I suppress a flicker of disappointment and force myself to remain optimistic.

Until we actually stop at our drop-off point, that is.

Our resort is known as 'The Oasis', which is the biggest misnomer I've ever come across. 'Arndale Centre', or maybe just 'Swindon' would be more appropriate. As would 'Inner City Estate'. The place is akin to a huge concrete shopping mall, dominated by bingo halls, fruit machines and the sort of restaurants I usually associate with egg, chips, weak tea, fag butts and provincial bus stations. And it's only when we're shown to our apartment that I suddenly remember the importance of reading between the lines when perusing the holiday brochure. It's absolutely vital to be aware of the following misleading phrases and their true meanings:

'Absolutely buzzing with lively hubbub well into the small hours' actually means, 'Directly under flight path, with planes landing all fucking night'.

'Close to all facilities and amenities' is more likely to mean, 'Sewage farm directly under balcony'.

Balcony itself, obviously, will be no more than a glorified windowsill.

And you can read 'Plentiful local flora and fauna' as 'Fungus and green mould in bathroom and kitchen full of bluebottles, all attracted by gastronomic delights of local sewage farm'.

Oh, and there's the bog standard 'Most resorts featured in this brochure are within a mere stone's throw of stunning, sandy beaches'.

Which, you can be damned sure, means, 'Yours isn't.'

Half our apartment block is covered in scaffolding and the view from our balcony is of a pile of rubble.

Let's face it. It's hardly an oasis. And it's about as exotic as Solihull.

Something tells me this holiday may well contain strong language from the outset. Mind you, at least George has paid for everything. So I shouldn't really give a fanny fart where we are.

Yep. Sod it. It's going to be absolutely boiling hot.

Which is enough for me.

Obviously, a ginger minger like me shouldn't really do sunbathing. It's just not nice, is it? But I do love the whole business of being able to lie out in it for five minutes and then sigh, 'Oh, it's too hot out here. I'll just have to have a quick dip in the pool then it's off to the shade for me for chips and lager.'

After all, that's what holidays are all about.

I'll feel a lot better when we've targeted some nice little place to have dinner.

But it's difficult to remain optimistic when the smell of drains is so overpowering we have to keep all the windows firmly closed. And when it comes to bagsying the bedrooms, I'm mortified when I realise I'm going to have to share with Sam.

How am I going to stop myself from craning to catch a glimpse of his willy every time he comes out of the shower?

Bugger Janice. She's insisted she has the single room. Apparently she's not sleeping too well. The thought that she'll soon look like Mr Greedy is bothering her at night. And she doesn't want to keep anyone else awake. Personally, I don't think there's anything wrong with her sleep pattern. She just doesn't want to share.

After we've freshened up, we congregate on our balcony/windowsill to quaff the champagne George bought at the airport. And, as we get giggly on bubbles, we declare the atmosphere to be distinctly more Suburban Starter Home than Spanish Villa. And Sam is only half joking when he bets me five thousand pesetas that the sound of cicadas we can hear is tape-recorded and played on a loop through speakers hidden along the pathway outside.

Our welcome meeting does very little to raise our hopes further. Dee (the orange-calved rep) welcomes us once again to our Top Wank holiday with a plastic cupful of watered down Sangria and shakes us all by the hand.

Is it my imagination, or does she look as though she's offering us her condolences?

She goes on to advise us not to drink the water, because, although it isn't harmful, it is full of minerals and tastes of rotten eggs. She also warns us that some of the beaches dotted around are full of naturalists, although I think she means naturists. And then she explains that the reason the resort is almost completely greenery-free and therefore looks as barren as Elizabeth I is that the Canary Islands only get six inches of rain a year. Luckily for us, most of this is forecast for the next few days.

As this news sinks in, she then cheerfully informs us that, as this particular resort is miles from anywhere and there's very little to do here, especially when it rains, it would make a lot of sense to pay a small fortune for the privilege of joining groups of noisy families in loud beachwear on some of the organised trips to places of not so local interest.

'Any questions?' she asks finally.

'Yes,' bellows George. 'Would you think it rude of me if I asked you to stop talking now?'

'Is this a joke?' someone else asks hopefully.

'Do we get complimentary Prozac?' Janice asks.

'Would you consider changing the description of this holiday in your brochure?' asks George.

'To what?' Dee is confused.

'A Helliday.'

As it turns out, this is no joke. We're not the unwitting victims of *Candid Camera* or *Beadle's About* or any other light entertainment show for that matter. And, as we toddle off to explore our surroundings, we soon realise that 'hell' is a pretty good description of our position. The resort is a pleasure-free zone. Slap bang outside our complex there's a building site the size of a small country. And we don't have hard hats. I jump as a crane with a rusty bath attached to it swings high above our heads. Janice bursts into tears as her Jimmy Choo scuffs against the head of an abandoned doll, its eyes rolled back into its hairless head and its knickerless, genital-free bum twisted at an awkward angle to the rest of its body.

'Sorry,' she squeaks. 'It's the hormones.'

'It's OK.' We all rush to comfort her.

Nevertheless, I take it as a bad omen.

The only places to eat are downmarket Chinese restaurants or sports bars, and everything comes with chips and mushy peas. By the end of the day we still haven't seen a fresh vegetable or a Spanish person and I'm so hungry I've eaten a whole packet of Rennies.

The resort bar isn't much better. Crowded with noisy families, you'd have been forgiven for thinking someone was staging a Westlife concert.

'Let's just try to have a nice time.' Sam puts a protective hand on the small of my back and I try to ignore the delicious shiver which runs the length of my spine. God. I have to get a grip.

'This is Katie's hen weekend,' he reminds everyone. 'She deserves to have fun when you think about what she's giving up for you, George.'

'*Okay*,' huffs George.

'Thanks, Katie,' David, rushes. 'We do appreciate it, you know.'

'I know,' I say. 'And I'm fine with it. Really.'

And I *am* fine with it. Although, obviously, I'm also absolutely shitting myself.

Sam goes to the bar.

'San Miguels all round, please,' he says firmly. Even Janice has to have a quick drink to overcome her disappointment in finding herself in a shopping precinct instead of a tropical paradise.

'All English beer 'ere,' the barmaid informs us proudly. 'Yous can 'ave 'Eineken, Stripe or Stella.'

'Stella's not...' I begin, but George shushes me.

'Forget it,' he snipes. 'Her idea of going Continental is changing her fags.'

We spend the evening drinking beer and playing cards until Janice rubs her back and says she's tired. So we all troop back to the apartment together to see her safely back. After all, as George points out, this might be a holiday resort but it's probably just as dangerous as any London ghetto.

Then we all get shitfaced.

Sam is strangely quiet as David and George produce bottles of melon liqueur and champagne and introduce drinking games into the equation. When we get up to our room, Sam produces two vodka miniatures, hands one to me and pats the bed beside him.

'I owe you an apology, Simpson.'

'What for?'

'Pussy.' He opens a tonic can.

'What about Pussy?'

He sighs. 'There isn't going to be a wedding.'

A surge of hope fills my chest. I try to quash it, telling myself that of course this isn't because of me. There's another reason the wedding's off.

'Why?' I stammer.

Sam draws a deep breath, hoofs back the vodka in one go and starts to tell me.

It turns out that, just before I arrived at his house to get the food ready for his party, Pussy dropped a bit of a bombshell. She told Sam she was having a baby. That she'd suspected for a while but that now it was confirmed. Her friend, a doctor, had done a test, and it was positive. And it was his.

'What could I do?' He shrugs, frowning. 'I couldn't abandon her, could I? It would be wrong. Although I didn't exactly want a baby. Not with her.'

'Oh?'

'I knew it was never going to be serious between us, but I just thought, well, if I can't have the woman I love, I'll have the one who loves me.'

'Oh.'

He looks so adorably confused that it's all I can do not to ask, 'So who is the woman you love?' But I manage to stop myself. Because every nerve in my body is screaming 'Let it be me' and I know that's not true. It's probably Cindy Crawford. So I say nothing.

'And then Dad and Mary announced they were getting married, which, yes, I did know about before you, and I'm sorry for not telling you but I thought you should hear it from them,' he gabbles, 'and then she came out with that announcement about us, well, I was more surprised than anyone.' He frowns. 'But I couldn't humiliate her in public, could I? How could I say I didn't have the first clue about it? Not with her having my baby and everything. I had to stand by her. So I just went along with it.'

I feel a huge surge of affection for him. He's so reasonable.

'So why change your mind?' I say. 'What happened?'

'She made it all up,' he says.

'What? About wanting to marry you?'

'No,' he shakes his head, 'about the baby. There was no baby.

Never had been. She just wanted to get me up the aisle, so she said she was pregnant.'

'No way.'

'Way.'

'How did you find out?'

'I happened to mention the whole thing to the doctor friend a few days later. And she said that, although patient advice was confidential, she thought I ought to be aware that she'd never *given* any advice. She had no clue about any baby. She was as dumbstruck as I was. So I confronted Pussy. And she confessed.'

'Did she cry?' I ask.

'Yes.'

'Good.'

'Oh, Simpson.' Sam suddenly looks up and smiles at me.

'What?'

'I just remembered why I love you to bits.'

'To bits.' That's the operative word, isn't it? It's the difference between 'I love you, I want to spend the rest of my life with you' and 'I love you, you're a mate'. But Sam pulls me to him and hugs me anyway and we go to sleep, curled together like spoons in the big double bed.

When I wake up next day, he's gone. There's a note on the table.

'Gone to get breakfast.'

I open the shutters excitedly, looking forward to a day of sunbathing. I'm disappointed. It's cold, grey and lashing down with rain. I can't help feeling depressed. The six inches of rain the Canarians get on average per year are clearly all arriving today. I pull on a pair of jeans and a sweatshirt and go outside. In the rain, the resort is even more depressing than before. And with no sign of Sam, I feel empty inside. I can't wait to go home.

In the resort bar, all the other guests are watching UK Gold and eating crisps. I turn on my heel and start to walk out when I spot George, teetering along by the edge of the swimming pool.

'All right?'

'No,' he tuts. 'I'm somewhat concerned about the amount of gold jewellery around. And look at the ruddy food. God, I'd do anything for a sundried tomato.'

I glance quickly around. He's right. The people here are—let's just say they're different. Vermilion-faced girls from Blackburn who are 'Out looking for mischief', and a large, fifty-year-old woman from Sunderland who, in a clingy orange dress made from waffle material and a tiny pair of matching plastic shoes with little pointy heels, looks not unlike an upside down space hopper.

'God,' George says again. 'It's like a miniature Mosside.'

'Stop it,' I say, trying not to laugh. At least he's cheering me up.

'It's true. The people here have probably all brought boxes of Shreddies with them because they can't eat foreign muck.'

I'm saved from replying by Sam, who saunters jauntily into the bar, a huge bag of fresh bread rolls swinging from one arm and a smug look on his face.

'What have you done?' I ask.

'Come back to the apartment and I'll tell you.' He grabs my hand. 'You too, George. I've got a surprise for you.'

Over the crusty rolls with butter and apricot jam, Sam tells us all that's he's had us transferred to a hotel across the other side of the town.

'What's it like?' George looks dubious.

'Oh, come on.' Janice, still in her towelling robe, looks at him. 'It can't be any worse than this dump.'

'Pack your stuff and come and see.' Sam smiles at me. 'It's my treat.'

'You mean you've paid for it?' I ask. 'Oh Sam, you can't—'

'Yes I can. Come on, Simpson.' He pats my shoulder. 'This is your holiday. You're doing something really unselfish here. You deserve to have a nice time.'

'Oh, Sam.' I smile at him. 'Thanks.'

'Any time,' he says. 'Come on. Let's get out of here.'

Everyone jumps up. Apart from me, that is. Despite myself,

I can't seem to move. I'm just looking at Sam, gorgeous in a pair of faded jeans and no top. And I want to hug him. I've never felt like this before. My tummy is flipping like a fish and I don't know what the hell is going on.

All I do know is that there's more to it than just fancying him. Bugger.

I *can't* be in love with him.

Can I?

Luckily, I'm saved from further thought on the subject by Janice, who suddenly shrieks like a banshee.

'Ohmigod.'

'Diddit kick?' We all rush to touch her tummy.

'No.' She pushes us away. 'Gerroff. It's way too early for that. I just thought. What if I get a fat one? A horrible fat kid. I'll have to put it on a diet and it'll be traumatised for life.'

'It won't be fat,' I reassure her.

'It might mind being called "it" though,' Sam points out. 'Anyway, you'll love it whatever it looks like. Won't she, Katie?'

'How the fuck would I know?' I ask.

He looks sad suddenly and I feel guilty. He's probably thinking about the baby he thought he was having a couple of weeks ago. Shit. Perhaps he really wanted it after all. Oh God. Have I made him feel worse?

Luckily we're all distracted by George.

'*Ooooh*,' he yells suddenly, rushing to the balcony. 'David, look. There in the leopard-print thong. Out in the rain and all. Pass the bollockspotters.'

David hands George their communal binoculars so he can ogle a piece of prime male meat as it struts towards the pool bar.

'Nice bod.' George hands them back.

'Looks a bit German to me,' Janice declares.

'You sure?' I pick up the binoculars myself. 'How many loungers has he bagged?'

We all burst into gales of giggles then rush to pack our stuff before Sam changes his mind about the nice hotel. None of us wants to stay here another minute. The poolside bingo is about to start and that might just send George over the edge. When we're ready, we go to find Dee. She's sitting in a corner of the dingy bar, a pint of lager in front of her.

'Drinking on the job?' I ask her. I feel a bit sorry for her. We're escaping. Imagine actually having to live here.

It doesn't bear thinking about.

'We're leaving,' I say, trying to be as polite as I can.

Dee shrugs, glancing around the bar area at the other tourists, with their screaming brats, their Superkings and their white raffia wedge heels. She doesn't blame us, she says. She's out of here once her contract's up. She's only doing maternity leave. The girl who covered this patch before her got knocked up by one of the locals six months ago and has gone home to give birth in a proper hospital.

''Ere mind, it was even worse where I was before. I was in Zákinthos, see,' she explains. 'You couldn't get pwoper English food for love nor money out there. It was all tawamasalata and that Gweek shit. Here, at least you don't have to go near a paella if you don't want to. And they do a lovely omelette and chips in the hotel down the road. And the local lads don't expect to kick the back door in every time you have sex with them.'

'She means take it up the arse.' George, coming up behind me with our bags, just catches the end of what she's saying. 'Up the stout and bitt—'

'Yes, thank you, George, I know what she means,' I say quickly. 'I don't think that's going to apply to me actually,' I tell Dee. 'I've seen some of the locals and I don't think I'll be taking it in either orifice from any of them. But thanks for the advice.'

We get two taxis to the hotel. George and David go with Sam, and Janice and I follow with all the bags. Janice pats my knee affectionately.

'You OK?' I ask her.

'Mmmm. Tired,' she says. Then, 'Katie, why don't you just tell him?'

'Tell who?'

'Sam, you ninny. Tell him how you feel before it's too late.'

'I don't feel anything,' I lie.

'Bollocks,' she says. 'I've seen the way you look at him.'

'I can't,' I stutter. 'What if he doesn't feel the same?'

'Don't be daft.' She hugs me. I'm shaking. 'I've also seen the way he looks at you when he thinks no one else is looking. Has done for ages. And he's paying for this nice hotel, isn't he? You surely don't think that's for my benefit, do you? Or George's? Or David's?'

I shrug. 'Dunno.'

'You *do* love him though, don't you?'

'Yes,' I say in a small voice that surprises even me. 'I suppose I do.'

'Then tell him.' She shakes my shoulders firmly. 'Before it's too late. Oh, and Katie.'

'What?'

'He's got a dick like a novelty draught-excluder, by all accounts.'

'How do you know?'

'That Paella told me that night we all got pissed on Pernod. Says he's hung like a bloody horse.'

At that we burst out giggling. Two minutes later, we pull up outside the hotel and I take a sharp breath.

It's gorgeous. It's even got a garden. The first green I've seen since we came out here. Except for the colour of Sam's face as we flew out. I guess the beautiful lawn is probably due to sprinklers and huge water wastage but who cares. It's so pretty.

Inside, it's just the same. Every room has its own bathroom, each the size of a small gymnasium and filled with piles of fluffy white towels and huge bottles of expensive bath oils and lotions and potions. George and David share one room, while Janice has her own. Again. Sam looks at me.

'I thought we could share again. If that's OK with you.'

'Sure.' I shrug. 'It'll save money, won't it? Ow,' I yelp, as Janice kicks my ankle.

That night, all much more relaxed, we eat dinner under the stars, which have finally come out now the rain has stopped. At eleven thirty, Janice goes to bed, giving me another ginormous kick under the table. At twelve, after two more ports each, George and David say it's time to hit the sack too. Sam and I are left alone.

And I'm completely tongue-tied. But I have to tell him how I feel. Janice is right. If I don't, it might be too late. And I only have tonight and tomorrow night before we have to go home. And back in London, with the pressures of work and the horrible weather, it just won't be the same.

When we get back to our room, Sam takes both my hands, pulls me to my feet and gives me an enormous bear hug.

'Do you like your surprise?'

'I love it,' I say truthfully, almost adding, 'If only it could include bonking you.'

I do love it. Our room has French windows, leading out to our very own deck. A jacuzzi bubbles away outside, and beside it are two steamer chairs covered in clouds of fluffy white towels. The complimentary bottles of citrussy bubble bath and lavender water in my marble bathroom are litre, rather than trial sized. As are the bottles of gin and vodka on the sideboard.

Plus, the fridge is stuffed with Belgian chocolates and Veuve Cliquot champagne.

Heaven.

I could get *very* used to this.

'You deserve a bit of luxury.' He shrugs. 'I'm glad you like it.'

I hug him.

'Consider it a wedding present,' he chuckles.

We luxuriate in the hot tub for a while, enjoying the warmer air and drinking the bottle of bubbly we find in the fridge (the label round the neck says 'Congratulations on your honeymoon', but we decide to drink it anyway). I find it almost impossible to be so close to him without telling him how I feel. But I just daren't. What if I have to face rejection?

But our legs are so close together, almost touching, that it's torture not to reach out and touch his thigh, which is already tanned a deep Mediterranean brown from goodness knows when. Next to him, I feel as British as beef dripping.

I chicken out of saying anything, of course, and we stay on separate sides of the big double bed. But I can't sleep.

Neither, it seems, can Sam.

'How do you feel about this wedding thing now?' he asks me suddenly.

'What do you mean?'

'Well, you're getting married in a few weeks and you and Jake are back together again. I just thought...'

'I have to be with someone, don't I?' I laugh. 'And I can't very well bonk my fiancé. Not with him preferring the old back door delivery.'

'I did offer to sleep with you,' Sam says. 'If you remember.'

'You did?' I don't remember that. 'When?'

'Your birthday. But you said you'd rather shag Neil Kinnock.'

'Are you sure?'

'Absolutely.'

'It wasn't Nicholas Witchell?'

'No.'

'I'm joking.'

And I am. But one thought goes round and round in my head.

He could at least have the courtesy to bonk me now.

Well, couldn't he?

Most blokes would surely have had a go by now. What with us being on holiday and all. In the same room. And we've had loads to drink, so he can't be shy.

And, every nerve in my body is screaming. It must be fucking obvious I fancy the pants off him.

But somehow, at some point, we both must have passed out. Because when I wake in the morning I'm not aware of anything having happened. And I wasn't *that* pissed.

Over a delicious breakfast of mango and watermelon, which we eat by the swimming pool, I bemoan my fate to Janice.

'It's up to you,' she says. 'You have to make the first move.'

'Why?'

'He still thinks you're with Jake, remember? And Nick. He can't make the first move. It wouldn't be proper. He's too much of a gent.'

'Is he?' I ask, surprised. Thinking back, I suppose he is. I've just never thought of him like that before. I mean, he was prepared to stand by Pussy when he thought he'd got her pregnant, wasn't he? When he didn't even love her. I mean, how gentlemanly is that? Pure bloody Jane Austen.

God. Come to think of it, he's bloody *lovely*.

Why the hell would he be interested in me?

'I'll tell him tonight,' I say.

'Good.' Janice gets back to her mango and asks the waiter if they've got any pickled onions to go with.

'You're rank,' I tell her.

I spend all day with Sam. George and David are both trying to windsurf and Janice prefers to flobber around in the shallows eating Soleros, so we both stretch out by the pool and read our books. And *still* I chicken out from saying anything. I'm cursing myself later that night. I've got one evening left. How the hell am I going to do it?

I don't, of course. We're splashing around in the jacuzzi, enjoying a packet of ham-flavoured crisps and a glass of wine before getting ready to go out for dinner, when Sam suddenly looks at me.

'What?'

'I need to ask you about Jake.'

'*Okay...*' I say cautiously. Hopefully this isn't the start of one of Sam's brotherly lectures. 'Cos if it is, I might just have to get a bit mardy. And that's hardly a suitable precursor to telling someone you can't stop thinking about them, is it?

'Do you love him?'

Wine comes out of my nose.

'God, no,' I snort. 'I don't even think I'll bother seeing him again when I get back. He's history, basically. I think I only shagged him to make myself feel better.'

'What about the others? Anything long-term going on there?'

I laugh. 'I got rid of Max,' I say. 'He made me feel sick. And Nick's eighteen, for beggar's sake,' I remind him. 'When he saw *Muriel's Wedding* on DVD he thought ABBA were an up-and-coming Australian band who were about to hit the big time. I don't think that exactly lends us much common ground, do you? So there's no need to rush that morning suit to Sketchley's just yet.'

'Well, there is, isn't there?'

'Huh?'

'You *are* getting married, aren't you?'

'What? Oh, shit. Yes. I suppose I am.'

I've sort of conveniently forgotten about my forthcoming nuptials. And I'd be lying if I said I'm not having doubts. Because I am. Big, fat, beefy doubts. But I'm not telling Sam that.

He'll only say, 'I told you so'.

'I might be getting married,' I swallow hard, 'but I'm not in a relationship. Not with David, not with Max, not with Nick, Jake or anyone else for that matter. Relationships suck. I've tried a few and I've never found one that matches up to a chunky Kit Kat.'

Even as I say it, I know it's true. I even hate the beginning part of relationships. The honeymoon period. OK, so it's the part everyone else loves because it's new and exciting but it's also extremely stressful. Perhaps things could be different with Sam.

Or perhaps not.

I think Janice would agree with me about the stress of early relationships. The waiting for phone calls. The agony over what to wear on a date. The expense of having to purchase new items all the time. And Janice couldn't even bear to go to the bathroom in the middle of the night for a pee when she first stayed at Jasper's. She couldn't stand the thought that he might not fancy her any more if he heard her emptying her bladder at full gush into his toilet bowl. So she used to creep downstairs

and find some receptacle—more often than not the teapot—
to piss into. Then she'd give it a quick rinse round and put it
back. And he was none the wiser. I chuckle now at the idea
that he must have thought she never needed to wee.

And pooing? Forget it.

'But if you were in a relationship with the right person it
would be like a chunky Kit Kat and more,' Sam insists.

'Yeah, right,' I say sarcastically. 'Like life might suddenly become one giant Godiva chocolate just because I had a nice
boyfriend. Get real, Sam.'

You see, I'm not like Janice was when she was looking for
Filthy Rich. I don't want a bloke who'll swathe me in Gucci
and take me to the Met Bar every night.

I don't even really want one who'll wine me and dine me in
restaurants where it's so quiet you're afraid to eat because everyone can hear you crunching your food.

I just want to be able to relax and enjoy life.

Oh, and I think I want Sam.

But what if I *don't* want him? What if he doesn't want me?
What if I go for it and he rejects me? Or what if I pour my
heart out to him and he says he feels the same. And then I find
that, with Pussy out of the way, I suddenly *don't* want him after
all? What happens then?

'What about you, anyway?' I think it's only fair he takes a
turn in the Mastermind chair. 'Pussy wasn't your chunky Kit
Kat I take it?'

'God, no.' He laughs. 'She wasn't even my Milky Bar. And I
hate Milky Bars. I couldn't even take her out to dinner and
enjoy it. It's no fun, Katie, I can assure you, always feeling like
you're eating alone because all the girls you go out with spend
their lives on some kind of diet.'

'If you didn't expect to go out with girls who look like Bic
biros the whole time, you might find a girlfriend you can have
fun with.' I take the stern approach. 'One who does food and
getting her clothes dirty.'

'I wish.'

'One who'll happily play Dutch ovens in bed on a Sunday morning just for the hell of it.'

'What, like you, you mean?' he jibes.

'Well, no, not like me exactly.' *Yes, yes. Exactly like me. I do farting. In fact, yes, it's me you want. Just me. Pick me. I love trumps.*

'I mean, not ginger, anyway,' I say hastily.

Why the fuck did I say that? God, I'm making one holy fuck-up of this, aren't I? I clearly have the seduction technique of a small pot-bellied pig.

'Why not?' he asks. 'Who said there was anything wrong with ginger?'

'Half the population?' I jest.

We go out and get drunk that evening. Again I drink more than usual, probably because Sam is making me so nervous. Janice keeps glaring at me over the table, willing me to get a grip. It's ridiculous really, the way the presence of my oldest friend who I've previously almost brained with a seaside spade, amongst other things, can suddenly have me shredding the skin around my thumbnails as though I'm noshing on spare ribs. And because I've had wine, and the odd beer, and a vodka marshmallow shooter and—oh, all sorts of other things, I suddenly realise I feel all squibbly.

I say I want to go home.

'I'll come with you.' Sam jumps to his feet. 'You OK?'

'Yep.' I look at Janice. 'Will you be OK? Will you boys see her home?'

'Course we will.' George raises his glass.

Janice gives me a silent thumbs-up. And, as we leave, Sam's hand is protectively on the small of my back, making me tingle with anticipation. Perhaps he *does* feel the same.

In which case, this could be it. It really could be it.

When we get back to the hotel, Sam makes me sit on the bidet, the only thing they're good for in both our opinions as neither of us get the point of them. Then he rinses a fluffy flannel in cold water and smoothes it across my forehead.

'Save you getting roomspin. Don't want your brain going round and round like a helicopter propeller if we can help it.'

'Sorry,' I say as he sits me on the crisp linen-covered bed and tucks a bit of damp hair behind my ear.

'No problem, Simpson,' Sam says. 'Lightweight,' he adds afterwards, for good measure.

'Bugger off.' I hit him with my flip-flop.

'Ow.'

So I hurt him. A bit. But he really should know better. I mean, I'm not the girl who used to make herself chunder in the Student Union toilets in order to fit in more booze for nothing.

'I'll show you, Sam Freeman.' I laugh, chucking my other flip-flop in his general direction.

'Show me what?' he teases.

'Don't be cheeky,' I scold. But I'm pink with pleasure nonetheless. At least, I think I am. I can't really tell because although I can see myself in the mirror, I'm having double vision. Or is that treble?

'OK.' I pull out a full-size bottle of vodka. 'What have we here? A nightcap, methinks.'

'Simpson, are you sure?'

'Course I'm sure.' I unscrew the top and pour us both a more than generous slug. 'Down the hatch, old boy.'

And Sam, good as gold, joins me in drinking half the bottle.

I don't remember going to sleep. But I wake with my jeans pulled down around my ankles so I must have tried to get undressed. I open my eyes slowly.

'Who took the floor away?' I grumble, struggling out of bed. Bugger. We have to leave so soon and we haven't even kissed, let alone bonked. We're back to cold old Blighty this evening.

'Not me.' Sam, delicious in nothing but a pair of faded denim shorts and a tan brings in a tray.

'What's that?' I ask him. 'And why are you so disgustingly bright this morning?'

'Breakfast,' he says. 'And you talk in your sleep.'

'Do I?' I look at the plump, flaky croissants, fresh straw-berries, orange juice and fragrant coffee laid out on the tray.

'You really shouldn't do that, you know,' he teases, poking my arm. 'A girl can reveal a lot of secrets that way.'

Shit. I didn't. Did I? But Sam's face is giving nothing away. So I guess I'll never know. I bite into a croissant and change the subject.

'I wish we didn't have to leave today,' I sigh. 'I could get used to this.'

'Me too.' He flicks through the TV channels. I don't know why he's bothering. Neither of us can understand a word any-one is saying. It's gobbledegook.

Suddenly, I realise I'm going to have to say something. But I can't. My tongue is like wet cement. Then Sam suddenly speaks.

'What we were talking about last night,' he says. 'Before you started snoring...'

'Mmmm?'

'Do you think you'll ever settle down? With the right per-son, I mean.'

'I don't know, Sam.' I shrug. 'I got hurt, you know.'

'I know.' He strokes my cheek and my loins almost explode.

'What about you?' I ask him the same. 'Don't you want to get married? Settle down?'

'Yes.'

'No.' I'm flabbergasted. 'Surely not. Sam Freeman? Casanova of Clapham?'

'It's still Balham, actually,' he points out. 'And why not? All my friends are doing it. Joff's got engaged to that girl he met at your birthday party.'

'What, Jabba?' I ask in disbelief. 'Chantal, I mean?'

'Mmm. The big girl.'

'But...when...Why?'

'You think he wouldn't want her because she's fat?' he asks me. 'We're not all that shallow, you know.'

'I didn't...I mean...I didn't know.'

'Well, it's true. Apparently she gives the best blow jobs he's

ever had. He's totally smitten with her. I don't blame him either. I've been out with them a couple of times. She's brilliant fun.'

'You've been out with them. When?'

'Like I said. A couple of times. She's great. Wicked sense of
humour.'

'I'm glad,' I say. And I am. Chantal's one of the few people I
actually liked when I worked at the magazine. I hope Joff makes
her happy.

'Even George has settled down,' he adds. 'And now you're
getting married.'

'Only pretend married,' I remind him.

'No,' Sam starts, then sighs. 'Actually married. I mean, God,
Katie. You look on this as some kind of game. Like two kids
playing at weddings. But you will be legally married. It'll affect
everything you do for the rest of your life. And you could get
into serious trouble, you know, if the Home Office find out.'

'God, don't be so square.'

'Sorry.' Sam holds up his hands in surrender. 'Anyway, all I
was saying is that, yes, one day I would like to get married. To
the right girl, I mean.'

'Not some pigshit-thick bird who looks like a lollipop
then?' I say.

'Pussy, you mean?'

'Of course.' I laugh. 'Do me a favour, will you? Next time go
out with someone normal. Someone who likes pies.'

Oh look! There I go, fulfilling all the criteria again.

He laughs. 'OK. I'll give it a go. I need to go out with someone who's my type for a change.'

'Well, who *is* your type?'

'Who's yours?'

'Well,' I say carefully, 'I suppose if the right person really did
come along, I'd have to reconsider my status on relationships.
But it would really have to be Mr Right. Mr OK For Now can
just sod off. I haven't got time for him. Even Mr Very Bloody
Nearly can get the hell out. Life's too short.'

'How do you know you haven't met him already? And what would he be like, your Mr Right?'

'Well,' I say thoughtfully, popping in a Revel from the packet he's suddenly found in his flight bag, 'he'd make me laugh, obviously. Until I actually wet myself sometimes. And he wouldn't be shocked if I did. He'd just clear it up.'

'OK.' Sam looks highly amused. 'Anything else?'

'He'd like having baths with me, instead of saying I got in the way, like Jake always did. And he'd always take the tap end.'

'Uh huh.'

'And he'd let me sit at the front of the top deck on the bus without calling me a baby.'

'Yes?'

'And he'd let me eat jelly beans in the bath. And he'd always eat the orange Revels, even if I'd already bitten into them first. Because you can never tell, can you? Between the orange ones and the Maltesers, I mean? You see, the orange ones make me feel sick. Like, really really sick. And he'd bring me Brannigans roast beef and mustard crisps for breakfast in bed on Valentine's Day because he knew they were my favourite. I mean, I'm not an idiot. I wouldn't expect it to be a bed of roses all the time. I know that heady feeling wears off after a couple of years. But there should be something left, shouldn't there? Otherwise, what's the fucking point? Oh, yuck.'

'What?'

'Orange one,' I say, spitting the chocolate into my hand. 'Want it?'

'Sure.'

'What about you then?' I ask. 'What's your type?'

'What do you think?'

'Don't be stupid,' I say, my tummy suddenly going all funny. 'I'm not a fucking mind reader. I mean you said the other day that if you couldn't have the woman you loved you'd settle for the one who loved you. Do you really think that?'

'Not any more, no.'

'So who is she then, this mysterious woman?' 'Cos, let's face it, I'm jealous as hell of her. 'Come on, Sam,' I urge him. 'Spill the beans. Who's your chunky Kit Kat? Did you meet her at work?'

'You might be surprised,' he says. 'You see, I want someone who'll make me laugh too. Someone I can take out to dinner. Who'll eat something really lardy smothered in butter and not care that it might make her fat. And she'll still order chocolate mousse afterwards. With extra cream.'

'You've never been out with anyone like that in your life,' I say in amazement. There's a funny, butterflyish feeling in my tummy which is steadfastly refusing to budge. I mustn't make too much of it. I mean, there's definitely anticipation, but it seems that Sam has met his ideal woman already. So this feeling I've got is probably just because Sam and I have never properly talked like this before. OK, so there've been times when we've touched on serious subjects, but never like this.

It feels as though we've crossed a line.

'Perhaps that's because no one like that has ever wanted to go out with me.'

Is it my imagination, or is he a bit closer to me than he was before?

And why is my heart thumping like a fat girl on a trampoline again?

More to the point, why are my nether regions playing up like there's no tomorrow.

Sam would probably laugh the end of his willy off if he knew how I was feeling.

Or would he?

Suddenly, almost imperceptibly, he moves closer to me until we're actually touching. Then he strokes a stray curl off my cheek.

'Do I have to spell it out?' he asks, as a nervous, fizzy sort of pain shoots from the tip of my toes to the top of my ponytail, taking in my minky in a big way on the way up. What the hell's going on?

'What?' I ask nervously.

'I ate the orange one, Katie,' he says. 'Isn't that enough for you?'

'The orange what?'

'The orange Revel.' He puts a finger under my chin and turns my head so I'm facing him. We're so close I can smell him. He smells of last night's beer and strawberries and outside. Delicious. For a moment, it reminds me of being a teenager again.

'I always eat your orange Revels, Simpson. I have done since we were six.'

'So?'

Shit.

Why is my heart refusing to beat normally?

'You, you dizzy mare,' he says gently, pulling me towards him until my mouth is nearly on his. '*You're* my type.'

There's something incredibly, wildly exciting about kissing someone you know really well. And when we've finished, we're both incredibly bashful. And this isn't like the time at Poppy's wedding, when we both tried to brush what had happened under the carpet. I mean, I was confused then. I didn't know what I wanted.

Now I do.

And it's Sam.

Chapter 22

For the rest of the morning, I can hardly look at Sam.

It's a bit like when you've had one of those freakish dreams. You know, the kind where you're having sex with someone you know really well in real life.

In real life, of course, you don't fancy them at all. But when you wake up after dreaming about them you're confused. Somehow, this person you see every day in normal situations, at work, at the bus stop, serving your Caffe Americano in Starbucks, gets mixed up with the person who was rutting you senseless from behind last night.

Then, just for a day or two, you really start to find them attractive. Being near them makes you nervous. And you find you can't look them in the eye.

Janice had a dream like that once about one of our lecturers. In real life, he smelled of stale Cheddar and had hairy nostrils and a flobbery blue mole on his chin. But that didn't stop her from shaking so much when he came over to help with an experiment that she set her fringe alight with the Bunsen burner.

And the fact that Sam and I kissed this morning almost seems like a dream. And it's so surreal, I can't help feeling all sort of Rice Krispyish and squirmy inside.

But I can't deny that, every time he looks at me, there's a connection that wasn't there before. It's a whole new facet to our friendship I never, until recently, knew was there. I think it's taken us both somewhat by surprise.

And what about all my well-intentioned resolutions? What about Behaving Like A Bloke? Humping and Dumping? Loving and Leaving?

What about not letting myself fall in love again? Ever.

Oh well, it's too late to go back now, I tell myself, as I crumple my bikini and shorts into my tote bag. I'm happy. Really, really happy. Sam looks over at me and smiles.

'It's weird, isn't it?' I grin.

'Not that weird.' He comes and rests his hands on my shoulders.

'No?'

'Not really. I love you. I've always loved you. I've probably loved you since we were kids. I told you this morning.'

'Since I smashed you over the head with that spade?' I smile.

'Well, perhaps not then. I actually thought you were a bit of a bitch on that particular day. Especially when the stitches came out.'

'That wasn't very Christian of you,' I say. 'Bearing a grudge like that.'

'Perhaps I'm not a very Christian sort of boy.' He smiles at me slowly. 'You might get to find out if you play your cards right. Still, Simpson, that was completely unnecessary, that spade-bashing. I hope you're not going to do the same thing to my father if your mum lets him sit on her lap.'

But I'm not listening.

'How can you love me?' I ask, stupefied at what he's just told me. 'I'm ginger. I eat like a bastard. And we've only just kissed.'

'You're stunning,' he says, gently bending down to kiss my cheek. 'You're you. And I've known you for ever.'

'But I haven't got big tits.'

'You've got lovely tits.' He runs his hand over one of my breasts so gently I think I'm going to scream with lust.

I've never felt so turned on in my life.

'You can shag me if you like,' I tell him. 'I won't break.'

'I think we should wait till we get home.' He grins. 'So it'll still feel real when we get back.'

'OK.'

Obviously, I'm slightly disappointed. I was really looking forward to finding out if the novelty draught-excluder was an accurate description. But if I have to wait...

Besides, no one's ever told me they love me *before* sex.

I mean it's far more usual for them to tell me as we're actually doing the nasty. Right as we're bumping uglies in a back alley. Let's face it, it's usually just as they're about to come.

And at least he knows me well enough to understand we can't get married. Not until my divorce from David comes through, at any rate. And anyway, do we have to follow the conventional route of house, marriage, children? Can't we just be us? Two friends who happen to have monogamous, loving sex. On the face of things, that's far less scary.

I'm just finishing my packing when Sam slips away and comes back with flowers.

'What are these for?'

'I wanted to ask you to marry me. But there's nowhere to buy you a ring. Unless you want a lime-green plastic one from the machine in the amusement arcade.'

'Oh, Sam.' I smile at his sweetness. 'You know I can't do that.'

'Why not?' he asks. 'Not because of that New Year's resolution rubbish, surely? All that being single nonsense?'

'I'm marrying David in two weeks,' I tell him. 'Remember?'

What happens next will always be a bit of a blur.

'I thought...' he stutters. 'I thought that now...I mean, with me and you and...'

It honestly hasn't occurred to him that I'll still go ahead with my plans to help David and George stay together.

He's allowed himself to believe that us getting it together would change everything.

'I never said that,' I snap. I don't mean to, but I can't let my friends down. Not even for Sam. I've made a promise. I have to keep it.

'You didn't have to,' Sam shouts. 'I mean, if you loved me you wouldn't even have to think about it.'

I'm so cross at him shouting, I decide he's probably only engineered this whole situation to stop me from getting married to David. And I yell at him for that.

Sam tells me I'm talking rubbish, saying that of course he loves me, he always has and he always will.

'Then can't you just let me marry David and still go out with me?' I ask him in desperation.

Sam stares at me for a moment, and I feel a flicker of hope. Then, ever so slowly, he shakes his head. 'No, I can't. It's all or nothing, I'm afraid. Black or white. I don't want there to be a whole big grey area where it's all confusing. And I can't really bear the thought of you marrying someone you don't love.'

'But I do love David,' I say in surprise. 'And George. And I've made them a promise. If I don't marry David, he'll have to go away. And now we've realised how we feel about each other, surely you can understand how awful that would be.'

'George only thinks of himself,' Sam snaps. 'And he's quite happy to watch you forego your happiness, isn't he?'

'Stop it,' I say, bitterly disappointed. 'Just stop it. George doesn't even know about us yet. So how could he think I was giving up my happiness? And I don't have to. You and I can still be together if I marry David.'

'But we can't.' Sam shakes his head. 'I don't want to share you.'

'Then you'll have to forget it.' I'm angry now. Angry at how selfish he's being. Can't he see that I can get married to David and it won't change a thing between him and me? If he loved me, then he'd understand.

'Forget what?'

'It. Us. Just put that kiss we had down to the booze and the scenery. I'm glad we haven't had the chance to have sex yet. I wouldn't go near you if I wasn't on holiday. Do you know something, Sam Freeman? I'd rather—'

'Shag Neil Kinnock, yes, I know,' he says sadly.

Chapter 23

'I'm not sitting next to him.' I wrinkle up my sunburned nose and scowl at the air hostess, stamping my chunky trainer to show I really mean it.

Janice, squeezing herself into her seat, glances at me sympathetically. Thank God she's on my side.

I feel so stupid. What was I thinking of, believing Sam and I had a future together? When all along he's too selfish to let me marry someone else if I feel like it? I mean, call me old-fashioned, but...

Whatever happened to unconditional love?

Sam merely raises his eyebrows to heaven as though this is exactly the kind of behaviour he might have expected from someone as childish as me. Then he puts on his 'I'm so reasonable' voice and asks the man next to him if he'd mind moving up one so he can sit between us.

Like a sort of central reservation.

'Trust me, mate,' he assures the man who, not surprisingly, looks reluctant to give up his comfy aisle seat. 'You'll only have to listen to her nagging at me all the way back to Heathrow.'

'Been married long, have you?' asks the man, standing up to let me pass.

'God, you're so pathetically predictable,' I snarl, leaning in front of the man so we can continue our conversation. 'All men together, eh? Nagging is a term invented by men to stop women from getting what they want, you know. How sexist is that?'

Even with the man sitting stiffly between us, the journey back to London is a total nightmare. For one thing, he's one of those people who sticks his elbows out at right angles to his body when he eats, so that I'm forced to do the same, even though I wouldn't normally want to, just to make the point that I haven't got enough room.

What's more, on the other side of the aisle, a snotty brat complete with skinhead haircut, leather jacket and gold earring is having a hysterical fit because he can.

I know just how he feels.

To make things worse, when I arrive back at George's (George and David are spending tonight at the Savoy because they want to), Jake is sitting on the wall by the hedge outside my flat.

Talking to Nick.

And they're both looking extremely angry.

I've been rumbled.

Buggeration.

I slam the car into reverse, driving round to Janice's.

'I'm staying here,' I tell her. 'Jake and Nick are outside George's house. They're chatting.'

'Oh dear.'

'I just can't face the music.'

'Don't you think you'd better?' She gets up and I immediately feel guilty because she looks so tired. She's being sick all the time at the moment. 'I'll come with you if you like.'

'Can't I just stay here?' I look round at her flat, which isn't as calm, cool and collected as it usually is. Copies of *Parent* magazine and baby-name books litter the floor. 'I could come and hide here then help tidy up when you're like the side of a house.'

'Oh, hon, you know you can stay here.' Janice puts her arm round me. 'But no tidying. In a few months, this place is going to be full of posset cloths and primary-coloured plastic. With bells on. I might as well get used to living in a mess. But don't you think you ought to sort this out?'

'Why?'

'I dunno really. Call it closure. Moving on. You'll be a married woman in less than a fortnight, don't forget.'

'Oh God.'

'He won't help you now. Come on. Let's do it.'

Reluctantly, I climb back into the Rustbucket, pausing only to load Janice in through the passenger door. Then we pootle off to Islington to face the music.

'Oh look,' I say in mock disappointment as we pull up outside George's. 'They've both gone. Never mind. Closure is just going to have to wait. I have chocolate biscuits inside.'

But, as I open the front door, I soon realise we aren't alone. I can hear the clattering of pots and pans. The fridge door opening and closing. And my mum's voice, bright and cheerful, as she comes bustling out to meet me.

'Katie,' she grins, 'how was the holiday?'

'Lovely thanks, Mum.' I'm surprised by how pleased I am to see her. She seems so comfortable, somehow, after all that's happened over the past few days.

'And Janice.' Mum beams. 'How's the little one? Gosh, you're as big as a bus now, aren't you?'

Actually, Janice is still tiny, but that's just Mum being Mum.

'Fine thanks, Mrs S.'

'And how's Sam? Enjoy himself, did he? He said he'd ring when he got back but we haven't heard a thing. Not a sausage.'

'Hrmmph.'

'Oh, you haven't fallen out again, have you? Never mind. I've brought round some leftover casserole in case you were hungry. And all that paperwork I've kept up for you. And I found these two on the doorstep. Look. This nice young man says he's brought your pants back.'

Bugger.

Buggery, buggery fuck.

Sitting either side of George's kitchen table, each tucking in to a steaming plate of Mum's lamb stew and dumplings, are Nick and Jake.

'I told them they were welcome any time.' She bustles about finding a chair for Janice.

'Great.'

'Don't worry,' she whispers in my ear and points at Jake as I reach for a tea mug. 'You don't want to know what went into his.'

I grin. Despite my squibbly tummy at the prospect of a showdown, I can't help thinking how bloody marvellous it is that my mum has known all along exactly what Jake was like. And there was me thinking he'd had her duped.

'Is there something you'd like to say, Katie?' Jake looks at me angrily.

'Yeah,' I sip Mum's tea. 'You're a wanker.'

Nick says nothing, just tucks into another helping of Mum's stew. Silly beggar hasn't really clocked what's going on.

'I came round to offer to leave Tracy.' Jake is beetroot with anger.

I shrug. 'Well, you had to see sense sometime.'

'But it appears you've been seeing someone else,' he nods in Nick's direction. Nick looks up from a mouthful of mashed potato and flashes me a heart-warming grin.

'I told 'im,' he admits. ''Ope you don't mind. See, the thing is, I were coming round to give you them clothes back. Me mum's washed 'em.'

'Oh, er, thanks.'

'I sorta fort it weren't workin'. What with you and me. It's just that you're dead clever.'

'Well.' I blather, feeling a stab of pleasure at the look of fury on Jake's face.

'I mean you read them big newspapers and everythin'.'

'It's fine, Nick.' I smile at him. God, this is going to be so easy. Nick/Dudley, whatever his name is, doesn't appear to be hurt at all. In fact, as long as I don't get between him and his plate, I really think he'll leave here as happy as a pig in shit.

Jake, on the other hand, is a different matter. I really couldn't give a toss how he feels. And I've got my mum and Janice here to hold my hand.

'So it's true then?' Jake challenges.

'Well, you heard the man,' I say. 'And he isn't some highly paid actor I've wheeled out just to get one up on you.'

'I thought we were seeing each other.' Jake pushes his plate of food away with distaste and Mum, noticing this, looks as though she might be about to bang him over the head with the griddle pan she's washing.

'We were,' I agree. 'But I was seeing some other people too. Just like you. But now I don't really feel like seeing you any more. So you may as well go back to Fishpants. Go on. Get out.'

Stunned, Jake gets to his feet, grabs his mobile and looks at my mum. Mum folds her arms in the manner of someone Not To Be Messed With, and he scuttles for the door. Janice smirks. Worried he might be affronted, I look at Nick. But he merely looks up from his plate and asks if anyone minds if he finishes Jake's helping.

As Janice gets a bit bigger, she starts to feel sicker, so I stay at her flat until the day of the wedding, only popping to George's for recipe books and to feed the cats. Anyway, I'd rather not be at theirs at the moment. After all, it is bad luck for the bride to see the groom before the wedding. And the last thing I need is a visit from the Home Office.

I also hope that the constant company and girlie chatter will take my mind off Sam. But it's wishful thinking. After three days of convincing myself I hate him, I decide I have to try and talk to him.

Because I don't hate him. Not at all. And I can't bear to leave it like this.

I slope round the corner to his house and ring the bell. I push my hands in my pockets. I can't help being nervous. My heart is lodged in the pit of my stomach and I feel sick.

It takes him forever to open the door. But finally, I hear footsteps in the hall and the door is pulled open.

By Pussy.

'Oh.'

'Hi.' She smiles sweetly.

'Er. Hi.'

'Did you want something?'

'Is Sam here?'

'No,' she smiles again, 'he's out.'

'Oh. Right.'

'Did he tell you we're back together?' she asks.

'No.'

I feel as though I've been kicked. In the stomach and from behind. The shock of hearing that Sam's gone running straight back to Pussy is almost too much to bear. He can't have loved me at all if he can do that.

Can he?

I don't bother to say anything else to Pussy. Can't even hide how upset I am. I leave, with tears in my eyes, a lump the size of Jupiter in my throat and my dignity in tatters. Then I leg it back to Janice's without even stopping at the Dog Shop for chocolate and fags.

One look at my face sends Janice waddling to the Dog Shop for chocolate and fags.

'Bastard,' she says when I tell all.

'Bloody bastard,' I agree.

'Bloody, fucking bastard.' She wipes my face with a hanky. 'I really didn't think he was like that.'

'Of course he's like that.' I slurp at my teary top lip and have a good blow. 'He's a bloody bastard bloke.'

'True enough.'

On the morning of my wedding to David, Janice and I watch videos to calm my nerves, a glass of Bolly each in one hand and a handful of caramel popcorn in the other. Laurence Llewelyn-Bowen, on the other hand, is slapping lurid zebra-striped wallpaper all over the oak-beamed walls of an eighteenth-century farmhouse in Shropshire.

'Not wishing it was a case of Changing Grooms, are you?' Janice squeezes my hand.

'Changing *Wombs*, more like,' I blurt. 'I've got period pain like you wouldn't bloody believe. I must be the only bride in living history to be jamming on her wedding night.'

'Just as well the groom will be spending it shagging someone else, isn't it?' She giggles. 'You can swap wombs with me if you like. Mine's getting a bit full.'

'Still, I'd rather be marrying David than that chintz-loving, frock-coated twit any day.' I nod in the direction of the telly and take a huge gulp of champagne as if to quash any doubts I might still be having.

'So would I,' Janice admits. 'No regrets then?'

'No regrets,' I say. 'I've never kept a New Year's resolution in my life, so I don't see why I should start now. And I'm not *really* getting married, you know. Not in the true "strap a mattress to my back and tie me to the kitchen sink with a wooden spoon in my hand" sense of the word. In theory, I'll still be Young, Free and Single.'

'Old, Feckless and Stupid, more like.' Janice smiles, taking a big swig of her own champers ('one glass only, mind') and turning her attention back to the screen, where Linda Barker is rough-plastering the kitchen walls of a tenth-floor council flat in Ilford with a fetching terracotta colour to make it look like the interior of a Tuscan villa.

'But I wasn't talking about you getting married.' Janice puts an arm round my shoulders. 'You know what I mean. I'm not talking about breaking your daft resolutions. I'm asking if you're wishing you'd held out a bit longer for Mr Diet Coke Break?'

'You mean Sam?'

'Exactly. Or someone like him.'

'Not really,' I tell her. 'At least I found out what he was like. I can't believe he just went straight back to that stupid little cat. Anyway, I'm doing my bit for true love, keeping David in the country so that he and George can be together. David's the first person George has loved you know, apart from himself. And his mum. It would be so unfair if he was thousands of miles away cracking open cold tinnies on a beach on his own.'

'Instead of making himself useful mixing daiquiris for George, you mean,' says Janice and we both burst out giggling like we haven't done for the last week.

And laughing feels good.

I don't mention that without George and David giving me a room and an office and a place to stay, I'd never have got Neat Eats off the ground. They've given me a career to be proud of. I can't throw it back in their faces, now can I?

OK, so I conveniently forget it was Sam's idea in the first place. I can't think about that now. I've got enough to worry about what with the very strong likelihood of my forgetting my vows. And the possibility of the Home Office getting wind of the fact that I'm marrying a gay foreigner and paying a visit to our wedding.

And not just to throw confetti.

It's nice to see George and David so happy. And I'm relieved to know that Janice is going to be OK. She took this week off work to help me as I baked an enormous pink wedding cake and decorated it with love hearts, silver balls and pink Jelly Tots. Together, we made tiny prawn toasts with sesame seeds sprinkled all over them, miniature crispy duck pancakes and cooked up huge vats of hot and sour soup, chicken with cashew nuts and squid in black bean sauce.

Visiting Sam that one last time has taught me one thing.

I've definitely made the right decision.

I know who my friends are.

And I won't be sleeping with any of them.

As I pull on my dress—a long, elegant sweep of sheer pinky gold (Didier has done me proud) and Janice puts the finishing touches to my hair and takes me outside to the waiting taxi, I squash any remaining doubts I might be having and decide to treat today as one big party.

My party.

And I'll cry if I fucking well want to.

But then I might just as well laugh.

The way I'm feeling, who can tell?

'Just one thing,' Janice whispers as we climb into the black cab. 'You may well be entering a sexless marriage but where there's a will there's a way.'

'What?'

'Remember when Rory Wilsher dumped me?' she says, untwisting one of the spaghetti straps of her Barbie-pink maid of honour's outfit. 'I used to spend a fortune on taxis. Even to work.'

'Oh yes,' I remember. 'You did. I thought that was because you were too grief-stricken by your loss to manage to walk.'

'Bollocks it was.' She grins. 'Now, sit there. Right in the middle.'

I obey, shifting along a bit, almost dropping my bouquet of pink rosebuds on the floor of the car.

'There,' she says. 'Feel anything?'

'Yes,' I say, a grin spreading across my face. 'I think I do.'

'There you go. Better than a vibrator any bloody day.'

We're still laughing when we reach Chelsea registry office.

I'm still a bit pissed from all the champagne I've drunk that morning, but George—bless him—remembers to put a blanket over my head as we trot from the car to the building, so that in the likely event that my mother is doing a Peter Jones run this fine Saturday morning, she won't spot me and have kittens all over the pavement.

'People will think you're a pop star,' he says as we make our way up the steps.

'That's what I'm afraid of,' I grumble. 'Hurry up, will you? I can't see fuck. And I don't want to attract attention to myself.'

David's friend Straight Rigby gives me away in the end. I've never met him before but he seems very nice. And though it all seems very strange, being the only straight person (apart from Rigby and Janice) at my own wedding, I realise I don't really mind one bit.

At least there's no one from the Home Office here. The whole thing looks suspiciously gay.

I don't think all the pink helps. And the glitter confetti's a bit the wrong side of camp, too.

I sneak a quick look round the audience and notice that there are actually other straight people here. Poppy and Seb have turned up. Poppy, pregnant and blooming in a tube of dark purply-pink silk. Seb in a dark suit with a matching purply-pink tie. Bless them. This *so* isn't their thing but I'm glad of their support. And—ohmigod—sitting in a seat at the front on the other side, twinkling away at me as if her life depended on it, is George's mum. She blows me a kiss. I look at George, who is beaming.

'I told her,' he mouths.

My heart fills with pride. I knew he could do it. And it's all obviously fine. His dear old mum has come to his boyfriend's wedding.

I knew she was cool as fuck.

The only person that's definitely missing is Sam.

I sigh. No matter how much I've been trying to pretend otherwise, I've been half hoping he might turn up and stop the wedding in its tracks. Bang on the floor, *Four Weddings and a Funeral* style, when it gets to the bit about 'If there is anyone present who knows a reason why this marriage should not go ahead'.

But he doesn't. And in the event the ceremony is so quick, that I hardly realise when it's all over. No hymns. No readings.

Within minutes, I'm a married woman.

Buggery bollocks.

Time for a stiff drink.

George's boss has lent us his boat on the Thames for our wedding reception. It's strung with dozens of Chinese paper lanterns in every shade of pink imaginable. Bubblegum pink, Barbie pink, salmon pink, candy pink, peony pink, all fluttering in the breeze, along with the pink gerbera flowers George has hung upside down at intervals from a wire suspended around the deck.

Three waiters in penguin suits with pink bow ties are serving pink cocktails in tall glasses and several guests already look a few sheets to the wind.

'Come on,' says Janice, sensing my unhappiness at not finding Sam among them. 'Let's get hammered. Well, *you* can,' she adds, laughing. 'I'd better not. Jasper junior might not like it.'

'You're *not* calling it after him?' I say, shocked.

'You never know.' She smiles. 'I'm joking,' she adds hurriedly, seeing I might be about to suggest she put the poor little beggar up for adoption after all. 'I'm not even going to call it anything beginning with J. So Jerome, Jemima and Jessica are all out too. And Josh. You'd better get thinking.'

'Why me?'

'I want you to be godmother.'

'You do?'

'Of course.'

'Oh, Janice,' I say. 'Thank you.'

And then I burst into tears.

'Mum's excited, you know,' she tells me. 'She's knitting already. She can't wait until it's born.'

'And you?'

'Shitting myself. You *will* come to the hospital, won't you?'

'Of course I will.' I accept a sea breeze and plonk myself at a table on the edge of the deck, forgetting for a moment that I'm wearing a dress and displaying my gusset to all and sundry. 'I'll be waiting outside with fat cigars and champagne.'

'Oh, not cigars, please.' She laughs gently. 'I've had enough of those to last me a lifetime. And I rather hoped you'd be there to hold my hand.'

I look at my best friend. She seems a tiny bit scared. And so I give her a huge, reassuring hug.

'Of course I will,' I say. 'You know, I fucking love you to bits.'

'I love you too.' She smiles back gratefully.

It's definitely a party to remember. And, much later, as the sun is setting over the river and all the drag queens, ice queens and acid queens that are George and David's friends are making for home, David takes me to one side.

'Thank you.' He gives me a huge hug. 'More than anything. Thank you from the bottom of my heart. Not many people would have done what you did today. It was very unselfish.'

Too fucking right it was, I thought. You don't know how unselfish.

But he does.

'I know about Sam,' he says. 'Janice told us. I know how you gave that up for me and George. And I'll never be able to make it up to you. I love you.'

'Love you too.' I hug him. 'And you're very welcome.'

It's ironic, really. There I was at the start of this year, so determined to stay single, so determined to shag around as much as I wanted that I didn't realise I was falling in love by accident.

I fell in love with Sam by default.

Still, where has that got me? He certainly doesn't want me now, does he?

I honestly thought he might turn up this afternoon, if not to the service, to the party at least. And it *has* been fun, this party.

'*I* wouldn't have done it,' George agrees.

'I know you wouldn't, you selfish bastard.'

He smiles. 'Life's almost perfect.'

'It's not so bad, is it?' I say.

And it isn't, I realise. It really isn't. I may have lost Sam, but I have three friends who love me dearly.

And I'm going to be a godmother.

How lovely.

'*Almost* perfect?' David asks. 'What more do you need?'

'A baby?' George suggests. 'Katie darling, are you sure Janice won't sell?'

I laugh. 'I'm sure.'

He'll never change.

'And what about you? Is the answer still no?'

'Put it this way, I'm not exactly hanging out the Womb To Let signs yet.'

'I'm glad to hear it,' says a familiar voice.

My heart lurches.

David and George instinctively melt into the background, and I'm left alone.

'You did it then?' Sam asks me.

I nod, slowly. 'Yes, I did it.'

'No regrets?'

'None,' I say truthfully. 'I was helping a friend. Two friends I just wanted to make happy. They *do* love each other, you know.'

'I know,' Sam says. 'I'm sorry things have turned out the way they have. Between us, I mean.'

'I know.'

'Do you think we can still be friends?'

'I hope so.'

'Would you like to?'

Slowly, from somewhere deep inside, I manage a small smile.

'Yes,' I answer truthfully. 'We don't exactly have any choice, do we? We're going to be related. Remember?'

'Oh yeah.' He smiles ruefully. 'You'll be my sister.'

'So it's probably just as well we didn't, you know...'

'I know.' He gives me a hug. A brotherly one this time. And I feel a twinge of regret.

But only a very tiny one.

'Bye for now,' I say, trying to be brave. 'Perhaps we can go for a drink when it's all a bit...you know.'

'I know.'

It's weird, making my way home alone from my own wedding. I'm just about to climb into a cab at Kew Bridge when I hear running behind me.

Sam.

'Can I keep you company?' he asks. 'This evening, I mean?'

'I don't know.' I shake my head. 'I'm not sure...'

'Please?'

'OK.'

When we get home, I feel strangely flat. All I want is a hot bath and bed.

'Will you feed Graham and Shish for me?'

'Sure.'

I don't particularly want the bath for the bath's sake. I just feel the need to get away from Sam. I'm confused. Why is he here? And where's Pussy?

God, this hurts too much.

OK, so we're friends again. And I'm glad. Really glad. We've known each other for ever. I would have hated to lose him.

But how long is it going to take? Getting over him, I mean.

And how will I manage to be a good sister to someone I'm head over heels in love with?

Especially when I'm going to have to watch him and Pussy being so bloody happy together.

I lie back in a mound of patchouli-scented bubbles, glancing down at my white gold wedding ring with a wry smile. George insisted that I wasn't to have gold, because it would look common.

I close my eyes, sinking underneath the surface to scrub away the rigours of the day.

Suddenly, as if from nowhere, I'm being pelted with stones.

'What the fuck?'

I come spluttering and coughing to the surface.

'What...'

Sam is climbing into the bath with all his clothes on.

'What the fuck are you doing?'

'I'm taking the tap end. What does it look like?'

'I don't understand.'

'Don't you?' he says gently, sitting down suddenly so that water slops all over the side of the bath and onto the floor.

'And what's this?' I feel underneath my right buttock to see what's digging into it. 'It bloody hurts. Why are you throwing stones into the bath?'

And then, with a tiny flutter inside, I realise that it isn't a stone.

It's a jelly bean.

A red jelly bean.

And there are packets of Brannigans crisps all over the floor of the bathroom.

'I love you, Katie,' says Sam, looking utterly ridiculous in his black Diesel jacket, sitting in a full bath, stinking of patchouli and surrounded by floating, brightly-coloured sweets. 'You can make me take the tap end as often as you like and I'll still love you.'

'But you're still marrying Pussy.'

'Whatever gave you that idea?'

'I came to see you. And she was there. Moving all her stuff in.'

'Dope.' He flicks a mound of bubbles at my nose. 'She was moving it out. I gave her my keys because I wanted her to remove the rest of her things from my property. She had loads of stuff just lying around.'

'So she made it up?' I ask, my heart suddenly lifting.

'Of course she did,' he says. 'I'm surprised you didn't twig. You know what she's capable of.'

'So why didn't you come to the wedding?'

'I didn't want to stop you from doing whatever it was you wanted to do. And it doesn't matter. You being married to David, I mean.'

'Honestly?'

'Honestly. I thought it would but it doesn't. All that matters is that I love you. Married or not. I mean, it's not as though you're married in the true sense of the word, is it?'

'Well...' I begin, then seeing his face I start laughing. 'I'm joking.'

'So will you? Can we?'

'Oh, Sam.' I laugh, finally feeling completely happy. 'Go and cut me a bit of my wedding cake and I'll think about it.'

Epilogue

Janice had the baby, a girl. She wanted to call her Katherine (after me) but I managed to convince her that was a boring name, which no one ever knew how to spell, so she chose Lucille. She's beautiful. She looks a lot like Janice and nothing like Jasper—thankfully. Janice's mum has come to live with them and looks after Lucille while Janice is at work. Janice's mum loves not having to live in a horrible flat where the lifts never work any more. And Janice is seeing someone new. His name is Ethan and he has a little girl too. They take the kids to the park every weekend. I don't know that they're in love, exactly, but they do seem very happy. I'm glad.

George pops in to see them all the time. He's a doting godfather. He's given up work now, and he and David are travelling around a lot at the moment, because they're hoping to buy themselves a Third World baby. So far, I don't think they've managed to get one to match the upholstery of their new car, but I'm sure they'll find something suitable soon.

Jasper's name turned out not to be Jasper at all. His real name is Archie Higgs and he's been wanted by police for questioning over an illegal porn ring operating in the Hampshire area for some time. I saw it in the *News of the Screws*.

Poppy had twins Molly and Holly in September. Being Poppy, she had a perfect, painless birth. Not like Janice's, which left the delivery room looking not unlike an abbatoir and her perineum in tatters. And, being Poppy's, the twins are perfectly behaved. They only cry in extreme circumstances and are hardly ever ill. The only time Poppy saw Janice's baby, Lucille barfed up all over her, to Janice's and my huge amusement.

I don't know what happened to Max, because, thankfully, I never saw him again.

Nick and Mum bonded over the stew and he pops round to her and Jeff's for supper every now and again.

Jake and Fishpants got married not long ago. The bridegroom wore Hugo Boss and the bride's knickers were showing.

Pussy's wedding to a minor royal was splashed all over *Hello!* the other week.

And I finally got to have a shag on my wedding night after all.

And, yes, the novelty draught-excluder was definitely not a disappointment.

My mother is in seventh heaven now that Sam and I have got it together. She keeps hinting about wedding bells and it's becoming difficult to keep my looming decree absolute from her.

But I don't think Sam and I will get married.

I mean, you can't exactly have a wedding where the bride and groom's parents are one and the same?

Can you?